CW00573616

NOVELLAS

OF THE DEAD

RICK MOORE

ADAM P. LEWIS

ALAN SPENCER

PATRICK MACADOO

KELLY M. HUDSON

OTHER LIVINGDEAD PRESS BOOKS

THE TURNING: A STORY OF THE LIVING DEAD * MEN OF PERDITION
THE DEAD OF SPACE BOOK 1 AND 2 * THE BABYLONIAN CURSE
PLAYING GOD: A ZOMBIE NOVEL * THE JUNKYARD
PLANET OF THE DEAD * THE HAUNTED THEATRE
ZOMBIES IN OUR HOMETOWN
NIGHT OF THE WOLF: A WEREWOLF ANTHOLOGY
JUST BEFORE NIGHT: A ZOMBIE ANTHOLOGY
THE BOOK OF HORROR* KNIGHT SYNDROME
THE WAR AGAINST THEM: A ZOMBIE NOVEL
CHILDREN OF THE VOID * DARK DREAMS
BLOOD RAGE & DEAD RAGE (BOOK 1& 2 OF THE RAGE VIRUS SERIES)
DEAD MOURNING: A ZOMBIE HORROR STORY
BOOK OF THE DEAD: A ZOMBIE ANTHOLOGY VOLUME 1-6
LOVE IS DEAD: A ZOMBIE ANTHOLOGY
ETERNAL NIGHT: A VAMPIRE ANTHOLOGY
END OF DAYS: AN APOCALYPTIC ANTHOLOGY VOLUME 1-5
DEAD HOUSE: A ZOMBIE GHOST STORY
THE ZOMBIE IN THE BASEMENT (FOR ALL AGES)
THE LAZARUS CULTURE: A ZOMBIE NOVEL
DEAD WORLDS: UNDEAD STORIES VOLUMES 1-7
FAMILY OF THE DEAD, REVOLUTION OF THE DEAD
KINGDOM OF THE DEAD * DEAD HISTORY
THE MONSTER UNDER THE BED * DEAD THINGS
DEAD TALES: SHORT STORIES TO DIE FOR
ROAD KILL: A ZOMBIE TALE * DEADFREEZE * DEADFALL
SOUL EATER * THE DARK * RISE OF THE DEAD
DEAD END: A ZOMBIE NOVEL * VISIONS OF THE DEAD
THE CHRONICLES OF JACK PRIMUS
INSIDE THE PERIMETER: SCAVENGERS OF THE DEAD
BOOK OF CANNIBALS VOLUME 2 * CHRISTMAS IS DEAD…AGAIN
EMAILS OF THE DEAD * CHILDREN OF THE DEAD

THE DEADWATER SERIES

DEADWATER * DEADWATER: Expanded Edition
DEADRAIN * DEADCITY * DEADWAVE * DEAD HARVEST
DEAD UNION * DEAD VALLEY * DEAD TOWN * DEAD GRAVE
DEAD SALVATION * DEAD ARMY (Deadwater series book 10)

NOVELLAS OF THE DEAD

Copyright © 2011 Living Dead Press
ISBN Softcover ISBN 13: 978-1-61199-019-5 ISBN 10: 1-611990-19-X
All stories contained in this book have been published with permission from the authors
All rights reserved. No part of this book may be reproduced or transmitted in any form or by any means, electronic or mechanical, including photocopying, recording, or by any information storage and retrieval system, without permission in writing from the copyright owner.
This is a work of fiction. Names, characters, places and incidents either are the product of the author's imagination or are used fictitiously, and any resemblance to any actual persons, living or dead, events, or locales is entirely coincidental. This book was printed in the United States of America.
For more info on obtaining additional copies of this book, contact: www.livingdeadpress.com
Cover art by CJ Hutchinson   Edited by Anthony Giangregorio

Table of Contents

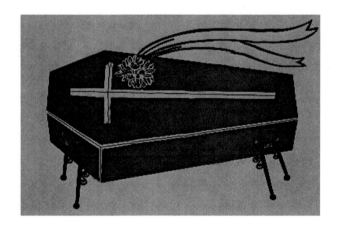

HOTEL HELL

RICK MOORE

They were boxed in, surrounded on all sides. Not low on ammunition yet, but they soon would be. There were hundreds of the undead pushing in on them, hundreds of the slimy sons of bitches, like this was some sort of zombie hot zone.

Cal knew they were as dead as the piece of shit red pickup truck they'd had to abandon. Plain old overheating. Simple to fix, but in a living dead world, mechanics 101 were out the window.

Zombies were slow, but not so slow you had time to wait for an engine to cool. Bad luck was followed by a bad decision. Not just bad, fatal. The hotel was huge, towering into the sky, and its presence had drawn them; the last hope of safety it represented luring the group into a trap of their own making.

The hotel, called The Villagio, stood in total darkness. It did not stand alone. The lights along the Las Vegas strip had been extinguished, the hotels like monstrous tombstones for a city that was dead. The MGM Grand, Caesar's Palace, The Sands, The Monte Carlo, The Excalibur—every other building for that matter, no matter how great or small—was silent now, the hotels now vast prisons that housed the dead trapped inside them.

All three of the group knew this, but still they headed for the Villagio hoping they'd somehow make it inside. That hadn't happened, and now they were screwed.

Behind Cal, Greg rattled the revolving glass doors, like doing it for the umpteenth time would somehow magically make the locks turn.

"Greg, give it up!" Becky yelled. She fired her handgun twice, taking down two of the dead. One of them tripped backwards over the edge of the enormous marble fountain that once served as the Villagio's first wow factor for arriving guests. The creature crashed into the water, the head shot ensuring it would never rise from the algae green murk. "Greg, we need you here."

About that Becky was wrong, Cal thought grimly. A third person firing at the advancing horde wouldn't make much difference. It would be like spitting into the flames of a forest fire. What they needed was an Uzi. Hand grenades. A tank. The Army. Throw in all that and maybe they'd stand a chance.

Maybe.

In his peripheral vision, Cal saw Greg had made the choice to die side by side with his friends, to fight to the end, instead of scrabbling at a blocked exit like some cornered animal, as the predators moved in for the kill.

Too bad he wasn't a better shot. One missed entirely. Another hit a moldy woman dressed as a crossing guard, tearing open her neck and exposing the dark wet redness within. The only effect the bullet seemed to have was to make her slowly lift her eyes and turn the stop/go sign in her hand a few times, before continuing on toward them.

Becky and Cal did their best to make up for Greg's mistakes. But for every piece of hot speeding lead that drilled through flesh, bone and brains, dropping the front line of zombies to the ground, there was more to take their place.

Inexorably, inch by laborious inch, the undead closed in: a wall of bodies packed so tight there was no chance of pushing through them, no chance for escape.

Before many seconds had passed, the three of them were forced to retreat to the revolving doors. There were six in total. Typical Vegas. Why have one when you can have a bank of them?

Cal recognized the design as the type that were motorized, operated from inside the building as a means of security. If memory served, such doors rotated so that only one quadrant could be accessed, the central axle moving the base and door simultaneously. The fourth door in the row offered a glimmer of hope. Due to the power outage, the position the glass-sided quadrants had stopped and locked at afforded access to two of the partitioned areas. The first was wide open and in under a minute, slime-coated teeth would be ripping them to pieces. The gap between the steel outer frame and the second quadrant looked too narrow for even Becky—the smallest of them—to squeeze through, but if they could get in there... If they could somehow get the door moving...

No time for 'ifs.'

"Becky, get inside!" Cal yelled, turning to look at her and seeing she was already ahead of him. Grunting, she struggled into the narrow gap, wincing as the metal edges pulled at her t-shirt and scraped against her skin. Cal and Greg emptied their guns into the walking dead. Reloaded and emptied them a second time.

"I'm through!" Becky called. "Greg, hand me your pack!"

Inside the backpack were the few supplies and canned food items they'd managed to forage. Greg shrugged it off his shoulders and pushed it into the opening. Becky yanked on the straps, and pulled the pack inside.

The zombies were so close now that Cal knew he was in danger of infection via the splatter effect. Ahead of the pack was a skinny dead teenager, with hair dangling in his eyes and wearing a skate shirt, baggy pants and Vans with the laces untied. He reached out for Cal, the touch of his fingers so cold Cal flinched. Cal centered his aim. The teenager wasn't torn up like some of them, didn't have an arm missing or his guts hanging out. Unlike many of the dead, decay had yet to set in, making the teen a rarity these days. To someone who didn't know better, the boy could have been mistaken for one of the living. There were just a couple of bite marks on his neck that at first glance appeared to be hickies. That is, until you saw the flesh was broken and that the hole was packed with wriggling maggots.

Cal shot the teenager in the forehead. Felt the cool splash of blood on his cheek. Brains, too, probably. Disgusted, hoping like hell none of the stuff had gone in his eyes or mouth, he instinctively wiped the wetness away with the sleeve of his leather jacket.

Four feet and closing.

Three...

A backward glance between head shots showed him that Greg had finally struggled through the opening and made it into the narrow space. Cal tore off his jacket, threw it at the nearest zombie, a long dead naked thing that used to be a woman. Cal tried not to notice the stuff leaking out of her withered breasts and running down her thighs between her legs. The jacket landed on the zombie's head, and the creature stood there, arms outstretched, too stupid to realize the cause of her sudden blindness.

Cal knew the gap between the steel frame of the enclosure and edge of the revolving door was going to be too tight to squeeze through, but he had to try. He turned sideways, and got his right arm and leg inside.

Becky grabbed his hand, Greg his forearm. Together, they heaved. The metal edge of the door tore through Cal's t-shirt in front, scraping away the top layer of skin on his chest, drawing blood. Cal gritted his teeth against the pain.

Keeping his head to the right, he tried to wriggle forward. He made it as far as his ears, then felt the cold metal pull against them on either side. No chance. He'd never make it. And now he was wedged in good—stuck.

Becky's eyes went wide.

The dead were right behind him.

Cal felt it then. A hand grabbed his left wrist. It was cold like the dead teenager's, only worse. What made it worse was not the putrescent spongy wetness of the flesh. No, what made it worse was there was no way to shrug the hand off. No escape. No way for this to be anything other than the moment before the end. The lips attached to his flesh gave him the same tactile sensation as shoving his hand into a garbage disposal to retrieve what had fallen inside, the touch of those lips akin to the wet rank stuff that sat rotting in the darkness. The creature's teeth clamped down on his wrist, and tugged at his skin.

Cal reacted as though he'd just received a hefty belt of electricity. He jerked. Twisted. Wrenched his body forward, his friends dragging him the rest of the way through. He didn't feel his left ear tear away from his head, didn't feel the steel edges abrade more skin on his chest along with his back. Cal tumbled inside the door, plowing into Becky and Greg. All three of them slammed against the rear glass wall, which was in fact not regular glass but solid polycarbonate. It bounced them off, sustaining no damage, just as it was designed to do.

Cal freed himself from the tangle of limbs and got to his knees. He looked at his wrist. Teeth impressions were there, but the skin was intact, unbroken. Becky leaned over his shoulder, the loose curls of her hair brushing against his face.

"I got lucky," Cal said. His voice sounded strange—distant.

"Right," Greg agreed, picking himself up off the floor. "Better to live disfigured than die and live as one of them."

Cal was about to ask what he meant, but then he felt a throbbing sensation, like the pounding of his pulse at the side of his head. With every thrum came a pain worse than any he'd known. The side of his head and neck felt warm and wet, the wetness soaking into the collar of his t-shirt. He kept away from the center of the wound but explored the wetness around it. When he looked at his fingertips, he saw red.

A second later he knew why. On the floor of the quadrant within which they knelt, was Cal's severed ear. He scooted forward and reached out for it.

Before he got to the ear a hand shot through the gap and snatched it away. Lifting his gaze, Cal saw the crossing guard zombie shove his ear into her mouth and bite into it. She lay flat on the concrete outside the revolving door.

Above her, at least ten other zombies pressed in, shoving against each other, their outstretched arms reaching through the opening, their hands grasping. Cal instinctively backed away. Every one of the dead with their faces pressed into the gap was drooling. Cal could smell their rancid death-breath. In the adjacent quadrant, the one most open to the street, more zombies had gathered. Those up front were being pushed from behind, causing their faces to press against the polycarbonate glass. Drooling at the sight of the three humans, they beat a slow relentless pattern against the barrier with their fists and open hands, smearing it with dirty hand prints.

Cal got to his feet and turned to the others. Greg was helping Becky off the floor.

"Now what?" Cal asked. Inside his head it was like the volume on everything had been set for low, his own words included.

"Let's see if we can move this thing," Becky suggested. "If all three of us hit it at the same time, maybe we can shunt it forward enough to squeeze through into the lobby."

Greg eyed the zombies pounding the glass and the hands reaching through the gap. "Let's hope so," he said.

On Becky's 'go' they ran at the rear panel, shouldering it with everything they had. The revolving door didn't budge an inch.

Greg screamed his frustration and drew his gun.

"Wait!" Becky grabbed his arm. "This stuff is a hundred times stronger than regular glass. You shoot in here and that bullet will ricochet off the walls until it ends up inside one of us."

Greg gestured at the zombies staring in at them, still beating the glass. "Then what the fuck are we gonna do?"

"All we can do is wait and hope they lose interest," Cal said.

"We're dead," Greg added. "There's only one way out of this now."

Greg raised his gun, stuck the barrel in his mouth and pulled the trigger, but the *splat* of brains never came out the back of Greg's head.

His gun merely clicked, empty.

Greg just stood there blinking. Slowly, he slid down the glass panel to the floor, drew up his knees, and covered his face with his arm.

"If we just wait," Cal said, "then maybe…"

Becky raised her arm, her finger pointing past him. "Cal, look."

He turned.

A zombie was trying to squeeze through the gap. It must have pushed past the others who'd been reaching in, shoving them out of the way. One arm and leg were already inside. The stink of the thing, a cross between a garbage can that had gone weeks without being emptied and rancid meat, filled the confined space. Cal covered his nose and mouth with his hand, resisting the urge to gag.

The dead man, who wore a gray sweatshirt and matching pants but no sneakers or socks, and didn't have the sense to turn his head sideways. As he struggled through, the steel edging that framed the glass abraded the skin on his forehead and cheek, sloughing it off. The outer layer of crusty skin flaked away, falling from the man's face like pieces of dandruff, exposing muscles dripping with clots of pinkish-yellow fluid. His head got through as far as his nose. A sudden wrenching of the head tore the nose away, cartilage snapping with a loud cracking sound. The man's nose dangled from his face, a dark red jelly oozing out of the hole.

Cal took out his gun, aimed it at the zombie.

"Is there any point?" she asked.

He looked at Becky. "What do you mean?"

"If we kill this one," Becky said. "Another will do the same thing. Then another and another, until there's no more bullets to kill them."

She didn't have to say anything further for him to know what she was thinking, and as much as Cal hated giving up, he knew she was right. Unlike Greg, he would make sure the gun was loaded before his finger curled around the trigger.

Greg lifted his head from his arms, looking up at him. "Do it, Cal. Quick, before you have time to think about it."

Cal nodded. He aimed the gun at Greg.

Only it was too much to ask. He couldn't kill his friend. He'd already lost everyone he ever loved. These two people, who he'd known less than a week, were all he had left in the world.

"You want me to become one of them?" Greg asked. "You want to see them eat Becky alive?"

Cal shook his head.

"Then do it, Cal," Greg pleaded. "For Christ's sake, kill me."

The gun wavered as Cal prepared to shoot, and after Cal shot Greg in the face, he would turn the gun on Becky, ready to do the same to her. But the man whose face Cal now saw in his mind's eye, the man he was about to shoot, was his father.

It was a few days after the first reports on the news. His father had been bitten, but none of them knew the facts of the virus. He went out for antibiotics. The Osco Drug was deserted, and Cal just vaulted the counter and found what he needed and took it.

He was gone thirty minutes at most. But in that time his father had turned. When he got home, he found his dad scooping his wife Julie's internal organs out of an opening in her stomach. When Cal returned from the bedroom with a gun, his father was sitting in silent contentment as he tore into Julie's liver with his teeth.

One at a time he'd shot them in the head.

Cal buried them in the backyard, lowering both bodies into the same hole. Then he'd placed his gun in his mouth and stood there looking down at the bodies of his loved ones for what seemed like hours. Cal knew he belonged down in the hole with his family; without them he was already dead, but his survival instinct wouldn't let him go through with it. When the sun sank and darkness spread across the sky, Cal dropped the gun and picked up the shovel and got to work filling the grave.

It was that same survival instinct that Cal battled now. The internal conflict made him feel woozy, so much so it seemed that the floor was moving.

Wait...the floor was moving, along with the revolving door.

From the ceiling, beneath a molded canopy that hid the electronics, came the quiet whir of a motor. There was someone inside the hotel. Someone was operating the door via the security controls.

As the door moved, Greg fell backward, crying out in pain. The door shuddered, halted, the back of Greg's head smacking the polycarbonate glass. Cal saw the cause of the obstruction.

It was the goddamn zombie, trapped between the panel and frame of the enclosure. Even with his diminished hearing, he caught the sound of the motor overhead, its low whir escalating, becoming a high-pitched whine. Whatever safety features were set in place at the time of the door's installation must have been disabled.

There was no other explanation for what happened next. Instead of rotating clockwise on its vertical axis to release the trapped object, the door continued to push in the counter clockwise direction. The pressure on the zombie's wedged head caused it to split open like a ripe watermelon.

One second the head was there, the next it was gone, all the individual parts that made it up reduced to a bloody slaw of brains, bones and unrecognizable chunks of meat and flesh.

Pushing past him, Becky grabbed the decapitated corpse's arm. "We've got to get it inside before that motor burns out."

Heedless to the mush flowing down from the corpse's neck, Cal clamped his hands around the sodden sleeve of the sweatshirt, his fingers digging into the corpse's bicep.

The atrophied muscles felt like saran wrap filled with Jello. Cal, Greg and Becky heaved together, wrenching the body the rest of the way through the gap and inside the quadrant.

With the blockage removed, the door almost silently completed its revolution. Greg tumbled out into the hotel lobby, rolling across the floor and coming to his knees. Cal and Becky staggered out after him, the door halting its rotation behind them. The area was so unnecessarily large that Cal felt like they'd entered a cavern.

At the front desk, where the controls for the door must have been located, Cal saw a figure crouched low on the opposite side of the counter. In the darkened lobby, lacking the benefit of lighting and relying on what little moonlight seeped through from outside, it was impossible to tell whether the figure was a man or woman.

"Hey," Cal called, his voice echoing. He raised a hand. "It's okay. None of us are infected. Thanks for taking a risk and…"

Behind them the revolving door turned. The zombies packed into the cramped space that was open to the street, were then transported from the exterior of the hotel into the lobby.

Cal and the others backed away. He turned to face the front desk, about to ask whoever operated the security controls what the hell they were doing, but the figure was gone.

"What the fuck?" Greg asked while quickly loading his gun.

The zombies stumbled out of the revolving door, their bodies swallowed by darkness as they stepped away from it, which was dimly lit by the moonlight, and moved deeper into the lobby toward their prey.

There was no time to try to figure out why the dead had been allowed inside, only time to react to the situation. Though there were no more than ten, the almost impenetrable darkness made it impossible to tell where all the zombies were located or accurately deliver head shots.

If they were going to survive this, Cal knew they'd need better visibility. He remembered the glow sticks stashed in Greg's backpack. Without wasting precious seconds explaining, or pulling the bag off his dead friend's shoulders to search for the glow sticks, Cal located Greg, released the clasps, and dug around until his hand closed around what he needed.

He pulled a glow stick from the bag and snapped it. Initially only part of the stick lit up, but as the two chemicals contained within mixed further, the entire stick glowed florescent yellow.

Ten shambling corpses, now washed bright yellow by the light, shuffled toward them, the closest just a few feet from where Becky stood. The creature's lips peeled back, drool dripping from its mouth, arms raised toward her.

Becky raised her gun, eliminating the threat with a single shot to the head.

Cal tried to fire at a zombie one handed, but missed completely, the recoil making him stagger. They made aiming with one hand look easy in the movies, but in reality, he wasn't proficient enough to pull it off.

Five of the zombies were grouped together, giving Cal the idea of throwing the glow stick at their feet and freeing the other hand. When the glow stick landed in front of them, all five zombies looked down at it, momentarily transfixed by the light.

The first bullet out of Greg's gun was wasted, the shot ripping away the side of a zombie's cheek, exposing the blackened gums and decayed teeth. Greg cursed in anger.

Cal was about to help Greg out, but saw that the zombie he shot was far enough away to pose no immediate threat, and figured Greg needed the practice. Instead, he focused on the five with their heads bowed, eyes still downcast, fascinated by the glow stick.

Even after he started cracking open their heads and serving up scrambled brains, the other zombies were too ga-ga over the bright yellow light to show the slightest bit of interest in the heads exploding around them.

How anything so innately stupid could take over the world was a mystery Cal knew he would never solve, and yet take over the world they had.

Mankind had failed to unite, and that was a major part of it, everyone out for themselves, everyone in a total state of panic, and the emergency services totally unprepared for a catastrophe of such immensity.

But even then...

To think civilization had collapsed at the hands—and teeth—of these moronic barely ambulatory bags of rotting flesh and bone, so infuriated Cal that as he went on firing his gun, finishing off the five and helping Becky with the three that remained, he became aware of how deeply he despised them. How much satisfaction he gleaned every time he wiped one out, eradicating the ugly bastards' sub-infantile level of awareness once and for all.

When it was over, and all the zombies were dead and leaking fetid fluids into the hotel's expensive deep pile carpet, Cal saw their work wasn't quite finished after all.

Greg's second shot must have taken the zombie with the ripped-open cheek down to the floor. He'd hit it in the eye, which was an improvement on his earlier efforts, but the bullet hadn't gone through to the brain. Striding forward, Cal aimed for the head.

But before he could pull the trigger, something unexpected occurred. So much so, that it took him several seconds to comprehend the cause of his sudden blindness.

When his vision returned, he had to shield his eyes with one hand against the brightness that suddenly dominated the lobby. Someone, the person who'd operated the revolving door presumably, had turned on all the lights. In his mind's eye, Cal pictured the Villagio's generator, and a hand flipping the switches in a breaker box located somewhere close by it.

Becky and Greg shielded their eyes also. Greg just stood still, looking around. Becky had the smarts to take cover behind an antique conversation couch.

Cal's first good look at the Villagio's lobby showed him the space was even larger than he imagined, the combined effect of all the marble and gold accents and all the art and antiques creating the impression he stood not in a hotel, but in a palatial throne room. Which was precisely what whoever designed the hotel had intended.

"Somebody's playing games with us," Becky said.

Cal didn't disagree. But he didn't bother to take cover either. If whoever it was wanted them dead, they already would be.

"First they let the zombies in after us," Greg cried. "Now this. What the fuck, man?"

Figuring out the answers would have to wait. Right now, a more pressing matter needed to be dealt with. Cal's attention returned to the remaining zombie.

The creature had once been a middle-aged man with a balding pate, a schoolteacher perhaps, who at some point prior to his death had placed two Bic pens—one black, one red—in the pocket of his short sleeved shirt and had matched it with cream-colored permanent press pants.

Now he lay on his back, his blackened and swollen tongue lolling from the hole in his cheek. A bloated black fly crawled out of the opening, and another took a leisurely stroll out of one of his nostrils, feasting on some dark crusty stuff stuck to the man's upper lip.

The flies then turned around and disappeared, heading back up into the nasal cavity. The right eye socket was empty, the orb it had been designed to house, completely obliterated. All that it contained was a dark milky mess.

The schoolteacher zombie kept trying to get up, but every time the dead man lifted his head, it thudded down again, smacking against the carpet. The zombie didn't use its arms or legs, didn't use its spine, seeming to think raising its head would provide sufficient leverage to get the job done.

Unlike the early days of the outbreak, Cal felt no pity for the creature. All that lived within him now was utter contempt—absolute hatred. Here this thing lay, a miracle in the flesh. Life where there should have only been death, and as incredible as the virus living within the creature had to be, it had turned its host into a being so lacking in intelligence, it couldn't even figure out how to lift itself off the floor.

Becky and Greg came to stand beside him.

"Cataracts," she said. "This thing was almost blind even before Greg shot out its eye."

The zombie's pupil was glazed a milky whitish-blue, the proteins that composed the lens clumped together, clouding it.

"Buddy," Cal said to the zombie. "I've got good news and I've got bad news. Good news is we can save the eye." He raised his gun, then aimed at the creature's forehead. "The bad news is that brain will have to go."

The schoolteacher lifted its head, strained to sit up.

Cal fired.

It didn't take long for one of the flies living inside the schoolteacher to crawl out of the nostril and move up the face, over the open-clouded eye, stopping just before the hairline, where there was now a fresh wet hole to explore. After a few seconds of exploring the outer edges, the fly disappeared inside.

Out of the silence that followed, the three of them became aware of buzzing deep inside the body.

If we cut him open, Cal thought. *A hundred of those fuckers would probably come pouring out.*

And if they looked closer? Maggots no doubt. The internal organs would be riddled with them.

A squeal cut through the insect hum.

"Hello and welcome to the Zombie Hotel!" said a man's voice. "We trust your stay here will be an unpleasant one."

All three of them spun around, looking for the owner of the voice.

It came from the hotel's PA system. Small, wall mounted speakers used at one time to make announcements to the guests, or call specific staff members to duty. If a guest demanded the manager, or if there was some sort of catastrophe, like a fire, the front desk would employ the PA. But the front desk sat empty.

Before Cal could ask his question, Becky answered it. "He must be using the hotel's security center," she said. "Somewhere around here, probably on this floor, there'll be a room with banks of surveillance monitors; plus a link to the PA."

"Surveillance? Greg said, looking up to where the wall met the ceiling high above. "The jerk who let those zombies in behind us is probably spying on us right this second."

"No 'probably' about it," Becky agreed.

Cal had to wonder what kind of shit they'd stepped in. Over the PA, music played. Cal recognized it: *Shake you Down*, an 80's soul ballad

"We need to get out of here," Becky said. "Allowing a bunch of zombies inside just to fuck with us makes me think our host has to be a little unhinged. But playing Gregory Abbot as an encore? That's just pure evil."

"Hey," Greg complained. "For your information, I got laid thanks to this song back in the day."

"TMI, Greg," Becky looked at him. "Way too much information."

Greg laughed, then went to check the bodies. Unlikely though it was, there was always a chance one of them still carried a weapon from before they'd turned.

At the revolving doors, the throng of pressing bodies were becoming fewer, those at the back already moving away. The zombies had forgotten why they were there, had forgotten they'd just been denied a meal.

Even with the lights on inside the lobby, Cal knew their eyesight was so deteriorated that they could see no further than a few feet away. He knew this from his prior encounters with the undead. To his understanding, they didn't so much hunt their prey as stumble onto it. They were drawn to sound, and such things as a car engine or gunfire would attract every one of them within range. But most of all, they seemed to rely on their own kind to guide them. A few walking in one direction would invariably be joined by a few more, then more, until there was a horde of them.

In a few minutes the zombies outside the Villagio would be gone and the coast would be clear. All they had to do was wait them out, and hope the nutjob inside the hotel didn't try anything in the interim.

Becky saw Cal looking outside and approached the front desk, a long slab of dark granite that topped a rich brown wooden base. It was, like everything else in Vegas, almost offensive in its size and grandeur. She went around to the opposite side, walking the length of the front desk until she found what she was looking for.

Although they'd been traveling together less than seven days, Cal had gotten to know her well enough to read her expressions. "What is it?" he asked, seeing the slight frown and the crease on her brow. "What's wrong?"

"Better come take a look for yourself," Becky said.

Cal approached the desk, walking around to the other side. He passed a bank of mail slots to the right and dead computer monitors to the left.

"Son-of-a-bitch," Cal said when he stood beside her.

The operating system for the revolving security doors required a key. The slot was empty. Without it the buttons to the doors were inoperative. Beside the buttons were two small surveillance monitors. One showed the doors facing the street, the section that would admit its occupants into the lobby when the door turned. The other showed the approaching walkway to them.

Out there the zombies were few and far between. Before too long their number would be sufficiently dispersed that little threat remained—an easy getaway. Except now that the three survivors were inside, there was no getting away from the hotel. Not by using the front exit anyway.

Becky tried the drawer nearest the operating system. Inside, all she found were a stack of room key-cards—useless unless activated—and the last thing on their minds was checking in for the night. Sleep deprived as they were, they were in no position to lower their guard and allow themselves to rest.

"Wait a second," Cal said as Becky started to close the drawer.

"I miss something?" she asked, pulling it open and looking inside again.

"A security card," he said. "It won't get us out but flash it at a reader and it might get us through some locked doors."

Becky found the laminated card with a young man's picture on it. The card said it belonged to Ralph Hines, Assistant Manager.

"How's your ear?" Becky asked Cal.

He smiled grimly. "The one I still got or the one inside the crossing guard's belly?"

"Sorry..." Becky said. "I meant..."

He smiled. "Hurts like a motherfucker."

"There's gauze in Greg's pack. I'll clean it with Iodine and wrap it. If you can take the pain, maybe you'd best pass on the painkillers. Now seems like a bad time not to be alert."

"What's up?" Greg asked, approaching the desk.

"Zombies outside are all gone but…" Cal said with a frown. "But there's a problem."

"Doors are jammed," Becky explained. "Our friendly neighborhood wacko pocketed the key. Without it, the controls won't work."

Greg nodded, and thought about it for a second. He turned and looked around the lobby. "Aha," he said, his gaze falling on a small marble-topped table positioned beneath a column, a dead plant inside a pricey looking vase sitting on top. "Problem solved."

Cal was about to tell him not to bother, but thought it better to let Greg find out for himself.

"Greg, wait…" Becky began, but said nothing further, evidently also deciding that where Greg was concerned, actions spoke louder than words. Greg went to the table and swept the vase off, shattering it. Soil and jagged fragments of ceramic scattered across the carpet.

"Used to be a time," Becky said, "that seeing something like that vase being destroyed would have bothered me."

Cal knew what she meant. The vase had been no cheap imitation. It was an antique, its value likely in the thousands, but the time of appreciating the care and skill taken in its crafting was gone. Mankind faced almost certain extinction. All man's achievements had been for naught. Now beauty served only as a reminder of all that was lost, and as such, its destruction meant nothing.

Greg lifted the small table, raising it above his knees. He turned the table over, held it by the back two of its four legs, and ran toward one of the large plate windows to the right of the revolving doors. Stopping a few feet short of the glass, he hurled the table sideways.

Upon impact, the marble top separated from the base and two of the legs snapped. The top and base clattered to the tiled floor, one of the broken legs snapping a second time. The glass remained unmarked.

Greg stood a moment looking at the window, then picked up the marble top and threw it. Again, the piece of shaped stone bounced off.

"What the fuck?" Greg cried, whirling around, looking at them.

"Too many pissed-off drunks in Vegas to take any risks with regular glass," Becky mused. "Some guy loses his shirt in one of the casinos, comes back to the hotel, sees this towering tribute to opulence and success, and gets to thinking throwing a brick through the window might be just the thing to make him feel better about being a loser."

"But it's glass," Greg said. "You hit it often enough, it's gotta break eventually."

Cal shook his head. "It's not glass. It's either a solid polycarbonate or Kwarx. You could hit it all day with a sledgehammer. Wouldn't make a damned bit of difference."

"Then there must be other windows," Greg suggested. "Windows with regular glass."

"On the ground floor?" Cal said. "Doubtful. You're in Vegas don't forget. Why have natural light when you can have light that's artificial?"

"So we're stuck here," Greg approached them. "Us and that psycho and who knows what else."

"Five minutes ago we faced certain death," Cal said. "Maybe we still do. But right this second we're alive, and that's all that matters."

The song playing over the PA ended and a new one started. It was Bobby McFarren's *Don't Worry, Be Happy*.

"Maybe we're not alive," Becky suggested, raising her gaze to the speakers. "Maybe we don't know it, but we're already dead and in Hell."

"Hey," Greg said. "Come on now, this is a classic."

They ignored him.

"Not that I think we'll have any luck," Cal said. "But first thing we should do is go try the fire exits."

Greg slapped his palm down on the marble counter. "The fire exits! Of course. Fire exits can always be opened from the inside. They have to, by law."

When neither Cal nor Becky said anything, Greg looked at them in exasperation. "They don't?"

Becky explained, "A resort casino this size would have an automatic fire alert system and exit control locks to deter people from opening them as a prank. If a fire alarm sounds, then the doors open, otherwise when you push down on the bar nothing happens. Through the computers in security you can access the system, disabling all the alarms and effectively locking all the exit doors at once."

Greg stood blinking at her. "And you know all this because..."

"I used to work the front desk at the MGM Grand," she said. "Until now I always thought it was just useless information, like a lot of other stuff inside my head."

"So the fire exits are out," Greg said.

"Probably," Cal agreed. "But we'll find one and break an alarm, just on the off chance the guy messing with us knows less than we're giving him credit for."

"Couple of other things you might want to forget about before you suggest them," Becky said. "The only rooms with ground floor balconies open directly onto the Laguna."

"Shit." Greg had a sense of wonder in his voice. "This is that place? With the artificial beach and that huge pool with a wave machine?"

"It is," Cal said. "That mean something?"

Greg shook his head. "Nope. Just always promised myself I'd check it out one day. Never thought I'd get the chance though. Not with the rates this place charges. Make that 'used' to charge." His voice became quiet, wistful. "Guess I'll maybe get to see it now, after all."

Upon seeing Becky shake her head and roll her eyes, Cal had to smile.

"Are you done revealing your inner eight-year-old?" she asked. "Or should I wait while you tell us about your dreams of visiting Orlando, Florida?"

"No, I'm done," Greg told her. "You were saying there are no ground floor balconies."

"Right," Becky continued. "None except those opening onto the Laguna. And the Laguna itself, the whole pool area and beach, the bars and cabanas, the restaurants, they're all enclosed by a wall that's at least twenty feet tall, if not higher. If memory serves, the wall runs right and left all the way to where it connects to the other side of the hotel."

"If memory serves?"

She looked at him. "Yes, Greg, if memory serves. See, unlike you, I had my dream fulfilled of staying here at The Villagio. It was where Mike and me spent our honeymoon."

"Jesus," Greg said. "Sorry, Becky."

Overhead, Bobby McFarren went on advising them to be happy and not to worry.

"Jesus," she said, blinking away a tear threatening to fall from her eye. "This fucking music. I swear to God, for that reason alone if I come face to face with this guy I'm gonna kill him and not even hesitate." She pulled it together and looked at them. "Like I was saying," she said. "The Laguna's walled in. Service doors set in them might lead outside, or maybe back into the hotel. I don't know. But either way, it doesn't matter because something tells me they'll all be locked. The other side of the hotel mirrors this one.

The second lobby's identical in layout to this, complete with revolving doors and windows that can't be broken."

All three were silent. There was nothing to say. They were trapped.

"Wait a second..." Greg started.

Barely containing his irritation, Cal cut him off. "What now, Greg?"

"Rooms on the first floor have balconies right? Balconies that look out onto the strip?"

Becky nodded. "Sitting about seventy feet off the ground. Your point?"

"Well," Greg said. "Maybe I'm missing an obvious flaw to my thinking here, but couldn't we just tie a whole bunch of sheets together, tie one end to the balcony rail, and lower ourselves down to the ground."

Becky and Cal looked at each other, both slowly nodding.

To Greg, Cal said, "We could. It would take a lot of sheets. But we could give it a shot."

"We definitely could," Becky said and smiled at Greg. "But not before I jump over this counter and give you a kiss."

* * *

A central staircase located to the right of the front desk led to the other floors. The three of them approached cautiously, looking up.

Cal, with his wound cleaned and a fresh bandage wrapped around his head, caught sight of his reflection in the banister and realized he looked more than a little like Van Gogh. Specifically in the self-portrait following the slicing incident. He was certainly as skinny as the great artist after all the meals he'd gone without these last months, and most surely his eyes looked as sad and haunted.

All that remained, Cal thought, was for him to completely lose his mind, then he'd have old Vincent down to a 't'. Thinking he was probably halfway there after all he'd lived through, Cal broke contact with his own distorted gaze and gripped the gold banister situated at the staircase's center. He climbed the first three stairs, the deep red and gold carpeting soft beneath his feet.

"Just a second," Becky said. "There's something I want to check."

Cal didn't question her. He just followed silently, moving down off the stairs back to the ground floor. Beside the staircase were six elevators.

Becky pressed the down button on the first panel. In the hotel's silence they could hear the elevator moving down through the upper floors.

"Back up," she told Greg, pointing her handgun at the elevator door.

Greg took several backward steps. Cal drew his gun also, following the direction of Becky's aim.

"Not sure that's a good idea, Becky," Greg said. "If that guy cut the power with us inside, we'd be screwed."

"Relax," she said. "We're taking the stairs. But if things get bad up there, and they could, it's not gonna hurt any to have an alternate escape route. Just checking to make sure there's no nasty surprises lurking inside."

"You think there's zombies roaming loose in this place?" Greg asked.

"The guy said, 'Welcome to Zombie Hotel,' didn't he? I'd say that means more than a few people checked in and never checked out again."

"But why…"

Becky held up a hand, silencing him. A single ding sounded from the panel, intended to alert guests that the elevator had arrived. The doors whooshed open.

Empty.

They stared into the elevator until the doors closed, then turned back toward the staircase.

"Something I don't get," Greg said, following them up the stairs. "All along the strip, there's not a single neon sign lit anywhere. Meaning…"

"Meaning the power's out," Cal finished for him.

"Right," Greg agreed. "But not here."

"All the big hotels have their own generators," Becky explained. "There was a major power outage here in '04. The entire city went dark, except for on the Strip. But here, the lights kept flashing and the reels kept rolling. When it comes to emptying money out of people's pockets, Vegas doesn't play around."

"So if we could get into another casino," Greg said. "One without a crazy psychopath running around…. And if we found a way to clean house…"

"Turn the generator on and dig in?" Becky asked. "Not a bad idea, Cal?"

"Let's concentrate on one problem at a time," Cal said.

Becky nodded. "Right."

Above them, the outer rail curved outward on either side, continuing on through the mezzanine. An enormous oil painting of an angel at sunrise dominated the space. Victorian conversation couches were placed against the walls beneath it. Between these and the elevators were two swinging doors, leading to the first floor hallways.

Cal took point, Greg was second, and Becky brought up the rear.

Easing one of the swinging doors open slowly, Cal looked left with gun in hand. It was a clear view of a long hallway.

Silent.

Empty.

Greg placed a hand against the door, allowing Cal to ease through the opening. Cal swung right, ready to shoot at the slightest indication the dead were waiting. Again nothing.

No movement.

He glanced back at Greg, and motioned with his hand for him to advance. Becky came through after Greg.

"You hear that?" Becky asked.

Greg listened. All he heard was silence. "What?"

"No bad 80's music is playing up here," she said. "Now I can die peacefully."

"I hate to be the one to break this to you," Greg said. "But you have no taste whatsoever. Eighties music was the best."

"Oh yeah?" Becky laughed. "You think so? Name one act out of the eighties that's still going strong today."

"One?" Greg said. "I could name fifty. U2 for starters…"

"Hey," Cal hissed, looking back at them. "You really think this is the time and place for this conversation? Newsflash, Bono and the rest are zombies, just like everyone else in the world. Now do us all a favor and get your heads back in the game."

Cal glared at them both. When Cal was again facing forward and slowly advancing, Becky wagged an admonishing finger in Greg's face. Her schoolmarmish expression was so spot on Greg had to clap a hand over his mouth to contain his laughter.

"He's right," she said, suddenly serious. "Let's go."

They moved along the hallway, Cal with his gun pointed straight ahead, Greg and Becky with theirs angled toward the floor. None of them had any firearms training, but Becky knew from seeing it on TV and in movies, that this was the safest way to enter a potentially hostile environment. Greg hadn't known this, but he did now. Some days back, after the first time he walked behind her with his gun pointing straight ahead, practically pointed right at her head, Becky reeducated him, the key points of her lecture punctuated by words blue enough to make a sailor blush.

Becky cut in front of him, leaving Greg to take the rear. A sideways glance from Cal told Greg all he needed to know. Cal was thankful Becky was beside him, relieved that his immediate back-up wasn't Greg. At least that was how Greg interpreted it.

Greg knew he wasn't the sharpest tool in the shed, knew he wasn't the greatest shot, but it bugged him, the way Cal and Becky acted superior. They volunteered nothing unless he questioned them, and shot down most of his ideas, like he was third billed in the shittiest show on earth.

Before the dead went and messed everything up by coming back as zombies, he'd been '*A number one*,' the star of his own life. Maybe not the greatest life, but it was his. The life he chose. He didn't have to answer to anyone, didn't feel like he had to seek anyone else's approval.

As far as Greg was concerned, anyone who judged him could go fuck themselves. But now all that had changed. It was bad enough being surrounded by dead people who wanted to eat him, without also having to deal with the only other survivors he'd found in weeks treating him like he was inferior.

Escaping by tying sheets together was his idea, hadn't it? It was him who had come up with a solution to save their asses. So where was the respect? He was about to suggest for once maybe he should be the one taking point, when he noticed they were passing rooms and not slowing down at any of the doors.

"What happened to the plan?" Greg asked.

Becky looked back at him. "We're sticking with it."

"Is that why we're passing all these rooms?"

"Suppose we break into one of the rooms," Becky said. "Suppose there are sheets on the bed. How far down you think we're gonna lower ourselves with only one set of sheets?"

"Not far," Greg had to admit. "So where does that leave us?"

Cal stopped, and turned to look at him. "Leaves us looking for a clean linen closet, the kind maids use to load up their carts."

Greg wanted to slap his forehead. He grinned. "A supply closet, of course. I knew that. I mean, it's obvious, righ…"

Becky held up her hand, silencing him. All three listened.

They were fifteen feet from the corner, where the hallway turned to the left. They heard a thump and then a squelch, a thump and then a squelch. For five seconds there was silence, then the sounds started up again.

Thump—squelch—thump—squelch—thump—squelch.

Something just around the corner was moving toward them. There was barely time to raise their weapons before they got their first look at the thing. It crawled along the carpet toward them. First they saw a cauterized stump, the arm removed just above the elbow, the flesh blackened where it had been burned. Then the head came into view—the side facing them like ground hamburger meat. Then the other stump, burned the same as the first, along with the shoulders.

The thing kept crawling.

Then they saw the origins of the squelching sounds. Its stomach had been torn open and its intestines pulled out. Beneath its exposed genitalia were two more blackened stumps, ending at the thighs.

It rounded the corner, dragging its limbless torso toward them, the unraveled intestines trailing behind, ending somewhere out of sight around the corner of the hallway.

Cal raised his gun and aimed.

In the same instant the limbless creature lifted its head. Set in the swollen and pulped mess that had once been its face, they saw a pair of eyes looking up at them—eyes that were full of pain and fear, eyes that were all too human.

"Please..." the creature—in actuality a living man—rasped. "Please...kill me..."

Someone cried out and somebody whimpered and someone gasped, but no one knew who.

"He's alive..." Cal said. "Jesus Christ, he's alive."

"Save me," the man sobbed. "Don't let him get me again."

Thump—squelch—thump—squelch.

The limbless man reached Cal's feet, and still there was no telling how far behind his innards ended. "Save me," he begged in a cracked whisper. "Save me."

"For Christ's sake, Cal," Becky said. "Do it."

Cal straightened his arm, and pressed the nose of his gun against the man's forehead. With his other hand he wiped tears from his eyes. "What kind of a man could do this?"

"Not a man," the limbless man said. "A demon. A demon in the flesh."

All Cal could think to say was, "I'm sorry,"

Then he pulled the trigger and the man's suffering was over.

* * *

They found the supply closet ten feet or so beyond where the dead man's entrails ended. On the door a message awaited them, neatly printed in red magic marker. It read: ***If you're looking for this door, then you really are shit out of luck.***

The door operated on an ID card reader, and Cal reached for the laminated square of plastic he'd shoved into his back pocket, then pressed it to the reader. Ralph Hines, Assistant Manager, was evidently still in the system. The door beeped and the lock clicked open. Becky and Greg aimed their guns, ready for any surprises. Cal pushed the door open. The supply closet was empty. No towels, no sheets—just bare shelves.

"He must have been listening in," Greg said, "and got up here ahead of us."

"Possible," Cal said. "But I doubt it."

"Are you saying this psycho's working with someone else?"

Cal shook his head. "Based on what just happened, I'd say we're not the first people to arrive at this door."

"Christ," Becky hissed. "You think this guy's been going out to find people, and bringing them back here to play cat and mouse?"

Cal shrugged. "That or using methods to get them to come here."

"Methods?" she asked. "Like what?"

"Wouldn't take much," Cal replied. "Since the emergency services went under, people have been turning to ham radios to communicate. I spent three days in Reno with a small group of survivors that had a CB rigged up and were using it to speak to others who were still alive. Imagine some guy comes on saying he's got this resort hotel all secured, that it's safe and has its own power source and enough food in the freezers and pantries to last for years. The only question most people would be asking is: when do we leave? And maybe he plays Mr. Nice Guy until he's got them locked inside. Soon as he does, he turns the tables."

"Mr. Nice Guy becomes Mr. Serial Killer," Becky said. "And the games begin."

"There's a billion fucking zombies out there," Greg stated. "This sick fuck can't get his rocks off killing dead folk? He's got to prey on the last few people still alive?"

"Sure looks like it," Cal said.

"So what now?" Becky asked.

"We could break open the room doors," Cal suggested. "Hope we get lucky and find the one where he stashed all the sheets."

They looked along the hallway, at the doors stretching all the way to the end.

"I don't know about you guys," Becky said, "but I'm running on empty here. We kick in one of those doors and I see a bed, I just might decide I've gone as far as I'm gonna go."

"Take a hot shower," Greg said. "Call up room service. You know it would probably be frozen meat, but I bet the kitchens in this place are loaded to the max. Hell, I bet they got every kind of steak known to man."

"Only one problem, Greg," Cal said. "The room service attendants along with the chef who'd cook that steak for you are dead. They'd just as soon eat you as feed you now."

Greg scowled. "Man, why you gotta be such a kill joy? Messing with my fantasy and shit. You think I don't already know they're dead? Still doesn't mean a guy can't dream..."

"He's right though," Becky added. "The freezers and pantries in this place must be fully stocked. It would be sweet if we had this place to ourselves. Tell you what, Greg, you put a bullet in Mr. Psycho's head or his heart, I'm not particular, and I'll cook you that steak myself."

Greg turned and hollered down the hall, "You hear that, Mr. Psycho? You're all that stands between me and a steak dinner. Guess that means you're going down."

"Some advice, Greg," Cal said. "You want to get this guy, and get your steak dinner, too, you might want to try to avoid giving away your position. Otherwise all you're gonna get is dead."

"Good advice," Greg conceded. "Maybe we better move out."

* * *

There was no telling the manner in which they would be attacked. They only knew at some point their foe would make his presence known. Whether that was by a direct assault or an attempt to set a booby trap remained to be seen. Nonetheless they had no choice but to move forward, to try for the other side of the hotel and hope by some means the doors there were operable. No other option was available.

They retraced their steps to the main lobby. From there, nine wide hallways stood in silence before them, all leading off to different parts of The Villagio. There was a directory to their right, and Cal went to study it. One hallway led primarily to conference rooms, the others included bars, restaurants, spas, hairdressers, clothing stores and a chapel.

"Doesn't matter which one we take," Becky said. "There's a concourse where they all rejoin before you exit this side of the hotel and go through to the pool area."

"Straight through the main casino looks like the shortest route," Cal suggested, then looked at the others for confirmation. They both nodded.

"One thing," Becky added. "Assuming what just happened upstairs wasn't a set-up to give us a scare, and we just chanced on one of his victims, then this guy might still be watching us on the security monitors. If that's the case, then as soon as he sees which hallway we go down, there's a good possibility he'll make his move. So be ready."

"There's something else," Greg said.

"What?" she asked him.

"The music. He turned it off."

Cal looked up at the tiny wall mounted speakers, then back at Greg. "You think that means something?"

"Yeah," Greg said. "I think it means playtime's over and this guy's about to get serious on our ass."

They entered the hallway with the same degree of caution as before. Other than the plush carpeting and occasional fire extinguisher, they saw nothing. The walls were absent of eye candy, the intention being to keep the casino itself as the only attraction. In the distance they saw double glass doors, and a brightly lit area beyond them.

"Shit," Cal muttered upon seeing the doors.

"Think they're locked?" Becky asked.

"Probably."

"Hey," Greg said. "You guys hear that?"

Even with the doors closed, the sounds of hundreds of slot machines couldn't be fully contained—which of course was the original intention. Hearing the machines before seeing them had once filled gamblers with the thrill of anticipation; as the three survivors drew closer, the sounds of the machines intensified.

From five feet away they could see that the locks were engaged; they would need to find another way through. Still, they approached the glass doors and peered inside. Greg tried one of the handles regardless, just to be sure, and all the door did was rattle. The casino was designed on a sunken level, requiring those entering or exiting to use a short flight of carpeted stairs.

Looking down, they found a vision of total absurdity. Hundreds of people were inside the casino; playing the slots.

* * *

Some sat on chairs while others stood. The three survivors stared, mesmerized at the odd scene before them. There was a slapdash manner noticeable amongst the gamblers who hit the buttons; an uncoordinated

24

gracelessness in the ones who lurched to pull the handles. They were dead—zombies, every one of them.

"What the fuck?" Greg wondered aloud.

"How can they..." Becky shook her head. "That's impossible."

A woman wearing a wedding dress grabbed for the handle of the slot she was positioned in front of and got caught by the hem of her long train. She tumbled- thumped to the floor, the face veil she wore knocked askew. Her face was grayish-blue, her eyes sunken deep in her skull.

On hands and knees she crawled across the carpet toward a lone quarter. Her ragged, bloody fingers grasped at the coin. When she had it in hand, the bride clumsily stood. She staggered toward the nearest unoccupied machine, shoving the quarter at the slot, until it finally found the opening and went in.

She pulled the handle, watched the reels spin with eyes that were hypnotized by the blur before them. Again and again she yanked on the handle, the reels turning more times than the credit bought with her coin should have allowed.

"He must have reset the machines to endless credits," Cal said, thinking aloud. "Not that these poor bastards have the sense to know it," Becky added.

"They don't have the sense to know that part, but they suddenly remember how to play the fucking slots?" Greg said. "Am I the only one who thinks something else is going on here?"

Becky looked at him. "Something else?"

"You heard him," Greg said. "Don't tell me his words didn't strike you as odd."

"Who?" Cal asked. "What words?"

"The guy with his guts pulled out," Greg said. "Before you...before you did what had to be done. You asked what kind of man could do this, and he said, 'Not a man, a demon. A demon in the flesh.'"

"So what about it?" Cal asked. "If someone did that to you, cut off your arms and your legs, ripped you open and pulled out your insides, wouldn't you call him the same thing?"

"Look," Greg said. "All I'm saying is, until a few months back, the idea of dead people getting up and walking around would have been the most ludicrous thing in the world, but now the dead own that world, and none of the big shots with brains came forward to say why. Sure, there was a lot of conjecture, a lot of theories. But no one had an answer. Only thing we knew for sure, was that the dead were slow and stupid and they ate the living.

Motorized instinct. Maybe they could figure out how to open a door, but a simple thing like walking up and down stairs guaranteed they'd stumble if they tried to go up, and trip and fall on the way down. Now those self-same dead fucks are in there playing slot machines. Well, there's only one way that could happen, and that's if something's controlling them, something with the power to make them act on command."

"What? A demon?" Cal laughed. "Greg, that's the biggest pile of..."

Greg jabbed a finger toward the glass. "Look at them, man. Why not a demon? Because things like that don't exist? Zombies didn't used to exist either, Cal. Now there's close to what, six billion of the motherfuckers crawling over every inch of the goddamn planet? If it's not some kind of seriously messed up supernatural bullshit going down in there, then explain to me how a bunch of corpses with about as much brains as the maggots crawling around inside 'em, are in there playing the fucking slot machines."

"You want an explanation?" Becky asked, keeping her eyes on the zombies inside the casino. "Take a closer look."

"What are you..."

"Just take a look," she told him.

Greg and Cal turned their heads.

"Okay, I'm looking," Greg said. "They're playing the slots, same as before."

"Gotta agree with him," Cal said. "What are we looking for?"

"Okay," Becky said. "Watch what happens when one of them hits a win."

This time they paid more attention. Before long they saw a fat zombie wearing khaki shorts and a Hawaiian shirt land three double bars in a row.

The machine—called Top Dollar—flashed its lights and bleeped a maddening tune. While the credits clocked for the win, the fat zombie slowly lifted its head and looked up and across to the other side of the casino, to an empty bar built to overlook the floor, and accessed either by a flight of stairs over on the left, or a central glass elevator.

The cracked scabby lips of the Hawaiian-shirted corpse parted, and drool that was black with clotted blood ran down its chin. At another machine, a zombie who bore a remarkable resemblance to Donny Osmond got two cherries, racking up a small win. Like the fat man, Donny also raised his head, looking up toward the casino's high domed ceiling, then over to the balcony bar.

Time and again, Cal and Greg saw the same pattern of behavior. Whenever a zombie landed a win, they went into neck-craning mode, eyes fixed on the empty bar, waiting until long after the machine's lights quit flashing, until it seemed whoever or whatever they waited for didn't show, before going back to yanking handles and crashing their hands against the buttons.

"Looks like someone taught these doggies a new trick," Cal remarked.

"Which means?" Greg asked.

"Like Pavlov's dogs," Becky said.

"Pavlov?" Greg said. "Who the fuck is Pavlov?"

"Like teaching a dog to sit up and beg. You know how you teach a dog to sit up and beg, Greg?"

Greg shrugged. "You know, Cal, in my vast wheelhouse of knowledge, I can't say that's something I'd ever need to know. I hate dogs, almost as much as I hate zombies. I got bit by one of the yappy little fuckers when I was a kid."

"You train a dog by giving it a reward," Cal said. "A treat, and it looks like what works for dogs, works for zombies, too."

Greg grimaced. "I don't even want to think about what constitutes as a zombie treat."

"I don't think it would take much imagination to figure it out," Cal said. "The question though, is why? Why go to all the trouble of corralling these things into the casino, of setting up these machines and waiting for enough trace memories to kick in, so they'll associate standing hour after hour at the slots with the concept of a reward?"

"This guy's sick in the head," Becky said. "Why does any psychopath go to such elaborate extremes to fulfill his demented fantasies? Because they get off on it. Simple as that. And whether you want to think about it or not, Greg, it looks like you're about to find out what these things get when the house is around to pay out on a win. It seems like the woman in the red dress just hit it big, but I'm guessing her prize gets divvied up, based on a first come first serve basis."

Cal and Greg spotted the woman in red immediately. She stood beneath a slot machine named Cash Attack. From their position, it was impossible to see the reels and tell how much she'd won, but judging by the number of flashing lights and the noise the machine was making, once upon a time the casino would have been writing her a check.

The woman—who was in her mid-twenties and still had a killer body, despite one slightly deflated boob that had been bitten into and had leaked blood and collagen down her dress—wasn't interested in the machine's light show. Instead, on some level, she responded to what the flashing lights signified.

Her head, which was crowned with a mane of long-matted black hair that must have once been beautiful to behold, craned all the way back on her neck. She remained that way for several seconds, looking directly at the ceiling. Then, slowly, her head turned in the direction of the balcony bar. This time there was movement up there—a dark shape that hurried amongst the shadows.

The woman careened to the left, staggering as she moved away from her machine.

One of the zombies working a slot near the bar also caught sight of the motion above. By the time he'd dragged his feet a few steps away from his machine, other zombies did likewise, abandoning the slots and moving to the rear of the casino.

A few of the zombies climbed the stairs on the right that led to the bar, but the majority waited beneath the glass elevator, looking up.

"It's him," Greg said. "It has to be."

"He must have used the service stairs," Cal said. "A place this size, with this many businesses, it probably has a network of delivery tunnels that run behind all the stores, bars and restaurants."

"Delivery tunnels..." Greg said. "Holy shit! That's it."

"What?" Cal and Becky asked simultaneously.

"The way out of here," Greg said. "Those delivery tunnels have to lead to bays for unloading trucks, and those bays have to have shutters that open from the inside. Even if you disable the motors they can be opened manually on a winch. Even if you removed the winch, I'll bet there's small plastic windows set in them, big enough to crawl through, easy to knock out if you rammed it with a forklift."

"Sounds like we've got a new plan," Cal smiled. "Good thinking, Greg. Now we've got to find a business we can access, something that isn't sealed off and..."

"Christ," Becky said, interrupting him. She pointed to the casino floor and the zombies. "Look."

Up in the bar, all the lights came on, and they got their first good look at the man Becky had dubbed Mr. Psycho. Only he didn't look like any of them might have expected. He wasn't the plain nondescript nice guy next door type. He wasn't the grinning bedraggled loon caught in the grip of psychosis. What he looked like was Elvis Aaron Presley, circa 1974. Not only did he wear an authentic looking one piece white jumpsuit, embroidered with rhinestones, but he also had a matching cape, big buckle leather belt and TCB sunglasses. Even his jet black hair looked exactly the way Elvis had worn it back in the day.

Below the balcony bar almost all the casino zombies were now gathered. Some stood with raised arms, reaching up. Others were stock still, like statues molded of rotting flesh. Those that arrived at the door turned the handle repeatedly, but didn't have the brains left to understand it was locked.

In his hand, Psycho Elvis held a cordless radio microphone. He clicked the 'on' button, moved to the balcony's edge, and looked down at the horde of zombies gathered below.

"Ladies and gentlemen," Psycho Elvis said, his mimic of the King faultless. "Looks like we got us a winner here, and if there's one thing we all love here in Las Vegas, it's a winner. Now sadly, on this occasion I'm only gonna have time to play you one song. See, some friends dropped in on me, kind of unexpected like, and I'm committed to seeing to it they have themselves a good time." Psycho Elvis looked across the casino, to the doors Cal, Greg and Becky stood behind, and waved. "Hello, friends." His attention returned to the crowd of undead down below. "But even a one song show here at The Villagio comes complete with a bite to eat. It's buffet style, which means ya gotta eat it with your hands, but somehow I get the feeling that's the way you good folks like it."

Psycho Elvis clicked off his mic, placed it on the table, and with a twirl of his white cape, about faced, and headed for the back room behind the bar. He went through the door. When he returned seconds later, he was pushing a man and a woman ahead of him, prodding them with a knife when they halted. Over their heads were cloth sacks and their hands were tied behind their backs.

The woman was stripped to her bra and panties and the man his boxer shorts. Psycho Elvis guided them to the elevator doors. He leaned forward and said something, and the two people halted. His hand reached out for the button and the elevator door slid open.

A prod to the woman's backside with the tip of the knife got her moving again. The man received the same treatment. He hurried into the elevator with such haste that his head banged into the outer facing glass wall. He staggered but managed not to fall.

Psycho Elvis used his foot to stop the elevator doors from closing, then used the knife to free the couple's hands. Finally, he grabbed the sacks covering their heads, pulling them off simultaneously. Before the man and woman could get their bearings, Psycho Elvis removed his foot and stepped away from the elevator. The door closed.

The answer to Cal's question came to him then. He wondered what was the purpose of going to such extreme measures to teach the zombies the slot machine trick? Now he knew. There, on the faces of the man and woman, he saw terror so absolute, that their panicked dread reached out and grabbed him, closing around his throat. And Cal's pain was Psycho Elvis' pleasure. From where Elvis stood, close to the front of the balcony, he could see directly into the elevator. He'd removed his TCB glasses, and on his face, even from this distance, the euphoria was plain to see.

Then the elevator descended. The man and woman could only stand there, looking down at the zombies waiting beneath them. There was no way out. No escape. As soon as the door opened they would be mobbed by the undead.

Psycho Elvis laughed, nodding, and ran a hand through his jet black hair. He grabbed the radio mic and turned it on.

Through the casino his voice drifted, his mimicry of the real Elvis eerily accurate. "They love meat tender," Psycho Elvis sang. "Love meat they gotta chew... All their dreams fulfilled... You will make their death complete... When they dine on you."

Inside the elevator the man looked at the woman, then said something to her. She shook her head, refusing to accept whatever he was suggesting. He continued to look into her eyes. Cal watched his lips move.

It's the only way.

Seeing the way they looked at each other, watching them embrace, Cal knew they were more than two people who'd separately fallen into the clutches of this madman—this maniac who'd turned a potential safe-haven into Hell's playground. The man and woman kissed. Both were sobbing. The elevator was halfway to the ground floor.

"Fuck this guy," Cal said. "Stand back." He aimed his gun at the door.

"What if it's bulletproof?" Becky asked, but even as she said it she was pulling on Greg's arm, dragging him away from the glass.

"If it is we'll worry about it then," Cal said. "All I know is that I don't want to be here when that elevator opens. Watch out for ricochets."

"Wait a minute," Greg said. "Ricochets? What do you mean ricoch..."

Cal fired and the door shattered. Before the shards and fragments had finished falling, Cal moved, kicking in the larger jagged pieces left attached to the frame, making it safe to go through. As he stepped through the opening, he felt the sleeve of his t-shirt snag on a shard and tear. Then he was inside, running down the stairs. Up in the bar, Psycho Elvis leaned forward against the balcony's gold railing. He was smiling at Cal, his entire face lit with surprised delight.

"Smile on this, fucker," Cal said, bringing up his gun. It jerked in his hand, and somehow it happened as he planned. Somehow the bullet found its target. It ripped a hole in Psycho Elvis's face, tearing the right side open wide. Psycho Elvis's head snapped back and when it came forward again, the cheekbone was obliterated and the splayed fingers he held to it were dripping blood. He tottered, looking confused and spat broken teeth.

Into the microphone he sputtered, "Hush now, little zombies, don't you cry, you know your daddy's bound to die."

He fell forward over the railing, tumbled through the air, and landed face first on the carpet below. Seeing him laying there, his body twitching, Cal thought it a pity the zombies moving in to claim a piece didn't get to chow down on him alive and fully conscious.

Cal saw a streak of movement on either side of him. He ran then, following Becky and Greg as they dashed across the casino. All around him, slot machines were flashing and playing their irritatingly catchy tunes. To Cal's ears, the cacophony sounded like a symphony sent straight from the bowels of Hell. The popping sounds that accompanied the racket came from Becky and Greg's guns.

Cal passed a row of slots and the elevator came back into his line of sight. He raised his weapon, taking down the dead things with shots to their heads. But it wasn't enough. Even with all three of them firing, they could only shoot the zombies on this side of the elevator; couldn't get at those waiting at the door.

And they were out of time.

The elevator had arrived.

The woman's back was pressed against the glass wall that faced out, designed so that people riding inside had a bird's eye view of the casino. She looked over her shoulder, looked right into Cal's eyes. Her gaze flickered to the side, to where Psycho Elvis lay, most of his body obscured by the zombies piled on top of him, feeding. She faced forward.

Cal and the others were still some thirty feet away when the elevator door slid open. Through the glass wall, Cal saw everything. He saw the man, who was positioned in front of the woman, charge forward, barreling into the throng of zombies pressing in. He knocked them back, clearing them away from the door.

"Run!" the man yelled to the woman, as countless hands grabbed at him and teeth sank into his flesh. "Marcy, run!"

There might have been a split second of opportunity, an opening through which Marcy could have slipped by, but seeing Psycho Elvis dead must have given her an idea, a better one no doubt than the man had come up with.

If only it had it worked

With so many dead still remaining, and with them right in the thick of it, Cal and the others could do nothing but watch the woman make her fatal decision.

She ran forward, her finger jabbing at the button that would close the door and return the elevator to the bar above. As the door began to close, the man collapsed under the weight of so many bodies bearing down on him. He screamed as their teeth sank deep, wrenching free gobbets of flesh; one free arm flailed wildly.

Lying there, blanketed by the dead, and soon to die and become one of them himself, the man unwittingly sealed the fate of the woman he loved. Two fingers was all it took. Two fingers on his outstretched arm that crossed the threshold of the elevator and activated the door's safety mechanism.

Cal shot the closest zombie in the head, recognizing her as the woman in red with the collagen oozing out of a bite to her breast, then looked again at the glass elevator in time to see the door slide slowly open.

As the horde clambered over each other to claim the woman, filling the doorway and shuffling forward, she backed away and turned and beat at the glass. Cal knew it was pointless, knew the glass the elevator was constructed of would be impenetrable. He fired a shot regardless but not so much as a nick appeared. He could only stand there, watching as her fists pounded uselessly, his mind recording the terrible fear in her eyes, as the hands of the dead spread across her body like a swarm, and the damage done by their teeth sent spurting jets of red down the glass.

"I'm almost out!" Greg yelled. "Becky?"

She dropped a dead man ten feet away, then yelled, "The same. Cal, we gotta go!"

He nodded wearily. With a single shot he'd defeated the man who would be the King, but the two lives wasted made it a hollow victory. Why did he even allow himself to hope there was a chance of saving them? He'd led his companions into the casino. They had wasted all their ammunition, and had breached their only shield against the dead by shooting the glass door. Of course, their self-elected nemesis could have freed the zombies at any time. And of course, he was now no longer a threat. But to Cal, it felt like they'd lost as much as they'd gained.

Even now, some fifty zombies remained. At least half were occupied, the feeding sounds so sickening he was almost grateful the loss of his ear made him partially deaf. The other zombies were making their slow shuffling way toward the three survivors. Soon, when Psycho Elvis and the man and woman became the walking dead, too, and those feeding lost interest, the shattered glass doorway would draw them away from the casino and out into the lobby. After that, it was only a matter of time before they spread, like an infection, across this side of the hotel.

"Cal," Greg pleaded. "Come on, man, it's over. There's nothing else we can do here."

Cal looked over and saw that Greg and Becky were backing out of the area, heading for an open aisle of slots.

"Wait," Cal called. "We need to think this through."

"Think this through!" Greg called. "Get real, man, we gotta go."

They were missing something. Something obvious. Something that under less tense circumstances they'd think of in a second.

Cal's gaze shifted to Psycho Elvis. The zombies had shredded his white jumpsuit, the blood gushing forth as they'd bitten into his flesh staining it red. Half a dozen zombies or so were still at work on various limbs. A frail looking elderly woman, who'd made her way into Elvis' stomach, pulled out a handful of internal organs and shoved them into her mouth.

Then Cal saw it, there, at Elvis' waist, the big buckled belt remained, soaked with gore but intact. Hanging from it, on a clip-on bungee key chain, was a ring of keys.

Cal took one of the two remaining clips from the back pocket of his jeans and reloaded. His finger squeezed back on the trigger as he walked. With each shot, bodies toppled silently. By the time he reached Psycho Elvis, only the old woman remained. She didn't even look up at him, just went right on eating what looked like a kidney. Cal felt the kick of the gun in his hand.

"Cal," Greg urged from behind him. "Let's go."

He pushed the woman out of the way, dropped to a crouch and unclipped the key chain. If he had a million dollars, he would have bet one of the small, wedge-shaped keys would activate the door controls. Cal grinned at his friends, gave them his best shot at an Elvis voice, and called, "Keys to the kingdom, baby. Keys to the kingdom."

Every locked door was now open to them. They could access the pool area and from there the other side of the hotel. If there was a stockpile of weapons, they could find them and clean house. Make this place theirs. If Psycho Elvis had other victims locked away, like the man and woman, they could find them and set them free, and if they wanted out, they could leave, at any time at all.

With these thoughts in mind, Cal started to stand. The change in expression on Becky and Greg's faces alerted him that something was wrong.

Cal spun around.

Psycho Elvis was sitting in an upright position. He'd returned. Cal had one bullet left. He aimed it at the zombie's forehead, and prepared to fire.

Psycho Elvis looked up at him…and winked.

That wasn't right. Not for a zombie.

That wasn't right at all.

* * *

Becky frowned, confused. The lunatic in the Elvis costume had returned. After he sat up—his chewed on guts spilling out onto the flower-patterned casino carpet— he just remained motionless, looking up at Cal.

Instead of using his gun and getting rid of Elvis once and for all, Cal only stood there, looking down at the dead man. Meanwhile, the undead crowd moved ever closer.

"Cal!" Becky called, for what seemed like the umpteenth time, and when he didn't respond, she decided he must be having some delayed reaction to the shock of everything that had gone down.

He was the last one she would have expected to crack—she'd assumed if any of them lost it, Greg would be the first to come unhinged—but apparently the deaths of the people in the elevator had sent Cal over the edge. She knew one thing for sure. If the erstwhile Elvis-impersonating-psychopath-turned-zombie didn't take a bite out of Cal first, the undead shuffling across the casino floor most definitely would.

Becky's feet moved a step before her mind caught up to what she intended to do. Raising her gun, she ran across the casino, dodging the living dead blocking her path. She didn't know how many bullets remained in her gun—not many for sure—and reloading might be all the time Elvis needed to make his move and take a bite out of Cal's leg.

A young man with a pale face, no nose, and wearing a dusty tux with a decayed carnation fixed to the jacket's lapel was the last to stand in her way. He had that wide-eyed, permanently shocked expression she'd often seen before; a look that gave the poor dead bastards an almost endearing quality. As Becky moved closer, the zombie who looked sorry about wanting to eat her scissored his arms, his hands clawing at the air, putting her in mind of a toddler grasping for some out-of-reach crib mobile dangling down from above. Becky ducked under his outstretched arms, the brush of his sleeve jacket against her hair the closest he came to making contact.

Ahead, Cal and undead Psycho Elvis remained as motionless as before, like the zombie and the man were having some sort of staring contest. Becky aimed, and at five feet away took her shot. The bullet did what it was designed to do. A hole appeared in the middle of the Elvis' forehead and his brains exploded out the back of his skull.

Becky grabbed Cal's arm and pulled him.

He turned to her, confusion in his eyes. "What..."

"Come on!" she shouted. "Time to go!"

Cal nodded, still looking unsure of where he was, but when she pulled on his arm a second time, he followed.

*   *   *

Minutes later, they were back at the lobby.

"Guys, hold up," Greg said. "I need to catch my breath."

No one disagreed with him. Greg and Cal fell ass first onto the nearest couch, sucking air into their lungs. Becky remained standing, bent forward with her hands on her knees, occasionally looking up the hallway that led to the casino.

"We gotta formulate a plan here, you guys," she said. "There has to be at least fifty of those things still standing back there, and it's only a matter of time before they come stumbling along that hallway. Fifty zombies means fifty head shots—and I don't know about you two, but that puts me somewhere in the ballpark of close to fifty bullets shy."

Greg checked his backpack and found nothing. He worked the cylinder release on his revolver. "All I have left is three shots," he said. He searched all his pockets and came up with a single bullet. He pushed it into one of the empty chambers. "Make that four."

"How 'bout you, Cal?" Becky asked. When he didn't answer, she walked over to him and squatted down. "Cal?"

Again, it seemed as though he was in some sort of daze. Years earlier, Becky's grandmother had been stolen away from her, killed by Alzheimer's while her body continued to live. First hand, she'd seen the woman she loved erased. If she didn't know better, if Cal wasn't forty years too young, she would have sworn he was suffering from the same disease.

"Cal?" Becky said. "You still in there?"

The blankness dropped from his eyes, and he looked up at her. He gave her that easy smile she'd come to know so well since meeting him.

"Barely," he said.

He must still be in shock, she decided. It wasn't what she would have expected from him, not after all they'd lived through—all they'd seen—but maybe when she reached her limit and finally cracked, Greg would be looking at her and thinking the same thing.

He just needs to rest, she thought. *He needs to eat and sleep, time for those frayed nerves to mend.*

"How are you for ammo?" she asked.

Cal reached into the back pocket of his pants and pulled out a full clip.

"That's it?"

"That and what's left in the gun," he told her.

Even if they made every shot count, it still wouldn't be near enough to eliminate the threat.

"We need to move out," she said. "We should continue going to the other side of the hotel."

"What about the loading bays?" Greg argued. "I thought we agreed it was our way out of here."

Becky waited for Cal to point out the blindingly obvious fact, that for reasons known only to the workings of his own mind, Greg had failed to grasp. Greg wasn't stupid, he just lacked the ability to apply foresight, living only in the here and now.

In the good old days, she suspected he'd been the family screw up. How he managed to stay alive this long was truly open to speculation. When Cal remained silent, she chalked it up to a continuation of the mental fallout he was suffering from after seeing the hapless man and woman he'd tried to save eaten alive.

Becky looked at Greg. "Let's say we make it outside. Then what? Even if we found another vehicle, one we could hotwire or find the keys to, where would we go, Greg?"

"Unless I'm mistaken," Greg replied. "Before the pickup crapped out, the plan was to head for the desert and look for one of the underground bases."

"Greg, get real," Becky sighed, sounding weary. "If there really is a base out there, if it's not just some pipe dream the survivors we've met cooked up to give themselves a last glimmer of hope, even then, how the hell are we supposed to find it? It's a secret underground base. You think they put up signs when the shit went down, saying, 'If you're still alive and haven't been bitten by a zombie, we'd really like to invite you to come share our limited food supplies?' "

"So what're you suggesting?" Greg asked. "That we stay here?"

"We've got the keys," Becky said. "This place has to be stocked with food, and above all, it's completely secure."

"Secure?" Greg laughed. "We've got no ammo, and thanks to hero boy over here shooting out that glass door, we just made it onto the menu of who knows how many goddamn zombies. You call that secure?"

Becky leaned in close, giving him a close-up look at how angry she was. "Hero boy here just saved your ass from a psychopath who more than likely would have been feeding it to those zombies before sun up, so show a little appreciation."

"Hey, I'm grateful," Greg said. "I really am. But that doesn't change the fact that we've got who knows how many of those things heading our way from the casino. Plus, who knows how many more of them are either loose in the hotel or locked behind a door just waiting for us to open it so they can sink their teeth into us. Case in point. One dead woman's heading our way right this very fucking second."

The first of the casino zombies plodded into view. It shuffled forward along the hallway, halted a few seconds, then continued at geriatric pace toward the three of them. It was the bride they'd seen earlier. The veil they'd seen knocked askew had somehow repositioned itself on her head, covering her face. Behind her, another two zombies turned the corner. Both were men. The one on the left was dressed as a dealer, from the tables. He either tied one hell of a knot or the bow-tie he wore was permanently fixed and held in place by elastic. Like the bride, the dealer zombie appeared relatively intact.

The other man was tall, in his thirties, wearing slacks and a striped button-down shirt. He wasn't so put together. The sleeves of the shirt were missing. So were the arms that were supposed to go inside them. His shirt hung unbuttoned, and though their position made it impossible to tell, Becky thought they'd likely popped off when the shirt had been ripped open.

Evidence of this theory was supported by the open cavity that used to be the man's chest. That the ribs and heart and lungs were gone made no difference, of course. The dead man took a shambling step and lost his balance. He was close enough to the wall that when he fell sideways, it stopped his descent. He leaned against the wall a moment, using it for support, then continued on, the stump of his arm leaving a dark smear behind him.

"We better move," Greg said, getting to his feet.

Cal stood up. His face, which had shown all the expression of a somnambulist these last minutes, suddenly became animated. The grin was too wide and the boggle eyes and raised eyebrows were a possession most often claimed by the insane. In those eyes ticked something that didn't belong.

Becky and Greg looked at Cal, speechless, both thinking this couldn't be the man whose cool dependability they'd never once questioned.

"Move?" Cal said. He snickered as though responding to internal stimuli, his features lit by schizophrenic glee. "We're not moving because of those brainless meat puppets. You have nothing to fear. Not from them. Not with me running the show. You don't believe me? I'll prove it to you. Stay right there. Don't move an inch. Kick back and I'll take care of business."

Cal marched across the lobby, arms swinging in exaggeration, heading for the hallway where the zombies were located. There were more than a dozen now. At the front, the bride and dealer were side by side, just arriving where the hallway ended and lobby began.

"Cal, stop!" Becky cried. "What are you doing?"

Cal halted, looked back at her and grinned. "TCB, baby. Taking care of business."

The small, wall mounted fire extinguisher snapped free of its bracket with one firm yank. Gripping the extinguisher by the neck, Cal advanced. Emitting a high pitched 'woo-hoo,' he swung his improvised weapon.

The thunk of metal on bone rang out as the extinguisher met the card dealer's forehead. The dealer staggered sideways and collapsed to his knees, then dropped face first to the floor. Next the extinguisher's base went slamming into the bride's face, her silk veil blotting the blood from her nose and mouth, the spreading redness causing the veil to cling tight to her features, painting an outline of her face. With flailing arms the toppling bride back-slammed the carpet.

Cal adjusted his grip on the extinguisher, turning it right side up. The blast that doused the armless zombie turned its entire head into a mass of frothy whiteness. The foamed-up zombie, to whom balance had been a trial even during the best of his post-life times, managed a complete three hundred and sixty degree turn before his feet got caught up in each other and gravity took him down.

"He's out of his freaking mind," Greg said. "It's the only explanation."

Becky said nothing. There was nothing to say. Impossible as it seemed that a man like Cal could lose his sanity in a matter of mere seconds, the evidence was right before her eyes. Then again, maybe he'd been close to losing it all along, and kept it somehow hidden. Either way, he was one hundred percent lunatic now.

"Here comes the bride," Cal sang, a metallic *donk* sounding between each word as he used the base of the extinguisher to bash the bride's head in. Here—*donk*—comes—*donk*—the—*donk*—bride.

The musical accompaniment of Cal and head-extinguisher continued with, "Now she's red—*donk*—and brain dead—*donk*—there goes the bride—*donk*."

"But wait!" Cal called, theatrically mimicking a ship's lookout holding a telescope. "What's this I spy? It's the man of the hour. Ladies and gentlemen, I give you the groom!"

The groom was a mess. A large bite out of his neck had resulted in the ruination of his wing-tipped shirt, which blood from the wound had cascaded over. The blood on his shirt front had dried completely, hardening to a shining purplish-black, suggesting he'd been dead for quite some time.

Further evidence of the duration of his death could be found on the groom's face. The ashen skin was pulled taut across the cheekbones, the eyes sunken deep in their sockets. On one side of his face, the skin had split open, revealing the gleam of bone beneath. On the other side, a bite out of his cheek had left an injury that served now as home to a nest of wriggling maggots.

While the dead were particular about the freshness of their meat, flies and their offspring were evidently not so choosy. The groom lumbered along the hallway, nearing its end, more of the casino's undead on either side of him.

"Hate to be the bearer of bad news, pal," Cal said, approaching the groom. "But your bride has runaway brains—running all the way down into the carpet, from the looks of it."

The groom halted in front of Cal, swaying back and forth. His mouth opened wide, revealing gums that were black with decay and contained only a few remaining brown stubs for teeth. A low moan came from his throat.

"I know you're disappointed," Cal said. "What man wouldn't be? But fear not, my fine fellow, I can't throw in all the bells and whistles, not on such short notice, but if nothing else, I can give you a taste of the big event. You deserve that much, don't you? Sure you do. After all, it's such a nice day for a white wedding."

Becky and Greg knew Cal was as good as dead. He had to be: the groom was less than a foot away from him and the other zombies emerging from the hallway into the lobby were closing in on either side. But the groom just stood there, looking at Cal, tottering like someone who'd downed a pint of Jack Daniels.

"Why doesn't he attack?" Becky wondered aloud.

"Didn't you mopes hear me?" Cal roared at the approaching zombies. "I said it's a nice day for a white wedding!"

He let them have it then, blasting the zombies on both sides of the groom with foam from the fire extinguisher, white particles dancing in the air over their heads like confetti. Lacking the brain power to wipe away the foam covering their faces, the dead wandered blindly in every direction, some colliding with each other and falling to the floor, some doing complete turnarounds and returning the way they'd come. Some shambled away across the lobby, their arms outstretched, hands grasping at the air in front of them.

One zombie continued toward Cal. It was the woman from the elevator, the one whose life a very different Cal had tried to save and failed only moments ago. Rivulets of blood ran from the countless wounds covering her face and arms. The zombies had made quite the feast of her. Chunks of the woman's flesh had been greedily gobbled, the teeth marks apparent.

Now, there remained only one small area of her forehead that had not been bitten into and devoured. The rest of her face was dripping wet with blood, much of the exposed sinew ripped to ragged shreds. Her nose was gone and her jaw ripped clean off, leaving exposed a dark stump where a zombie had bitten into the meat of her tongue and devoured it. Somehow, only one of her eyes had been plucked from her head during her mass mauling and the other stared glassily out at Cal, intelligence no longer residing within.

Cal clicked his fingers twice, pointed at her. "Say," he said. "Don't I know you?"

The woman—Marcy—took a step toward him.

Cal aimed the extinguisher, prepared to spray her. Over his shoulder, Cal called to Becky and Greg, "I told her they love meat tender, and I told her they love meat they gotta chew. Well, guess what, you guys? Now she loves it, too."

"W…w…what's he…" Becky stammered, the tingle of fear chilling her spine. "W…what…"

"That was what that psycho sang," Greg whispered, his face blanching, goosebumps prickling his arms. "Jesus, Cal's gone totally wacko."

Cal worked the extinguisher. It sputtered, the nozzle dribbling a thin watery trail of foam. He frowned at it, then shook it. He tried the lever but got nothing. He shrugged, grasped the extinguisher's neck, and used it instead as a club to repeatedly pound the top of Marcy's head.

Blood bloomed atop her skull, wetting her already gore-matted hair, running down her face as she fell to her knees, the sound of the empty canister contacting with her cranium creating a *ding ding ding* sound that was bizarrely musical. Marcy finally toppled, to lie still at Cal's feet. He tossed the extinguisher over his shoulder and a second later it landed with a clatter somewhere behind the front desk.

The groom remained as before, swaying but making no attempt to attack Cal. With a dramatic swing, Cal wind-milled his arm, making three complete circles, swiveling his hips to face Becky and Greg. Ceasing the momentum, he lifted a single finger, pointed directly at the two of them. Looking through the hair dangling in his eyes, he said, "Greg... Becky... Psycho Elvis has officially reentered the building."

The two of them could only stand in shocked incomprehension.

To the groom, Cal said, "Okay, big fella, now is the winter of your discontent made glorious summer, by this son of Hell." To Becky and Greg he called, "You two think you got a zombie problem? To that I say, zombies are the least of your fucking problems right now." He looked at the groom and said in a voice that belonged not to a man but a woman, "You better not drop me, David. I swear if you drop me, I'm gonna ask for an annulment."

Then Cal draped an arm around the zombie groom's neck and hopped up into his waiting arms.

The groom groaned, his atrophied muscles straining to take Cal's weight. Across the lobby, Greg and Becky saw something they would have never expected. In the groom's eyes there was a look of dim awareness. A look that told them something shone within the blankness of the creature's mind. The instinct that relentlessly drove these things to seek the flesh of the living had been subdued.

The groom made no attempt to feed on the man he held in his arms. Instead, he shuffled forward, an expression of wonder forming on his face, and it was clear that somehow, in some way, the groom's mind had undergone a partial rejuvenation.

Under the veil of illusion, the creature was compelled to transport Cal across the lobby, believing he held in his arms his bride, and that he carried her now over the threshold.

"No fucking way," Greg said, shaking his head. "That's impossible."

"Quite the contrary, Greg," Cal called. "You see, it's all a question of power. In this case the power of consciousness. Your own, for example, was born of the body that now contains it. Mine, by contrast, needed no such corporeal form, because where I'm from, there is no type of existence beyond consciousness."

Becky brought up her gun. "What do you mean, 'where you're from'?"

The groom zombie continued to plod toward them, holding Cal in both arms.

"Naturally, you have many questions," Cal called. "And before you die, I may even give you the answers to one or two of them. On the subject of consciousness, on what is and is not possible, I'll offer the following analogy, Greg. Yours is like a forty watt light bulb, while mine is the electricity that powers that bulb, that powers the coffee maker, and the refrigerator, and your flat screen TV and everything else in your house, and everything in everyone else's house all along your street, and everything else in your neighborhood, and all across your city. Do you get me now, Greg? Do you get me?"

"He's flipped," Greg said. "Cal's totally flipped."

Becky shook her head. Tears welled in the corners of her eyes, before rolling down her cheeks. "I don't even think he's still in there. I don't even think he's still alive."

In a clipped English accent, Cal said, "By Jove, I think she's got it."

"Got what?" Greg asked. "What's he saying?"

To the groom Cal said, "Okay, big guy, this is good for me." The groom responded by lowering his arms slowly, until Cal's feet were again planted on the floor. In his English accent Cal told the groom, "Now be a good chap and run along."

The groom didn't run. That would have been asking too much, but he did do an about-face and shuffle away, dragging his heels across the carpet.

Cal raised his arms until they were stiffly outstretched in front of him. He took a lumbering step toward Greg and Becky. "I'm coming to get you, Becky," he said in a sonorous voice.

Becky wiped her eyes with the sleeve of her jacket. Her finger closed around the trigger of her gun. Cal took another lumbering step.

Becky aimed for his heart and warned, "Stay back, whatever the fuck you are. Stay back or I swear to God I'll shoot."

"Do you really think it's going to make a difference?" Cal asked, arms out-still stretched, inching forward.

Greg brought his gun up and made a target of Cal's head. "I don't know what the fuck's going on here, Cal," he said. "But either you back down or you're a dead man."

"There's a line from a movie," Cal said, taking another step. "When there's no more room in Hell the dead will walk the Earth." Cal's Ken Foree was faultless. "But I have my own version," Cal said. "When there's no more room in Hell, the dead are not the only things that will walk the Earth."

"For once will somebody tell me what the fuck I'm missing here?" Greg asked.

"You really have no clue, do you, Greg?" Cal said, sounding a lot like his old self now. "Just like old times, huh, buddy?"

"With one exception," Becky said, the tears flowing freely down her face. "You're not Cal. Something tells me you'll never be Cal again."

"Well, if you won't put poor Greg out of his misery," Cal said, and took another step. "Then I will." His mouth suddenly opened wide. Though his lips didn't move, a voice carried clearly from within. *"You heard him. Don't tell me his words didn't strike you as odd."*

"That's me," Greg whispered. "It's what I said about the guy we found upstairs. Jesus Christ. What the fuck..."

Out of Cal's widely stretched mouth, Greg's voice continued to travel. *"You asked him what kind of man could do this and he said, not a man, a demon. A demon in the flesh."*

"A demon in somebody else's flesh," Becky said. "Flesh that bleeds. Let's see if it also feels pain."

Becky aimed for Cal's foot and fired. The echo of the shot continued to bounce off the lobby walls long after Cal—or the thing now in command of his body—had dropped to the floor.

"Son-of-a-bitch that hurts!" the demon hissed, writhing on the floor. Like a soccer player preparing to strike the ball, Becky ran at Cal, raised her right foot, and let him have it, delivering a kick straight to his face. Cal's head snapped back on impact, blood rushing from his nose.

"What the fuck, Becky?" Greg cried. "You shot him!"

Snapping the keys free from Cal's waistband, Becky turned to look at Greg. "Cal's gone. I know it's hard to accept, but this isn't him. This thing took him; moved out of the other body after it was dead, then took over Cal's body and destroyed his mind in the process."

"Cal's gone?" Greg asked. "Dead?"

The demon sat up, wiping blood from the face of the man whose body he now inhabited. "Sorry, Greg," the demon said. He used a finger to tap the side of his head. "But this town just wasn't big enough for the both of us. Cal's dead and gone. Becky too..."

From the waistband of his jeans, the demon drew a gun and aimed it at Becky. An instant after the gun went off, a spray of blood appeared at the back of her head. Becky's lifeless body dropped to the floor.

"Now," the demon said, wearing Cal's face. "It's just me and you, Greg."

"No!" Greg yelled, running to where Becky lay. One look at the brains leaking out of the head wound told him all he needed to know. "You fucking killed her, man." Greg sobbed. "She's dead."

"Do you really have to say 'fuck' all the time?" the demon asked, the palm of his hand pressed to his nose to stem the blood flow, making him sound like he had a cold. "I mean, it was okay while you were on sidekick duties, but you've been promoted. You're the main character now, and frankly, it's just not fitting for an individual of your newly acquired standing."

"Oh yeah?" Greg said and walked over to where the demon sat. He raised his gun, his voice clotted with raw emotion. "Well, fuck you, fucker."

Holding his gun inches from Cal's face, Greg squeezed back on the trigger.

"Go on," the demon said. "Do it. Believe me, I'm really not sold on staying in this body now that it's damaged, anyway. Yours is physically inferior, but beggars can't be choosers."

Doubt entered Greg's eyes. He eased off the trigger. "If I don't shoot, you'll kill me anyway, so what do I have to lose?"

"Greg," the demon said in Cal's skin, his tone affectionate. "You were the one I was interested in from the moment I let the three of you inside. The only one. Those other two were just too damned decent. But not you, Greg. Oh no, not you. You see, I only have to look into your eyes to know of all the times you let darkness reign. Oh, you tried to step back into the light after the world went to shit, and I applaud you for trying, but all the bad things you did? They're still in you, Greg."

"You're wrong," Greg said.

The demon with Cal's face shook his head, his expression one of sad regret tinged with a hint of mockery. "No matter how much you try to forget that you beat your ex-wife, or try not to think about all those hookers you fucked, or the houses you broke into and the shit you stole, no matter how much you tell yourself you didn't rape that girl and that she was drunk and really wanted it, no matter how much you try to forget the kid you hit that time when you were driving home from the bar shitfaced, no matter how much you try to kill them, those things are always going to be alive and inside you. Always."

Greg's hands were shaking.

"But that's okay," the demon said with a smile. "Now is not the time for heroes. Now is the time for men like you and beings like me. Join me, and I'll give you more power than you ever dreamed of. I'll give you the gift to control the dead, Greg. Armies of them, all yours to command. Together, we can rebuild this world. Together, we can conquer the few remaining scraps of humanity and emancipate them from the dead in exchange for their loyalty."

Greg sneered in contempt. "You mean for their subjugation into slavery."

"You say potato, I say po-ta-to." The demon spat a bloody wad of phlegm into his palm and extended the hand. "So how about it, Greg? Are you gonna eat that bullet and prove that you're really one of the good guys after all, or are you gonna take my hand and help me up off the floor so we can go get our evil on? I've got one hell of a show in mind for this town. More vile than anything it's ever seen. Which frankly, is really saying something. I've even picked out the venue. All I need now is my audience. It's time to shit or get off the pot, Greg."

Greg looked from his gun to the bloody palm of his former friend.

The right choice was a no-brainer.

So Greg made it.

DEATH WALKING TERROR

ADAM P. LEWIS

Chapter 1
The House Call

Midmorning on Friday, March 31, 1888, I heard the loud, rumbling clops of horse hoofs and the crackle of wagon wheels reverberating over the cobblestone road from my second floor office.

The driver yelled, "Whoa there, whoa!" followed by muffled talking.

I pulled back the window curtains and looked through the glass. In an instance, I recognized the carriage driver and the overweight servant woman Clarabelle, a former slave who moved north after the Civil War. She jumped down from the carriage, ran up walk, and leapt up and over the steps. Her large frame landed atop the stoop and her unbalanced momentum pushed her into the heavy oaken door, creating a startling thud.

She pounded on the door, screaming, "Please, Doct'r Myerburg, come quick!"

I scurried from behind my desk and out of the office. I ran down the staircase skipping steps. In one quick motion, I stepped onto the landing, glided across the hardwood flooring to the door, and twisted the doorknob. The front door swung open. But before I could greet or invite Clarabelle inside, she pushed me aside, rushing through the door.

She spoke quickly while crying. Her words were accented by her arms and hands flailing in the air. With each syllable chattering between her teeth, I tried piecing together her words. But her nose, dripping mucus over her lips and often blown into a handkerchief, distorted her words more than her crying.

"Oh Lord, dat gal, dat gal!" she babbled.

I grabbed her hand and tried to console her. "Calm down—calm down. I can't help you unless you relax and tell me what brought you to me this morning."

She continued ranting through a prayer, one for a sick child. "Heavenly Fath'r, watch wit' us over yo' child!"

As she rambled, she followed me to my study. Her hysterics made it difficult for her to act peacefully. She kept grabbing her chest and waving her hands at the heavens, chanting prayers. Her eyes fixed on the ceiling as though she was looking through it to the clouds. She kept stumbling over her feet, causing her shoulders to bang into the wall. Then she fell to her knees, where her praying would be considered prim and proper.

After entering my study, I handed her a glass of water and instructed her to breathe slow and deep between sips. She snatched it from my hands like a hungry dog and soon thereafter, her hysterical praying subsided enough to comprehend every other word coming out of her mouth. But her southern drawl and broken English still made it difficult to understand what had brought her to me.

Between deep breaths she explained her visit. "Karen...gravely ill...Mr. Chapman...ordered...me...ta fetch you."

"Karen? What's wrong with her? Tell me of her symptoms," I ordered, leaving the study to gather my medical bag from the adjoined examination room.

Clarabelle calmed enough for me to understand. "I knocked on Miss Chapman's bedroom this mornin' because I heard her coughin'. It were a' awful coughin' fit, all filled wit' mucus dat made her throat all clogged up a' all. I called through da door a' asked if she be okay. She answer me wit' a moan so I enter. I fell back through da doorframe when I saw her pale face an' dat blood 'round her mouth. Oh Lord, save da child, she done no one no harm!"

"Has she an appetite and drinking plenty of liquids?" I asked while latching my medical bag.

Clarabelle grabbed my arm and with all her weight behind her. She yanked and pulled me off balance. "No need fo' more questions, Doct'r Myerburg, hurry now!"

Clarabelle almost dislocated my shoulder. Annoyed, I jerked my arm from her tight grasp, grabbed her by the arm, pushed her on floor and yelled, "I cannot help you unless you allow me to do my job correctly! Do we have an understanding?"

She coward by pulling her legs and arms up in a fetal position, shaking her head yes. Her eyes closed tight and her lips quivered in fright. She kept flinching at each motion I made. It was obvious she was experiencing flashbacks of her former slave owner beating her for doing a job not up to his standards.

I offered my hand to hers and pulled her up. I apologized, "I'm sorry, that was no manner for a doctor to act in. Especially to a lady."

She smiled and accepted my apology. " 'S'all right. Wit me actin' all wild I don't blame ya."

I smiled in return. "Come now, take me to Karen so we can help her."

I pick up my medical bag and put on my overcoat. We left my office. Clarabelle was still winded and lagged behind. I reached the foot of the stairs and exited the house. I waited on the porch for Clarabelle. She was moving slow and breathing deep. Her overweight body couldn't handle the excitement and stress; if anymore was piled atop her shoulders, I feared she would collapse and die. She exited the house, started down the front stoop and lost her balance. I stretched out my hand for support, and she grabbed it and made it down the steps safely.

From behind, a male voice asked, "Hey, Doc Myerburg, you need any help?"

I turned to thank the carriage driver for offering his assistance. To my surprise, it was Ben, the town's blacksmith.

"No thank you, Ben, much obliged!" I said.

"Everything all right?" Ben asked, holding open the gate for Clarabelle and me.

I raised my eyebrows and said, "I hope so, Ben, I hope so."

Clarabelle climbed into the carriage and I followed.

Before we sat down and the carriage door closed, the driver yelled, "Giddy up!" A loud crack of reins broke the air as they whipped down upon the horses' backs. The carriage lurched forward, causing us to fall back into the seats. Clarabelle stumbled and fell into my chest; her obese body knocked the wind out of me. She stood up, flushed with embarrassment. She apologized and straightened out my clothes.

I grabbed her hands and stopped her. "Thank you, but I think I'll be fine."

The carriage sped away with the driver whipping the horses, making them gallop faster down the street. The crack of the whip was deafening, as was his yelling for patrons crossing the street to make way.

"Hey there, clear out—clear out. Get outta the way!" he warned, followed by cursing and name calling from those the horses almost trampled.

The carriage wheels dipped into potholes and bounced over loosened cobblestones, making the ride bumpy and dangerous. The carriage tipped on two wheels each time the horses rounded corners, causing the carriage to almost fail to navigate each turn.

Clarabelle came close to falling out the window when the carriage tipped. She would've done so if it weren't for her wide shoulders that wouldn't fit through the window frame. When the carriage landed back on all four wheels, our bodies bounced off the seats and our heads hit the roof.

After exiting the town and entering into the countryside, the hair-raising dash in the carriage settled to a steady ride. I used this moment to ask Clarabelle questions pertaining to Karen's illness. With each question, she became quiet compared to her dramatics back at my office. Not wanting to hear further questions, she turned her face from me and stared out the window. She pressed her lips together and folded her arms over her chest. Frustration began to settle within my mind as answers regarding Karen's infliction and the possibility of others being stricken went ignored. The rest of the ride was quiet. There was something she was not supposed to speak of, perhaps under direct orders of her employer, Harold Chapman. In due time however, that piece of information would be revealed.

Upon entering through the front gates of the Chapman Estate, the house created an overwhelming sense of awe. I had never visited the Chapman's estate nor have I seen it. I've never ventured this far south from town even on a house call until now. My longest trips were for hunting and fishing north to Canada. The townspeople would often gossip and exaggerate about the size and appearance of the house, but those rumors were far from true. The house was bigger and more extravagant than the rumors led me to believe. The Chapman's were wealthy, but no one figured their wealth to be so extensive.

The house was erected upon the eastern hilltop within a fifty acre, gated estate and was architecturally styled in American Queen Anne. This style was most popular among those worthy enough to afford the high construction price, which the Chapman family most certainly could. Those jealous of their wealth called the Chapman's spendthrifts and rightly so, the house was magnificent and the amenities extravagant.

The facade was asymmetrical and accented with two gables, and the apexes complimented a bell-shaped tower between, which was the dominant feature of the front elevation. A pediment porch that cornered around the left side of the house surrounded a large oriel window sectioned into thirds. The siding resembled fish scales and were painted light tan, accented by trim painted in a dark brown, as were the dentils. The shingles were slate with a natural gray tint.

Another tower constructed in the background eclipsed the size of the bell tower, soaring approximately twenty feet higher in an octagonal shape. This open aired balcony resembled a gazebo, allowing those who stood within to get a clear view of the grounds surrounding the house.

On a day when the sunshine wasn't constricted by clouds, one could look down over Saratoga Lake as well as the mountain terrain beyond it. Those on the ground also have a clear view of the balcony and its occupants. Its openness created a voyeuristic appeal.

As I gazed in wonderment, Clarabelle jumped from the carriage before the carriage came to a complete stop. Her pear-shaped body was off balance, causing her to land on her side and tumble onto the grass. Before asking if she was injured, she stood and ran up the stoop, skipping every other step between strides. She then flung open the front door and yelled inside, telling her employer she had returned with me.

Before exiting the carriage, an old, plump man with a gray mustache came down the steps. He hunched over and waddled as he walked. He was dressed in a morning suit indicating he was the Chapman's butler.

"Welcome to the Chapman Estate. My name is George. If there is anything I can assist you with during your examination, please do not hesitate to ask," the butler said in a scratchy, winded voice.

"Please, call me Dr. Myerburg."

He extended his arm to help me climb down from the carriage. "My apologies, Dr. Myerburg, and thank you for arriving on such short notice."

"Much obliged, but there is no need to assist me down from the carriage, I can manage."

The seasoned butler smiled. He most likely never experienced respect from a visitor or perhaps even from his employer. Harold Chapman had an unfavorable disposition towards the city of Saratoga Springs that one could assume carried over to his employees.

George opened the front door and rushed me down a long hallway decorated with exotic paintings and statues. At the end of the hallway was an oaken door leading into the parlor. Inside and kneeling by his daughter's side was Harold Chapman. He turned and greeted me. His lips were turned downward in a frown. His eyes were watery, his arms shook, and his voice cracked from nervousness.

"Thank you for coming, Doctor," Harold said, shaking my hand as he motioned with his other to his daughter. She was sprawled out on a couch and staring at the ceiling without expression.

Visuals gave the first impression of the illness affecting her body. Trailing from the corners of her mouth, bloody spittle encrusted over her chin and neck. Her skin was a ghostly hue, giving her face a waxen complexion. Her eyes sunk into their optic canals, lips flushed in a crimson tone, and her body had turned frail, taking on the appearance of a walking corpse.

"How long has she been in this condition?" I asked Harold, taking his daughter's wrist in my hand to check her pulse.

"Clarabelle heard Karen coughing this morning and checked on her," Harold answered. His voice cracked as he held back tears.

The condition of his daughter filled him with worry and stress. Sweat beaded on his forehead, his lips clasped together and curled back. His eyes were squinted and glossy. He tried keeping his feelings bottled up, but it was clear he was grieving as if she'd already passed to the other side.

Harold needed to relax before he broke down and upset his daughter. I smiled at him and said, "At first glance I can tell she has tuberculosis, but just to make sure I'll do a full examination. I can heal your daughter if the illness isn't too advanced, which it doesn't seem to be."

I lied. Her illness was in its late stages. I didn't need Harold turning frantic on me or threatening. The parents of children I've examined in the past often turned violent upon hearing their child had no possibility of recovery. Against their will and mine, we had to allow their illnesses to overwhelm the children and quicken their deaths to lessen their suffering.

Harold's voice turned from sobbing to defensive and irate. "No, you're wrong, Doctor. She doesn't have tuberculosis, she's dying from…" He stopped talking and placed his hand near his mouth, trying to conceal any body language that would indicate he was keeping a secret, but by trying to cover his mouth, he told me the exact opposite

In response, my eyebrows rose in suspicion, signaling he'd failed to keep his secret.

"Is there something you need to tell me that would help me diagnose your daughter? If so, you must tell me now," I demanded.

His demeanor turned defensive. He looked at his servants, and when his eyes met with theirs, they turned away. Some looked at the floor as others turned their faces to the wall and ceiling. Some folded their arms over their chest, rocked on their heels or hid behind their hands by scratching or rubbing their temples. It was obvious they were uncomfortable and tried to ignore the situation.

"There's nothing anyone in this room needs to tell you, Doctor, please continue," he said, waving his hands at me as if he were shooing me away like a rodent.

Knowing he was keeping information from me, I found it odd he said we. It was obvious by his servants' gestures and his own that they knew something. As a group they were keeping it private.

I took a chance that one of them would speak up and expose the secret so I directed my suspicion to them and asked collectively, "If anyone here knows anything that would help, please tell me now."

Not a single person offered information and some of the servants' body language suggested they were eager to tell me something important. They cleared their throats, eyes opened wide, their lips separated as if they were about to talk, but they feared backlash if they spoke so each servant became reserved.

I myself became frustrated with them and continued the examination. I checked Karen's pulse while glancing at the clock, timing and counting it. While doing so, the parlor turned from a medical examination into a theatrical event. The servants gathered around the couch looking on. Though I am a professional, their eyes felt uncomfortable, as though they were prying, and above all I was observed by a group that was keeping a life-saving secret from me.

As a public servant myself, I didn't want to degrade Harold's employees by ordering them out of the parlor. Instead, I insisted on moving Karen to her bedroom to complete the examination, much to the dismay of Harold himself.

"I need to continue my evaluation in private. She must be moved to her bedroom!" I demanded.

Harold snapped back. "In her condition she needs to stay where she is. It's written on her face that she's in pain and moving her will only make her feel worse. You don't even know what her illness is. Moving her may kill her!"

"If she dies from being moved then I will take full responsibility for her death," I said. "But as I stated before, your daughter needs to be comfortable and this couch is not meant for a sick person to recover or be examined on. She needs to be moved."

"And as I have stated before, she's fine where she is," Harold said, mimicking the demanding tone of my voice with a sarcastic attitude.

"I haven't been able to perform a complete examination." I raised my voice. "I don't know if she has a communicable disease. It's quite possible that even before I diagnose the illness she's spreading it to me, you, and every one of your servants. That is if we all haven't contracted the disease already."

Harold shook his head and pointed at me. He was stern with his words and tried to make it obvious who was actually in charge—him. "If everyone is already infected then your point in moving her is moot. She stays where she is."

A plan to twist control in my favor entered my head. "If you insist on the examination continuing in this parlor and on this couch, then you'll not reject to your daughter's breasts being exposed in front of you and your servants as I check her breathing."

Harold walked to the door and opened it. "All servants must leave and return to their living quarters." The servants looked around at each other and at me without budging until Harold yelled, "Now!"

Before they reached the door, I ran to it and ripped it from Harold's grip, slamming it closed. "If Karen cannot leave the room then no one can. If everyone here is infected then the rest of the servants not present may contract the disease. They must not be allowed to freely roam the house. If they fear they could die then they could leave the property. No one can do such until I know what her illness is."

I returned to Karen's side and started unbuttoning her nightshirt. From the corner of my eye, I saw George staring at Karen's chest. My head turned to his. The left corner of his mouth curled up, his eyebrows crimped in towards the bridge of his nose, and his head tilted down. His palms rubbed together over his groin and his breathing became loud as he licked his lips. My first impression of the little old man was docile but it seemed he was sexually perverted as well.

Harold noticed George's sudden giddiness and halted the examination before the third button on Karen's nightshirt was undone. "Stop, take her upstairs. She should be examined in private."

I rose and ordered, "No one leaves this room until I have concluded the exam, including a diagnosis. Is that understood?"

The servants muttered in agreement and Harold folded his arms in annoyance. He was incensed with the way I was ordering his servants around, but more aggravating to him was the way I took control over him as well.

I helped Karen to her feet with Harold's help. "I will be present while you examine my daughter," he said.

"I cannot allow that, sir. Like I said, I'm not sure if you're infected or not."

George rolled his eyes, let out a quick laugh, and muttered under his breath, "Like the others."

Again my head turned to his. If he indeed did say *like the others*, then their identities, whereabouts and symptoms needed to be known. If their symptoms were the same as Karen's, then a pandemic was staring to flourish, if it hadn't already done so.

After George mumbled his statement, my attention turned to Harold. He scowled at his butler with teeth pressed together, eyes nearly hidden under lowered brows, and muscles twitching his cheeks. The angry expression caused George's face to go blank and his head to droop, and his eyes to stare at his own feet. There was something the old man knew and Harold's glance caused George to keep that information locked away.

Whatever the old man knew, I had a feeling he was never going to tell me. Perhaps he knew the family's medical history; after all, he had been the Chapman's butler before the children were born. My gut feeling told me he wasn't going to talk to me, even in private.

Chapter 2
Vomit the Soul

Karen's knees buckled as she tried to push up on the first step with her leg. For support, she draped her arm over my shoulder and held on to the railing. With each step, she let out a soft moan laden with coarse coughing. She was suffocating under asthmatic attacks.

Midway up the staircase, she collapsed. Her arms were frail from her sickness, making it difficult for her to brace her fall. She fell into the wall and hit her head on the railing, almost knocking herself unconscious. With all my strength, I lifted her up to her feet and piggybacked her up the rest of the way.

Within two steps my legs weakened. I felt as though I were trekking through knee-deep snow in the Adirondacks with one hundred and fifty pounds of dead weight attached to my back.

The climb to the top step was a struggle but we made it without further mishaps. In a gentle motion, I lowered Karen from my back and stood her up on her feet. She supported herself on the wall with her shoulder while fighting the limpness within her legs. Her shoulder slid across on the wall as she shuffled her feet to her bedroom. After two steps, she paused and started choking until she coughed black mucus from her lungs. Unable to wipe it from her lips or spit it out, she let it drizzle from the corners of her mouth, allowing it to seep down her chin and under her collar.

Unable to continue walking, her back slid down the wall until she rested on her buttocks. I lifted her to her feet and draped her left arm over the nape of my neck, then wrapped my other arm around the middle of her back. She gripped my clothes within her hands to support herself as I helped her down the remainder of the hallway to her bedroom.

We entered her room, and before she reached her bed, she clenched her stomach as the pain intensified. Tears began trickling down her face and she doubled over and collapsed to her knees. Her head jerked forward and her mouth opened, forming an oval shape as she proceeded to vomit stomach bile. The vomiting was violent and extensive. Her face turned blue from lack of oxygen. She fainted; fell onto her stomach and the vomiting ceased.

Minutes later, she regained consciousness and her body curled up into the fetal position. Without warning, she became stricken with seizures. Her body thrashed about the floor and her head bucked against a nightstand, creating a deep gash across her forehead.

I pulled her into the middle of the room, away from the furniture and other dangerous obstacles. Straddling her body and forcing open her mouth, I removed my belt, folded it in half, and shoved it between her teeth in order to keep her from biting off her tongue.

Her body continued thrashing. She nearly bucked me off and onto my back. Pushing her shoulders down with the bulk of my bodyweight, she became stabilized. I tried keeping her from rolling in fear the belt would loosen from between her teeth, causing her to bite off her tongue.

As quickly as the seizers appeared, they ceased. I bandaged her head and helped her to her feet. After removing her vomit-covered nightgown, she climbed into bed and pulled a sheet up to her chest, hiding her naked body. From my medical bag, I retrieved a stethoscope and began the examination.

Pressing the stethoscope upon her chest, I examined her coronary functions and noted heart palpitations that were, in relation to healthy heartbeats, faint and erratic. Her pulse couldn't be determined through her neck because of the erratic heartbeat nor by pressing my thumb upon her wrists because of her heart rhythm's anemia.

Her respiratory function, which couldn't be evaluated through triangular auscultation of the lungs due to her body position, was examined through her chest. Her breathing as noted was labored, shallow, and spotted with wheezing. Both tests indicated she was dying. Her illness was more advanced than even I believed at first glance when I was downstairs with her in the parlor.

I turned to place the stethoscope back in my medical bag when her body shot up in a seated position. The quick lurch forward knocked me from the bed as her chest bumped into my head.

She swatted at her arms while screaming, "Get them off me!"

Her arms were bare.

"Please…get…them…off…help…me!" She begged, thrashing her head in circles as if something was attached and biting her scalp.

I jumped up and grabbed her upper arms between my hands. "Relax so I can help!"

Her head whipped forward and crashed into my jaw, knocking my head backwards. I lost my grip of her shoulders, fell off the bed, and onto my back. Her screams continued, the girl crying out for help as she again pleaded with me to get *them* off her. She scratched at her arms, drawing blood with every rake of her fingernails across her skin.

I stood up and grabbed her left arm, holding it steady, while glancing from her wrist to her shoulders, looking for whatever was crawling across her skin. Still, her arms were bare.

"What is it that you feel? What do you see?" I asked, looking at her skin.

"The bugs, they're eating away at my skin. It hurts so much! Please get them off me, please!" she begged and ripped her arm free from my grasp and continued clawing at her skin. Her fingers dug deeper, peeling back layers of skin that curled up under her fingernails.

"You're only hallucinating. There are no bugs on you. You must relax!" I yelled, holding her arms apart and against the mattress, trying to stop her from scratching and drawing more blood.

Her head whipped back and forth as she screamed, "My head is burning! I feel them slithering out from under my hair! Please get them off me!"

My fingers raked through her hair, spreading apart the follicles while searching for the things that were hurting her. Again, nothing was found. Not a single bug or creature was slithering on her skin.

Her pain threshold reached it limits as she begged, "Please…help me…kill me…end my pain…please!"

There was nothing I could do but beg her to stop. "I can cure you. Just let me help. Please stop yelling and calm down!"

With what little strength she retained, she pushed me off her body to the foot of the bed. She rose to her feet, opened a desk drawer, and pulled out a letter opener. She put the point against her chest, and at the same moment she pressed down, I lunged forward, grabbed her wrist, and overpowered her. Her arm twisted, causing her to spin around and scream out in pain. The letter opener fell to the floor. Before she picked it up, I opened the window and tossed it out to the ground below.

She collapsed to the floor, lying motionless, becoming too weak to claw at her arms. "Please, let me die!"

I helped her stand and walked her back to the bed. I started cleaning and bandaging her self-inflicted wounds without resistance from her. Whatever images she was experiencing vanished. She no longer flailed her arms about and kicked her legs or thrashed her head back and forth. I was no longer in danger of being hit and thrown to the floor.

From outside her bedroom, we heard footsteps running up the staircase and down the hallway. Her father called out to his daughter in hysterics, "Karen—Karen, Daddy's coming! Hold on!"

Seconds later, Harold burst through the door, pushed me away, and held his daughter in his arms. Upon seeing the bandage on her head and her arms bloodied and scratched, he glared at me in anger. "What've you done to her? You're supposed to be saving her life, not making it worse. This is why I should've been allowed to be present during the examination!"

I grabbed his arm and pulled him away his daughter. "I told you to stay downstairs. Now look at yourself, you've got her blood on you and now you may have gotten yourself infected. Stop being a stupid hero and start listening to me!"

He pushed me away. "Don't come into my home and order me around like you're the man of my house!" He turned his back to me and folded his arms over his chest.

I walked around him and looked him square in the eyes. "You asked me here, sir. I didn't come here out of pleasure. As long as you want my medical advice then you need to listen to me!"

He grabbed the front of my shirt and slightly pulled me to him, stopping me inches from his face. His warm exhale of breath could be felt on my face as he grumbled at me. "You listen to me, Doctor, you're going to stay here and heal my daughter and then leave this house and never return. Until then you're going to listen to me. Do we have an understanding?"

Rage swept through me. My pulse rate increased and my face flushed. I was angrier than I'd ever been over my forty-five years of life. I wanted to drag him down the hallway and pushed him down the staircase to his death, but the health of his daughter was more important to me than releasing my anger. My fantasy of doing harm to Harold would have to suffice.

I took a deep breath and spoke calm and respectful but still my tone was filled with tension. "I understand. I will stay here if needed but if I'm called upon by another patient, I will tend to them and come back here and check on your daughter. When she stabilizes, I'll need a carriage ride to my office to leave a note on the door explaining my whereabouts."

Harold shook his head in disagreement. "If no one else in this house can leave because they may be infected, that means you have to stay here as well. You may also be infected. Those are your own words and demands, Doctor, not mine!"

I did not argue. He was right. I also knew that if I was going to save Karen's life, I would need help. I extended my hand in friendship and asked for assistance. Seconds later, he rushed out of the room to retrieve fresh water and clean bandages to rewrap Karen's wounds. The initial bandages were now soaked with blood that seeped through and began to be absorbed by the mattress. After Harold retrieved the bandages, together we rewrapped the wounds and continued the examination.

Karen's pulse strengthened, and while counting heartbeats and tracking seconds, I glanced around the bedroom. It was bare compared to the extravagance that decorated the downstairs, except for a vase holding roses and a wall lined with photographs of the Chapman family. In one of the photos, Harold and a much younger Karen stood next to a young boy and another girl. With them were their wife and mother, Jane. The boy looked like uncannily like Harold, tall, thick-haired but missing a beard. In the picture, Harold was much thinner than he was now. The girls were a spitting image of their mother, which made for very attractive young women. Their hair was long and curly, faces heart-shaped with stout noses and thick lips. Their eyes were big and round and accented by thin eyebrows.

Jane and the other two children were absent in the house, which raised red flags to their whereabouts. If Harold had sent them away in order to protect them from becoming ill, then a pandemic could arise if they were carrying a hazardous and highly contagious bacteria. Yet, I didn't recall seeing his wife or other children in quite some time.

In a calm voice, I said to Harold while nodding at the photographs, "You have a beautiful family."

"Thank you."

"I haven't seen them around town in quite a long time, maybe a year or so. Are they on an extended vacation visiting her family in the south? I ran into Clarabelle a few weeks back at the market and she said they've been there a while because her father fell ill."

Harold's voice trembled in nerves. "No, they didn't go south."

"Oh, I must've misunderstood. Then I'd like to examine them as well when they come home. Even though I believe Karen has tuberculosis, I haven't definitely identified her infliction yet because of her violent outbursts. Your wife and children may be carrying a bacterial infection that may spread quickly, so I need to make sure they are healthy."

"You don't need to worry about my family spreading what has befallen Karen. My wife and children have passed on. They suffered from the same illness Karen has now."

Harold started crying and I was about to erupt in anger but refrained. For Karen's sake I needed to remain somewhat calm. But it was impossible to ignore the fact that he hadn't confided in me about his family today or in the past.

"Why did you keep information about your family from me? It may be important. It could save your only surviving child's life!"

"I didn't want to explain to an educated man, especially a man of medicine, of an unseen and supernatural plague that has affected my family."

"Unseen or seen you must tell me what has killed your family. I am a doctor and open to all possibilities."

"The cause of their deaths isn't a disease that you or anyone else can cure with medicines, Doctor. That's why I didn't tell you when or how they passed. That's why I told my servants to tell those who asked that they were away. I didn't want people to think I was murderer or a practitioner of witchcraft or worse yet, Satanism. My youngest daughter Maggie, like her brother David and their mother Jane before them, fell ill and died under the spell of an unearthly god's consumption. Only such a disease could be explained as evil conjured up from the depths of Hell."

"Well, sir, whatever the case may be, you kept this a secret. You could have very well put a death sentence on the entire village of Saratoga Springs!"

"You know how the people of this town look at my family and especially me," he said. "They would think I killed them for financial gain or in some scheme. If you were married and lost your family to an unseen force then you would also be targeted as the cause. This town is very religious. I'd be put on trial for witchcraft and hanged!"

I became annoyed with him and almost collected my medical belongings and left his house. Not only because he failed to inform me of his family's medical history, which directly related to Karen's plight, but also because of his reputation and what it caused him to hide. But in respect of my medical teachings and practice, to which I devoted my life, services, and expertise regarding the healing arts, I set aside my differences for Harold to help the girl.

In doing so, I decided to maintain my professionalism by examining and watching over his daughter in an unbiased opinion. Neither my devotion to the practices of medicine or my ill will toward Harold would construe my findings.

However, before the horror that we were about to experience is described, I must briefly clarify my cynical regards and understandings toward Harold's social standings. In doing so, one would easily understand why a man such as Harold kept this secret to himself.

Harold, self-disparaged from high regards within the village of Saratoga Springs, distinguished himself unfavorably as a grifter. He'd swindled schoolchildren of mere cents and drunkards of whiskey bottles through dishonest schemes. Magical illusions, marked card decks, double-talking, and various aliases were his foray to stupefy gullible and unsuspecting individuals. The leery, sober and those citizens displaying qualities of culture and learning were not dumbfounded by his trickeries nor easily corrupted into collaborating with him to commit similar schemes upon unsuspecting travelers. Hence, his reputations to surround himself with naïve schoolchildren and alcoholics in order to lie, cheat, and steal.

Twenty-five years earlier, he tried to make his mark within Republican politics. He moved south, rather I should say he carpet-bagged and in vain touted himself as trustworthy and sympathetic.

Offering false promises to rebuild sections of the Civil War ravaged south if elected to office, he solicited benefactions from disparaged, displaced, and needful Southerners. But he didn't use the donations for the good of a recovering nation, but rather indulged in countless bottles of alcohol and women. Both of which could be assumed as being cheap. Upon returning north, after wedding a wealthy southern girl named Jane Bottington, he was greeted indifferently and considered aloof.

Personally, my only interactions with the Chapman family, other than examining the children since birth, are sidestepping Harold's alcohol-comatose body sprawled in front of tavern stoops. All my other negative feelings stem from stories of moral decay, featuring none other than Harold Chapman himself.

Therefore, taking account of his known reputation and my own feelings, for him to falsify Karen's illness for personal gain and attempt to dupe a rational doctor such as myself, the scheme is far too complex for a man with his level of ignorance to conspire and execute. Additionally, Karen's illness was too complicated to forge.

I stared out the bedroom window and Harold put his hand on my shoulder. "Doctor, I apologize for not telling you of my family's past. I ask for forgiveness."

"I don't need an apology," I said. "I just need you to be straight forward with me from here on out. If there is anything else you need to tell me then you must explain it to me this instance."

"There's one more thing I need to tell you but now is not the time or the place. And you wouldn't believe me if I told you, you've have to see it for yourself. You need to see it to believe it."

"By all means, Harold, whatever it is, then show me," I demanded in a gruff tone.

"After the sun sets meet me out under the gazebo," he said, pointing out the window. "For the sake of believing my story, Doctor, I hope you experience the *lights*."

Chapter 3
The Lights of Cole's Woods

Hours passed and the sun settled on the horizon. Karen's condition stabilized; she hadn't experienced further hallucinations. That was when I decided it was time to meet Harold outside and experience the 'lights.' Moments after joining Harold under the gazebo, George walked out from the house and supplied us with blue-veined cheese, two wine glasses, and a bottle of Port. We sat under a gazebo as a summer's breeze washed across our faces. The breeze was cool and created a mood of relaxation and content.

Harold sipped his Port and sat quietly. For a moment, my mind escaped from the stressful events back in the house. I reclined in an Adirondack chair, stretched out my legs, and closed my eyes, indulging in the tranquil moment. The feeling was much overdue.

Many minutes later, I began taking pleasure in my second glass of Port and third piece of cheese. Harold was sipping his third glass as he began to stimulate my imagination with tales of the mire just beyond his property. The stories were fantastic and frightening as they spoke of demons and ghosts. I didn't interrupt him, figuring he was leading up to an explanation of the lights. After all, he did mention a supernatural cause to his family's suffering just hours before.

"Have you ever heard of the Jersey Devil, Doc?"

I shook my head while chewing a piece of cheese.

"Over a century ago, in the Pine Barrens of New Jersey, a woman named Leeds became pregnant with her thirteenth child. She said that child would be born the Devil. And on the baby's birthday, he was born normal but soon changed into a winged and hoofed creature with the head of a horse. The beast flew up to the ceiling and whipped a forked tail around the room until impaling the midwife with it. It's said that the mother was a witch and the father the Devil himself!"

My reactions to his stories, if I were sober, would normally be to scoff, which I had at first. As a doctor of medicine, such tales of supernatural events are automatically ruled out as created explanations of events and sicknesses people don't understand the causes for. Karen's symptoms and Harold's actions lead me to believe just that. But being that my belly was full of Port, my personality turned lighthearted and naive.

"Do you suspect that this...this Jersey Devil as you call it, has come for your family?" I asked.

He shook his head no and continued speaking of tales that turned ominous. He spoke of insecurities so ghastly they induced phobias too haunting to alleviate minds through psychiatric therapies. He described demons whose evil minds constructed treacherous plights in which no man could forge through with sanity intact. None of which were more apparent then when his speech wavered in frightful intonations as he began speaking of the light that manifested within the mire, which he described as a torturing pestilence.

"The torturing pestilence is what has attacked my family. Like the Jersey Devil, the pestilence is a horrific monster conjured up from the bowels of Hell," he said, holding his wine glass out with his index finger pointing to the general direction of the mire. "It can clearly be seen from this very gazebo."

I sat up in the Adirondack chair and adjusted my posture to give Harold my full attention. I had never heard of the torturing pestilence during my years of study or during my practices. And having my mind clouded under an inebriated state, he grasped my attention at the mere utterance of the words.

"They are spectral lights. They form over the marsh at nightfall. A small ball of light appears out of thin air and can be seen drifting through the trees."

I interrupted him with a soft snicker and interjected my thoughts. "What you are seeing is only natural discharges of swamp gas. Spectral lights, this torturing pestilence as you label them as being, are nonexistent. It seems you've been tilting Port to your lips more often than not!"

He held his wine glass over the table before us and dropped it upon the maple tabletop. The glass base bounced and clinked as it spun and vibrated in rapid thumps before resting upright. He gave me an ill-tempered glare infused by my badly timed quip. He wasn't convinced by my explanation of the lights, which was evident by the bottle drop.

His abrupt anger, which scorned my scientific suggestion, withered under sudden fear. His teeth clattered. His brows rose exposing the whites of his eyes. They stared deep into my eyes that were trustless to all subjects of the paranormal.

His voice spoke in fear as he continued his account of the spectral lights. "As twilight sets, you can hear the bullfrogs croaking and crickets chirping within Cole's Woods. Soon however, they stop in unison as the torturing pestilence manifests. A small ball of blue light burbles from underneath the water's surface and rises into the air. The horrific light then climbs to an approximate height of ten feet and contorts into the shape of a human being. I can hear its shrill of pain-stricken wails as it searches Cole's Woods for victims and the house it lived in when alive."

He turned and looked past me at his house. "The house being the one in which my family resides. We were doomed from the moment the pestilence found us."

He glanced back into the woodlands without speaking a word. I took his moment of quietness to state my case once more. "Harold, if I may, it's only swamp gas you're seeing. Please trust me."

He stepped out from under the gazebo, pointed at the mire again, and turned his head towards me. "The first time I saw those lights was not a coincidence. It was just after Jane passed away. Soon after seeing the lights, Maggie died followed by David a week later. On the eve of each of their deaths, I saw those very lights form over the mire and float through Cole's Woods."

He cleared his throat and continued. "The lights have no simple explanations, such as natural occurrences of swamp gases discharging from the mire. It's the specter of my wife coming to feed on her own children like a vampire sucking blood from necks. I laid Jane to rest in my family's burial grounds that are just beyond the mire. I've dreaded her return for the past two years, fearing she would come for Karen. Now, being that the lights have returned, she has come to take her last child. If that's the case then I fear I'll fall soon thereafter."

I set my Port down on the table. "If I may ask, how did Jane die and why do you think she has come back for the rest of her family?"

Harold breathed in deep. "Two years ago I woke up to Jane moaning. She was holding her stomach and huddled over a vessel sink. I hurried out of bed and stood by her side, asking her what was the matter. She didn't answer me, instead she vomited blood. After the vomiting stopped, I insisted she call upon you right away. I even had the driver get the carriage ready, but she continued to refuse your help."

"Why didn't you make her come to me?" I asked, confused to why her illness was kept under lock and key by her own doing.

Harold shook his head and shrugged his shoulders. "I don't know. I suggested that as well but again she argued. She said she was too tired to go through an examination and didn't want the children to think there was anything wrong with her. All she wanted to do was rest in bed. That was what she did for three straight days. I kept watch over her and was ready to call upon you if she needed me to. But she never asked. She just kept getting worse. Then on the fourth day, I woke to find her dead. There was blood encrusted on her mouth and neck, so much that her nightgown collar was drenched in blood. Her skin was white as a ghost and her eyes had turned black."

I rose to my feet and stood next to him. "Who did she have contact with before she fell ill?"

He closed his eyes tightly and breathed in deep, trying to hold back his emotions. "She'd just returned from her parent's plantation in the south," he explained, his voice broken with grief. "Her father was ill and wasn't expected to live more than a month more. She arrived there a few days before he died and left two weeks after his burial. During that time her mother fell ill but also recovered."

"What were the symptoms before her father died?"

"He had the same symptoms that my entire family had including Karen. David's was more severe and he died after two days. Maggie lasted two weeks before perishing."

"Why didn't you ask me for help?"

"The circumstances of their deaths were not from illnesses. They fell ill because of an evil entity," he said, banging his fist against the gazebo as his voice turned angry.

I placed my hand on his shoulder and squeezed in sympathy, which calmed him down. "Why would you think that?"

Harold's anger subsided and he began to cry. "When my wife returned home, she told me about a ritual she participated in a day after her father's death." He wiped tears from his eyes. "This ritual started our family curse!"

"What kind of ritual?" I asked.

Harold paced around the gazebo without making eye contact with me. He was embarrassed. "Two months before, she traveled to pay her last respects to her brother Jack, who fought for the south in the Civil War, retired from military duty, and returned home. He had been ill and received an immediate discharge. He had a terrible cough and was vomiting blood. The military doctors diagnosed it as tuberculosis. Many soldiers contracted it; it spread easily throughout their camps. It was determined some of them got it during the war but never died from it. Instead they just carried it in their bodies and infected those around them. This went on for many years and the disease continued to kill soldiers. Jack happened to be one of many who became ill but didn't die, not right away that is.

His mother tried to nurse him back to health but he died soon after arriving home a few weeks after being discharged. Jane received a message telling of her brother's death but she missed the funeral. We were planning a trip south to visit his grave, but before we worked out the details, another message came telling of her father's illness. She hurried south without me or the children. Like I said before, after she arrived her father died."

Harold sat down. He started crying again and I gave him a moment to collect his thoughts and composure.

Minutes later he continued. "After her father's funeral, a family friend who attended pulled Jane and her mother aside and expressed his concern about the loss. More importantly, he was concerned for their health. He filled their heads with superstitions of rising souls from graves feeding on the living and draining them of life. He convinced them to exhume her brother and father, remove their hearts, burn them, and drink the ashes to ward off evil spirits. He said if they didn't, the spirits of the deceased would return for them and continue to feed until their resting bodies could again walk the earth. They did so and I believe that was how my wife fell ill, she engaged in this ritual and at some point it went wrong. All I can assume is that they missed a step and eventually suffered the ultimate consequence— death." His sobbing slowed.

"When Jane returned home she wasn't herself. She stopped talking and kept to herself. She loved reading books and riding her horses but now she did none of those things. She became withdrawn. I figured she was just grieving so I gave her time to herself but as the days went by, she never came around. That's when I forced it out of her, and upon hearing her confess that she cannibalized her family, I was shocked and sickened. She told me that her father looked like a vampire and her brother a zombie. Their bodies appeared to grow fat, as if they were still eating and drinking, and their hair and fingernails continued growing. I'm not a man to believe in the supernatural and found her story absurd. It wasn't until after she died that I began to think maybe there was something to her story. After David died, I became a true believer."

Harold turned from me and covered his face. He was embarrassed for his wife and what she had done. To him she was a southern lass filled with charm, manners, and highly respectful toward the Catholic Church. He couldn't face me so he stood up and walked out from under the gazebo. I could hear him sniffling and I felt uncomfortable being in his presence as he reflected and became saddened with memories of his family dying.

I wanted to explain the situation to him from a doctor's point of view. I wanted to say that to the uneducated and superstitious, the bodies rotting appeared as though they took on the appearance of zombies and in some cases vampires. The bodies lost their pigmentation as if they were malnourished, similar to how a vampire's complexion appeared. After death, the bodies would begin to bloat as if they were still alive and feeding. But the bodies were naturally releasing gases expelled during decomposition. The skin would also shrivel back from the fingernails, giving the appearance they were still growing. The skin around the skull would also shrink, giving an effect of hair growth.

He didn't have to tell me of his wife's story in full detail, but out of respect I didn't stop him. I understood what he was explaining to me. I already knew of such a ritual from colleagues who witnessed such events first hand. During the night, the victims woke up in coughing fits that were filled with mucus clogging their throats. By morning, they were in dire conditions.

Relatives would wake to find their love ones either dead or at death's door. The victims showed the first sign of their illness marked by blood trailing from their mouth, ghostly skin and sunken eyes. Each of the victims died from their disease, which was called the vampire's consumption. As a medical doctor however, I knew that they died from tuberculosis, a sometimes-treatable disease depending on the stage and severity of the illness the patient displayed.

To combat and stave off infection and protect their families from consumption, surviving family members would exhume those who died from the disease. To stop the nightly visits and drainage of life from the living, the family would remove and burn the heart and feed the ashes to the sick to cure them. The healthy would also consume the ashes to ward off supernatural infliction. Then the family members would mutilate the corpse by decapitation, remove the limbs, and arrange them to confuse the evil spirits and rendering the corpse useless.

It was that final step, the removal of limbs and their rearrangement, that I figured his family forgot to do. Because of this, they allowed the cause of their plight to rise from the grave and commit hellish acts. I kept this theory to myself to not upset Harold any further. I decided that seeing the lights he spoke of was the least important detail of the night. His grieving, his daughter, and his own metal well being were more important and he needed to deal with this before the lights.

I rose and stood by Harold's side and stared along with him down Cole's Woods trail leading to the mire. I thought about the conditions his family took upon falling ill, the blood trails, ghostly skin, sunken eyes, and quick deaths.

Knowing how they suffered and died, because I witnessed similar horrific inflictions killing Karen first hand, I could no longer mock him or try to convince him otherwise.

He'd swayed my opinion of the subject at hand. I no longer tried to will him into disbelieving in the supernatural or try to discredit him for explanations that are more scientific. I decided to leave him be so he could mourn in peace.

"I must check on my patient before I turn in," I said through a drawn-out yawn. "Thank you for the cheese and Port, your hospitality today has turned very cordial…"

Before I could finish, he covered my mouth with his hand and placed his index finger in front of his lips to shush me. He pointed into the woods, saying nothing. He didn't have to; the images I laid my eyes on spoke on his behalf, validating his story beyond belief.

Drifting through the woods was a dim light. I had to focus my eyes away from it to see it clearly. It was ball-shaped, and for five minutes or so, it remained suspended in one spot about five feet off the ground. Its brightness intensified slowly and it began rising higher as its shape distorted into a full-bodied apparition of a human being. It then began moving parallel to the property.

"The torturing pestilence," Harold whispered. "It has risen!"

Shocked by it presence, we did nothing more than stare and watch. We were unprepared to deal with the apparition that materialized amongst the trees. We affixed our eyes to the light as it illuminated the surrounding trees and bushes.

To our surprise, the light metamorphosed into a vaporous, winged creature. It soared above the branches canopying the forest floor, taking the shape of the Jersey Devil that Harold spoke of. I figured the form to be the Jersey Devil, but my own imagination formed the image as the thought of the creature was implanted into my subconscious. The creature's appearance, more than not, was just a coincidence.

We stood and watched the specter's form contort into shapes that looked like arms and legs, which grasped at movements created by the breeze. I thought if it had intelligence, and there were victims within its reach, it would act. These arms and legs mimicked an angler's fly-fishing line skipping across a pond's surface, coaxing prey to its bait.

As it scoured the woods, its disembodied voice groaned in drawn-out tones in repetitions that haunt my dreams to this very day. *"Harold...Karen...Harold...Karen..."*

Tortured by this terror and the unearthly voice, we froze in shock. Neither of us dared to move an inch nor did our heads turn to follow the light, only our eyes kept constant contact with it. We muttered not a single word, fearing the light would hear us. We drew in not a single breath, fearing the light would smell the Port upon our exhale. Scared to death, we stood petrified in defense, fearing the light would attack and dispossess our souls of sanity and worse yet, our existence if we moved. Then all of a sudden and without warning, the light dematerialized without a trace, much to our delight. We were relieved, and began breathing deep and loud.

Over the next ten minutes we cowered within the gazebo, fearing the light's return. Only our eyes scanned the woods, searching for the light that ghosted from sight. We were thankful the light hadn't resumed its spectral state.

After figuring it was safe to move, we turned and walked to the house in long, quick strides while glancing over our shoulders into the woods. We hoped the light didn't detect us and double back. Neither of us muttered a single sentence for we were lost for words at what had transpired. My mind ran wild and became overwhelmed with various thoughts pertaining to the paranormal, and more importantly, the torturing pestilence. Nothing I said at that moment would have sounded sane, which to Harold, everything I wanted to say would have sounded rational.

Upon entering the house we checked on Karen. She was still in dire condition. I checked her vital signs but they hadn't changed for the worse or the better. This sign gave me hope that she could be nursed back to health unless what was seen in the woods was in fact coming to take her life.

After my quick examination, Harold's spirits rose when I determined that his daughter could survive. He ordered Clarabelle to keep a vigil over Karen, and if her condition were to change, to retrieve us without hesitation. We then said our goodnights and retired to our respective bedrooms.

Chapter 4
The Deed and the Mire

With permission from Harold, I dressed in nightclothes worn by his late son, David. After climbing into bed, I pulled the blankets up to my chest and hoped to take full advantage of the bed's comfort until morning. My eyes fluttered closed but opened as thoughts of what had transpired within the woods kept me awake. Attempts to fall asleep failed numerous times for what seemed to be an eternity. In reality however, it was no longer than an hour.

Redirecting my attention on sleeping rather that the light's haunting aura was difficult, its ghastly vocal pattern and overall terrifying presence turned my state of mind into paranoia. All shadows of tree branches shifting across the bedroom walls turned into monsters coming to take my life. These eerie shadows reminded me of the light and how it moved through the woods as it swooped, changed shape, and floated to dizzying heights.

I felt lethargic by the alcohol I'd consumed. My inebriated mind was clouded and all attempts to confront the true origin and meaning of the light were misinterpreted. All sensibility was numbed. My perception of rationality was dull and confused. I lost my ability to reason. Furthermore, the alcohol fueled my emotional state. All sense of terror intensified, impairing my ability to become fearless. The visions of the light were dreadful and too mystifying to understand.

With much relief, I fell asleep and woke just as the sun was climbing over the horizon. I woke with the same questions in which I had no answers for before I drifted to sleep. How could a body rise from the grave in the form of an apparition without illusion?

To me, it was impossible but I saw it with my own eyes. How could this ghost think, speak, attack and feed on the living?

This was a deep mystery, one which would never be uncovered by mere brainstorming alone. To uncover the answers one would have to examine Jane's body or at least her grave. Exhuming her body was out of the question as asking for permission at this time would infuriate Harold against me once more. We had managed to set aside our differences and I didn't want anything to ruin it for Karen's sake. She didn't need the added stress of two grown men continuing to argue right from wrong, bark orders at each other, and fight like two toddlers over a toy.

I lay in bed thinking, perhaps an hour or more. After a short time, I decided a rational explanation of the torturing pestilence to my own satisfaction was impossible. I decided that what I saw could possibly not be a hallucination. If it were a mirage created by alcohol or an overactive imagination, then only I would have witnessed the spirit. Therefore, I wouldn't have shared the experience with Harold and vice versa. What I saw was real and I began to dread that I had come to the Chapman Estate.

After rising from bed, I splashed cold water on my face to liven myself up. After that, I dressed accordingly for the weather in David's clothes. Outside, a hard, steady rainfall pelted the roof, creating quick, muffled thumps. The air was chilled and a fog blanketed the property. Visibility was poor. The edge of the Cole's Woods and the trail entrance leading into it could not be seen. The gazebo was eighty yards away, give or take, and silhouetted by the fog.

Only an outline of its masterful construction could be deciphered. Its beautifully painted trim in pastel blues and siding of white had turned gray and dreary.

When Karen woke, Clarabelle was to fetch for me to check on her condition. The decision had been made the night before that it was better for Karen to get plenty of rest rather than me waking her up in the morning.

Neither Harold nor his servants were about the house yet. I took it upon myself to prepare coffee in hopes it would help suppress the hangover effects brought upon by the alcohol from the previous night. I'm not used to consuming that much in such a short time. I headed downstairs and into the kitchen.

While the water heated for coffee, I heard Clarabelle's voice yell throughout the house, "Mis'er Chapman, come quick, Karen gone an' be attacked. Da child been attacked!"

The instant Clarabelle called for me, I was racing up the staircase and down the hallway to Karen's bedroom. Clarabelle sped past me, weeping with her head buried in her hands, while shouting, "Forgive me, forgive me! I done da best I could've, oh lord!"

Upon entering the bedroom, Harold was found kneeling at his daughter's bedside with his head pressed against the mattress. At first glance, it was clear that Karen was nearing death.

Dried, bloody spittle encrusted the corners of her mouth and also over her chin. Her skin turned pale, lips crimson flushed, her eyes sunken in. Her breathing labored with accents of crackled exhales, suggesting her lungs had filled with mucus. It was obvious to both Harold and I that our worst fears had come to fruition. The spirit we saw drifting in the woods came back to claim Karen and the girl was now knocking at death's door.

I ran from Karen's bedroom and into David's room to collect my medical bag. Before settling into bed last night, I'd placed it on the windowsill. When I reached for it, I glanced out the window and saw no trees growing near the house. The nearest tree was growing near the edge of the woods. The shadows drifting across the wall I saw last night weren't made by tree branches. They were made by the light I saw floating through and over Cole's Woods. I turned away from the window and left the room, blaming myself for Karen's condition. If I hadn't been drinking the night before, I would have thought with a sober mind and checked in on Karen and perhaps protected her from being attacked.

Harold, hearing me re-enter the room, cried through his hands, "That demonic light, it—it circled around and entered my house. I'm losing my last child to it. You have to help me reverse this plague before it takes her from me. You have to help me destroy the cause of this torturing pestilence—the corpse of my wife!"

To make sure I understood his request correctly, I asked, "You want to exhume your wife and disturb her resting body?"

"It's not disturbing the peace of the dead when the dead rise and commit devilish deeds, Doctor!"

Without further hesitation or thought of the gruesome request, I obliged. I knew what we were to do and I didn't find it objectionable. If I hadn't seen the lights in the woods and heard that eerie voice then I would have called him mad. But I had seen the lights, and the deed he asked me to commit with him would also give me the opportunity to examine her corpse. In doing so, the truth behind the torturing pestilence would arise and prove that we both had gotten caught up in the moment of this odd situation.

That afternoon Harold led me into the basement, where we collected a crowbar, spaded shovels, a large knife, oil lanterns and other supplies necessary to complete our task.

While I placed the smaller tools into a large sack, Harold said, "If by chance something were to happen to me, I want you to run away. Don't hesitate, don't turn back, just continue to run. Come back to the house and leave the property with Karen. Do what you can for her."

"Don't talk in such a grim manner," I said, pulling the drawstring on the sack tight. I had my doubts anything horrible would happen. But at the same time, I was reluctant to go into the situation haphazard. "We're both going to return safe and sound."

"I can only hope so. But if you were to die and I survived, then I would feel a great amount of guilt. This is my family's curse, not yours."

"As long as a patient of mine is dying, it's my ordeal as well."

Harold nodded his head in agreement. "Then make this deal with me, Doctor. If one of us is to parish then the other must return to the house without regret to save Karen's life. As a father, I will give my own life to save my child."

"And as a doctor, I would give my own life for my patient."

Harold extended his hand and we shook in agreement.

George appeared at the bottom step of the cellar staircase. He cleared his throat to get our attention. "Excuse me, sirs, I have your boots and coats laid out by the backdoor as you requested."

"Thank you, George, and please keep an eye on Clarabelle. She seems stressed from the situation. If she cannot watch and care for Karen as the doctor has instructed, relieve her until our return."

"As you wish!" George bowed his head, turned, and climbed the stairs.

We followed behind and headed for the back of the house. Once there, we laced up the boots and pulled on our jackets. The sack of tools was heavy and rested over my shoulder and Harold carried the shovels and pickaxe under his arms.

We left the house and walked across his backyard. Behind us, the dew clinging to the blades of grass left impressions of our footsteps in our wake. The rain that had fallen throughout the day was now a mist, which dampened our clothes and slicked the tool handles. Harold kept dropping the shovels, and the sack over my shoulder became heavier from the mist soaking through the fabric. The fog failed to lift, keeping visibility down to about the same distance it was during the morning. We passed the gazebo and soon came upon the entrance to Cole's Woods. We followed the trail inside, which led to Harold's family plot.

In the woods the visibility was barely ten yards. The trees looked like skeletons, their trunks and branches etched within the fog. An overactive imagination turned the branches into crippled and boney arms, contorting in various directions. These arms lurched down, giving impressions they were ready to pluck us up from the ground.

The breeze jostled tiny twigs resembling fingers splitting off the ends of the branches. As our shoulders brushed against them as we walked, they teased and tapped our shoulders, tricking us with images of monsters. The tree bark, highlighted by murky shadows, formed faces with eyes that followed our every step.

It was evident by Harold's shaking legs and jerking head movements that his imagination was running rampant as well.

We heard the crackling of brush, which froze us in our tracks. Hairs stood on the back our necks and goosebumps popped up over every inch of our bodies. Neither of us had been this frightened in our entire lives. We listened in the direction the noises came from and stared into the fog. The breeze that once swooped through the trees was still. The chirrup of insects and animals became silent. Something unseen and horrific was lurking in the trees. We could sense its presence as it had sensed ours. It froze the moment we stopped dead in our tracks. Unwilling to become sitting ducks of whatever was shadowing our movements, we ventured on.

Soon, we were twenty minutes into our hike. We cautiously kept our ears poised to detect the slightest of noise. Every now and then we would hear a twig snap and a dead leaf crunch off in the distance. Whatever we sensed earlier was gaining ground on us. Neither of us spoke of the noises, we were too scared to speak and we continued hiking.

Our eyes darted back and forth, focusing on the negative spaces between the trees, searching for movements, but all was still. The further we moved into the woods, the more chilled the air became, numbing our exposed skin and dulling our sense of touch. Only the smell of rotting peat moss drifting within the breeze from the mire was detectable by our senses, which reminded us we were getting closer to the gravesite and closer to committing our plan; a plan that was blasphemous and unforgivable.

Harold stopped and sat on a fallen tree. I dropped the sack of tools that became heavier with each step and rubbed the pain out of my shoulders.

"Are you okay?" I asked.

"I just need a few minutes of rest. I haven't hiked through these woods since I buried my wife. I forgot how hard the walk is. The fallen trees that have to be climbed over; the sharp drops and steep hills are a bit too much on my old body. Since my wife died, I stopped taking care of myself. I've gained many pounds from drinking and eating too much."

"We should not rest long though, I still fear we're being followed," I said, sitting next to him.

I opened the sack and removed a canteen, unscrewed the cap, and handed it to him. After sipping the water, he handed it back to me. I sipped from it as well and screwed the cap back on. We sat for another ten minutes, not speaking a single word to keep our ears poised to the woods around us. That silence was broken when Harold's head jerked to the left and grabbed my forearm with such force that I almost screamed out in pain.

"What is it?" I whispered.

He pointed into the woods. "See those two boulders?"

"Yes."

"Just to the left there is a bush. I saw something dart behind it. If you look close, you can see a dark figure crouched behind it through the branches."

I stared at the bush, seeing nothing. "I don't see it. What did the figure look like?"

"Human," he said.

I squinted, studied the bush harder, then saw it; a short figure trying to keep still. It was hiding from us and waiting for us to move, to then possibly attack.

"I see it now. It's curled up in a ball."

Harold stood up and held the pickaxe over his head, ready to strike down anything that lunged forward. "It's the corpse of my wife; she's trying to sneak up on us from behind. We have to get her before she gets us."

I pressed my hand against his chest, holding him back. I lowered the pickaxe with my other hand. "That isn't her. It's something else."

"What else could it be?"

"I don't know, but we have to find out. If we let our guard down it could attack, then we'll never save Karen."

I opened the sack and removed the crowbar. Holding it like a sword, I crept towards the bush. Behind me, Harold held the pickaxe in front of his body. The head of the axe was level with his shoulders and the end of the handle at his waist. Through the fog we saw the dark figure darting out from the bush and hobble behind a tree. It was short and pudgy. It limped, causing its body to dip to the right and its arms to flail out to keep its balance. Behind it a tail whipped into the air and flapped in the draft as it ran. Its breathing turned heavy and gruff as though it was growling.

Without speaking, I motioned for Harold to go right as I went left. We circled around the tree and raised our weapons. I held up my fingers and counted down from five. As my thumb curled in to zero, we jumped out from behind the tree and bore down our weapons.

Harold belted out a violent scream with his eyes closed tight.

"*Harold no!*" I yelled, while looking down at our target.

In one swift motion, I turned my wrists up and redirected the crowbar skyward, into the pickaxe Harold was thrusting down. With all my strength I pushed up on the pickaxe and broke it from Harold's grip. The tool spiraled through the air and landed on the ground behind us.

I looked down at man on the ground that we were about to kill and asked, "George, what are you doing out here? You almost got yourself killed!"

Before George could speak, Harold lifted him to his feet and began scolding him. "You old fool, you're supposed to be watching over my daughter and Clarabelle. What are you doing out here?"

George's voice shook as he held his hands up, pressed his palms together, and interlocked his fingers. "I...I...I'm sorry, sir. I just needed to tell you that most of the servants have fled. There aren't many of us left. The ones that stayed fear you aren't returning and demanded an update on your progress. Even Clarabelle is threatening to leave if I did not check. She needed to know you were still alive. So I came out here to find you."

"Why did you hide behind that bush?" Harold asked, angrily pulling George up to his feet.

George favored his ankle, bowing his head like a scolded child. "I couldn't tell if that was you, the fog is too thick to make out familiar faces or bodies. That is why I hid. Then I ran because I saw someone coming towards me, but I twisted my ankle and fell behind this tree."

"You could have been killed if I didn't recognize you," I said, placing a consoling hand on his shoulder.

George looked up at me with an apologetic smile. "I'm sorry, sir. I just didn't want the remaining staff to leave."

I sat George on the ground and pulled off his shoe and sock, then felt his ankle for breaks. "Nothing seems to be broken. Is your ankle strong enough to make it back to the house?"

He replaced his sock and shoe, stood up, and walked on his ankle, testing its strength. "It is, Doctor, and I do apologize again." George began to hobble back to the house.

Minutes later, we reached the mire without further incident. The fog churned over the water and thinned making visibility reasonably clear, allowing us to see across it. Alarmed bullfrogs, aware there were strangers amongst them, hopped off the peat moss and into the water as we neared. Rotted trees, with trunks implanted into the murky slush comprising of the mire's bottom, rose out of the water. Some snapped off midway up their trunks, while others broke off at the water's surface. Perched on one of the trees, a spooked owl quickly spun his head around, caught sight of us, flew off, and disappeared into the fog. Beyond the water, the fog re-thickened, cloaking the trees behind a drapery of cold, dense, and drifting fog.

We walked around the perimeter of the water and found the opposite side of the trail. We continued another fifty yards until the path came to a dead end in a thicket.

"Where do we go from here?" I asked, placing the sack of tools on the ground, giving my shoulder a rest.

Harold pointed into the mangled brush. "My family's plot is beyond that thicket. My great grandfather created the plot here to hide it from grave robbers. It worked. Not a single grave has ever been disturbed. We'll have to crawl under the thicket to reach the plots. I'll go first, then you hand me the tools after I make it through."

The thicket measured no more in width as the length of an average person is in height. It was dense with intertwined vines weaving throughout wild raspberry and burning bushes, both displaying their fruits and flowers. Sections of the thicket were comprised of fallen tree branches. With our imaginations running rampant, the branches looked like broken and strewn bones. Even some branches of the thriving bushes were void of life. Their thin branches snapped off with the slightest touch. The ground, littered with broken off branches and dead, rotten berries, resembled scattered remnants of deceased humans in various stages of decay. For those whose bravery would labor at this suggestive and ominous sight, they would turn back. For us however, it was an encouraging sign to completing our mission.

Harold dropped to his knees and then his stomach. He jostled his body through and under the entangled brush by contorting his torso around the curvature of each limb and trunk. Upon reaching the opposite side, he called for the tools. I pushed them along the ground under the bushes, then followed.

After crawling through, I stood and brushed my clothes free of dirt and other debris. I looked up and gazed upon the cemetery's unfortunate condition. Its dilapidation was to the extent that future burials, under normal circumstances, would be banned until renovation deemed the site safe. Sinkholes sporadically pockmarked the ground. Weeds and wild flowers sprouted between thigh high patches of sunburned crabgrass. Fallen trees, rotted by over hydrated roots that grew through the soil into the mire, crumbled to the ground and became stricken with insects feeding off the proteins and reproducing within.

A dozen wooden crosses marked the deceased family members' resting places. However, no visible inscriptions were carved upon them. Only the rate of decomposition afflicting the crosses gave clues to who occupied the grave and for how long. The weeds and grasses grew over and wrapped around the older crosses, encasing them within a chrysalis of rotted stems and leaves, some of which were ridden with termite mud tunnels and other insects inching over and burrowing within. Thin wooden strips peeled from their facades and flapped in the breeze. The more recent crosses were merely sun bleached and blemished with small, crusty bird droppings. These effigies of the forgotten created a sense of sadness within my heart.

"Which grave is your wife's?" I asked.

Harold pointed to the far left corner. "That one!"

We approached the grave and examined the ground around it. The turned, darkened soil, void of weeds and grass, indicated that something or someone had recently visited the plot. Knowing something could be lurching about, possibly ready to trounce, I felt the tingle of bone-chilling fright slide down my spine, making my back feel as though fondling skeletons dragged their cold, boney fingers across my skin.

At that instant, I wanted nothing more than to exhume and exterminate the corpse and leave the gravesite. I no longer wanted to examine the body to deem my newfound belief in the supernatural false, I became too intimidated by the moment to do so.

Having the same worrisome ideas as myself, Harold handed me a shovel and said in an apprehensive voice, "We better hurry. The sun will be down soon. We'll not wish to disturb the grave after nightfall and allow the corpse's body access to the world."

Chapter 5
Ridding the Disease

The sun was still high on the horizon as we dug into the grave. The thickness of the mire's vegetation growth shadowed the gravesite, giving the impression that nightfall was moments away. The dig was harsh on our old bodies. Numerous times we had to stop and rest our muscles and catch our breaths.

Harold complained his back was cramping but forged on with the digging despite the fact. My back held up well under the strain, but my shoulders tired and burned from carrying the sack and from the digging. With each dig into the ground and toss of dirt over my shoulders, the skin on my hands turned raw as the wooden shovel handle twisted within my palms. Torn strips of cloth from the jacket I wore served as gloves used to protect my hands from the friction. This idea came too late as the rawness of my palms soon blistered over.

We took alternating breaks to replenish our bodies enough to handle the strain of digging. Harold took the first digging shift as I rested by sitting on the ground, sipping water from the canteen. I took time to rewrap my hands and rub the cramps from my shoulders.

Harold took numerous breaks to quench his thirst and to stretch his back, but with each break from digging, we stalled our advancement through the soil to the coffin beneath. There were roots that had grown directly over the top of the coffin, and we chopped through with our shovels. We also removed rocks of various shapes and weights, creating a bigger strain on our bodies. Because of this the dig took longer than expected and induced consequences and terrors unforeseen at the onset of the dig.

After he was done with his break, Harold resumed digging at a pace that was hurried and worrisome. I feared he would overexert himself and pull his back muscles to the extent he could no longer dig. I encouraged him to slow down to allow his muscles recovery time between shovelfuls and to conserve energy. He scoffed at my suggestion with a smile, suggesting he was *all right*. He also stated that the dig must be completed before the sun had set and before the monster buried within awoke. He continued digging and tossing dirt from the grave.

Moments later, he stopped and leaned on the shovel handle to support himself. "I'm starting to feel lightheaded and weak."

His breathing turned shallow, but should have remained heavy and deep from digging. I climbed into the grave and felt his pulse. It was weak and his body felt cold. His eyes darted back and forth. It was obvious he was experiencing a sudden dizzy spell. His body started swaying, his eyelids fluttered, and his knees bent as though he was trying to remain balanced.

"You must rest. I fear the digging and stress of the situation is too much of a strain on your mind and heart. It may sound selfish of me but I do not wish to continue this ritual without you. A family member of the deceased is needed to break the spell."

He looked at me and smiled. "It's not selfish, Doctor, it's the truth."

With my help, he climbed out from the grave and sat on the ground. He unscrewed the canteen cap and took a sip. As he rested, I continued digging, and after a few shovelfuls of dirt, I visually examined his condition. His breathing became deeper and his eyes stabilized. His health improved and his vertigo attack disappeared.

About ten minutes later, weakness began settling about my body. Breathing turned into a struggle. My lungs felt empty with each breath drawn and my diaphragm started to spasm. My heart rate dropped and I felt as though I was spinning around in circles in one spot to purposely make myself dizzy. I stopped digging as Harold did moments before, propped myself up on the shovel handle, and closed my eyes to stop the spinning. Whatever affliction weakened Harold's body began to hinder my health as well. This was no coincidence but some sort of unseen plague concentrated within the confines of the grave.

I opened my eyes and stared down at the ground, hoping my vertigo would cease, but it worsened. The soil churned with frightening images of ghouls. The faces of victims past wilted into human-serpent hybrids, feeding and mating upon mounds of dead carcasses, rotting and floating in pools of blood. The smell from the carcasses was that of decaying flesh and excrement. These carrion dreams exploded into liquefied sparks that burbled from within the dirt as it churned.

"Are you alright, Doctor?" Harold asked, sensing something was wrong.

"I feel weak," I said between short and choppy breaths. "And I'm experiencing transitory deliriums."

"Deliriums, I don't understand."

"Short hallucinations," I said with weakness in my voice before collapsing onto my knees without warning.

I could feel the density of the stench filling and clogging my lungs. The clog felt as if it formed into a sphere that expanded within and constricted my trachea. The sphere continued growing until it vibrated quickly and tore, as if hatching. Then I felt a small serpentine creature propelling in vertical undulations as it slithered down to the end of my trachea. I grasped for a breath of air but the girth of the creature suffocated my lungs. The creature wiggled and split into two separate serpents that slithered into my bronchial tubes, where they entered into my bloodstream.

I looked at my arms, saw my skin bulge, and wiggle from the serpents traveling through my veins and arteries. They then burst through the vein walls, burrowed underneath, and disappeared into my muscles. My skin stretched as the creatures grew in size and began multiplying in the same manner they were born. One serpent became two, two serpents became four, and four serpents became eight and so on. I lost count when they reached triple digits.

Too weakened to support myself, I collapsed onto my stomach and thrashed about as the serpents festered within and began devouring my organs. My stomach went sour as the bile sizzled the flesh off their bodies. My diaphragm violently constricted, forcing the digesting serpents to be vomited out through my mouth.

I looked down at the wiggling creatures. The heads of the creatures were void of eyes; their mouths opened like snakes with forked tongues that pulled my body's scent from the air. Their skin was covered in black and red scales with patches of raw skin where my stomach acid boiled away their hides. Their bodies had no appendages and the tail end formed a segmented point with a scorpion-like stinger with serrated edges. The creatures slithered towards me and hooked their tails over their heads, thrusting their stingers into and under my skin. The tails continued slicing and puncturing my skin until they formed a hole large enough to burrow back inside.

The pain was horrific and unbearable. It felt as though hundreds of knives were stabbing and slicing at my skin. I couldn't move my arms and swat them away. I was too weak. All I could do was lay and watch their bodies slither into mine. My heart raced as the first serpent wiggled its head into the wound. I felt every inch of its body slowly burrow into my flesh until its serrated stinger disappeared inside me. One after another, the serpents entered my body through the holes they carved in my arm and torso.

One of the serpents entered through my ear. Its body became wedged within my ear canal and it bucked about, trying to free itself. Angered at being stuck, it bellowed a squeal between hot, breathy hisses. I could feel it stretching its body, becoming thinner, and hoping to free itself and navigate deeper into my ear canal.

Suddenly, a loud popping and tearing sound exploded, followed by the feeling of the serpent dissipate into smaller serpents as its body ripped in half. The tiny creatures slithered deep into my ear and fed upon my eardrum. For a brief moment before I went deaf, I could hear them biting into and tearing away pieces of my eardrum.

The other serpents traversed through my arms, bent around my shoulders and gnawed their way into my chest. They gathered near my heart. Immense pain radiated throughout my chest. In an instant, my chest tightened and my heart ceased as the creatures ravaged it in a feeding frenzy. The light from the lanterns diminished as my eyes flickered closed. The pain in my chest subsided as I began to lose consciousness. I was dying.

A soft thump vibrated through the dirt inside the grave. My body lifted off the ground and drifted out of the grave. I began to lower and felt the stiff blades of the dead grass crumble under my weight. Within seconds of lying on the ground, I felt my muscles strengthen, my heart beating, and the rest of my respiratory system begin to function normally. My eyes opened and the heat and the light from the lanterns blinded me for a second. I rubbed my eyes until I could see once more. Harold was crouched over me, looking over my body and unsure of how to handle my sudden collapse.

"What should I do? Tell me how to help you, Doctor," Harold said, panicking.

I tried to sit up but the trees and grave markers spun around me. I collapsed to my side and closed my eyes while everything continued to spin.

Then, just as suddenly as it began, the pain and sensation of serpents consuming my body disappeared.

"You cannot help me. I'm not experiencing a sudden illness. Whatever is buried in that grave drained my energy through visions of torment. I'll be fine soon enough."

"What did you see?"

"Serpents, they hatched inside of me and started devouring my body and soul. The same would have befallen you if I had not noticed your body becoming weak and pulled you from the grave. I now know why Karen was hallucinating. The torturing pestilence was controlling her."

"I'm sorry. I should have helped you before you collapsed," Harold said.

"No need to apologize. When I felt my body succumbing to the torturing pestilence, I should have climbed out of the grave on my own."

He turned and looked into the grave. "If it's true that you experienced the plague that has attacked my family, then I'll finish digging. I'll sacrifice myself before I allow you to die."

"Very well, but if you collapse I will pull you out of the grave."

He shook his head and said, "No, don't rescue me. Leave the area and tell the remaining servants to flee, but take Karen with you. We made a pact and now you must own up to it."

I did not argue with him.

He jumped into the grave and continued digging. He dug fast and with intention of reaching the casket before he was overcome. Minutes later, he pushed the shovel into the dirt and a hollow thud was heard. He reached the casket and just in time. The sun was setting, and only our lanterns illuminated the gravesite. The torturing pestilence's witching hour was drawing near.

Harold scraped the dirt off the casket lid. The wood casket was rotted from lying underground for two years. It had turned dark from collecting moisture that seeped through from rainfall and the mire flooding over during the spring thaw. It was also apparent by the small crevices and holes decorating the coffin that insects were festering inside.

"Prepare for the worse if she's alive," Harold warned.

I nodded and held a pickaxe tight in my hands. My fingers and knuckles, wrapped around the handle, turned white as my hands shook in fear. I positioned my body so my right foot was pointing to the thicket. If I had to run, I was ready.

With a crowbar, Harold dug into the side of the coffin and pried off the lid. The wood was weak and the nails rusted, making access to the contents within effortless. The lid cracked and creaked as he lifted it.

A whoosh of decayed and stale air flushed over our faces, creating the feeling of asphyxiation, which in turn created a dizzying effect. I pulled up my shirt collar to block the smell but the air was concentrated with fumes too intense to filter. My eyes felt as though they were burning.

Blinking in hopes the pain within my eyes would subside, I stared down into the open grave. The sight of the corpse itself was horrifying, though as a doctor, it was engrossing in a morbid sense. I'd never seen a human body in such state of decay or any type of flesh in such a condition other than carrion serving as a meal to scavengers. The body was abundant with unrecognizable worm and insects that ate through the wooden casket and into the corpse, using it as a breeding ground and an abundant food source.

The corpse's skin was gray, leathery and shriveled around the bones. The skull was accented by clinging skin around its jaw line and the cheekbones looked waiflike. The eye sockets were deflated; giving the impression of large, vacant eyes that never blinked nor broke contact with ours.

This voyeuristic feeling made me uneasy, as though the corpse was studying our movements and timing an attack at an opportune moment. Its chin had dropped and the mouth was opened, creating the sense of silent screams in ghastly pangs of horror, some of which I thought I could hear. Perhaps it was only my futile imagination or residual effects of my hallucinations.

The burial clothes were gray and tattered, showing signs that time and insects had deteriorated the fabric. The clothes lay loose around the body. Underneath the body was a thin layer of sludge with an oily light spectrum floating about.

Harold knelt down and whispered into his wife's shriveled ear. The words were mumbled. What little words I understood and heard were assumed to be an apology. He then pulled a knife from his boot and sliced into the corpse's chest. The dry skin crackled as the knife cut through. The insects and other pests that ate into the corpse scrambled deeper into the holes.

I handed Harold a hatchet and he rammed it down upon the sternum. The blow, even though weak, was enough to break through the brittleness of the bone and crumble it into small fragments. He then pushed his hands into the dried entrails and pulled out the heart. It resembled that of a thriving human heart for it possessed healthy hue and muscular tone, which was a surprise. A corpse buried for so long should have had a decayed heart that was shriveled and discolored like a rotten apple. The corpse was not dead; it was alive and had in recent times consumed the blood and soul of man, which I felt was my own as I still felt weak and violated.

Harold turned and climbed from the grave. He placed the heart in a shallow bowl fashioned from stone. With a wooden mallet, he ground the heart into small pieces. After dousing the heart with lantern oil, he mixed it all together with a stick. He struck a match and dropped it into the bowl, setting the heart ablaze. It burned quickly and radiated a bluish glow. The smell of the burning heart was dry and reminded me of venison.

Several seconds later, the fire smothered itself. Harold ground up the larger pieces with a rock and turned the ashen remains into a fine powder. He carefully shook the ash from the bowl into a small, clear glass vial of water. He stirred it by twirling the vial, creating a concoction that if drank would ward off the torturing pestilence, or so we hoped.

"Here's to your health!" Harold said in a sarcastic yet hopeful tone, while raising the vial in the air as if in a toast.

He swigged a portion of the concoction. His face cringed and he gagged, almost coughing up the mixture. Then his face lit up with a smile as hopes that the supernatural elixir would stave off his own demise.

He handed the vial to me and I looked through the vial into the mixture. I shook it and watched the suspended powder that had not dissolved spin within. The more I stared at the vial, the more apprehensive I became. I thought about what the mixture was derived of and found myself arguing over the morality of consuming it. But the desecration of the grave, removal and cremation of the heart negated all morals.

I closed my eyes, held the vial close to my lips, and smiled. "Cheers!" I kicked back the vial like a shot of whiskey.

The taste of the elixir was dry and smoky. My eyes clasped together and my head jerked back, forcing down the mixture. I gagged, not from the taste, but knowing I'd consumed ash derived from a human heart. Pieces of the ash trickled down my throat as others remained in my mouth. I scraped my tongue on the back and fronts of my teeth, wiping off pieces of burnt and ground-up heart that lingered within my mouth.

I swished a bit of my saliva around and swallowed some of the remaining particles down my throat. The second swallow was more nauseating than the first, for it was thicker and the pieces more apparent.

Harold took the remaining mixture from me. He capped it and tucked it deep within his coat pocket for safe keeping until we could return to Karen's bedside and have her drink from it as well.

We waited several minutes to allow the mixture's healing capability to take effect. My stomach turned sour as my bile's acidity digested the elixir. A few times, I belched and regurgitated the mixture into the back of my mouth. I gagged and came close to vomiting but held back while breathing in deep, hoping my nausea eased.

"Are you okay, Doctor?"

I looked at Harold and smiled. "I'll be fine in a moment. I'm not sure if it's the idea of drinking the elixir or the ingredients itself that had turned my stomach ill."

He held his stomach and said, "I feel sick, too. Maybe it's the pestilence within the mixture that is making us feel ill. We may have swallowed the infliction voluntarily."

"If that is the case then we have committed suicide," I said with concern.

Chapter 6
Provoking the Disturbed

After several minutes, the nauseous feeling subsided but my stomach kept churning. Because of my medical training, my own aches and pains went ignored while keeping an eye on Harold. By the way he was standing, upright with his hands by side rather than hunched over holding his stomach, he was feeling better.

He leapt back into the grave with a sudden confidence heightened by the consumption of the elixir.

"Hand me the hatchet," he said, holding his hand up and waiting to grab the tool.

I lowered it into the grave, and before I let go, I looked him in the eyes to express my concern. "Be careful, we may have drunk the remedy but it may not have taken affect. Whatever lurks inside your wife's corpse may still be perceptive to our doings!"

Harold jerked the hatchet from my grasp. I took no offense, knowing full well he was eager to execute the deed. He was ready to incapacitate the corpse from reanimating and taking more lives. He pushed the corpse's head to the right, exposing a large portion of the neck, and raised the hatchet in the air. His hand waved back and forth inches at a time as he lined up the hatchet blade with the target. He glanced over his shoulder at me, and by the look on his face, it was clear he was worried.

The deed he was about to commit would either fail or cure his family of the torturing pestilence. I shook my head in a slow, approving manner, signaling to him I understood his apprehension and guilt.

He lowered the hatchet to the corpse's neck again, positioning his arm to strike the target cleanly. He then lifted his arm in a quick, jerking backswing and plunged the hatchet towards the corpse in a violent fury while screaming out in anger.

Before the moment of impact, Jane's corpse sprang to life in a sudden outburst of rage. The extremities Harold was about to detach from his wife's corpse and arrange them in each other's corresponding positions, wrapped around his torso.

Harold dropped the hatchet. He struggled, trying to free himself and grab the hatchet but it was out of reach. He kicked and punched but his blows were ineffective for Jane's grip was strong and constricting. Her arms pulled her husband closer to her body and the pressure bent his spine inward.

Surprised, I jumped away and fell on my backside. I pushed myself up and grabbed the pickaxe, holding it over my head. I sprang forward, ready to bury one of the points deep in Jane's skull.

But before I could bring the pickaxe down, Harold yelled, "Save yourself, Doctor! Save yourself!"

My rage ceased upon hearing his voice, heroics setting in. I dropped the pickaxe to the ground, reached into the grave, and grabbed Harold's arm, trying to yank him free from his wife's clutches. Not wanting to lose him, I broke our agreement to flee back to the house if the other met his doom.

"You fool...let...go...save...yourself...save Karen!" Harold struggled to speak, ordering me to flee as he was being constricted within Jane's arms.

I released his arm and turned to run but my body became stiff as a board and I stopped dead in my tracks. My feet sunk into the earth under a tremendous weight of dread. The leathery, eye-voided skull stared over Harold's shoulders and into my eyes.

Black cataracts pooled within my eyes as a black cloud surrounded my head. I could feel my life draining away and collect within the Jane's soul. My extremities went limp, muscles flaccid, my senses dulled while becoming deprived of all perceptions.

Jane cackled in joy. Her laughter was high-pitched and broke the bond that memorized me and linked my soul to her. I blinked and focused my vision through the cataracts that seeped from my eyes like molasses. I wiped the remaining residue from my eyes and my knees buckled. Black clouds swarmed around Harold's entire body, but were thin enough for me to watch the torturing pestilence ravage his life away easily.

He was alive when his body began to decay. His complexion turned gray and his muscles wilted. His skin broke apart like a crack upon a frozen pond. Through the cracks, a cloud of red dissipated into the air as his blood boiled within his veins. His head flopped over his shoulders and his eyes stared back at me. I saw nothing as I stared through the eyes of his dead body. His wife drained him of life within seconds.

Jane dropped her husband's body and stood over him, absorbing and feeding off the lingering vapors. The corpse that Jane once was, a shriveled bag of bones and decomposed entrails, began rejuvenating through a progression of evil.

Her muscles twitched and expanded under the skin and her expressionless face formed eyes that glowed red. The dry strains of hair thickened and glossed over in a healthy shine. Her fingers, stiff and boney, stretched and popped with a sound I can only describe as twigs stepped on and broken.

Jane stepped over Harold's body and reached out for me. With what little strength I still obtained, I turned and ran headlong from the burial ground. The light from the lanterns left at the grave faded into the dark abyss of the night and barely illuminated the thicket. I leapt into and burst through the thicket and upon the trail on the opposite side. My body was sliced open in small lacerations made by the jagged branches but the pain soon subsided under the sensation of a greater agony, fear.

Running down the darkened trail, unable to see, I tripped over a rock protruding from the soil and fell into the brisk waters of the mire. My heart, stricken with heavy and erratic palpitations, the pressure so great, worked as an anticoagulant, allowing my blood to seep from my body. My blood dissipated within the water. This bloodletting lured leeches lurking within the water to me. In seconds, dozens of slimy bodies attach their suckers to my skin and begin their feeding frenzy. They attached to my arms, legs, back, and on my neck. Their mucus worked like an anesthetic and numbed my skin. It was difficult to determine how many of the leeches latched on and began feeding on my blood.

In combination with the blood loss through cuts and leeches, I began to weaken. I forced myself to wade my head above water and try to swim, but I was too tired. I decided to float atop the water, hoping I would soon regain enough strength to swim and return to the estate and save Karen.

At the end of the trail where it met the thicket, Jane rustled through the branches. They snapped repeatedly, the leaves on the ground crunching under her bare feet. She was coming for me and I needed to escape, but due to the leeching of my blood and onset of fear, I was too weak to swim. By pure chance, I drifted to water's edge, where I could crawl out and flee, but fearing Jane would hear me slosh out of the water and capture me, I remained floating, leaving my body to the will and whim of the leeches. To me this was a better option than being tortured by a zombie.

Jane's footsteps crumbled dead leaves and twigs, which grew louder with each step as she neared the mire. Not knowing what would happen next, my heart pounded harder in my chest and louder in my ears. The water was cold but sweat trickled down my forehead. My lips quivered and my arms shook, causing ripples to form a target around me.

I gazed into the trail, watching and waiting for Jane to emerge, but the trail was too dark to make out Jane's silhouette.

Seconds later, she appeared in an atmosphere of death-walking terror. Her joints creaked from lying constricted within an oblong box for so long. Her arms hung and swayed by the side of her torso. Her back was hunched over, giving an appearance of an old woman stricken with osteoporosis. Her rigid walk was created by her knee's range of motion, which remained inflexible but loosened with each stride, as she slowly regained her land legs. Her head drooped with her chin resting on her chest as her weak neck could not support the skull's weight.

Her breathing was rasp and cracked with each exhale. She moaned and gurgled the names of her children: Karen, David and Maggie.

Dripping from Jane's body, dead bugs and worms fell as each footfall pounded the ground. Swamp flies buzzed and landed on her and instantly died as their lives were drained away.

Divots along the path tripped her up, causing her to roll her brittle ankle. Her bones snapped and popped like crumbling crackers as she stumbled to the ground. She lay on her stomach for a moment before pushing up on her hands. She rose to her feet and continued advancing along the trail, dragging her broken ankle and foot behind.

From the water's edge, a frog scared by Jane's presence leapt into the water. The splash caused her to stop dead in her tracks. She turned and scanned the water left to right, looking for signs of life.

I tried to remain calm. I forced my arms still to avoid making more ripples in the water that she would see. My body began sinking and my ears dipped below the surface. Water touched my lips and I tasted its flavor in my mouth. It tasted like dirt and raw fish. My throat tickled from the water seeping into my mouth and I began to gag.

Panic set in as my head sank deeper, the water leaking in and filling up my nostrils. In the back of my throat, water drizzled from my nose and down into my esophagus. I started gagging but forced myself to breathe through the water that was collecting in my throat. Drips of it leaked into my lungs. I was overwhelmed by the urge to cough but forced myself to push the water out with my throat muscles and diaphragm.

Tilting my head back, my nose rose above the water. I swallowed the remaining water down my throat. I breathed normal but could feel water droplets clinging to my nose hairs, creating an itch that built up a sense to sneeze. I fought it off, which if allowed would have given away my presence that would lead to my death.

In my new position, I couldn't see or hear Jane. All I could see was the fog rolling over the mire, all I could hear was the elevated blood pressure beating in my ears, and all I could smell was the fish odor of the water. I sensed no waves rippling against my skin, telling me she'd entered the water.

I continued floating, unsure if Jane had continued on or was circling the pond, waiting for me to drift closer to shore where she could pounce on me.

Then I saw her eyes.

They were glowing red and stared into the water at the area in which I was floating. I stared back while projecting positive thoughts, hoping to make her turn away in some form of extrasensory persuasion. Unfortunately, she felt my eyes penetrating her mind with unwanted thoughts. She turned her head and affixed her eyes to mine. I could feel her stare penetrating me, filling my mind up with her own demands.

She persuaded me to swim to water's edge and I unwillingly obliged. I lifted my feet from the bottom of the pond and paddled my hands through the water. When I was five feet from her, she waded in and lifted me out. She slumped me over her shoulder, walked me to dry land, and dropped me to the ground, where I landed on my stomach. My legs still dangled in the water and I could feel more leeches squirming into my shoes to latch onto my feet. The leeches were the least of my concerns; I was at the mercy of the dead.

I felt dripping water hitting my back. I opened my eyes and looked up over my shoulder. Jane was straddling my body and looking down at me. I closed my eyes, giving in to the fact that I was about to die. I was too weak to run or fight. All I could do was hope I would not suffer and I would die quickly.

As I waited to die, a black cloud filtered from Jane's mouth. The cloud's pungent stench of death singed my nostrils and chocked my lungs as it engulfed my head. My eyes slowly closed and I slipped into unconsciousness.

Chapter 7
The Carriage House

I don't know what transpired between the moment the black cloud filled my lungs and the instant my eyes fluttered open at daybreak. I woke and found myself still lying at the water's edge of the mire. Small cuts and circular bite marks covered my body where the leeches had latched on to me, turning my skin pale from blood loss. Dozens and dozens of leeches that fed off my blood were scattered around me, their tiny bodies shriveled like burnt bacon.

My arms and legs felt weak, my head dizzy. For nearly an hour I tried to stand but all I could do was crawl away from the water and onto the pebbles and sand lining the trail.

As I rested, I wondered if everything I'd experienced had been just a nightmare. That is until I looked at the wounds on my skin. Then I realized my luck had held out the night before when Jane had found me. I feared I was as good as dead and resided to the fact. My body was hers for the taking and my soul for her pleasure and torture, but a miracle occurred and she left the mire without bringing further harm onto me. All I could figure was when I passed out she considered me dead. What little blood and energy she fed off from the leeches she must have believed to be mine.

My thoughts of Jane left me as I thought about my body's condition. My throat was dry and I was tempted to sip from the mire to wet my mouth, but the thought of contracting cholera, typhoid and other diseases carried by microorganisms such as dysentery stopped me from doing so. Though in my condition, bruised and cut, I would probably contract any infections regardless if I drank the water or not.

Thinking of Harold and Karen, I forced myself to stand and gain enough strength to move. I rose to my feet and staggered down the trail and back to the thicket. Jane had cleared a path through the brush about the width of a doorway. I walked through and into the cemetery. With a great deal of caution, I approached Jane's open grave, unsure if she'd returned to her resting place before sunrise. I expected to see her within the grave and the appearance of her body back to its normal state. If that wasn't the case, though, then she may have wandered into the town and began attacking the citizens of Saratoga Springs.

I snuck on the grave, keeping one eye focused on it and another on my surroundings. The tools used to excavate the grave were still scattered about and the lanterns were burned out. Ten feet from the grave, I heard a crunching sound under my feet. I lifted my foot and bent down. The vial that had held the mixture we hoped could save our lives was shattered to pieces. The elixir had not saved Harold but I still held hope it could work for Karen. Within a few feet of the grave I stopped, leaned over, and peered into it.

At the bottom, Harold's corpse laid twisted and white. His clothes were torn to shreds and his shoes had been flung from the grave. His skin clung tight to his bones. His eyelids were open, exposing eyeballs that had turned gray and deflated. Insects scurried out from his ears while worms wiggled between his teeth and curled back under his tongue.

I turned, picked up a shovel, and buried his body within his wife's grave. My weakness was gone upon seeing him lying lifeless, a shell of a man misunderstood by the community. A man who gave his life to save mine, his daughter, those he employed, and his fellow citizens. Whatever opinions I had of him in the past were now gone, as I held him in the highest of regards. I decided at that moment I could not leave the gravesite until I buried him, a final thank you and show of respect that he was deserving of.

The filling in of the grave took only twenty minutes. I felt no fatigue, for the pestilence that had drained my strength the night before was gone. My body was still sore from blood loss but the pain was only noticeable if I focused on it.

As visions of Karen being killed went through my mind, the shovel fell from my hands and I ran from the gravesite, through the thicket and followed Cole's Woods Trail back to the Chapman house. I pushed myself to its limits. Karen, George, Clarabelle and the rest of the servants were in my thoughts. I had to save them if they weren't already dead.

The fog from the day before had lifted and sunshine pelted my face between tree branches and shadows. The eerie presence the woods induced by the fog and my imagination the day before was now replaced with a serene feeling. I felt the presence of woodland animals rather than fearsome and invisible demons. I smelled flowers and heard birds chirping, the breeze rustling through the trees. These feelings gave me the courage I would need upon reaching the house.

Through the trees, I could see the outline of the Chapman house. I emerged from Cole's Woods, ran through the backyard, and stopped at the gazebo. I leaned against it to catch my breath. My chest heaved, my stomach lurched, and I coughed and spit saliva from my mouth.

While resting for a moment, I glanced at the house. The once beautifully designed home had turned into a dilapidated shack. Slate shingles laid in piles at the foundation, window glass littered the grass, shutters tilted and hung from single nails, and the porch railing had toppled over.

My back slid down the post of the gazebo and my eyes began to blur as I looked at the grass in shock. Before my very eyes, the blades were morphing into bones, then into fingers, then hands. An army of skeletal hands that crawled towards me like spiderlings emerging from silken egg sacs. My eyes started to blacken and a feeling of dread swept over me. The same pestilence I felt in the grave had invaded me once more but it wasn't as power-ful.

Jane was near and I knew she felt my presence as well. If she was not, her aura lingered behind enough to slow my advancement to the house. The skeletal hands grabbed my legs and climbed up my pants. This time how-ever, I fought off the hallucination and rose to my feet and staggered to the house.

Lying next to the back porch was the letter opener I'd tossed out the window two days ago. I picked it up and held it like a dagger, ready to thrust it deep into Jane's chest if I found her lurking in the house.

The backdoor was locked just as Harold had left it the previous day. I leaned against the house, supporting myself as I shuffled around to the front door. Upon laying eyes on it, I froze. The door had been ripped off the hinges, ripped to pieces and strewn about the lawn.

I approached the entrance and peeked through the doorway. Inside, ly-ing on the landing of the staircase, was George's body. He was dead. The area of his wrinkled body that I could see was shriveled into deeper cre-vasses that folded over one another from his internal organs being removed. His clothes hung loose around his limbs. His face retained his last expres-sion—fright. His eyes were wide and his lower jaw slack. His tongue was curled back and his plump nose, crinkled and narrowed, had drooped off his face like wilted flowers.

I searched the house for other victims and more importantly, survivors. I forced myself to run up the staircase and into Karen's room. Her body was gone and the bedroom was in disarray. The top mattress was pushed off the bed and had been laid on the floor below the footboard. The sheets were torn to shreds and the feather pillow stuffing was strewn about as if a chicken had been attacked by a wolf. The vanity mirror was shattered as were the glass picture frames. With each step I took into the room, shards of glass cracked beneath my feet. All the clothes in the closest and dresser were tossed about the room, as is someone had been searching for some-thing. The windows were open with the curtains dangling out over the house siding. It was as if someone had tried to climb out to safety or something horrific had entered, murdered the occupants, then used the window to escape.

Bloody handprints were smeared everywhere. I could follow each print and reenact the struggles. Karen first print was over the top of her bed. The hands prints were inches from the ceiling. Then the prints moved down-ward at a sharp angle to the floor molding, then onto the floor itself. The prints then crawled across the floor where they stopped under the toppled mattress.

As I looked at the mattress from a different angle, I noticed curled up toes beneath it. I flipped it over and found Clarabelle lying face down on the floor. The handprints were hers and not Karen's. Her black skin had faded into a light tan with patches of white from being sucked of life. Her body had collapsed in on itself from being drained of organs, blood and tissue. Her excess skin pooled out about two feet from her bones like a bunched-up blanket. I could not see her face but I could tell by the outline of her jaw that her expression was the same as George's—fear.

Karen's body was missing. I could only at the time speculate about what happened. Either upon her death, Karen had risen and attacked Clarabelle, or Jane had attacked and killed Clarabelle and took Karen with her and turned the girl into the same creature Jane had become. If the second scenario was true, and I pray it is not, I fear there are now two demons walking the Earth, stalking, attacking and preying on the innocent.

I tore down a curtain from the window, covered Clarabelle's body and left the room to continue my search. With all the noise I'd made, I would have drawn attention to myself, and whatever demons lurking in the house would have attacked me if they were present. I felt safe for the time being.

The rest of the house was ransacked. Drawers turned over and contents tossed across the rooms. Clothes, shoes and personal artifacts were strewn from closets and dressers. The kitchen was toppled with utensils, bowls and food littering the floor and counters while trailing out into the dining room. Throw rugs were torn, curtains ripped to the floor, more holes pelted into the wall and more glasses crackled under my feet.

On the living room wall, a family portrait of the Chapman's hung untouched. This effigy of them displayed the healthy, living and loving family that had fallen into torment by an evil entity. I stared at their faces, their eyes, wishing I could have saved them. I whispered an apology before walking away.

Continuing my search, I found more victims of those unable to escape Jane's wrath. I found the cook in the pantry, the tailor in the nook, and the seamstress in the parlor, each lying in a mass of deflated skin. All had met the same fate and all were killed in the same manner, and all because the night before Harold and I were unable to complete our task and destroy the root of evil, the torturing pestilence—Jane Chapman.

I went outside to the carriage house to retrieve a horse to ride back into town to escape this nightmare and warn the townspeople. The large oak doors were closed and the windows covered in dust. I could not see inside and determine if the lurking fear that was Jane or Karen was inside and hiding from me.

I pressed my ear on the side of the carriage house and listened for any sounds coming from within. I heard nothing. Not a single horse snorting, rustling in its stall or neighing. I walked to the front of the stable and pulled open the heavy doors and stood in the entrance. The stale smell of horse urine and feces swept over me and diluted the bittersweet scent of hay.

I searched inside, but there were no signs that anyone was lying in wait or dead, which the latter came as a relief. I had grown immune to mutilated bodies over the course of the past twenty-four hours, but still, I did not want to find another victim. I was hoping someone had survived.

I took one step inside the carriage house and paused. It was quiet and this made me uneasy. I figured I had not heard any of the horses because the walls were built thick, but now that I was inside, their lack of presence was alarming. I crouched down and looked under the small gap of the stalls for the horses and anyone and anything else. Each of the six stalls was empty except the last. Underneath the gap, I could see a black mass of what looked like a pile of remains.

I stood up and crept toward the stall. The top of the door to the stall was level with my neck, making it hard to see inside unless I hoisted myself up onto the side wall of the stall or opened the door. Not wanting to put myself in a compromising position where I was not able to flee, I opted to open the door. With a slight push, the door creaked open enough to poke my head inside. When I gazed on the stall floor, I pushed open the door and stared at a gutted horse lying atop a bedding of hay soaked with blood.

Its head was intact as were its legs and back end. Its mane was dampened with blood as were its tail hairs. The belly was slit from the neck to the anus. The ribs were still attached, leaving the rounded shape of the torso intact. Strewn about the stall were its organs, leaving the body cavity hollow.

Without taking my eyes of the carcass, I backed out of the stall and began to close the door when I saw what looked like either human toes or pieces of intestine poking out from under the horse. I pushed open the door and removed a horseshoe hammer from the wall. I put the head of the tool under the torn lip of the belly and pulled up on the skin, then looked inside the body cavity of the horse.

Curled up in the fetal position was the carriage driver— still alive. When he saw me, he began weeping and shaking in fear.

"It's me, Doctor Myerburg," I whispered to him.

He turned his head away from the spinal column. His eyes were wide and stained red from the horse's blood seeping into them. His face was covered in blood and pieces of red and gray organ tissue. All of his clothes were drenched in blood and covered in viscera.

"I came back," I said. "I thought you were killed like the others."

I reached out my hand, and when he took it, I pulled him out from within the horse cocoon and helped him to his feet. His once curly hair was matted down with blood and chunks of flesh slid down his cheeks.

He stepped out from the stall, sobbing. "I killed the horse and crawled inside it. I killed it to save myself."

"I'm sorry I…" I began but was stopped.

"I said, I killed the horse," he said again.

"I know. I'm sorry I did not return sooner to help…"

Again he interrupted while pushing by me. "It was all I could do to save myself from that monster."

"Monster? Do you mean Jane?"

He turned and grabbed my arms in his hands and shook me, yelling between laughter. "That, that wasn't Jane, no…no, no, no…that was a monster. I heard screaming and I…I rushed through the backdoor and into the kitchen where the screams came from. I stopped dead in my tracks when I saw it kneeling on the floor, sucking blood from a hole it had made in the cook's chest. I screamed and the monster looked up at me. Then it and stood up. It stepped over the cook and reached its arms out for me. You see, it was coming for me. That was when I ran out of the house to the stables."

He paused and looked around the carriage house. He leaned forward and placed his face inches from mine. "I don't know why I ran out here," he whispered.

He paused again and his breathing shivered as he drew in a breath. He became less wild and calmed down as he continued whispering; all the while his eyes never broke from mine. "I suppose my only thought was to save the horses and not anyone in the house. I opened each stall and shooed the horses away except one. I meant it no harm. I was going to ride it away but in all the commotion its old heart must have gave out and it collapsed. Maybe it would have lived but I panicked. And that, that is when I did the unthinkable. I took a knife and I cut open its belly."

I looked down at his hand; the knife he used to open the horse was still clutched in his palm. His hand was twitching as he continued his graphic story while raising the knife and stepping away from me.

His voice turned wild again as his tale frightened himself. "I heard that thing, that monster, enter the stables and look for me. But it only found an empty carriage house and a dead horse. I saved myself by hiding inside the animal, you see."

He began creeping toward me with the knife raised above his head. "Did you hear that? I hid inside the horse, the horse that I carved open like a jack-o-lantern. And if it weren't for you and Mr. Chapman wandering the woods and doing acts only the Devil himself would cherish, then I would never have butchered that poor and defenseless animal!"

With each step he took towards me, I backed up, trying to convince him that he was in his right mind. "You did what anyone would have done in your situation. You needed to survive and tell the world that a monster is loose," I said calmly.

An evil smile came over his face, and he said in whimpers and chuckles, "You don't understand, Dr. Myerburg, a monster that was lurking inside of me has burst out. Not everyone would have done what I did to survive. Only a monster would do that to an animal, as that monster inside of Jane also did to the helpless cook. And as far as I'm concerned, you are the direct cause of my monster being unleashed. And before you cause me anymore trouble, my monster is going to end your life!"

He lunged at me with the knife, slashing through the air. I put my hand in my back pocket to retrieve the letter opener to defend myself but fumbled and dropped it. He jumped at me, and I pushed him away, at the same time ducking and rolling out of the knife's path to fall against a carriage wheel. My head hit the wheel and almost knocked me unconscious. I felt dizzy and could not stand. I pulled myself up on the wheel, leaned against it, and looked behind me to see that my attacker was now lying on a small haystack, and protruding from his back, dripping with blood, were four prongs from a pitchfork that had been lying in the hay, where he'd promptly fallen onto it.

I staggered over to the letter opener and picked it up, hoping by chance he was still alive. I'd once kept a man alive for a week that had fallen on a pitchfork accidentally years ago. That time the prongs had only embedded a few inches and had not impaled him. This instance might be was similar so I kept my guard up, knowing that the man could try and attack me again. I turned him over and the knife that he was going to stab me with was embedded in his throat. If the pitchfork had not kill him then the knife most certainly did.

I removed the knife and the pitchfork from the corpse and dragged the body back into the stall with the horse. Then I walked back into the house and wrapped the other victims in blankets and curtains that were not torn to shreds. Then I carried the bodies from the house and placed them into the same stall as the mutilated horse. Using the pitchfork, I buried them with hay. Before they returned to life like Jane, if they were to at all, I decided to cremate them to prevent any such resurrection. I searched the carriage house for lantern oil to use as an accelerant but found none, then I remembered that in the basement there was oil. With one last glance at the buried corpses, I left the stable and headed for the house yet again.

Chapter 8
The Pyre

I found the oil in the basement and was about to leave when I heard a scratching noise and began to smell roses. The scratching sounded as if someone had moved their foot across a dirty floor. The noise came from behind a stack of wooden storage trunks. The smell of roses reminded me about what Harold had told me about Jane in the cemetery; roses were her favorite flower.

I pulled the letter opener from my pocket, walking slowly, in a horizontal path along the trunks from a safe distance. I kept my eyes on walls behind the trunks, searching for shadowy movements. And there poking out from behind one of the trunks were the shadows of feet. I'd found Jane or possibly Karen. If I was lucky, I found them both. If indeed luck was indeed on my side, I could kill them before they killed me.

Still feeling adrenaline rushing through my veins from the brush of death in the carriage house, I was jittery and on high alert. I was not going to wait for another close call that might send me to my grave. I was going on the offense rather than defense again.

I moved to the trunks and could hear someone behind them breathing. I raised the letter opener in a striking position and placed my hand on one of the trunks. I breathed in deep, loud, and swallowed hard. My heart pounded in my chest and my hands shook. I felt my knees wobble to the extent they were knocking together.

I counted to three, then pulled down the trunk. It clattered to the floor, and at the same time the figure stood up. I closed my eyes and with all my might I buried the letter opener deep into the center of the figure's chest.

I let go of the letter opener and opened my eyes to see in my horror what I'd done. "Oh God, w-what have I d-done, p-please, n-no!" I stuttered while crying out.

With the letter opener implanted in her chest, Clarabelle staggered away from the trunks, fell into the wall, and onto her side. I pushed over the remaining trunks and stepped over them. I fell to my knees and held up her head.

"I'm so sorry," I said through tears. "I thought you were..."

Clarabelle interrupted me and looked into my eyes., "I figure you was too!" she said, coughing up blood.

Her left arm fell to the floor and her hand uncurled. A large, serrated knife clattered to the floor. I looked at the blade, knowing that if I hadn't stabbed Clarabelle first, I would now be the one lying on the floor with a knife wedged between my ribs. Next to her were two roses, from the vase in Karen's room.

My hands shook. "I thought you were dead. I saw your body lying on Karen's bedroom floor."

"No, sir. That is Karen. I was prunin' her roses when she woke an' started screamin'." Clarabelle's head rolled to the side and she coughed up blood that dribbled over her lips.

I wiped her mouth clean and she continued. "A horrible thing were a standin' over Karen and I runned from da room an' hid in a hallway closet. I return later when all da screamin' went quiet an' I found her body torn apart. I found all da others, too. I then 'eard someone enter into da house so I runs into da basement and been hidin' here ever since. I now know it were you dat came in."

"I can save you; all I need to do is find my medical bag."

"Please, sir, lemme die. Help me remove da knife from my chest." Again she coughed up blood as her chest muscles twitched.

"You don't deserve to die this way."

"Please, sir, lemme die."

I refused and stood up. "I think I know where my bag is. I'll be back. Just hold on."

Before I made it to the staircase, I heard Clarabelle grimace and the letter opener clanked on the floor. She had pulled it from her chest. I turned, climbed over the trunks and dropped to my knees. I tore a large section of fabric from her shirt and pressed it against her wound. The blood popped and burbled out, under pressure from the escaping air in her lungs. Her chest spasms increased and her legs and arms flailed. Her neck stretched back and the remaining air passed through her mouth, as did more blood.

"Stay with me, Clarabelle, stay with me!" I yelled, trying to keep her from slipping into unconsciousness and then death.

Her head drooped to the side. A slight trickle of blood drizzled from her mouth and nose as she let out a final cough. Her arms went limp and her heart rate dropped. Her eyes looked into mine as her eyelids fluttered closed. She let out a moan and stopped breathing. Clarabelle died.

I whispered my final apologies, pulled her body out from behind her hiding spot, and dragged her up from the basement. In the carriage house, I placed Clarabelle next to the others and spread hay over her body. I poured the oil and lit the pyre ablaze. The flames spread and shot up to the ceiling in seconds, the fumes of burning flesh a welcome scent compared to the decayed stench drifted through the house.

As the pyre burned, I stuck the pitchfork in, removed a pile of burning hay, carried it to the house, and tossed it through the open back door. The fire spread through the house quickly, and within minutes, the roof became engulfed. An hour later the house, weakened by fire, collapsed in on itself. If there was a curse lurking behind the facade, it was burned away with the house.

I walked away from the property to the front gate. Embers drifted, fell, and landed on the ground like snowflakes. The smoke drifted around me, making it hard to breathe. To escape the suffocating smoke, I began jogging across the property to the road. Off in the distance, I heard yelling and crying that a monster was loose. The townspeople were in danger.

I started running.

Chapter 9
The Black Cloud

From the outskirts of town, lights flickered from oil lamps and torches. The echoing screams and cries from the remaining women and children filled my ears with the anguish that Harold and I had spawned a monster no man could destroy. The men were yelling also but in anger. I sprinted and made it into town minutes later.

Upon arrival, the men were gathered in a large circle that was six bodies deep. In their hands, they held torches blazing in red-hot fire, and pistols and rifles pointing into the center of the circle. Men without firearms held onto sickles, axes and other tools they would use to fight, maim, or kill.

"Devil woman!" a man shouted, loud and rasped.

"Burn her—burn her to back to Hell!" another man yelled, throwing a torch at the center of the circle, followed by more cheers, as if the torch had struck its target.

Pushing my way through the crowd, my eyes caught hold of Jane in the middle of the circle. She still resembled a corpse but had rejuvenated more since our frightful encounter in the mire. Her eyes were glowing and foam bubbled out of her mouth. Playfully, she stroked the hair a young man who was propped up against her leg. The man had his eyes closed and didn't move but was still breathing. What little life he retained was being drained. His body was withering before the mobs' eyes as he turned into an old man. His skin became wrinkled and cracked from dryness, his black hair turning gray as it fell from his scalp in clumps.

Jane snatched the man off the ground and held him up by his shirt collar. She opened her mouth and a black cloud drifted out and engulfed his head. The man's head snapped back as his arms tried to break free from her grasp. His chest heaved and his legs kicked. He tried to yell for help but was being suffocated from the black cloud.

Jane breathed in deep, inhaling the cloud into her lungs. Her chest began to expand as her breasts ballooned under her ragged clothes. Her cheeks filled and flushed over with pink as her natural skin tone was replenished. Her torso began to fill out her clothes and her thighs began to expand.

The man's body flapped like a flag in a breeze. His skin had become black and any resemblance of a human being was gone. You wouldn't have known he'd been a man if his clothes weren't still intact.

"Burn her at the stake!" a man yelled from the back of the crowd.

Then in unison, the crowd began to chant, "Witch, witch, witch!"

I stepped out from the perimeter of the circle and into Jane's view. My movement caught her eye and she squared her body to mine. She raised her left arm, extended her fingers as if reaching out for me, and I could tell by the way her hand shook that she was still weak, but strong enough to kill each of us off one by one if need be. By the looks of the man she'd turned into an empty bag of bones, she was well on her way of disposing us.

"My maker!" Jane gurgled and pointed to me. Her voice was guttural and winded.

A loud murmur rolled over the crowd upon hearing her speak.

Ben, the blacksmith who'd offered his help days before, yelled from the crowd, "It's true. I saw Doc Myerburg a few days ago. I saw him; he was climbing into a carriage with one of the Chapman servants. He did this to Jane Chapman; he turned her into a demon!"

The crowd grew angry and began shouting while pointing their firearms in my direction. They chanted, "Devil-man. Devil-man!"

Two men grabbed me from behind and one held a knife to my throat, holding me captive. "You'll burn at the stake with the witch for this, devil-man!"

"Please, let me go. You don't understand. Let me explain!" I begged, as I stretched my neck and lifted my chin, trying to pull away from the knife.

"Slice his throat," one of the men said, "then we'll burn him. Make the devil-man suffer!"

The knife raked across my neck. The blade cut through my skin, and just before the knife slit my jugular and I was killed, a man galloping towards the mob on horseback yelled, "Fire, the Chapman Estate is on fire!"

My executioner lowered the knife and I pulled myself free, fell to the ground, and crawled away in the chaos. I felt my neck. The knife had cut into my skin but not deep enough to be fatal. I tore a strip of cloth from my shirt and wrapped it around my neck to absorb the blood.

The man on horseback leaped from the saddle, pushed his way through the crowd, and into the circle. "I just arrived from the Chapman Estate. The property is burning. The house has been destroyed by fire as well as the carriage house. There's a pile of bones smoldering in the yard. Someone murdered everyone there and tried to hide the deed by burning their corpses!"

The man's imagination was far from the truth of what really happened. I was trying to save their souls from coming back to life as a monster like Jane. I was anything but a killer trying to conceal a murderous rampage.

Ben raised his pistol at me and pulled back the hammer. "Whatever it was you did there has brought Hell on our town, mister. You spawned this demon. You're a murderer." He pointed at Jane as he talked.

"You don't understand, let me explain!" I begged, falling to my knees with my hands clasped together and fingers intertwined.

"Explain your actions to the Devil!" Ben shouted.

In my mind, his finger pulling the trigger moved in slow motion. My heartbeat rose in my chest and it felt as though my heart was tearing apart and exploding. The hammer dropped on the bullet, followed by a flash exiting the muzzle and chamber. I closed my eyes, not waiting to see the bullet enter in my body but I never felt it. A loud pop echoed in the night and the went over my head and ricocheted off a metal sign hanging over the shop door of the gunsmith.

I opened my eyes and saw Ben hoisted into the air. His legs were kicking and his arms were trying to reach around him and grab onto Jane. In the confusion and excitement of the moment, Ben forgot, as did the crowd, that she was standing there and waiting, feeling the need to attack.

Gunfire exploded around me and the expelled gunpowder singed my neck hair. The unending popping of pistols and rifles was deafening. It sounded like dozens of stringed-firecrackers were hung, lit and were popping around my head. I covered my ears, dropped to the ground, and watched in horror as the barrage of bullets pelted Ben's body as the men tried to shoot Jane. With each bullet that entered him, he twitched and grimaced.

Bullets passed through Ben and hit Jane, but they were ineffective. Jane continued holding Ben in the air, opened her mouth wide, and engulfed his head in a black cloud.

"Hold your fire. Hold your fire!" I yelled over the crowd, while rising to my feet and waving my arms.

The firearms ceased one by one until all went quiet. The fumes of gunpowder dried my nostrils and a loud ringing filled my ears.

The men watched in horror as Jane sucked the life from Ben. His body aged and shriveled the same as the last man who'd met his fate within Jane's evil grasp.

As she fed off Ben, I grabbed a torch from one of the men and circled around her. I inched towards her and made sure she could not sense my movement. Whenever she turned, I moved to stay out of her line of sight. Closer and closer, I came upon her back. My heart raced and rose into my throat. The force of my beating heart within my ears drowned out the yelling of the men and the random gunshots. I was within arm's reach of her when she tossed Ben away.

Then she spotted me and her arm swung around and hit me across my chest. I lost my footing and fell to the ground. The torch fell from my grasp and rolled out of reach.

Jane reached down and lifted my body from the ground. Only this time there were no leeches sacrificing their bodies to save mine. I was now hers for the taking, for the leeching of my soul for her to posses for all of eternity.

I turned my head away from her and yelled over the crowd, "Run away. Leave before she kills all of you!" Like Harold before me, I had to sacrifice myself for the good of mankind.

The majority of the men scattered like scared mice when a barn door is opened. But some men remained because they were either too scared to run or because they were too stupid. In order for the men who were running to get away to a safe distance, I fought Jane. I kicked my legs and pounded my fists into her head and chest, but my blows were weak and ineffective.

Jane slammed my body to the ground. She crouched over me, picked me back up and slammed me shoulder first into the hard earth again, followed by my face implanting into the dirt. She was playing with me, torturing me before she opened her mouth and engulfed my head in the black cloud of death.

My shoulder became dislocated and my nose broken. I heard a gunshot and saw the bullet exit through her chest. She turned and looked at the man who'd fired the shot. She staggered to him and he dropped the gun and ran. She chased him, only making it ten feet, before another bullet hit her arm, followed by more bullets.

I crawled to the torch, grabbed it, and stood up. After gaining my footing, I ran at Jane, but before I could thrust the torch through her back and into her body, a bullet hit her in the shoulder. She turned, caught sight of me and charged. I stood my ground and fought the pain of my dislocated shoulder, holding the torch in both hands like an axe.

Jane grabbed me and lifted me off the ground, her mouth opened wide. The black cloud dissipated from within. It smelled of rotten fish. The black cloud burned my eyes and suffocated my lungs. It was now or never. I had to kill her.

I raised the blazing torch over my head like a dagger. The heat began to melt my skin and the flames scorched my knuckles. I withstood the pain and rammed the torch straight down and into Jane's mouth. With all my strength, I held the torch in place and pushed the fire deep into her throat. I could hear the muscles and tissues within melting and crackling from the heat as she ignited from the flames, the sickly sweet odor of burned flesh filling the air.

Jane held on to me while stumbling around, then she fell over onto her back. As we landed, I held the torch in place and continued pushing deeper. Smoke billowed out from her nostrils followed by sparking flames. Her eyes melted before popping, and exploding black liquid sprayed onto my hands and face. She bucked her body, trying to kick me off. Her arms flailed, trying to grasp the torch, and when her arms found it, she tried wrenching it from my grasp and her throat.

She failed.

Seconds later, she stopped moving and her arms flopped to the ground. I stood up and staggered backwards. I regained my footing and turned and looked at the remaining men. They were silent. Their jaws were dropped, their firearms still pointed at Jane.

I walked over to the closest man to me and reached for his axe. He didn't fight me for it. He let me take it from him.

I turned and looked at Jane as she burned. The flames used her bones as a wick and her body fat as candle wax; she was being cremated from the inside out. Her skin bubbled and popped like a witch's cauldron over an open fire. Her skin began to crack open and smoke seeped from the crannies, followed by yellow-orange and reddish flames.

Soon after, her clothes caught fire and flames engulfed her entire body. Her hair curled up as it began to burn and her teeth fell from her mouth. Embers made out of pieces of her clothes and skin floated in the air and drifted back to the ground.

I walked up to Jane as she burned and raised the axe. Swinging it through the air, I slammed it down into her right shoulder. Embers plumed into the air as if a log had been tossed into a roaring fire. I wiggled the axe free from the ground and her melted skin fused to the cold, metal axe head. I lifted the axe and her arm slid off and dropped to the ground.

Next, I drove the axe blade into Jane's left shoulder, followed by her head, right leg and finally her left leg; with each chop from the axe, embers plumed into the air.

After the fire smothered itself, I collected the ashes and placed them in a coffin. What extremities didn't turn to ash, I arranged them accordingly to their corresponding positions.

Epilogue

The Chapman Estate sat dormant for two years, nothing but a pile of ash. It served as a site for those with a morbid curiosity to visit before it was cleaned and the property sold by the City of Saratoga Springs. A hospital now stands on the site, a hospital that I could never practice medicine in.

I've been deemed mad.

If I were indeed mad then I would have killed myself in order to escape my own personal hell. I can say that I may have even harmed others in order to prove my sanity.

There were moments when I thought I saw Jane, because from the corners of my eyes those who were mistaken for her shared similar body and facial features, but I never accused or attacked anyone. I know for a fact that Jane's body is buried, I dug her grave myself.

It has been five years to the day since I left Harold's property ablaze and took an axe to Jane's body. I've not taken in a sick patient to diagnose and heal them since. No one seeks my medical advice anyway. I don't blame the community for shunning me as they had the Chapman family over the years. Who in their right minds would call upon a doctor who'd exhumed a corpse, drank its burnt heart and afterwards returned to the estate only to find those remaining turned into bags of bones?

I've not opened the curtains to allow the sun to shine on my face. I've not bought food or drink nor have I relished in home cooked meals that I once enjoyed. I only eat when I feel weak and drink when I cannot form saliva to remove the dryness from my mouth. I don't deserve such pleasures. I've destroyed many lives. I'm the direct cause that Harold, Karen, George, Clarabelle and the remaining servants died. I'm the reason Ben and that other poor man was killed.

It was I that let my imagination overcome rational thinking and partook in a hellish act that night in the cemetery. I didn't have to accept the plan to exhume Jane. I could've talked Harold out of the ritual but I allowed myself to get caught up in the supernatural. In doing so, I unleashed Hell upon the land.

I struggle daily with the guilt of spawning the curse upon the Chapman servants. It wasn't their fault they were killed. And, if I was sure that Jane was dead, my guilt would have put a gun in my mouth and I would have pulled the trigger. I visit her unmarked grave behind the church each night to remind myself that indeed this horror is over, but I can never be sure it truly is.

I hear rumors of beasts ravaging sleepers during the night through the northeast. The stories are all the same. The victims' bodies are found drained of blood and internal organs. Their bodies are cold, deflated and are seen days later wandering the night hours. Following their sightings, a rash of death and destruction is left within their wake. More victims are found dead or nearing a death they cannot escape from.

I cannot erase the memories that I collected in the burial ground or the mire. The corpse, the sight of Harold expiring under Jane's wrath and self-imposing my body as a feast to innumerous leeches, has plagued my sanity with nightmares.

The accidental murder of Clarabelle still jars me awake from agonizing nightmares and plunges me deeper into self-loathing. Sometimes, I dream she got the best of me and plunged the knife into my chest.

Sometimes I dream the letter opener had been driven into Jane's chest, ending the nightmare in the grave before it got out of hand.

I see Clarabelle smiling and laughing as she continued to enjoy life. Then I wake, and see the pistol resting on my pillow, reminding me it was all more than just a nightmare. It was reality. It is reality.

I wait for the pestilence to emerge and rape my body of life. Because of this, I have not slept a moment during the night hours. I can only rest under the protection of daylight, for that monstrosity, only known through my own experiences, scavenges the land at night.

During those hours of restlessness, I sit motionless at Jane's grave while gripping a pistol in one hand and lantern fuel in the other. If and when Jane returns from her grave, a bullet will put her down and the oil will torch her soul. Then and only then will I rest in peace, my nightmares finally put to an end.

FEEDING THE DEAD

ALAN SPENCER

1

Feed the dead, and the dead won't feed on us...

2

The corpses were splayed delicately on the floor of the walk-in refrigerator with their arms stiff at their sides, one beside the other, ten bodies total—what used to be a thirty-one strong supply.

They were the remaining elderly patients in the hospice care building who hadn't escaped during the initial onslaught of the attack. Each was terminally ill and had died when their life support machines stopped functioning during the power outage. It had lasted for twelve hours before the lights miraculously flickered back on, and stayed on, giving the hope that someone was doing something to rescue them from the dangers lurking outside.

Gazing down at the floor of bodies, Andrea Brundage was one of the four survivors that had to make a decision. Overwhelmed by her job, she couldn't stare at the dead for too long, fearing they'd rise up from the floor and shamble after her with their arms outstretched and their teeth clacking so hard they could shatter—and she'd seen it happen!

"Who do we pick now?" Hospice care director Harold Price asked the group, the only man confident enough to stand inches from the dead bodies for a closer inspection, as if he could form a determination for selection by their still facial expressions. "Come on, people, they're drawing closer to the windows. If enough of those things get irate, they'll crash through the blockades. This has worked so far, so let's not lose sight of what's important. We have to keep buying time. Someone will come and save us, but for now, we have to save ourselves. This is why we're doing this, remember?"

"Yes, he's right, he's right," Vinny Wharton agreed, the beefy three hundred pound man who was nervous in the delivery of his words. His piggish face was awash in sweat, the fridge's air failing to cool him down. "We can't do anything for them. They're obviously dead. They'd want us to save ourselves."

"We've already been through this argument," Harold insisted, shaking his head at the rest of them dismissively. "And we decided together, so let's stick with our resolve. It's not pretty, it's not moral, but it's very necessary."

Andrea eyeballed the other survivor who happened to get along with her the best. It was an elementary school janitor in her fifties—a black woman named Edith Jackson. She looked for any indication as to who to pick, when Harold suddenly kneeled down with a crack of his knees and chose Mrs. Hillman, a woman who'd been in the terminal stages of lung cancer. She wasn't a person anymore, but instead a chilled body about to be dished out to the hungry zombies outside.

"Grab her legs, Vinny," he insisted, and together, the two men hauled the body into the cutting room. "Let's get moving. They're pounding harder on the windows. The bastards are ready to eat."

3

The patches over the windows vibrated against the pounding of the undead's fists, the insistent blows that would only escalate the longer they waited to feed on Mrs. Hillman's body. The noises were reinforced by the infernal moans of ten or twenty zombies, their dreadful voices without affectation.

Laden in death rattle fluids, the chorus of the dead kept chanting and baying. They'd do so for hours on end until they got their way, and if they didn't, Andrea knew they would strip the wooden barriers and take them instead. So the four of them, including herself, had decided to do the unthinkable and simply give the dead what they wanted.

What had kept them alive...for now.

Knocked from her thought processes, she returned to the situation at hand, which was standing outside the door in the hallway, when a jarring noise jolted her.

Swack!

She clasped both sides of her head, her hands acting as a vice to subdue the pressure building in her skull. Standing outside the hospital's break room door, with the access partially open, she paced back and forth, nervous and hating every second of the duty being performed inside.

The chamber served a new purpose.

They called it the 'cutting room.'

She was in charge of consoling Vinny during the unsettling duty of corpse preparation, and she kept talking to him despite the way her stomach lurched up her throat as she imagined the cuts he was making to Mrs. Hillman's body.

Andrea tossed out the words, desperate to block out the hacking of steel against bone sounds that repeated relentlessly, "Tell me about your wife; what was she like?"

The whoosh of the cleaver, he hammered the cutting edge through the neck bone, the connection sounding like two cue balls slamming into each other.

The butcher, doing his best to ignore the ghastly severity of his work, answered her question, "Jenny was a knitter. She got it from her mother..."

Four successive strikes later, and he was slicing through Mrs. Hillman's midsection, breaking into the hip bones, and then moving on, he gutted her by hand. The wet plop and drag of what sounded like wet socks slopped against tile floor.

"...her mother got arthritis 'cause she knitted so goddamn much..."

The sound of blood spilling onto the floor came to her and she imagined buckets of it flowing out of the corpse's dismembered body.

How many gallons did the human body hold? she wondered.

"...my wife, though, she'd make the knitting motions with her hands in her sleep, and I couldn't stand it. She'd keep me up for hours, twitching and crocheting sweaters, or oven mitts, or scarves, or God knows what in dreamland..."

Andrea clutched her belly, hugging herself tighter. She braced herself, wanting to retch, but she held it down for Vinny's sake—the man who took on the job no one else wanted. But he did it because he was a grocery store butcher in his normal life. She tried to help him through the harrowing ordeal of dismembering corpses, but once she overheard the scraping of the fire axe against the tile floors—his next dissecting tool—she had to bend down to her knees and let the blood rush to her head to avoid unleashing a scream.

When Vinny was done leveling the axe mercilessly into Mrs. Hillman, he shoved a large, covered rubber tub at her with his foot, then went about cleaning the mess he'd made inside the cutting room with a water hose.

"Take this. I'm done with her body."

4

Scooting the rubber tub forward by bending over and pushing it with two hands down the hallway, Andrea did her best to ignore the horrifying images of Mrs. Hillman's pieces settling and turning over inside the container as she transported it. Serving as a distraction, Harold rushed down the hallway to help her. He was a tall and lanky man who refused to dress down during the emergency situation. He wore a Men's Warehouse black suit and glossy dress shoes. He'd become a permanent mourner.

He helped her lift the tub and carried one side, Andrea the other, as they trudged up to the second floor, and then slowly to the third. Walking with him, she noticed how he stank of a freshly smoked cigar—a cheap grape Swisher.

He smoked one every hour on the hour, channeling the stress of watching New Haven Hospice Care Center, a small and privately owned facility, become a dormant place under his supervision as director of human services. A place where the dying perished prematurely and the rooms downgraded themselves into false tombs. During these evening runs of feeding the dead, she'd caught him grow weepy-eyed when he recognized one of his patients that had been butchered and stowed in the rubber container.

He worked hard to force himself not to succumb to the grisly nature of the work, and that was why he kept talking up their motives out loud, as she knew he was about to any second.

Edith was already working on the third floor, preparing raw beef and chicken meat on a large table to mix with the human parts. Flies buzzed rampantly in the corridors, perhaps too afraid to feast on the walking dead outside, and instead chose the poultry and beef.

The laboring woman was sweating heavily in her haste to ball up the wads of pink and white animal flesh, anticipating the undead's arrival.

The duty, as Harold was now describing, was stating the obvious, "All right, let's mix the meat with," he sighed, trying to find a respectful way to say Mrs. Hillman's remains, "...what's in the tub. Those things will think we're giving them many bodies instead of just one; it'll prolong our survival. They're dumb enough to fall for it, but they're smart enough to stick around wanting more. Damn them, they'll never leave. I wish they'd just rot to death already and let us be."

Vinny caught up with them ten minutes later, his swagger unsteady after taking what Andrea imagined was a heavy dose of booze. He fit on a pair of plastic gloves, as they all had, and delved into the gory job they'd already started.

She opened the rubber tub, trying her best to stick her hands in without checking to see which part of Mrs. Hillman she was selecting. She could feel the shape she carried without actually viewing it, knowing it was a leg from the knee cap up to the woman's gluteus region. Still cold, it was starting to perspire and grow slick in her grasp. She dropped the leg into another rubber tub, as each of them had an individual one, and she went back to Mrs. Hillman's container again to take out some guts. Handling them was like grasping soggy coils of cold, congealed pudding.

Dropping her portion of Mrs. Hillman into her tub, she then delved into the meat patties Edith had created. Scooping up a pound of mixed raw meat, she dumped it in with Mrs. Hillman's leg.

Ready on her end to serve the living dead outside, she dragged the container to room 309. It was empty except for a chair in the corner, a TV nailed into the wall up high, and a fake fichus plant by the bathroom. The lights were kept off, not wanting the other dead things in the city to see the light and catch on to their presence.

Harold suddenly blurted out the directives of their mission with astute surety. "Carry this mess to the windows. Then open them wide, but slowly. Give them a second to notice us, but stay quiet. We don't want to draw a crowd. And don't throw it out all at once. Again, we want to give them the illusion we're serving them a feast."

Ignoring the man's instructions, Andrea followed her own mind, opening the window and letting the night air wash over her. A tinge of warmth carried in the breeze, now being June, one of the hottest months of summer. They were near the city's hospital, in the heart of the metropolitan area, where parking garages and apartment buildings and libraries resided in the urban box.

She could view the undead in the streets, the foragers, since they were up three stories high. It was two in the morning, and the darkness was broken by swatches of working street lights, the squares of yellows and whites from various buildings still functioning despite no one being alive.

The dead were very dead, she thought, spying one of them wearing a hooded sweatshirt, the face literally a skull without skin except for what was left around the mouth and nose, the flesh wet spackle. It skulked at a sluggish pace, dragging its left foot behind it, and it turned at a dislocated angle when it noticed her window opening. The dead thing opened its lips to issue a grunt and picked up its pace—a crawl to a limp.

The other zombie near the window was a woman in a police officer's uniform, with her throat torn out and half her uniform in ribbons, showcasing the eaten up breasts and the bones of her sternum. More horrible, her long blonde hair was torn back, the headpiece flapping against her neck like a flaccid death toupee.

The dead woman crawled on her knees to below Andrea's window, her hands stretching upwards, audibly breaking rigor mortis, and she swatted at the air impatiently, awaiting the wet meat that would drop from the heavens and onto the pavement.

Fifteen others, the regulars for the past three weeks, were surrounding the building, groaning in their joy, their insistency for sustenance. Among the undead, a new zombie had arrived. The man was dressed in running gear; a college-aged man who was still listening to his iPod, his midsection eaten through and exposing an empty cavity where intestines and innards used to be, but now a gummed-up recess of rubbery fat and blackened rib bones.

The living dead were still growing in numbers, and that's what kept them here in this building, she reasoned after their nightly arguments that they should run and find help by themselves.

We don't know how many are really out there.

The dead aren't our only enemies. People out there will rob us blind. Kill the men and rape the women.

No, the choice is obvious. Stay here. Hole up until we have no choice but to do otherwise.

Help will arrive soon. The military. A local militia. Cops. Someone will come to our rescue. It's like anything else, good things take time to happen, but it'll happen. We will be saved.

Let's stick to the plan and keep feeding them.

But what happens when we run out of 'food'?

Returning to herself and the task at hand, thus avoiding that dangerous question of running out of 'food,' she dug her gloved hands into the rubber container. She turned away from the glop, aghast at the smell of raw meat and dead human, and hurled the mess out the window, rejecting what the bottom feeders below considered a murder-worthy delicacy. She did this until the container was dry except for puddles of watery blood at the bottom.

She couldn't resist watching the dead eat the pieces, though she checked to make sure they'd bought the rouse. Which they did. The female cop picked up the leg piece, and crawling under a nearby bench to enjoy her take, she bit off her own tongue in the process of chewing the knee bone stump, swallowing both with zest. The jogger squeezed two wads of beef in its hands, the greasy fibers oozing out between its fingers. Soon, it approved of the texture and the blood seeping free, and swallowed the mess whole in one big ball. It slurped the fat off its fingers, smacking voraciously, then stole a wad of raw chicken that was splattered on the sidewalk. The jogger, now out of food, ambled over to the cop, sparking a violent, shrieking battle for Mrs. Hillman's leg.

Turning from the shoving and growling fight, Andrea closed the window. Moving fast, she bypassed everyone in the hallway, uncaring if they were finished or not with their duties. She retreated to her room on the first floor.

5

Andrea's room used to be the patient waiting room for visitors when the doctors were busy running tests or declaring times of death. She had a decent couch to relax on, and a TV mounted to the wall, which she kept on channel 5 on a low volume, in case of a broadcast. For the past three weeks, it displayed only snow. The hand-held radio on the coffee table exclusively played static as well.

She'd made good use of the vending machines, driving the steel leg of a chair through the front glass and shattering it. She'd enjoyed her fill of pretzels, Snickers and Twinkies, and so much more. She was an admitted soda junky, and she praised God with every pop of the tab. The soda was the rush of energy she used to get through her job as a courthouse stenographer, typing the prosecutor's and defense's cross examinations and witness testimonies with unflinching accuracy. And just as Vinny's wife had knitted in her sleep, sometimes she'd feel her fingers type on the keys, recording information in dreamland.

Lying back on the couch with her eyes closed, she heard the snow play on the television, the sound strangely soothing, telling her that if anything did happen out there in the world, she'd be the first to know.

But sleep didn't come, her mind turning over the past three weeks and the events that had transpired, but her unrest was mostly a repetition of previous conversations.

First, it was Vinny, the man who'd convinced them to use the bodies of the dead hospice patients as zombie food, saying, *"I only lived this long because when the dead broke through the storefront, they sorted through my glass displays of butchered meats. They were distracted long enough, devouring sausage links and veal cuts, that I escaped, but then they saw me. The dead things looked me over, and as they were eating, they didn't want to hurt me. I wasn't needed because the meat was provided for them. They were no longer a threat to me because they were satisfied."*

Harold, agreeing with Vinny's reasoning with instant assuredness that the plan would work, gave the group his supportive spiel—a testament from

115

a man who'd seen terminally ill hospice patients suffer and die on a regular basis for over fourteen years. *"I'm not done living, and I don't care about anyone's opinion about me and what I have to say, because I know I'm right, and to hell with you people. I've seen the expressions on the patients' faces, and you know what I see? Regrets. Especially from those who didn't spend more time with their loved ones, or they didn't go to that vacation island, or have their affairs, or they married the wrong person, or they let their health go to shit. It all comes at them in their final moments as regrets. They see what they didn't accomplish, and they're horrified. I haven't lived my live to the fullest, and I see that very clearly now after facing off with those zombies. I'm not dying in here or out there, and I'll do anything to survive, including feeding those things anything they want."*

Edith's reasoning was less philosophical. *"My husband's out there. We talked over the phone before the lines went out. He said for me to stay where I am and to wait for him, so I'm waiting for him. Henry's coming for me. He'll be here any day now. Any moment, he'll show up. I'm not going anywhere until he arrives, period."*

Andrea, lying down on the couch with the mental mess circulating in her head, pictured her next door neighbor, Stacy Woodcock, bash through her apartment door with half her face eaten off, spitting blood and puss through flesh-choked teeth. Andrea would rush straight for the fire escape—having no boyfriend or pets to save—scale the ladder, and run for safety.

Pockets of the city were clustered with the ravenous, walking dead who appeared without reason or cause, even to this day. Cars had swerved off roads, wrecking and burning and being turned over, the drivers and passengers either missing or eaten. Storefronts were smashed through, everywhere she looked ransacked or being ransacked. Men and women were sorted out among the zombies, living buffets screaming in torment, until they were rendered into bloody dead pieces. It wasn't until Andrea had sprinted eight city blocks that she spotted the hospice care center, and Edith, who waved her to an open window and let her in.

She'd be dead without the other three survivors, and she had no choice but to cling on to what kept her alive, no matter how gruesome or wrong it felt. The loud knock on the door stirred her from remembering the past. It was Edith, with a piece of bad news to share.

6

Edith looked worn down, and had looked like this even before the recent events. It was thanks to working at the local elementary school, buffing floors and cleaning kids' puke with kitty litter and a dust pan, and the many other thankless tasks set out for her beyond her janitorial calling. Her dark brown hair—the color of a brownie—had turned metallic on the edges, giving further evidence of her fifty-seven years of age. Entering the room, she plopped down on the chair across from the couch with a tired groan, resting her two-hundred and ten pound body.

"You want something to eat, or to drink?" Andrea asked.

Edith shook her head, already knowing what Andrea had to offer. "If it's not whiskey, no thanks. And I don't know where Vinny gets his stash. He says he's out, though I keep smelling the sauce on his breath. The jerk thinks he's entitled to more than us."

"I guess he is," Andrea sighed, admitting the truth. "I couldn't do what he does, you know, chopping up Mrs. Hillman, like that."

"If only they liked people food," Edith said.

Andrea didn't mean to laugh so hard, but it came bursting from her lips, "I can picture them chomping down on a huge bowl of salad and fighting over who gets the croutons."

Edith gave her that *you're so silly, I like you* expression. "You're something else, girl."

After a long moment passed of enjoying the amusing idea, Andrea returned to the matter at hand. "So what's the news?"

"Harold has done another once over of the city with his binoculars. He says there are no signs of help, no choppers in the sky or military or anything, only more of those things. He saw a group on 119th and Vine smash out the windows of a turned-over bus, and over twenty of them spilled out of it. They'd been trapped in it for who knows how long. They haven't seen us yet, but they could still be coming."

"Jesus Christ," Andrea gasped, shaking her head. "There could be hundreds, if not thousands out there, just waiting in the ranks."

"That's why Harold says we have to stay here. Venturing out is too dangerous, and besides, we don't have any weapons here, except for a fire axe and some kitchen tools. That's hardly an arsenal." Edith rubbed her tired eyes, though added the next quip with undying determination, "Besides, Henry hasn't come back yet. I'm going to stay here, no matter how many pop out of the woodwork. Bastards could come in droves. I don't care."

"I guess the news could've been worse, though."

"That wasn't my bad news; that was Harold's bad news," Edith said.

"Oh." A pang like a blush hit Andrea, her cheeks stinging with the dread of why Edith had come to see her. "Then what's *your* bad news?"

Edith stared at Andrea, her face turning blank, as her eyes welled with tears. "It's...it's just that we used the last of the steak and chicken meat in the walk-in last night. All we've got left are the nine dead bodies, and then, well then, I don't know what we'll do after that. And Henry hasn't come back. He could be on his way; any minute, he'll show up. Harold keeps watch. He promised me he would. I've described him to Harold so many times. Tall. Strong. He's a strong man, my Henry. Really hard looking in the face, but friendly, he's so nice, he's so loving and kind, and he's coming soon, really. That's why we have to wait, Andrea. We can't go anywhere until he arrives."

Andrea hugged her tight as Edith broke down, losing her composure to a fit of tears.

Help wasn't coming.

And they were running out of zombie food.

7

The mornings and afternoons were the safest times. The walking dead hid in the shadows, in buildings or underground, away from the burning hot sun.

Andrea had seen the effects of the blazing heat on the dead many times. She witnessed a man literally melt as he stumbled out in the open. His flesh dripped down his face like caramel over an apple, slithering down in heavy bullets, until it sloughed off his dermis and muscle tissue, to finally break up into six pieces and collapse into a puddle of putrid remains.

"The elements speed up decay; it's basic Casper's Law," Harold told them all when they first witnessed it. "They're smart, in a way, hiding in the shade and seeking shelter from the sun. If only they didn't figure it out, we'd be in the clear. They'd just melt away."

Being morning, breakfast was served, a simple meal of boxed cereal and orange juice. The four sat together at a table to consume it in subdued quiet. The past weeks, meals were a time for sharing their feelings and thoughts, but now, one issue prevailed: what to do next once the corpses of hospice patients were used up.

Without guns, we wouldn't get that far without being attacked.

We can't keep this up. Time's running out. The plan won't work forever.

Then we stall as long as we can.

Reinforce the barriers, double them up. They won't get through. They're only so strong, right?

They always smash through, don't be stupid. The meat's the only—and ONLY—reason they haven't cannibalized us already, and you damn well know it. You could box us in concrete, and they'd find a way. They always find a way!

Then what do we do, huh, people? What do we do? Let's stop bickering and get some ideas out there.

Look, there's nine bodies left. We should be having this conversation when those are gone. Who knows, help might show up by then.

They're not coming. Everyone's dead.

But we're not dead.

We know nothing beyond the radius of those fucking binoculars of yours, Harold. There could be a way out, and if we stay here, we might not see it.

If the rescue wagon would've pulled up, I would've seen it. I keep using my short wave radio and calling out signals too. You people have seen me in my office do it. I sent out e-mails when the lines worked. I drew S.O.S. PEOPLE ALIVE INSIDE! in paint on the roof. What else can we do?

Keep feeding them.

Yes, he's right—you're absolutely right, Vinny.

This doesn't mean we shouldn't stop thinking about a Plan B.

Fair enough. Plan B. Let's work on that.

Then we're settled. After we eat, I want everyone to take a hammer and nails and double check the windows and doors before we go off and do our own thing tonight.

The group disbanded, still troubled by the enigma of Plan B.

8

When the painstaking task of checking each room's security had concluded, and they adjourned for a break, Andrea decided to take a shower. Locking the door to one of the patient rooms and double checking the windows, she stripped out of her denim shorts and v-neck shirt, then cleaned herself with the equivalent of a hotel's sample soap and shampoo, though it all smelled like urinal cakes to her.

She'd stop the shower every other minute, listening to make sure the dead didn't enter the room through one of the windows, or that one of the men weren't getting any fishy ideas about walking in on her.

Vinny had given her breasts a thorough visual inspection the day she arrived at the hospice, mentally cataloguing their shape and size, as if he was going to need to call the image up later when he was alone. Harold also gave her the once over with his eyes too many times during various times of the day, and she sometimes caught him staring at her ass. Both men, she'd learned through conversations, had lost their wives during the riots in the streets. Perhaps it was post-traumatic relief for them, she thought, so she cast their unwanted glances to the wayside in exchange for another day alive. They were all in a bad place, and thinking that, it was the only way to forgive their leering gazes.

After finishing her shower, she toweled off. When she was about finished, she overheard a conversation coming in through the vents, which conducted voices as if they were made solely for that. It seemed she only caught the tail end of the conversation, but she could tell it was Vinny and Harold in a heated debate.

"What do we do then? The bodies will run out. It's inevitable. What's your Plan B?"

She could tell it had been Vinny talking, and now, Harold piped up to soothe his henchman's concerns. "Don't worry, Vinny, we just need to stick with the plan. I know what to do. It's simple, and when the time comes, you'll realize how simple it really is."

Then they went silent.

She heard a door down the hall open and close, their private meeting concluded.

9

Lunch was pasta and boiled frozen vegetables, the four of them eating at the same table, unenthusiastic over the spread. Vinny had finished his plate and was now using a carving stone to sharpen his cleaver and the fire axe, each *schink, schink, schink*, grating to all of their ears, but they didn't say anything.

What could they say?

Stop it, you jerk, Andrea thought.

But the man had the harshest job of them all; who were they to criticize or judge him? Harold was jotting notes down on a notepad, gesturing with his hands, working through his thoughts.

Edith, always inquisitive, asked, "What're you working on, Harold?"

The man jerked upright as if caught, and keeping his hand over the page, explained, "I'm trying to write an apology to the families...to the families who've lost their loved ones, I mean, and how we've, had to, well..."

"Serve them sunny side up to the zombies?" Vinny joked, issuing a series of black-hearted sounds of amusement before returning to his carving stone without another word.

"Yes, in a matter of speaking," Harold replied, shocked by the man's lack of tact. "I have all the addresses of my patients' families. I've already written twenty-one apology letters."

"For each person sacrificed," Andrea blurted out, understanding his thought process. "It makes sense. If we don't use them all, there's no need to apologize to the ones we don't have to throw out there, right?"

"Exactly." Harold returned to his task, done with explaining to everyone the inconceivable errand. "Keep eating, everyone. You'll need your strength tonight."

10

Andrea stood on the roof with Edith, both of them indulging in a can of soda, as they looked out at the empty city. It soothed Edith to be able to search the streets and broken buildings to scout for Henry, no matter how futile the process.

Andrea had offered to venture out with Edith before, but she always argued, "If Henry comes, and I'm not here, how will I ever find him? He told me to stay here, so I'm staying. He wouldn't want me to risk my life out there. He'd never forgive me."

Andrea had given up on the idea of arguing the possibility of Henry being dead, and decided to raise another subject. "What do you think Harold writes in those letters?"

"You'd have to be a speech writer for the president to come up with something so convincing and genuine. Perhaps Bill Clinton could wiggle out of this, but Harold? He's no poet or politician."

"Still, how do you apologize to the families for what we've done?"

"You just do."

"I couldn't. Imagine, 'Dear so and so, I'm very sorry for slicing up your grandma and feeding those animated corpses her body so we could live that much longer.' It's just fucked up. Some things you just don't apologize for."

"He won't send a single letter out." Edith hardened her gaze, peering further out into the city. "And he knows it. It's for him—therapy. He tells himself that if he apologizes on paper, it's like apologizing for real. It works for him." She turned a shade of pale, averting her eyes from the city. "Oh my God..."

"What is it?" Andrea asked.

The shaken woman pointed under the shade of an overhang in front of a Chinese restaurant. A male zombie was cradling a recently dead man, sitting down with the body, and literally digging into the man's eyes, plunging its fingers deeper into the cortex to eat the raw pieces that came free. And as the zombie ate, its beady black dead eyes looked up at them in warning, as if saying it would be there next if the women didn't keep giving it what it wanted.

The two women ducked back into the building, retreating from the truth and seeking relief in the place that shielded them from the grim reality of their escalating situation.

11

"I'm sick of standing outside that door while he works. It's getting to me. It's like I'm listening in on the sidelines of a killing."

Harold flat-out ignored Andrea, dismissing her. "He's doing us a great service, Andrea, and if it's you he wants to stand outside the room to talk to while he works, then I think Vinny's not asking too much." He cleared his throat, the next words cementing his dispute. "If you don't want to stand outside the door, then why don't you cut up the body this time? Give ol' Vinny a break. I'm sure he'd appreciate it."

"Just forget it," she snapped, disgusted with him, and disgusted by what they had to do to survive every night. "I'll do it, but I don't like it. I fucking hate it."

He walked away from her, heading to his office, but he called out before closing the office door, "Well, no one said you had to like it, did they, Andrea?"

12

"There's a bit of good news in this." Andrea talked for the sake of talking, breaking the silence between her and Vinny. She'd do anything to avoid taking in the sounds of his cleaver breaking Mr. Birkenstock's body. "When we run out of bodies, you won't have to do this anymore."

He offered up a strange 'uh-huh' sound without opening his mouth, sucking out anything positive from her statement. "Then it'll be us next, right?"

Thwack!

The wet slice was punctuated by the splatter of meat striking the floor, possibly Mr. Birkenstock's head, because of the way it rolled and struck the wall.

Fighting her roiling stomach, she relayed the question cycling in her stressed mind, "What do we do when we're out of bodies? Seriously? No one wants to answer the question. I know it's hard, but don't you think it's important we figure it out? And soon?"

The hacking motions increased, and at the final succession, he slammed the tool down so hard the cleaver cut completely through the body and bit into the table. "Like Harold says, Andrea, it's not like we can run. Zombies are everywhere, and more keep coming, and many others are hidden that we don't even know about. Food is what's keeping us here, in reality. Food for us and food for them. Once both dry up, then we'll have no choice but to venture out, but until then, it's best we stay put. Harold insists that any minute we'll hear that chopper fly overheard or that tank roll down the street and end this once and for all. But for now…" He claimed his axe, and taking a double-handed swing, split open Mr. Birkenstock's torso, "…we stick to the plan, the great fucking plan we've created together."

His voice demurred into one of accusation, "Just imagine, without me, you could be doing this shit, Andrea. You're lucky, really. Lucky 'cause I see their bodies in my sleep and you don't. I see the axe split their heads in two, or sometimes they come apart without me doing a damn thing to them. I just look at them, and they break into servable pieces. In my dreams, they'll be laying on a slab, and their stomach will unzip itself, and their guts will roll right out, heaps and coils and piles of them—and so many pounds, too, impossible amounts. I'm wading in it, drowning in the mess, neck deep, and you know what's even more fucked up? What really bothers me, is that it's me who starts eating the guts, the skin, and sucking the marrow from the bones. And that's not all…" He sighed heavily. "What's the very worst part of my dreams, is that I start liking it. It's downright mouth watering, and I can't get enough, so I eat and eat and eat to the point I throw up, and I keep fucking eating…" He let out a loud grunt and shook his head. "So back to the point, it's chop-chop work for me until we run out of bodies, yes, it's me who's doing the dirty job, and when it's over, I'm going out there in the streets, and it's chop-chop time for those walking sons-of-bitches. I'll slice them up like I did these fucking old fogies with skin liked dried prunes and bones like fossils!" He began to laugh. "Old bastards. Old dead people. Old dead people…all they are is food. I'll split all their heads with my axe and maybe one day I'll have normal dreams again!"

She was taken aback, aghast by the man's maniacal rant, and quivering at each new word he spat with an icy edge, giving her insight into what haunted him. She realized it was actually the door that struck her when it was kicked open and not him. Her shoulder took the blow—and it was bruise-worthy—and he pushed out the rubber tub with his foot, but stayed inside the room, closing the door again.

The tub was slathered in wild streaks of blood over the top, as if he'd taken a giant paintbrush and flicked gallons of plasma at it. The rubber container glistened like a living thing, evidence of Vinny's breakdown, of what had brewed in his mind the entire time he'd been working.

Andrea called out for Harold, screaming his name by the time he hobbled out of his office and came to her rescue. He eyed the plastic tub, and breathing out his nose in one long sigh, he whispered to her, "Vinny's under a lot of stress. He's been doing the dirty work for all of us. Be grateful it's not you who had to cut up Mr. Birkenstock into chunks. Be very grateful..."

He turned and peered at the door as if trying to visualize Vinny through the wood. "I'll handle this, you just go upstairs. It's best I handle this alone."

13

She wasn't sure what had come of Harold dealing with Vinny, but when Harold returned upstairs, he was alone. He asked Andrea to come back down and help him lug the tub with Mr. Birkenstock's body up the three flights of stairs.

After carrying the heavy load to the third floor, each of the group—minus Vinny—selected the pieces they'd throw out the window to the zombies outside. While preparing for the drop, she thought about how Vinny had suffered the most out of the group, having to be the one to dispatch the corpses, but it was no excuse for what she soon discovered in the rubber tub. It was an accident she even saw it, because normally she kept her eyes shut. She was opening the tub to claim her selection when a zombie shriek caused her to stiffen in alarm, both her eyes shooting open, and she saw the deplorable sight.

She couldn't help but think the worst of Vinny.

Had he always been so cruel in his vivisections?

Impossible, she kept telling herself. He was allowed a bad day, and she dismissed the deeper implications of her findings.

But this wasn't a bad day.

This was psychotic.

Mr. Birkenstock's eyes had both been cut in half by the cleaver, and she couldn't count how many slivers and lacerations and gaping wounds were inflicted in the man's cheeks and forehead.

In that moment, choking on dry heaves, she tossed the head and guts out the window, where the expectant zombie cop, jogger, and the hooded dead man fought over the meal, but she didn't stick around to view the feast.

She retreated to her private room downstairs, the question repeating in her mind over and over again: how many times had Vinny treated the corpse as if it was his murder victim?

14

"This would be the first time I know of that he's ever done something so out of character," Edith insisted, sitting with Andrea in the waiting room, defending the butcher. "Are you sure about what you saw?"

"Yes, God YES! I keep seeing that poor old man's face defiled. I guess I'm the only one who ever looked at the pieces we're feeding those things out there."

"Maybe you're the one under too much stress. Don't forget, you were doing this in the dark. You might've seen something that wasn't actually there."

Angry that Edith would rather believe she was caving under the pressure than Vinny turning a dead man's head into a canvas for mutilation, Andrea fired back, "I'm not stupid, and I'm not seeing things. I know what he did, and it's scary. He's going to have a worse breakdown, and I for one pray he doesn't have his axe handy when he does finally flip out."

Edith believed her sincerity, and after what she said next, Andrea understood why Edith wasn't as riled up about the situation as she should've been. "Harold said he took care of it. Yes, Vinny blew a gasket, to put it nicely. It's being dealt with, Andrea. We're not ourselves, you know. I see things too when I sleep, but it's mostly Henry showing up here and me not seeing him, or he comes here, and he can't find me. Our minds each have a way of working out this bizarre situation, and Vinny's had the worst of it. Yes, it's not right what he did to those bodies, I agree, but what do we do? It's out of our hands."

"I don't care how stressed out he is, it's wrong. He needs to be evaluated. That's what we need to do. Surely there's something Harold can do, maybe give him drugs or something, to calm him down."

"Harold's taken care of it, I promise. So I say let Vinny get a good night's rest, and we'll put our ideas together in the morning on how to treat him."

15

Harold's words from a previous argument filled her head when she fell asleep in the waiting room. *It's not like we're murdering anyone. Yes, it's grisly. Yes, it's horrible. But you heard Vinny. If you feed them, they ignore you. They won't eat us, and we stay alive. My patients have expired. We're not denying them heavenly slumber by what we're doing. If I were one of them, I wouldn't want people to die just to spare my corpse. The soul is gone, the body is what's left behind. It's survival, so quit looking at me like that and really think about what I'm telling you.*

It's clear we have to stay here to survive. Out there, it's uncertain what may happen to us. Here we have food, walls as protection, and each other to fall back on, so yes, this is a terrible thing we have to do, but it must be done, and if you don't want to be involved, then get walking and see how far you get by yourself if you're so much better than the rest of us.

"Raaaaaaaaaaaaaaaaaaaaaaaaaaah!"

The terror-filled shout happened in one long succession, ejecting her from her troubled sleep. Fearing it was one of the barriers that had been compromised and one of her friends was losing the battle against the undead intruders, she lunged out of her room and b-lined down the hall. When she realized what had really happened, standing outside the door to the cutting room, she cursed herself for not acting sooner on her impulses.

Andrea backed up, shaking her head, when the door shot open. Then she cowered in mortal fear and shock when Vinny showed her what he'd done.

16

"I...I couldn't take the idea of prolonging my work anymore. I lost it tonight, Andrea; I'm losing my grip, and I know it. I wanted the butchering to be over—I never wanted to do it in the first place, but you people made me. *You made me.*"

"Calm down, Vinny." Harold had him cornered in the hallway, so he couldn't run in any direction except through him. "We understand. I hear you. And it's over now. It's done. No more, Vinny, no more, I promise you. Breathe. Take a moment and just breathe."

Andrea gawked at Vinny; he was covered in so much blood that his clothes were sodden and dripping on the tiles, his face contorted in denial and relief and sadness all at once.

She kept her distance as Harold closed in another step, Vinny blathering in reaction, "Get your hands off of me, Harold! You know nothing about it.

Not a goddamn thing! I did it for you people, and you thank me by looking at me like I'm some kind of lunatic! You think I'm a madman!"

"You're not a lunatic," Harold argued, well-versed in utilizing a calm voice in dire situations. "You're nothing but an upstanding man. You've kept us alive. You're a hero, Vinny. Everyone here appreciates what you've done. You're a good person. You've done nothing wrong."

The bloody man was up against the wall, pushed back by Harold's slow advances. It seemed the Harold's kind words somehow took Vinny down a notch. Taking advantage, Harold removed a syringe from his suit pocket with stealth and drove the needle into Vinny's neck, whispering, "You need rest, my friend."

After the man passed out seconds later, Andrea helped Harold carry Vinny to a patient's room, one taking his arms, the other his feet.

Vinny kept apologizing; worried Andrea had considered his actions too harsh.

"I gave him a mild sedative," Harold said. "I thought he'd calmed down after I spoke to him earlier, but...but he hadn't, and then he did the unthinkable..." He couldn't say more.

She let him off the hook. "Let's just put him in a safe place and talk about it later."

17

Harold kept Vinny in room 104, having to lay the man on top of a bed because he was out cold. He now stood outside the room with Andrea and Edith, consoling them.

"Are you two okay?" Harold asked.

Edith nodded with tears in her eyes. "Only if Vinny's going to be okay, then yes, I'm fine."

Andrea simply nodded in agreement.

"Okay then, good, we need to stay strong." He eyed the corridor up ahead, thinking about the deeds committed in the cutting room. "He'll need rest. I'll check on him later. Just leave him be. Talking to him will only work him up again. He had a nervous breakdown. No one's faulting him for it, but it happened, and I'll take up the duty of tending to him. He's locked in, and he'll sleep through the night with the sedative I gave him."

They were about to walk away when Harold added, "I need help, though, remember? To clean up the mess, I mean."

Edith sobbed harder, and she shook her hands, dismissing them, "No...I...I just can't!" With that, she stormed off to her room, which was down near the south exit of the wing. When her door slammed shut and they heard the distinct turn of the lock, it was the two of them standing together as forced volunteers.

"I don't want to do it either," he confessed, "but together we can get this done and put it behind us."

"Of course," Andrea agreed, swallowing back the dread in her throat. "We already made the mistake of letting Vinny do it alone. I guess this is our punishment."

He held her shoulder, showing his appreciation. "You're a good person, Andrea, under any circumstance, please know that."

Finished recognizing each other, the grim task remained ahead of them.

18

Andrea retched on and off throughout the process, taking in the battle-field of eight dismembered corpses. Half heads, broken jaws and eyes that gleamed in their sockets—dead but somehow watching her—seemed to turn and look at her as she moved about the room.

They seemed to be saying, *You let this happen, and here were are desecrated.* Torsos were independent of their appendages, the meat torn at their dissection points strewn like pink seaweed, wet and serrated. What was more horrible was the amount of entrails, so much, it was literally coating the entire floor. The drain gurgled non-stop with the slow trickle of blood, and she struggled to keep her bearings as she dumped another hand, another broken kneecap, another set of genitals, into the tubs.

All Harold could say in reaction was, "They suffer no longer. They lived a good long life. They suffer no longer...."

She lost herself again after picking up an eyeball drowning in pink or-bital tissue, a marble in a glop of rank mess. Her sleeves, pants, and her skin growing cold with blood and dripping in red, Harold sensed her distress and said, "You've helped me enough, Andrea. You can go."

19

Andrea showered until the water gurgling down the drain wasn't tinged pink. It was a while before she erased the image of herself blood-spattered like Vinny had been hours ago. Tonight, she knew her dreams would be plagued with images of the room turned into a butcher's block.

He only wanted it to be done.

Vinny couldn't take the idea of eight more days of cutting up dead people.

Jesus.

She couldn't blame him for wanting it over with, no one could, and that left them all back at the beginning: feeding the dead.

20

Harold knocked on her door hours later, solemn and in need of a friendly person to talk to. He carried a fifth of whiskey, offering it up to her as she let him in. "I have a confession to make. May I come in?" he smiled slightly.

Andrea sat across from him in the waiting room, accepting the bottle and taking a hearty swig, relishing the burn, even though it was the cheap stuff and it made her cough twice. "Wow, this stuff's hair of the dog quality."

"Worse," he admitted, winking at her when he enjoyed a taste himself. "I was quite the drinker working here. I'd take three hits a day, usually. It wasn't to get drunk, mind you. The sting of it snapped me out of it. I'd get done telling a family that their loved one had died, or it was going to be another week, maybe two, before they passed on. You see so many people cry—to the point you can anticipate it—and it affects you. It gets under your skin; it really stays with you.

"The worse day was when Mildred Kimm died. I was there in the room with her, and she was on her last moments, dying from complications due to pneumonia. Mildred and I, we'd been friends during her stay. The day she died, she whispered to me that Death was coming, and she could see what it really was." He paused, closing his eyes as if trying to expel the images filling his head. "She said she was utterly terrified, that she wanted me to do everything in my power to save her. She asked me not to let her die, for once Death had her, it would never let her go."

She grimaced at the scene he was painting, and she fought it off by asking, "Was she with it enough to know what she was saying?"

"That's the thing, she was in her right mind, though she was in a lot of pain." He hit the bottle hard, a dribble of it running down his chin. "Her dying moment kept coming back to me during our situation. I fear death, too, Andrea." Grave-faced, he said, "I'm not done living. They won't take my life, at least not those things out there. This is why I was able to finish Vinny's work without you. My determination to live. It's why I decided to follow the butcher's logic when I first met him. This entire situation has gained me a new level of perspective, and I hope you can see where I'm coming from. That's why I came here to talk. I had to know if you were willing to fight for your life, regardless of the reasons."

After two more hits, she was tipsy, but not drunk. The severity of his words, the sheer seriousness of the talk, she couldn't help but answer him immediately, "Of course I'm willing to fight for my life."

His face was unreadable. "I'm glad to know you value your life."

21

Harold woke up earlier than the others and cooked pancakes. Andrea sat with Edith while eating the meal, the older woman gaunt-faced and keeping to herself. Harold was wrapped up in writing letters to the families of the dead bodies Vinny had butchered the previous night.

After Andrea was finished eating, she deemed it appropriate to wash the dishes and leave the two alone with their thoughts. She considered visiting Vinny, but she wasn't sure if he was awake or even wanted visitors. After thinking it over, she wasn't certain she wanted to see him yet anyway.

Alone, she decided to check the windows again to ensure they were solid. Each of them had gone over their work time and again, the act a form of reassurance that the dead wouldn't get in—and if they did, all would know it well before they gained access by the level of noise it would produce.

She was on the east wing, peering out at the topmost corner of a reinforced window at the empty street. She sensed the zombies were out there, within buildings and in the shadows, staying safe from the sun.

Edith walked up and hugged her.

"I'm sorry I left you alone last night, it's just that I couldn't..."

"No need to apologize," Andrea said, understanding why she fled from the task. "I didn't want to do it either, but I don't want what happened to Vinny to happen to Harold, too. We need both of them sound of mind to survive this."

"Seeing Vinny bloody like that and out of his head, I had to get away from everything. I'm so sorry for what you had to see; I can only imagine what you went through," Edith said, apologetic.

Yeah, you can only imagine, because you weren't there, she thought.

She did her best to live down any resentment and move on. "Vinny finished what he needed to finish. He doesn't have to butcher them anymore. I'd imagine he feels better now."

They heard a door close, and Edith followed the sound, moving down the hall, thinking it was Vinny leaving his room, but when they walked together far enough, they discovered Harold was leaving Vinny's room instead. He noticed the women coming and stood in place, awaiting their questions.

Edith was the first. "How's he doing?"

"Tired and stressed, but a little better," Harold replied. "He'll be sleeping it off for a while. I gave him another sedative. He said he wanted to be alone some more to clear his mind. He's a bit ashamed by what happened last night, and he's afraid you two consider him crazy, so give him some time to come around. He needs his privacy."

With a smile, he returned to his office with his notepad tucked under his arm. "Now if you excuse me, I have some work to tend to. I'll see you both later on tonight."

He went on his way, and the two women stared at Vinny's door for a moment, before leaving the corridor and walking up to the roof for some fresh air.

22

"He's sauced on the job, huh?" Edith was entertained by the notion. "It makes me think if he has all this booze, what else is he holding out on us?"

"We might have to sneak in that office of his and find out," Andréa stated.

"I already have, and there's nothing but a desk, his short wave radio, his computer, and a bunch of file cabinets. The door was unlocked. He's got nothing to hide. I wouldn't bother."

"But he's got booze."

"We don't need alcohol," Edith said. "It's not worth the trouble, if you think about it. It's hard enough to get along with each other the way things are."

A staggered scream resounded from deep in the city, lasting minutes, then ending abruptly.

Edith studied the buildings in the distance and quickly took back her words, "On second thought...I could use a stiff drink."

23

A week had passed, and now it was night again, and they had only two more corpses left in their stock. Vinny had returned to the group three days ago, and without an explanation to his mental status, he took up his station upstairs and flung down a set of remains to the hungry zombies below. When tonight's duty was finished, instead of disbanding, they met in the cafeteria to have a talk on the argument they had yet to finish.

"It's not like I can produce more bodies. That's it. Two left. Period."

"No one asked you to produce more corpses. We need an escape plan. Screw finding more bodies."

"If we go out there, we'll get attacked, or worse yet, we'll make progress, run out of food, and starve—the end of the story all leads up to them eating us."

"We can fortify the windows and doors better then."

"It's a waste of time. You could barricade every entrance, window and nook, and they'd still find a way in. I'm surprised they haven't scaled the building to the third floor yet, and I've seen it happen. I saw one make it three flights and sneak into an open window and kill everyone inside. In any case, our hammer and nails skills won't save our asses..."

"...the goddamn bodies were saving us, I know, I know, but..."

" I know, I know, but'...don't be an idiot, we have to find more bodies."

"Find more bodies? How do you suppose we do that? Are we going to scrape them off the pavement and give those dead fuckers leftovers?"

"That's the problem, there isn't anyone left to even do that."

"What about the county morgue? There's got to be bodies on ice there."

"That's five miles from here, and that's not mentioning how we could transport them from point A to point B."

"I'm not going out there, no way."

"No one asked you to, Edith, because we all know you're a coward. The biggest coward out of all of us."

"Do you hear yourselves? That's a terrible plan, anyway. Whatever happened to packing it up and leaving this place? Harold, you said you had a car in the parking lot. We can take that and drive as far as we can. If we find nothing, we'll circle back."

"And who's to say they don't overrun the place while we're gone? They're good at hiding, too. My aunt was calling me on my cell phone when one popped out of her closet, and it'd been hiding there for hours. It killed her, ate her alive, and I heard every moment of it. I'm with Edith; I'm not going out there. I'm staying right here and figuring it out."

"That's what we're trying to do right now."

"The problem is simple: without anymore bodies, they have no more reason to hold out on killing us."

"If you want to stay, Harold, fine, but me, I'm only running when we have no other choice. If no one's with me and I'm alone, then so be it. You're not finding anymore dead bodies to use as snacks for those dead things. That much is clear."

"There's always a way, if we think."

"I am thinking."

"Andrea, you're getting angry, and we need to stick together."

"The time's come to make decisions, and I've made mine. I'm running when I have to, and if I die, then I'll die out there as likely as I'll die in here. Now if you excuse me, I'm exhausted. Good night."

24

Andrea was bombarded by stress, imagining the moment she had to strip a door of its protective components and reenter the city alone. Edith was too overweight to handle it on foot, and Harold and Vinny were too obsessed with obtaining more bodies to see the obvious: their time was up. Help hadn't arrived. They were on their own, as they always had been.

Channel 5 was still nothing but snow. Harold's short wave radio wasn't catching any signals. Perhaps the scream she'd heard earlier in the week on the roof was the last living person in the city. Was that victim occupying the many hordes of the walking dead in the city even now? And if so, would they be coming here for their human supply next?

Andrea locked the door and wedged a chair beneath the knob to secure it, knowing it would wake her if it rattled.

Not that she'd sleep any easier because of it.

25

The numbers of the dead had doubled the next night, perhaps forty now surrounded the hospice care center, patiently waiting for what would drop from the sky and into their mouths. Andrea was talking to Edith in a patient's room about her new observations. "Did a set of zombies tell their friends this is where the buffet's at, so head on this way?"

Harold broke in, standing by their window, assessing each angle of the street and finding the same devastating situation. "There's too many. We're going to have to give them both of the bodies tonight."

Vinny was right behind him, arguing, "But that's it. That's the last of the bodies. We can't just do that. No more, means no more…for good." Vinny trailed off, knowing Harold was right, especially when Harold said, "If they decided to take their empty stomachs out on those barriers, we're done for. Let's bring every last piece upstairs. We've got work to do."

26

Andrea had dumped three armfuls and ten pounds worth of guts onto the pavement below, and now she clutched Mr. Unger's head, ready to drop it. The ten zombies below her raised their hands and issued their broken chorus, begging her to feed them. She released the head, thinking it would be the end to their perfect plan. Tomorrow, their fight for survival would truly begin.

27

The emergency meeting happened right after everyone had removed their bloody plastic gloves and washed up after the night's efforts. Harold led the discussion, having pondered their situation throughout the day while witnessing the numbers of the walking dead increasing.

"Okay, we can't run. Here is where we stay. If they doubled in one day, imagine how many more are hidden throughout the city. You're right, Andrea, I apologize for my crazy thinking yesterday. It's a terrible situation we're in, so let's stay realistic. I propose that early in the morning, when they hide from the sun, we go to town on the windows and doors. This place will be a fortress by the time we're done with it. But we'll have to be on guard when those things start pounding the windows and doors tomorrow night. We'll carry weapons and patch material, so we're at the ready. All four of us will have to be prepared to fix a broken slat and fend off the dead if they break through. But we have to all agree that this is the best plan. If we go into tomorrow night with doubts, they'll certainly get us."

Vinny stood with his arms crossed and a hard expression on his face. "I'm in."

Edith looked frightened, her eyes shrinking from the idea of having any contact with the dead, whether it be hand-to-hand combat or through a window. "It's what we have to do, then I agree. I'm in, too," she hesitantly acquiesced,

The three turned to Andrea, all of them worn out and ready to retire for the night. She absorbed the team's beady eyes, the people who could either save her life or push her expediently to the end of it, and she gave in, picking the only viable option for survival.

"I'll be up in the morning, ready to get to work. I'm in," Andrea said as she met the eyes of each of them.

28

None of them could sleep, so before the sun rose, announcing the dawn, the four survivors had already been combing the building for scraps of wood and metal to use on the windows and doors.

At first, it was the cafeteria tables, which they placed against the first floor windows. The problem was that nails were in short supply; the utility closet wasn't stocked for such situations as a zombie siege. Harold claimed that the window or door that needed to be the strongest would get the nails, but the others would require someone pushing their weight against them when the time came and the dead wanted inside.

They used the hospital beds to stack up against the main double doors at the front and also the back doors. Vinny resorted to breaking the blades off the ceiling fans in each room having them to use on each of the upstairs windows, covering them with the weak, but necessary, pieces.

The privacy curtains around the beds were also used to drape over the windows, held flat up against the wall, so the dead couldn't get inside without tripping or falling first. By four that afternoon, every scrap of wood was accounted for, every nail driven, and every option explored in defending their haven.

29

The sun wouldn't go down for another hour, and the four survivors sat in the waiting room, eating snacks and trying to rejuvenate themselves for the night to come. It was quiet between them until Andrea, trying to maintain her sanity, blurted out, "If we make it through this, drinks are on me."

Everyone laughed at that, temporarily delivered from the direness of the situation. Vinny was the most amused, smiling at her and giving her an approving eyeful. "Guys, if I were trapped with anyone else, I don't know how I would've fared." He gave them all a thumbs up. "You guys are the greatest."

Vinny turned to Harold and patted his back. "You were kind to me, Harold, and very patient. I just broke down, and I'm sorry. I wanted to reassure everyone that I'm okay, and I'll fight tonight with every ounce of my strength."

"We never doubted you," Harold said, returning the gesture, and smiling proudly at each of them. "And Vinny's right, you ladies are upstanding people. It's a shame we didn't know each other before this mess." He thought for a moment, before adding, "I guess no one really gave us an answer as to why this mess happened."

"No one left to give an answer," Andrea added. "The news, the military, everyone was attacked literally overnight by this shit. It's barely a month later, and here we are. But we're still alive."

Edith only nodded, taking it all in without a reaction. She was lost in deep thought and kept to herself.

Andrea absorbed the moment for what it was, shifting the conversation to their previous lives, and talking of families and loved ones, but the conversation soon ran dry at the initial pounding on the doors and windows.

Four sets of hands smashed through the window in room 102, shattering the glass and ruining the wood covering it. Andrea charged into the room, swallowing fear and the instinct to run for her life. She was forced to use her only weapon, a meat tenderizer, upon the intruders. Their flesh was sopping wet and spit out blood in syrupy consistencies with each strike. The pale hands relented after she'd broken enough bones, and she could finally re-patch the window.

In the next room, a hand was tearing at Harold's hair, the zombie trying to pull the frightened man into its gaping mouth. Harold had been caught by the dead man while he was running to help Edith on the opposite side of the room when the emergency exit door was forced open, the zombie claiming hold of him. Andrea rushed to Harold's aid, as blood trickled down his forehead, his scalp bleeding.

She utilized one of the broken boards on the floor with a long nail sticking out of it, and jammed it through the attacker's eyes with the spurting of whitish pus and a jet of yellow bile.

Winded and free, Harold shouted, "Everyone, look out for each other! They're coming in!"

30

"Both of those windows are down, for God's sake, patch them up!"

"Edith—Edith where the fuck are you? You better not be hiding! Shit!"

"Two have gotten in through the double doors, and they're crawling this way! Vinny, quick, club the one on the left, I've got the one on the right! Andrea, throw the bed up against the door and hold it up straight!"

"I heard a window shatter upstairs, I'm going up!"

"Edith, why aren't you coming out? We need you out here right now! Quit hiding! Goddamn it, why aren't you helping us?"

Andrea used a fire extinguisher to coat the four zombies that had climbed into room 204. Layering their faces in white muck, they were blind, and she shoved them back out the window one at a time, and began spraying the other undead figures who tried to climb up. The entire west side section of the building was being scaled by dozens of living people.

"They've given up breaking in downstairs. They're trying to climb up!"

"Use your clubs and hammers on their hands and knock them down. The sons-of-bitches can't climb up without their hands. *Yaaaaaaaaaa!*"

"There's too many. They're striking all of the windows at once. There's at least a hundred out there, and they keep coming!"

"Edith, Edith—you bitch, come back here and help us before we all die!"

"She's not helping, so give it up, Harold! We've got to deal with this by ourselves, so let's deal with it!"

"I'm going to kill that bitch when this is over, mark my words!"

Andrea ran back down to the first floor, hearing a collection of doors slamming down onto the floor in unison, crudely ripped from their hinges. From both emergency exits and ten rooms, dead bodies stumbled inside, their grumbles and verbal mastication rising upon sighting her. Trapped in the center of them with nowhere to run, she waited to be attacked viciously as they closed in.

"Hold tight, Andrea, I'm coming!"

"They won't hurt you, I promise."

"Then hurry the fuck up!" She searched for Edith, the woman hidden in the waiting room, the door not budging, even as Andrea's screams escalated to the point her throat gave out and she cowered against the wall, knowing she had seconds before the first dead man touched her body and defiled her flesh.

"Andrea, duck!"

Wet splashes, something was shot out into the crowd, but she didn't know what it was. Then the dead turned from her, studying the two men who'd re-entered the hallway.

"Run to us, just shove right through them. Crawl if you have to, but quick, before it's too late!"

"Don't think. Just run!"

Crawling on her hands and knees, no room to shove through them standing up, she weaved through gangrene stinking legs, the flesh coming apart in ribbons and raw meat strands by the force of gravity. Clawed hands bent down to reach for her, tearing at her clothes, and she kicked and flailed to retaliate, but once they had her legs, she couldn't squirm to escape. She was pinned in place, and vulnerable on the floor, the entire horde of thirty shifting to pounce on her.

"*Noooooooooooooo!*"

"Don't start yet, Harold! Not yet!"

"She's dead!"

"If you kill her, I'll fucking kill you!"

The smell of decay encapsulated Andrea as each of the zombies bent down to reach for her. With each passing second, the throbbing, burning, emanating pain along her skull increased, flaring up to the point she cried out as if it was her last chance to curse the world and what it had done to her.

She finally closed her eyes, knowing it was the end. Then she was turned over, and she struck the wall. Something was grasping her hair, and after seconds of reeling from being thrown, she learned it was Vinny who had seized her hair and flung her from the crowd of undead.

He told her to back away, as the two men kept tossing the contents of one gallon paint cans at the zombies, the paint taken from the janitor's closet just down the hall. Browns, greens, and whites covered the walking towers of death as they closed in, and without giving them a chance to come any closer, Vinny splashed them with turpentine and threw a lit match onto a puddle of the liquid, the bodies lighting up with an awesome *whoosh* of flames.

Instead of flailing, the zombies bumbled about in confusion, unable to see their prey, they were soon herded out of the building as Harold and Vinny chased them out with their hammers and bludgeons, literally forcing them out one-by-one.

The zombies shambled in pathetic strides, collapsing and burning in the street. The lit bodies fidgeted and fought the flames, until they stopped moving altogether, the corpse pyres warding off the rest of the dead who wished to gain entry.

31

The three stood in the hallway when the sun came up, the dead now hiding in the shadows for protection. The moment meant excitement and victory. All was quiet, and Andrea had recovered from the assault. Everything appeared to be okay, she'd made it, and everyone else had made it, but her reassurances ended when she caught Harold slamming the fire axe into the waiting room door and shouting Edith's name. Vinny went to Harold, and Andrea followed behind him.

"She abandoned us!" Harold shouted, seeing them approaching out of the corner of his eye. "They might not have gotten in if she stayed at her post. The bitch could've gotten us killed! She can't be trusted!"

Vinny was trying to calm him down, trying to level with the stark-raving lunatic as he swung the axe once more, creating the fifth wedge in the door. He began kicking through the slashes he'd created. He was about to reach through and unlock the door when Vinny got within arm's reach.

He raised his hammer as a weapon and warned, "You can't do this, Harold. This isn't like you. You're a patient, understanding, and caring guy. Yes, it's been hell, and yes, and she left us, but she was scared. We were all scared. But we survived. We'll come up with a new plan tonight. One she can participate in."

Cradling his axe with both hands, now face-to-face with Vinny, Harold was spitting his hatred of Edith who wailed and cried and begged God for help inside the waiting room. "She's shown her true colors, Vinny. She'll get you killed. But most of all, she'll get me killed, and I'm not dying in here. I've been surrounded by death for years, it's been my job, and I want as a far away from it as I can get—and that means I'm not dying in here!"

"Take a deep breath, and hear what you're saying," Vinny said. "Hear what you're saying, man."

Andrea was close enough to view Edith up against the far wall in the waiting room through the slashes in the door. The woman was quivering, her face animated with horrors beyond imagination.

Edith knew Harold wanted to kill her, and he had all the reasons in the world to do so, whether it would be murder or not.

Before Vinny could voice another line of negotiation, the door to the left of him burst open, and out came a dead woman—the police officer Andrea had seen on the streets—to close in on him.

Seizing Vinny's neck and turning his head aside to expose the area where his jugular vein was, the zombie sank its yellowed teeth into his flesh. The dead woman clamped down hard, antsy to quench its hunger, and as it reared back its head with a chunk of meat in its teeth, Andrea could see Vinny's exposed trachea.

Broken arteries spurted blood and dripped down his chest and onto the floor in an unending splatter session. Mortally bitten, he sank to his knees, gasping for air, choking, and crying.

Andrea froze, a sudden chill sucking the very life from her, and she stayed stationary as she watched the dead woman chomp on the fleshy morsel, staring at her the entire time.

You're next, the zombie's crusted-over eyes promised, leaking black jelly from the tear ducts. Finished with Vinny, the dead woman trudged over to

Andrea, half of her back bent forward, as if its spine was curling into a sideways U.

It reached out to Andrea, its greasy hands touching her forearm and causing her to stiffen, but she couldn't move, so terrified at being so close to one.

The zombie bent down to partake of the flesh on Andrea's forearm when Harold finally swung the axe. It landed squarely on the top of the dead woman's head, braining her, with a skull to steel *clack* sounding.

Bending the axe to one side, the left section of the corpse's skull broke off, spilling out its brains that were swimming in dead maggots and mealworms. The putrid mess splattered onto the wall and onto Andrea's shirt, smelling so awful that she bent down to throw up.

In doing so, Harold gained his opportunity for revenge.

"YOU KILLED VINNY! LET ME IN, YOU BITCH! EDITH!"

Vinny was on his knees, one hand on the floor, the other around his throat, as blood continued to leak through his fingers in staggering amounts. His mouth kept opening and closing like a fish out of water. He reached out to Harold, though weakly, begging him not to hurt Edith, but Harold sidestepped his reach to swing the axe once again. This time the axe chopped off the door knob, and he was able to kick open the door.

"Noooooooooo!" Edith screamed, trying to dodge his advances. "I'm sorry, Harold! Please don't do this! Think about it! Hear me out! Okay? Listen to me! It's not what you think! I was scared! I was so scared!"

Andrea, frozen in fear, tried to force herself into action, to race forward and stop Harold, but she still couldn't move. All of her was numb. She was so terrified of Harold and his transformation. She was gaining movement, but it was like running upstream, stuck in sinking mud, and each moment prolonged itself.

Harold's writhing grimace, his bulging eyes popping open wider at the prospect of sweet murder, Edith tripping over the coffee table and landing on her back, Edith pleading to him to spare her life as she raised her arms over her face to avoid the axe. Vinny crawling into the waiting room to stop Harold, but as he crossed the threshold, he lost consciousness.

"Please don't kill me!" Edith screamed; one last appeal.

"You'll get us all killed, Edith," Harold garbled, his words sharper than his axe. He tittered as he stood with the axe in his hands, his smile jerking as if being jump-started but not quite kicking over. "I have a better use for you now!"

Andrea was running now, finding her body again, and shot forward in a full-out sprint, only seconds away from stepping over Vinny's body and reaching out to stop the axe's swing.

"I'm not dying because of any of you people!" Harold screamed when the axe swung down and cut into Edith's forearm, slicing through to the bone.

Screaming in horror, Andrea inches from pushing Harold aside, he had the upper hand and momentum on his side, and the next swing cut Edith's head vertically into two pieces.

Andrea stopped, turned, and ran away after seeing Edith's head split in half. Now racing away from the room Andrea had been scrambling to enter a second ago, Harold began to stalk her, the axe's head dripping with Edith's blood.

"We have two bodies," he called out, rationalizing the killings. "They'll last us at least another night. Think about it, Andrea, we're safe for now. Come back, talk to me, I won't hurt you. There's no reason to now...not now...so come back and..." He said the next sentence as calmly as if he was chatting over coffee. "Help me cut up these bodies into smaller pieces."

Would it be safer to go outside among the cannibalistic dead, or could she take on Harold? As long as he was armed with the axe, she was defenseless against him. The man had lost it worse than Vinny; his breakdown was permanent.

After witnessing Vinny attacked by the zombie woman and then ultimately killed, Harold's face had changed. He'd gained a snarl and flicker of rage in his eyes, forming the package of an overall blood-thirsty maniac.

His steps pursued her, his pace slow, confident. He knew she wouldn't leave the building. She would be another body to chop into pieces, to feed to and fend off the dead for another night.

She blurted out mid-stride, "And then what, Harold? I help you, and then what? You chop me into pieces the next day after you run out of bodies again? Where will _you_ go then? What will _you_ do? How are you any better off two days from now than right at this moment?"

He babbled, not answering her directly, talking to himself, "Help might come any day now...I won't die...I can only protect myself...I killed them to stay alive...I've seen death in my patients' eyes...they fear death for a reason...they cower in their final moments...the dying have told me many things...I see it in the walking dead's eyes too...they hate their undead existence...I want out of this place...life is precious, and I want to live...help will come...minutes from now, days from now....any moment...they'll be here...need more bodies...I have them now...everything's okay...I won't die...because I have more bodies..."

Andrea knew she had to run and hide. Find a place with a weapon, anything to use against him.

She was trapped in the east wing, the windows were blocked, the emergency exit was blocked, too, and she had no choice but to run to the closest place she could. Before the axe became colored with her blood, too.

She ran to Harold's office and locked herself inside.

32

Regrets plagued Andrea's mind about choosing the office to hide in as soon as she heard Harold lurking outside the door. Any moment, the axe would plunge through the wood, the door would topple, and she'd be an easy kill.

Waiting for it to happen, she stared at the door and the two shadows of his feet through the bottom crack.

She could beg him not to hurt her, to spare her life, to give rational thought a second chance, but he was completely insane. His breathing was erratic, like a panting dog with rabies coursing through its veins.

His logic was skewed to the point he was incoherent. He was unnoticing of the blood covering his face and clothes; he cared nothing of the evidence of murder pasted all over him from the killing earlier.

He made no move to chop down the door.

Instead, he walked away.

Was he leaving her alone?

What was he doing?

The minutes dragged on with no answers or clues until she overheard the turn of wheels, and he wedged up one of the beds against the door, and then another, and another...

He was blocking her in! Saving her as an emergency body for when Vinny and Edith's corpses were used up.

Regretting her decision to hide in the office more so than ever, she balled up her hands and punched the wall twice, knowing she had no choice but to wait for Harold to make the next move.

33

Harold spent half the day repairing the windows and doors. The hammering continued as Andrea's trapped situation didn't change. Once he was finished securing the hospice, he returned to the office to perform another job.

Corpse preparation.

He talked on and on to her, and she stayed silent, afraid of saying the wrong thing, or the right thing to set him off. He was in permanent chatter mode; it was as if she was already dead, and he was alone, rationalizing and hatching the next step in his survival plan.

"Edith is large enough, she'll feed them for a night...but maybe not...I can't know for sure and I won't take unnecessary risks..."

The axe swung down on what Andrea assumed to be Edith's corpse, the impact of the axe muffled by flesh; where ever the blade hit the thick torso.

"But we've attracted more of them, so I might have to cut up Vinny, too. I can't save him for the next day if they come in after me, now can I? You understand, don't you, Vinny? Yes, I think you do. You were always smart and were willing to do what it takes, as am I."

A long pause, and then Andrea jumped at the sound of Harold's jarring laughter as he talked to Vinny's corpse.

"You were a genius, Vinny! A genius butcher!" He was babbling. "It's a good thing I've got Andrea's body, too. Won't feed many with her body, but she's easy on the eyes. I'll have plenty of time to enjoy her before the next night. She won't be putting up a fuss then. It'll be just me and her. No one will care. No one's alive out there anymore to care, except for me, of course, and I don't give a shit!"

He'd dismembered Edith's body while talking, and when he finished, Andrea could hear him plop the pieces into a rubber tub.

The new butcher moved on, dragging the tub to the door, then he went to work once again, the axe breaking bones and severing extremities with a slough of muscle tissue and the heavy splash of curdled blood.

He didn't talk anymore, as if he felt worse about cutting up Vinny than he did Edith—or he didn't receive the thrill from dissection now.

He had to be exhausted, Andrea thought. After fending off the dead all night, repairing the windows alone, and now playing butcher, he had to be on his final wind.

He stayed quiet other than the chopping, and when the work was done, he transported the pieces upstairs.

Soon, it would be dark, and the dead would arrive once more.

34

The office had no windows, so there was no real way out except through the one door. Andrea couldn't get it to budge so much as an inch, and after an hour of trying, she couldn't bring himself to make another futile attempt.

Resigned to being trapped, she considered protecting herself, so she searched through his file cabinets and desk drawers for anything to use, even a letter opener. All she found was a pack of gum, a fifth of whiskey, which she kept on the desk for later, and files, notes, bills, and requisitions for funerals for past clients. No food. No weapons. Nothing of good use.

Sitting on the swivel chair behind the desk, she tipped back the fifth of burning liquor, sending it down her throat with a groan and a shake of her head. She needed something to abate her raging stomach and her amped up nerves. Relaxing, the room spinning slightly, she happened to find Harold's steno pad on top of the desk, face down.

She picked it up, having nothing better to do to bide her time.

35

Reeling in terror, Andrea studied the pages, learning that Harold hadn't spent his time in the office writing letters of apology, but instead, he wrote...

Edith definitely will be the first to go. She's lazy. Can't hammer a nail straight. She's always scared. Crying. Doing her woman thing. No, she'll be the first body to use. It's logical. It's an easy decision, killing her...

Vinny can't hack it anymore. He's unstable, at best. He's cracked. If I'd known he couldn't chop up a body without crying on the inside later about it, I'd have done it myself. I could overdose his meds, it'd be so easy. I could say he committed suicide. His body would come in handy later when we run out of corpses. It'd buy me more time, too.

Lazy whore can't put down a fucking bag of chips long enough to save her own life!

Bitch might be pretty, but her skinny ass couldn't fight them off worth a damn if they broke in here. She can't protect herself, never mind the rest of us. Why should I spare her any longer than the rest of them? Killing her wouldn't be too much of a loss.

A real man like Vinny has got my back. He'll fight until his death, and if he dies first, then it works out for the better. He should stay alive the longest. The women are the weakest. I should pick one of them before Vinny. Save Vinny for last...it's decided.

Edith's the number one choice. She's got the most meat on her bones. She could feed them all for one night. It'd be better than wasting two bodies. Bitch can be a buffet for those dead people, and no one would miss her.

Andrea, I'll save for last. End of the world type thing. Last man on Earth. She'd make love to me. After all, I'd keep her alive for last. The bitch would owe me. She'd owe me big time.

Vinny's sane again. I guess I won't drug him to death. It's too late anyway, he's up and around and productive again. No one would buy him committing suicide now. And he's got good ideas. The best at erecting the barricades, too. He's got a strong back. Not like that bitch, Edith. At least Andrea tries to look like she's working hard.

I can't kill her...I keep thinking about her...I love her. I'm in love with her. She'll be the last to die. It's settled. Edith goes before Andrea.

I still can't decide who to use first. We're out of corpses. Tonight will determine who lives and who dies. I should let them pick themselves. Whoever performs the weakest will die, and I'll convince them to help me, whoever's left. They'll be so scared, they'll understand my thinking. And if they don't, I'll kill them all. Yes, then the choice will be very easy.

Andrea's hands sweated as they clutched the sides of the paper, her perspiration soaking into it. The words weren't the only disturbing thing on the pages. There were drawings of Edith hanging by her neck, the rest of her body on the floor with dead men devouring her oversized pieces, the artist emphasizing her weight two-fold. The sketches of Vinny were created with morbidity, as the man was not only cutting the hospice corpses on the floor with a cleaver, he was also using his other hand to split open his own stomach as he sorted out the pieces and dumped them into a rubber tub.

What struck Andrea the hardest among the three dozen rough sketches were the depictions of herself spread eagle on a slab, Harold always standing in front of her or near her with a cleaver, axe or a hammer. She had cartoon bubbles over her head with comments like: "Thank you for saving me for last/How can I ever thank you for sparing my life?/What would it take to be the last one to die, Harold?/You've done so much for us, Harold, now it's time for me to pay you back/The dead won't hurt me as long as you're here to protect me."

Her entire body shuttering in horror, her core ice cold, her skin clammy and breaking out in a nervous sweat, she threw down the notebook and shook her head in denial.

He had been planning their deaths the entire time.

Harold's fear of death was accentuated by his career, and this situation had allowed him to commit wanton acts of criminal immorality.

She was certain once the bodies were used up, he'd charge through the door, and she'd be dead; butchered and fed to the corpse masses.

He was obsessed with her. The drawings and words kept passing through her mind, powerful as they were haunting—a foreboding warning of things to come. Would he rape her body, whether she was alive or dead?

What removed her from her inner turmoil were the groans and moans of the walking dead approaching the building, then their inevitable feasting on the bloody pieces of human meat that dropped from the third story, filtering through the walls with stark clarity.

36

Andrea stood next to the only door in the office, clutching a lamp in her hand, imagining the object being driven onto Harold's head, just moments after he stopped outside the door. He didn't remove the beds.

"I'm coming in for you, Andrea, and you know what for, so don't fight me."

You can go to hell, she thought, now arched beside the door with the lamp ready to use.

"Help's not coming tonight, Andrea. You understand what I'm saying? It's only me and you, and I'm not dying, so it has to be you. I'm sorry, but it's the only choice. I saved you for last. Doesn't that mean anything to you?"

She knew the battle against her and the axe wouldn't play out in her favor.

"We could leave here together, Harold," she said as calmly as possible. "We could find safety. Watch each other's backs. We'd be okay. How 'bout it? We leave, and forget any of this ever happened. It'd be so easy, right?"

His tone demurred into one of stone-cold hatred. "You'll tell on me. Yes, we'll be rescued, and then you'll tell the police I killed Vinny and Edith in cold blood. They won't understand why I did what I did, because if you can't understand my actions, then why would they? You're tying to trick me, you bitch? You'd pull the trigger at my execution. Put the fucking bag over my head and suffocate me, you *bitch*!"

The beds were shoved aside, and then the axe plunged through the door with a splintering of wood, the steel edge of the axe head jutting out until it was ripped back. Then another swing, another sliver breaking over and over again until there was a large hole. She expected another swing of the axe, but instead, he jammed his arm into the hole and opened the door.

Shoved aside when the door flew open, Andrea landed on her side, the lamp crashing beside her, the only weapon she had now ruined. Reeling from the blow, her entire shoulder aching, she watched helplessly as Harold stomped his way into the office, his body reeking of dead flesh and iron, from the blood coating him.

"No, Harold, please, think about what you're doing! I'm on your side. I wouldn't tell on you. It's a bad situation, and bad things happen, they do, Harold, listen to me, I understand. I hear you. We'll work this out together. Please stop and listen to what I'm telling you!"

He turned his head to the side, half his face smeared in splatters of red. Viewing his contorting face, his eyes exempt of human emotion, she confirmed that Harold wasn't Harold anymore. She could be a poet laureate, and her words wouldn't reach him.

Under his breath, he let out a whisper, "No, Andrea, I can't let you live. I'm sorry, so very sorry."

She was weeping, losing herself to the fear and the paralysis that was working into her limbs, the moment exaggerated by the stand off with her pending murder. Trying hard to keep up the fight, she forced out her argument whether he'd hear her or not. "I'm in this situation just as you are…we threw the bodies to the dead, and…and…" She blatantly lied, trying to win his trust again. "I could've stopped you from killing Edith and Vinny. I had every opportunity, but I chose not to, and do you know why? Do you know why, Harold? Because I want to live. I'm with you, I don't want to die. I'm scared shitless of death. I'll keep our secret. It's between us, because we share the same burden. Are you hearing me, Harold? Please say something. Please!"

He unleashed a lungful of air, audibly squeezing the axe as the blood painted on the handle squeaked in his turning hands. "You do fear death, I see that, and that's exactly why it has to be either you or me, Andrea, and it's not going to be me."

Raising both hands over his head, the axe up high and bound to be driven down into her skull, she couldn't remember what words she yelled out at him, but the next moment was over in a second.

Another life was taken.

37

Harold's lips spilled out gobs of crimson. He was sprawled out on the floor, the axe head penetrating the side of his skull. Andrea imagined a part of the blade was behind his right eye because of the blood seeping free around the edges of the orb. Airless words were mouthed, and she couldn't understand him. She didn't want to. His hands kept digging in the carpet fibers of the commercial carpeting, channeling his pain. Second by second, his death twitches grew weaker and his eyes fluttered in the back of his head, until he finally expired.

A moment of accidental genius had prevented her from being brained. The moment Harold jerked forward to render the blade into her skull, she moved into action, a spasm that was pure instinct. Her mind worked beyond herself, and out came her leg, pegging her shoe against the side of his knee. With an unlocking of his knee bone, his leg was bent crooked and broken, and launching into fits and screams of elevating pain, he shuttered to the floor, the axe falling first before him.

The fall didn't killed him, but landing on his axe did.

38

The boards on the windows and doors were in place in every room. Andréa checked each access for security with meticulous diligence.

Once more, the sun was going down.

Help will come, she thought, *and if it doesn't, I'll leave this place. Maybe help is just around the corner. Or nowhere at all. That's the plan.*

Peering down at the crowd of zombies coming out of their hidey holes and shelters from the third floor, she knew one thing for certain as she dropped Harold's severed head and spleen down into the undead mob.

For one more night, she was safe.

KATAKALYPSE

PATRICK MACADOO

GLOSSARY

Agora - marketplace, place of assembly

Asklepiad - devotee of Asklepios, a supremely skilled physician eventually elevated to godhood

Duszeus - literally 'Bad Zeus,' a sacrilegious epithet

Greave - a shin guard

Haides - a more accurate phonetic spelling of Hades, signifies both the god and the underworld

Helios - the sun

Hyperion - the sun god reigning before Helios

Katakalypse - a covering up, the opposite of 'apocalypse'

Mantis - a fortuneteller

Mysterion - a mystery or secret doctrine

Palaestra - wrestling area

Pharmakon - medicine, potion

Phoebe - one of the Titans, the gods who ruled before Zeus' hostile takeover

Pluton - Pluto, in the word's Greek, rather than Latinized, spelling

Polis - community, city, village

Ergates stroked his jaw, savoring the texture of his soft, newly-sprouted fuzz. Feeling manly and thoughtful, he surveyed the scattering of both sheep and goats in the lush green valley below. Under the early-morning shine of Helios, Ergates thought that his father might be shrewd enough to hide his flocks from mortal men, but how could he hope to hide the fattest and the best from the gods?

A shaggy ewe ambled toward him. He reached down and plunged his fingers into its deep fleece. He buried his hand to the wrist before his nails grazed its rough hide. He scratched its haunches, eliciting a shiver from the gratified beast. He smiled, imagining the time when his beard would be as wooly, not scratchy and shit-colored like his father's, but black and glossy like his mother's draping tresses.

"Why do you smile so?"

Ergates looked up and saw Ixos, wearing sandals and his loin-wraps, striding towards him. The two of them had eschewed proper clothing the day they had set up camp in this isolated valley. This temporary exile had reminded Ergates of when they were little, running about barefooted and often playing bare-assed. With no one else around, they had fallen into the habit of not bothering to dress after their customary morning wrestling bouts, only pulling on clothing when the cool evening breezes stippled their naked skin with goosebumps.

Ergates grinned. "I think I shall not pin you today, little one." He was fond of teasing Ixos about his narrow waist and bony chest, but the truth was that Ixos was barely shorter than Ergates and his shoulders were just as broad, and he was quick, a tough opponent in the palaestra. Still, Ixos' cheeks remained hairless, and so he was forced to endure Ergates' gentle gibes, even though down below he had finally grown a golden thatch, which matched his curly blond locks above. He had inherited his fair hair from his mother, who had come from a distant land and died when Ixos was very young. As long as Ergates could remember, his own mother called them Night and Day, not only because of their contrasting manes, but also because one always followed the other.

"That ewe seems ready to go home and be sheered," Ixos said.

"Soon," Ergates said. "It's been eight days now. The tribute collector should be departing soon. We had better pack up our camp and start rounding up the herd."

"Your father is a clever man indeed."

Ergates scoffed. Stinting on rites, hiding flocks, sending his sister, Sunnoia, along with most of the rest of the virgins of the polis, into the mountains, from where so few ever returned, his father was perhaps too clever for his own good, and Ergates was about to say so, when the death scream of a sheep rent the tranquil air.

The ewe recoiled and darted in the opposite direction.

"Wolves!" Ergates said with wide eyes.

They dashed to their campsite and snatched up their spears and long daggers, then sprinted up the rise, zigzagging around the bleating sheep and goats, which were stampeding the other way. They both skidded to a halt at the summit and gawked down into the next valley. Ergates blinked. He barely heard Ixos whisper, "Barbarians."

A pack of filthy men...no, not all. Ergates saw that two of them were women, their sagging breasts swinging free from their ragged clothing, had torn a sheep apart, with blood-matted fleece adhering to their faces and hands as they shoved gobbets of raw meat into their maws. The gory squelches of their open-mouthed chewing made Ergates' stomach bile rise to the back of his throat. Their fecal stench assaulted his nostrils, then mingled with the astringent odor of his own involuntarily bladder release.

They were stick thin and starving to death, he prayed, because starvation was the only human excuse for this outrage. A pair of the barbarians, grayish-blue, diseased or grime-spattered, Ergates could not say, flailed a few steps away from the pack towards Ergates and Ixos.

Each grisly barbarian clutched an end of an intestine, the abomination on the left with two hands, the other with one, his left arm flopping useless at his side. As they staggered and leaned contrary to one another, the intestine stretched taut between them and drizzled black blood, fouling the grass below. The intestine, strained viper-thin, lashed free from the grip of the barbarian with one good arm, and whistled through the air, then thwacked the other in the face. Both fell ass first to the grass.

The victorious barbarian used both hands to begin cramming the prized intestine into his mouth, smearing a fresh film of grease over his already crusted and slimy beard. Unable to watch this desecration, Ergates turned his eyes to the loser, who sat dazed, his head weaving back and forth as he stared at the feasting victor. Thick strands of mucus drooled from his nostrils over his mustache and into his blood-stained beard. His head snapped to the rise, the mucus strands swaying back and forth, and his yellowed eyes burned into Ergates dark blue orbs.

Ergates and Ixos spun as one and fled. Ergates felt his pulse beating in his ears, twice as fast as his panicked feet pounded the ground. They ran down to the nadir of the valley, and as they started up the next rise, Ixos began to outpace Ergates. When they crested the rise, Ergates saw portions of the dispersed herd, some still bolting in all directions, others coming to rest in small clusters, already resuming their graze.

Ergates stole a glance behind him. There were no barbarians in sight. He slowed his pace and Ixos surged ahead of him. He opened his mouth to call out to his comrade to slow down, but before he could get a word out, Ixos tilted too far into his stride and stumbled, pin-wheeling his arms for balance, long dagger and spear still in his hands, to then tumble head over heels, somersaulting to the bottom of the valley.

Ergates ran to his fallen comrade. "Are you hurt?" He looked over Ixos while helping him to his feet, searching for wounds inflicted by Ixos' own weapons. The grass had skinned up his back, leaving pulpy green streaks on his flesh, but otherwise he seemed unharmed.

Ixos shook his head. Ergates placed his palms on either side of Ixos' skull and forced him to look into his eyes.

"We must go back for the flock," Ergates said.

Ixos swallowed, and a bit of fire returned to his gaze. "Certainly. Your father will be furious if we do not. We shall be shamed before the polis if we do not learn more of the invaders."

Ergates nodded and released Ixos. His friend was right. Certainly they must warn the polis, but first they needed to take the measure of the barbarians, if they wanted to avoid a life long rebuke.

Ergates gathered up his weapons. "Come."

They crept up the rise and laid themselves flat in the grass at its apex. The barbarian with the useless left arm, the one that had locked eyes with Ergates, sat lolling on the valley floor. Ergates judged that the barbarian was a victim of his own headlong tumble.

"Did you see any of them bearing arms?" Ergates whispered.

Ixos hesitated, then shook his head.

"What kind of invader comes unarmed?" Ergates asked.

Another barbarian appeared at the top of the next rise. Through his torn and flapping frock, Ergates could see the soiled wretch's skin hanging loose from his bones. The barbarian took two tottering steps, then toppled and careened down the slope, flipping ass over elbows, and bouncing airborne near the bottom. The barbarian landed flat on his back and laid still, a puff of dust rising from his dirt-caked body. The other barbarian ignored his motionless fellow.

"They are stricken," Ixos said in a quiet, awed tone.

Ergates knew what Ixos meant. Ergates didn't want to say the word, 'plague,' either. He tapped Ixos on the thigh. "Follow me."

They gave the barbarians a wide birth while traversing the valley. Once again they stole to the crest and flattened themselves against the grass. They crawled up and looked over the next valley. They both gasped.

Barbarians had overrun the dale. Hundreds at least, maybe more than a thousand, reeling and jostling along the valley floor, some beginning to struggle up the slope towards them. Ergates could see still more reaching the peak of the opposite rise. He gagged. Their putrid reek made his eyes water. He had seen enough. "Let's go," he said.

He rolled over and saw the two barbarians almost upon them. He sprang to his feet and leaned back out of range of the attacker's clumsy swipe, then drove his spear into the man's unarmored chest. The spear-tip splintered breastbone and burst through the barbarian's back. Ergates released the spear as the man fell backwards, the spear's haft cracking off as he crashed down the slope.

Ergates whirled to aid Ixos and saw him locked in combat, the barbarian with the bad arm throttling Ixos one-handed and gnashing his teeth an inch away from Ixos' nose.

Ixos' dagger was plunged to the hilt in the barbarian's belly. Ixos drew the blade upward and the man's guts slopped onto the grass.

Ergates lunged and smashed his dagger through the barbarian's blackened teeth. The tip pierced the soft palate and angled into the brain before slamming to a stop against the interior of the skull, the jolt traveling back up Ergates' arm and rattling his shoulder.

Ergates' blow broke the barbarian's grip on Ixos' throat and sent the gutted wretch whirling to the down-sloping ground, with Ergates' dagger-handle protruding from his mouth. With his head pointing downhill, the barbarian slid to a stop on his back several paces below. The mortally wounded man lay twitching, his innards coiling out of his gashed belly and winding up the slope to Ixos' sandals.

Ergates spun and checked their rear. The erratic vanguard of the barbarian horde was still struggling up the other side of the rise. He turned to Ixos and saw that his friend was bleeding from a narrow scratch on his throat. Ergates watched Ixos pluck a rotted greenish incisor from a bite mark on his forearm, the bite also seeping blood.

"Do you wish to retrieve your dagger?" Ixos asked.

Satisfied that Ixos was well enough to travel, Ergates shook his head "No, let us go."

Then they ran.

Porphures watched the low rays of the setting sun strafe the western fields, and he exhaled a long, relieved sigh. The excruciating task was finally complete. He crouched and scratched the dog, a short brown mutt, behind the ears, its rough, wiry hair making a scratching noise under his fingers. The dog was already filling out in the belly, due to Porphures' charity, though it had attached itself to him just eight days ago. A villager claimed that the dog was good for herding, as were the other appropriated dogs and pups, but they looked more like ratters to him.

He straightened up, his knees and ankles popping, and he looked at the wagons. The oxen were rested and ready to be yoked first thing in the morning. He smiled, imagining his troops herding goats and sheep back to the capital. The wagons themselves were loaded, fowl in wicker cages, wheat and barley, food and drink, goblets, jars, and mixing bowls, textiles and skins, and best of all, it included the prize, at least from the villagers' point of view—a lion's pelt.

Porphures' smile faded away. He turned and surveyed the grain-thick fields and green pastures rolling out to the horizon. He still wasn't sure what the Fat King expected to extract from these farmers and herdsmen. There were no mines, no factories, just rustics and a few craftsmen in the polis, and the mystics dwelling apart in the mountain caves to the north. His orders were to fill all three wagons. He had distributed the goods evenly between them, but anyone could see that the entirety could fit into two.

He rubbed his forehead, trying to smooth the sharp edges off the day's headache. He simply did not possess the stomach for fleecing these folk down to the hide. No matter how long he massaged his head, he could not erase the image of the old woman, dressed in rags, living in a hut off the edge of the north quarter, where the poorest of these folk clustered. The look of bleak resignation on her wrinkled face, and at her hems the pair of skinny young children, both with hollow smudges for eyes, and his men seizing hens from the dirt in front of her hovel…he shuddered. He had compelled his men to return the hens, along with baskets of grain and meat, but he still kept seeing her face, kept feeling the decaying vibrations of her broken spirit.

He pressed his palms into the small of his back and arched it, working the kink out of his spine. It was not bad enough that he was expected to take from those who scratched a living through backbreaking work. The rest of his time was spent quibbling over every little crumb with those who were blessed with plenty. On the first day, the town elders had balked at quartering his troops.

In order to maintain the peace, which was already unstable on account of the friction between the native lads and the younger soldiers, he agreed to establish the camp in field tents outside the walls of the polis. The veterans had grumbled about proper customs, but Porphures had insisted on treading lightly. He guessed that cunning-eyed Drimutes, the unofficial despot of the polis, had inferred from that first day's compromises that he did not possess the necessary cruelty to perform a thorough reaping of the local surpluses, and so Drimutes grew both vociferous and prolific in lodging protests against the smallest of levies.

Looking over the wagons' contents, he had to admit that Drimutes had worn him down. He shook his head. The grains, the cheeses, the rustic wines, and the herd animals, taken altogether, might not be sufficient to provision one of the Fat King's feasts, if the gluttonous monarch would even choose to sup on such coarse fare.

He reached into the nearest wagon and fingered a thick blanket, admiring the rigor of its weave. The textiles and handicrafts were of sturdy quality, the sort of items made to last through hard use, but he knew that the royal assessors would judge them to be substandard, not even fit for the Fat King's servants. The Fat King would maintain a magnanimous silence, while his advisors spread the word of the provocative tribute and manufactured justification for the inevitable execution of Porphures.

He snatched up a flat stone and flicked it eastward. The dog dashed after it. He smiled tight-lipped against the bitterness rising in the back of his throat. He had intended for this expedition to be the balm that would heal the wound between himself and the Fat King.

Volunteering for a duty well beneath his station, a duty considered distasteful, traveling so far from the capital and culling tribute from a remote polis, all meant to assure the Fat King that he was no threat, that he was loyal. The Fat King had been assassinating his way through the nobles of the rival faction, and although Porphures was but an obscure, bastard offshoot of the challenging bloodline, the sudden death of his cousin Criton—stabbed to death in the gymnasium—had elevated Porphures to the status of the rival line's preeminent adult male.

He watched the dog as it sniffed the tossed stone, then wandered away, snout to the ground while tracking a more interesting scent. He nodded. Perhaps the dog was an oracle, showing him the way. He and Pragmates were in agreement that, at the very least, the Fat King had secreted spies in the troop, and very likely, an assassin, and if such an assassin skulked about, he was bound to strike on this night, in order to make it seem like an incensed villager—feeling overtaxed—had murdered him in a fit of rage. But if he should survive the night, as well as the trek back to the capital, his eventual reward would be either a knife in the back or a goblet of poisoned wine.

He turned to the west, raised his head, and held his open hands up to the sky.

"O Apollo, many and noble sacrifices I shall offer in thanks for granting to me the foresight to send my sons to the north. I beg you watch over them," he said.

He crouched and dug up a handful of soil, crumbling the moist dark clod through his fingers. The dog padded over, no doubt hoping for a treat. Porphures smiled and took a thin strip of dried meat out of his pocket. The dog dropped into a sitting position without delay and wagged its tail. He held the meat out to the dog, who took the treat out of his palm, leaving behind a light smear of drool. He roughed the dog's head.

"I ought to remain here."

Only this morning, he had caught himself scouting a piece of land not far from the polis, a green and healthy plot that was probably owned by Drimutes. He could do the carpentry and masonry himself. He had never worked the land, but he harbored no doubts that he would figure it out, given enough peace and tranquility.

Erupting from the center of the polis, brash shouts made him wince and re-ignited his headache. He slumped. He considered ignoring the now familiar torrent of sneers and taunts, which broke out several times a day, seemingly whenever his youngest soldiers ranged within hailing distance of a gang of local pubes. He was long past caring who started it. Of course, if he caved and allowed them to fight it out, he knew precisely how it would end.

"Patience, Porphures. But one more night," he whispered.

The dog gave him a quizzical tilt of its head.

"Seems ten thousand times a day, my friend, and neither party will be satisfied until blood stains the earth," he snorted.

He stood, his joints crackling again on the way up. He kicked the tightness out of his thighs and strode toward the polis, toward the hullabaloo. He passed through the unguarded gateway and glanced at the polis' walls, which in their highest portions, reached his hips, and at their lowest points, he could step over without adjusting his gait. From what he had gleaned, the issue of raising funds for fortifications had been out of favor for longer than a generation. He was not surprised, given his struggles against the tight-fistedness of Drimutes and the other elders.

He wended through the twisting passages between the mud-brick homes. His stomach rumbled as he savored the fading fragrances of roasted meats and tangy spices. He waved to the men who poked their heads out of windows and doorways. He considered it a genuine victory that many returned his greeting, unlike the first days, when they glowered at him with open hostility.

He entered the agora, halting just inside the east passage. The tiled, rectangular expanse was torch-lit and empty of vendors, the wooden stalls and tables carted away or stacked against the south wall in designated spaces, a privilege for which Drimutes charged a fee. Between market days, as well as during the evenings, the agora served as a gymnasium, the young men wrestling and boxing while their elders drank wine on the benches and couches lining the walls.

Porphures had found it a bit reckless, that while leaving the outer walls in such a state of disrepair, the town fathers had seen fit to finish the walls with a portico overhanging the north side. Instead of intervening, the townsmen lounged against the walls while passing wine jars and enjoying the spectacle. In the center, six younger men and nine local youths were puffing their chests and taunting one another, neither group having yet worked up the nerve to cross the line into fighting words.

He spotted Drimutes under the portico, his hairy legs stretched out on a couch, his left arm across his broad chest, his left hand gripping his right bicep while he stroked his dung-colored beard with his right. He caught Drimutes glancing his way before the big man's eyes shifted back to the fracas and his sealed lips wormed into a smug smile.

Porphures took a deep breath and relaxed his jaw. He knew that Drimutes sanctioned these juvenile confrontations, but he could not see what the patriarch hoped to gain by instigating a brawl. Even if Drimutes' undertrained and under-armed fellows managed to drive out Porphures' battle-tested veterans and lusty rookies, without the tribute due, this rebellion would only provoke the Fat King, who would send an army to devastate the polis as an object lesson to other potentially-defiant communities.

Porphures made eye contact with some of his veterans. A group of them, all unarmored, but with swords girt about their waists, watched with bored expressions and passed the jar while slouching against the south wall among the stacks of tables and stalls. Shrugs and unconcerned head tilts answered his questioning gaze.

Only Pragmates was poised to intercede, the worry-line between his flashing green eyes creased deep. Pragmates' short brown beard could not conceal his grimace. His sturdy frame, not yet shed of all of its youthful slenderness, quivered with tension, but still he checked his temper and strove to broker a peace with cooling words.

Porphures noticed that his deputy's hand remained free of his hilt, and he nodded his approval. He stood back, content to monitor Pragmates' management of the situation, as long as matters remained verbal. He judged it to be a good experience for the lad, bolstering his confidence and preparing him for leadership.

A dark-haired youth, hollering for his father, burst into the agora from the west, with a pair of men behind him, the men supporting a limp, blond-haired boy between them. By the way Drimutes sprang up from his couch and rushed to the newcomers, Porphures reckoned that the dark lad was his son. Porphures could not remember having laid eyes on either of the boys.

Porphures shouldered his way through the young men, both the townies and the soldiers forgetting their quarrel while crowding around the dark boy, who was reporting to his father in rapid, high-pitched bursts.

Porphures pushed to the front of the mob and heard Drimutes say, "Take him to my house and put him in my wife's care."

Porphures got a good look at the blond boy as they bore him away. His face was a ghastly blue-gray, as if he were asphyxiating. His head lolled. Flecks of yolky spittle speckled his lips. His body hung limp between the men supporting him on either side. Dried blood crusted his bare torso and legs, with rusty flakes peeling away and cascading to the brown clay tiles below. Porphures doubted the afflicted boy would live much longer.

"I demand protection!" Drimutes said, his face showing red through his beard and his eyes blazing, as he stamped in front of Porphures.

Porphures took a step towards Drimutes, forcing the irate townsmen to take a backward step. "Protection from what?" he asked.

Drimutes snatched his son by the shoulders and shoved him in front of Porphures. The soldiers, vets and rookies alike, pressed in to hear. Porphures scrutinized the dark boy's face. Purple bags hung under his exhausted blue eyes, but Porphures saw no sign of the disease afflicting his comrade. Fine black hairs fuzzed the boy's pale cheeks and dimpled chin. Porphures could not see how a brute like Drimutes had fathered a specimen like this small lad.

"Invaders. Barbarians. Hordes," the boy said. "They bring disease. They…"

Drimutes jerked the boy to the side. "We pay tribute, therefore we are entitled to protection!"

Porphures did not need to turn around to identify the soldiers already murmuring about retreat. The sons of aristocrats, bullies, the first to pick fights with crudely-armed rustics and to gripe about the lack of women, although Zeus knew they spent most of their time gratifying each other, these pampered children obliged to serve on this expedition, their fathers no doubt hoping that a trip to the fringes of the fatherland would mature their wayward offspring.

"Bostrukhos will muster the company, prepare for both evacuation and siege," Porphures said. "Pragmates and I shall go with the boy to see this barbarian horde."

"Ergates shall not go," Drimutes said, glaring at Porphures.

"Ergates, are you able to run?" Porphures asked as he looked at the filthy, half-naked, and worn-down boy.

The boy squinted at Porphures and swallowed. Porphures was cheered by the steel in the nodding boy's gaze. Porphures turned to Drimutes and said, "Your son's companion cannot travel. Time flees. If you oppose me, we shall throw you in chains."

The color drained from Drimutes' face. The big man stepped aside. Porphures gathered up Pragmates and Ergates, and hurried them to the weapons dump.

"We should take more men," Pragmates suggested.

"I fear we might, by chance, include a partisan who could not resist the opportunity," Porphures said. He watched Pragmates glance sidelong at Ergates, who appeared to ignore their exchange, a studious ignorance that Porphures knew, from the long experience of raising his own boys, actually signified undivided attention. He wondered if the boy was sharp enough to guess the unspoken remainder. The opportunities that a siege offered an assassin were bad enough. He would not hazard a scouting foray into the wilderness with potential murderers at his back.

Melissa wrapped a small, soft cloth around the handle of the bronze pitcher, which sat next to the white marble basin on the wooden table. The table was flush against the wall. She stood with her back to the others as they prepared her mourning garments. She heard their soft bustling. She appreciated that they were maintaining silence out of respect for her grief.

Melissa lifted the pitcher with her left hand and poured clean water over her bloody right hand. She heard them fussing over by the mats. She wanted to help them wind the shroud around Ixos' corpse, but she did not want to show her tears.

Her right hand cleansed, she unwrapped the pitcher's handle and placed the cloth on the table. She began washing her left hand. So many times she had scrubbed the motherless boy's hands before feeding him at her dining table.

She closed her moist eyes and tried to replace the image of the blood-crusted, blue-faced, convulsing young man with that of Ixos as a small child, bright Day giggling and chasing dark Night through both the narrow town walkways and the green pastures outside the walls.

She remembered another time when he came to her bloodied. He had been very young, no higher than her waist, a few seasons after his mother's death. He had tumbled while he and Ergates had been playing, and a sharp stone had gashed his forehead, the blood oozing over his eyes and coating his face with a dripping red mask. She had cleaned the blood away and bandaged the wound while he, pale and trembling, yet stoic and silent, endured her ministrations like a brave little man. When she had finished he had stared at her with grave eyes and had asked her if he would be all right. His solemnity had tugged hard at her heart, as the memory of it did now. When she had said yes, he would be all right, the relief and the trust in his eyes had touched her so deeply she still felt it now.

She fought against it, but couldn't stop a wail from wracking her guts and escaping her lips. She surrendered to it, her naked anguish echoing in the chamber.

She hitched in a breath and exhaled. She opened her eyes. She picked up a towel and dried her hands, then dabbed the tear tracks from her cheeks. She looked into the basin. The blood she had cleansed from her hands formed red ribbons which spiraled in the water. Ixos' affliction had been beyond her healing arts, even though he had exhibited only a scratch on the neck and a bite mark on his forearm, the skin hardly broken. She had discovered nothing in his throat that accounted for his suffocating color. All she had been able to do for him was to try and comfort him as the breath left his body, then wash his enemy's blood away and begin preparing him for the rites.

A shriek shocked her out of her fugue. She spun and saw Trimma, her younger handmaiden, standing in the doorway, gaping bug eyed and pointing at the far wall. Melissa eye's followed Trimma's indication to the mats.

Ixos, completely enveloped, had risen, and was struggling to free himself from the shrouds. He stumbled and cracked his skull against the brick wall, as Trimma continued to shriek.

"Thanks be to Phoebe...Ixos has returned from Haides," Melissa whispered. She knew it was so. She was no Asklepiad, but she knew death when she saw it, and Ixos had surely been dead.

Ixos shucked the shroud from around his head, revealing yellowed and red-veined eyes. Drool dribbled down his chin, a feral scowl distorting his face. Ripping fabric, he freed his arms and stumbled away from the wall toward Trimma. He slammed into the shrieking girl. Tangled, they dropped to the marble tiles.

Ixos' head reared back, his jaws open wide, then he snapped down on her cheek. He slapped a hand across her forehead, then he wrenched his own head backwards. With his teeth clamped tight, he tore a hunk of flesh away from her face, her teeth and jawbone showing through the hole before it filled with gushing blood. Her screams became a series of jarring, staccato explosions, deafening in the small chamber.

Gore glistened down Ixos' chin as he chewed, the flesh squelching between his teeth before he swallowed. The wad lodged in his throat. He gagged and dry swallowed, clawing at his neck, until he forced the wad down with a sloppy gulp. His head swayed over his screeching victim, then he buried his teeth in her throat. Trimma's screams died in a wet gurgle.

His hand still clamped on her forehead, he ripped his face back, a scarlet mist following in his wake, the damp cracking causing Melissa to shudder. He crunched on gristle and slender throat bones. Melissa emitted a weak moan.

She detected motion out of the corner of her eye. She swiveled her head but her eyes remained on the flesh-eating Ixos as he reveled in his meal.

Zeira, her trusty old housekeeper, flashed into her field of vision and brained Ixos with a heavy stone vase.

Ixos, stunned, began crawling away, his limbs sluggish and clumsy. Zeira raised the stone vase over her head with both hands, bowing her back, then brought the vase down on the crown of his head with a mighty *clang*. The blow fractured the vase into large, jagged pieces, the shards clattering to the tile floor. Ixos laid flat, his blond locks beginning to soak up redness.

Ixos spasmed, then struggled up to his hands and knees and lunged at Zeira. The shroud was still tangled around his legs, and he fell short, smacking against the tiles. Melissa looked away from him, her eyes coming to a stop on her twitching and savaged handmaiden, whose throat and face were now a rugged crimson wasteland.

Zeira unleashed a torrent of curses, drawing Melissa's numbed attention away from poor, ruined Trimma. Ixos was on his hands and knees, spattering the tiles with blood, forcing Zeira into a corner while the gray-tressed housekeeper beat him about the head and shoulders with a broom. Ixos swiped at the broom and managed to grip its bristles. Zeira, trying to tug the broom back, shot Melissa a pleading look. "Mistress, help me!" she bawled.

Melissa blinked. She wheeled and snatched the half-full pitcher from the washing table. She whirled and charged towards Ixos. She banged the bronze pitcher against the side of his head, the shock of the blow numbing her forearm. Water slopped out of the pitcher and splashed to the floor as Ixos' head bent so far that his ear caromed against his shoulder.

Melissa waited for his head to rebound to its normal position, then she drove the pitcher into him again, with such violence that the pitcher broke free of her grip and flipped into the air before falling to the floor.

Ixos dropped his end of the broom and raised his battered head. With a sudden lurch, he was on his feet and reeling toward Melissa, who shrank back from the cannibal fury on his blood-grimed face. The shroud, still tangled about his ankles, tripped him and he fell flat at Melissa's feet.

She took a step back. He stirred and began to push himself up. She screamed, the scream distorting into a wild howl as she turned and grabbed the marble basin, which she was barely able to lift from the table. She pivoted back and dropped the heavy basin on his skull. The basin crunched his head into the floor, then thudded off to the side. Thick innards oozed out from his smashed brow.

Melissa backpedaled to the wall and gasped for breath. She tore her eyes from the mess of bone and blood-tinged blond hair, and she looked at her housekeeper. Zeira, still clutching the broom, panted and stared at the motionless maniac. "Are you harmed?" Melissa asked.

The handmaid wheezed heavily. "No." She swallowed. "Are you?"

Melissa pointed at her slaughtered handmaid. "Trimma is dead."

"Mistress, look at her face," Zeira said, her voice husky.

Melissa squinted and saw that under the blood, Trimma was exhibiting the same blue-graying of the face that Ixos had. She glanced at the boy. He was still. She edged around him and approached the dead girl.

Trimma's eyes popped open. They were yellowed and red-veined. Melissa jumped back. Trimma began to lever herself up. Zeira bounded over Ixos and, with a low groan, lifted the marble basin, then scrambled over to Trimma and bashed out her brains.

"By Phoebe, Pluton sends them back!" Melissa said. "Zeira, summon Norops. I must warn Drimutes."

She ran through the rooms of the house. She sprinted along the alleys to the agora, heedless of the stares attracted to her disheveled appearance. She found Drimutes engaged in a heated discussion with other town elders.

"Husband, husband," she called out.

The men parted. She ignored their gapes as she hurried up to Drimutes. She parted her lips to speak and he backhanded her across the mouth. The hard-knuckled *slap* blurred her vision and spun her to the ground.

Drimutes loomed over her. "How dare you leave the house with your head uncovered?" He reached down, seized her upper arm, and yanked her to her feet. He grabbed her by the shoulders and shook her back and forth, then turned her around and shoved her, then kicked her in the ass. "Go home, now!"

She was halfway back before she regained her senses and her staggering became an outraged stalking. Once inside, she snatched up a veil and covered her face, more to conceal the slap mark across her cheek than out of duty to her fool of a husband. She found Zeira and old—but stout—Norops, the ranking manservant of the house, standing guard over Ixos and Trimma, both of them lying where Melissa had left them.

"Have they moved?" Melissa asked.

"No, mistress," Zeira said.

Melissa turned to Norops and said, "Gather some men and seek out the commander. He has gone west with Ergates. Tell him what happened here. Arm yourselves. Hurry!"

Norops hustled from the room.

"Should you not ask permission to send the servants on such an errand? Will not the master be vexed?" Zeira asked.

Melissa touched the veil where it overlaid her throbbing cheek. "He will show his displeasure, as always, with the back of his hand. Let him. The commander must know that the dead now rise."

The sun warmed Ergates' back. He had been lying on the ridge, on his belly, next to Porphures, with Pragmates on the other side of the commander, since daybreak, observing the ragged barbarians in the valley below. Porphures had pointed out that with the morning rays in the invaders' eyes, there was no danger they would spot them.

To Ergates, none of the barbarians seemed at all concerned about stealth. The largest pack, which Ergates put at around thirty, paid heed to nothing but the goat they had managed to encircle. The old goat battled, ramming and kicking, knocking more than one barbarian on his butt, but there were too many. Ergates looked away when they started tearing the poor beast limb from limb.

Porphures, without looking away from the rude feast, said in a pitch just above a whisper, "You and your friend were concealing flocks far from the polis. How far have they traveled since you first encountered them?"

"Three valleys," Ergates said, still averting his eyes.

"Then they should have reached the polis by now," Porphures said.

Ergates nodded. He almost added, 'If they were healthy,' but the notion of these blighted men and women on the march caused the nightmare of the previous day's flight to swamp his already overtaxed faculties. They had raced headlong. Ixos' face had turned ever bluer, then he had sickened so he could no longer run. Soon after he had lost the power to walk, and Ergates had propped him up and had dragged him along. All the while Ergates had cast fearful glances over his shoulder, expecting to see the barbarians giving chase, closing the gap.

"The barbarians display the same coloration as your friend," Porphures said.

Ergates blanched, unable to bear the image of golden Ixos gone blue and mindlessly chasing goats.

"Perhaps we may talk to them and discover if there is a remedy, or if the ailment will run its course," Porphures mused.

"Do you believe it could be so?" Ergates asked Porphures.

Porphures nodded. "They are upright. They must have been afflicted for far longer. So there seems to be some manner of recovery, at the least."

A surge of hope brushed the cobwebs from Ergates' mind. He turned his head and resumed surveying the barbarians. He did not want Porphures to see his eyes well up. He took a sidelong peek and saw that Porphures had also returned to looking over the valley.

"Most of the animals show little fear," Porphures said.

Ergates supposed he had been distracted by the pack ravaging the goat, but now he saw that it was true. Small groups of sheep and goats grazed at a safe distance from the barbarians.

"Most do not carry weapons." Porphures pointed to the northwest "Look at that one."

A lone barbarian, toting a spear, was trundling after a sheep. Whenever the barbarian neared, the sheep started and galloped a bit away, then stopped and went back to grazing.

"He carries the spear backwards," Porphures noted.

Ergates squinted and saw that the tip of the barbarian's spear was indeed aiming the wrong way. Ergates, fascinated, continued to watch the barbarian hunt the crafty sheep. The sheep grazed until the barbarian was almost on top of it, and when the barbarian lunged, the sheep darted away. The barbarian keeled forward and impaled himself.

Ergates cringed and heard Pragmates grunt at the sight.

"You could see that coming," Porphures added.

Ergates watched the barbarian pitch sideways and thud into the grass, then roll onto his back, the spear protruding perpendicular to his body.

"He made no sound," Porphures said. "Look. None of the others pay heed." As the impaled barbarian began a torturous struggle to his feet, Porphures shook his head in confusion. "They baffle me."

Ergates looked at Porphures, who was chewing his lip. Ergates looked past Porphures and met Pragmates' stare. The lieutenant shrugged.

"Honor dictates that I must at least attempt to parley. You two will stand down, whatever may come. If they attack, you will run," Porphures said.

"Commander..." Pragmates began.

"You will obey," Porphures said forcefully, cutting him off. "At least one of you must warn the polis."

Ergates watched Porphures descend into the valley, straight into the jaws of the invaders. As far as Ergates could see, the commander showed no fear. On the contrary, his back was straight, accenting the breadth of his shoulders under the precise cut of his leather armor. The bronze hilt of his sheathed sword flashed, reflecting the rays of the sun. Everything about Porphures seemed clean and correct, from his sandal-straps to his trimmed, salt and pepper beard.

Ergates tried to imagine what his father would do. Certainly he would not confront the barbarians face to face. No, his father would seek a way to turn the situation to his advantage, his calculating eyes shifting back and forth, measuring all the possible angles. Ergates was surprised by the relief he felt at not knowing exactly what his father would do.

As soon as barbarians noticed Porphures, they began to shamble towards him. In Ergates' mind, there was no mistaking their hostile intent. Porphures drew his sword, the iron singing against the sheath on its way out. The barbarians did not pause in the face of Porphures' brazen warning.

Porphures stood his ground, and when the first of the slavering barbarians groped for him, he lopped off the fiend's head. The decapitated wretch fell to his knees, then flopped to the grass, but inspired no hesitation in the rest, who continued to close in on Porphures.

Porphures did not hesitate either. He went on the attack. He became a whirlwind, minus the chaos. His every blow landed, doing catastrophic damage. As he stabbed, chopped, and slashed with his sword, he used his left hand to punch and shove, as well as to deliver devastating pokes and gouges to eyeballs. As the mute barbarians kept coming, the only sounds were the commander's grunts of effort, the swish of his blade, the clang of iron against bone, and the thud of severed body parts dropping to the grass.

Despite Porphures' jaw dropping martial skill, Ergates could not see how the valiant warrior could withstand the barbarian numbers for much longer. In their stumbling way, they had hemmed him in, now three deep behind him, blocking retreat. More were flooding over the opposite rise, apparently the sounds of battle attracting them.

Ergates looked at Pragmates, who was still on his belly, but he was flexing his fists and grinding his teeth.

"I cannot permit him to die," Pragmates told Ergates. "You warn the polis."

Pragmates sprang up and hurled his spear, the missile blasting through the back of a barbarian. Pragmates charged into the fray, sword in his right hand, shield strapped to his left forearm, and he cut his way to Porphures, who wasted no time in chastising his lieutenant, but rather the two of them synchronized, one striking while the other defended, and they cleared a good space. But the barbarians were swarming fast and thick, too fast for the soldiers to hack their way out of the crush of bodies.

Ergates gripped the sword he had borrowed from the weapon's dump. He reckoned that with him fighting from one side, and his allies on the other, they might be able to hack a path through the throng so that the three of them could flee. He breathed in a deep, shuddering breath before pushing himself to his feet. He swallowed the knot in his throat, then ran down the slope. The barbarians he targeted turned before his arrival, but were too slow to ward off his attack.

He went berserk. Blackness narrowed his field of vision. Anyone with a blue face and dressed in rags was fair game. Wherever he felt a clutching hand, he sent a wild slash.

"ERGATES!"

The hoarse but mighty shout slapped him back to his senses. He locked eyes with Porphures and realized he had just struck Pragmates' shield.

Porphures shot him a savage smile. "Madman!"

Ergates wheeled, and instead of the clear escape route, he saw a dense wall of barbarians, fresh foes trampling their fallen fellows into the blood-soaked grass. Their putrid stench forced him to gag, despair extinguishing his fury. The first ranks in front of Ergates plummeted, the fall of one clumsy brute creating a ripple of headlong tumbles. They crawled over one another like a pile of ants, those behind climbing over the top and crushing their downed comrades. The mass collapse created a respite in which Ergates faced constellations of unblinking yellow eyes, the feverish yellow shot with jagged red lines.

"Ergates, to me!" Porphures called out.

Ergates retreated two steps. He was back-to-back with the commander. They had cleared an uneven circle, but they had descended further down the slope to do it, and the barbarians were regrouping and pressing inward.

"Guard our rear," Porphures said. "Cry out when you need help." Porphures glanced over his shoulder, and Ergates knew that the commander had seen him shaking, and shame welled up within him.

"There is no disgrace in fearing death," Porphures said. "At the least it will save you from rebuke, for disobeying my orders." He narrowed his eyes and his lips formed a grim smile. "A shaking hand makes a wider wound."

Ergates barked out an astonished, yet relieved laugh. He swung his sword at the neck of the first barbarian to rise to his feet beyond the barricade of his writhing brethren. The sword's tip slashed the barbarian's jugular and released an arterial spray. Ergates stepped out of the way of his falling victim and focused on the next.

Over the slaps and slashes of iron through meat and bone, Ergates heard a familiar voice ring out from up the slope. He heard the whine of swift shafts through the air. "Commander!" he yelled. A rush of hope energized his limbs, and he began hacking his way towards that familiar voice, that of Norops, who was shouting orders. Ergates did not dare look up, the danger of the snapping jaws of the fallen demanding his full attention, but he deduced that Norops was marshaling a squad of servants.

Ergates brought the flat, hard sole of his sandal down on the skull of a snapping barbarian. He had no choice but to tread on the wounded and the dead, as he fought his way uphill, the commander and Pragmates now covering his back, urging him on. Pragmates wheeled around, and his expert sword doubled the pace of their push.

Ergates risked a glance upward. At the top of the ridge, Norops and two others were firing arrows into the barbarian horde, and three more had descended to engage the enemy hand-to-hand.

Ergates tripped and tilted forward, but a hand grabbed his shoulder and pulled him back to his feet. Porphures slipped around him, with blinding speed, cut an opening through the barbarian ranks. With his free hand, he thrust Ergates into the daylight and screamed, "Run!"

Ergates staggered past the first line of servants, who were all armored in leather and fighting with spears, and then turned. Pragmates, then Porphures followed, the two soldiers immediately whirling and attacking, allowing the servants to retreat a few paces. Ergates understood the tactic, and he lunged to Porphures' right. Arrows continued to wing overhead, Norops calling the shots.

"Now!" Porphures shouted. The three of them turned and fled, the servants behind them doing the same. They rushed up the slope and past the archers, who joined them as they sprinted down the next slope and up to the next ridge, where Porphures called a halt.

Ergates doubled-over and gasped. The barbarians were mounting a haphazard pursuit at best, the foremost being those who had tumbled into the bottom of the valley, and it seemed to Ergates that the absence of their prey perplexed the scattered pursuers.

Ergates looked at his fellows. Pragmates and Porphures were blood-smeared and dripping ichor. Ergates looked down at himself. He was covered in enemy blood, too. He looked up and saw Norops whispering in Porphures' ear, as the commander wiped slime away from his blade.

"Pragmates, go to the capital," Porphures ordered.

Pragmates did not hesitate. He turned and began to run eastward, charting a course that would bypass the polis to the south.

"Come, let us go. Ergates, run with me," Porphures said.

The commander's sober tone did not cheer Ergates as he fell in beside him.

"Woman!"

Even though Melissa had been anticipating Drimutes' ill-mannered summons, her jaw tensed. She could not recall the last time he had called her by her name.

The other wives, along with their female servants, all gathered with her to await the outcome of the battle, began to bear the basins, cloths, towels, and fresh clothing to the courtyard, where the men awaited. Melissa carried a basin, the water warmed, and strips of clean cloth draped over her shoulder. She had taken pains to assure that her hair and face were properly veiled.

When she saw the defeated countenances of the men, she did not need to ask if they had been able to break through the eastern horde. She scanned the survivors. Ergates was not among them. Her heart pumped rapid, irregular pulses. Ergates was absent.

"*Woman!*"

Drimutes' second shout roused her. She hurried to him, telling herself that maybe her son was still fighting, maybe her son was in the company of the soldiers…and she continued to manufacture unlikely maybes as she began to strip off Drimutes' leather and bronze armor.

The men sat silent.

Each click of a buckle and swipe of a loosened strap grated on Melissa's nerves. With a great effort she swallowed a portion of her anguish, enough to notice that Drimutes' armor was nearly pristine. Underneath, he was slick with a slimy layer of perspiration. She suspected he had done more running than fighting. She tried to lock eyes with him but he ignored her.

She began to scrub his back, the water causing the long, wiry hairs to clump. She went over his shoulders, the muscles grown squishy and soft from luxury. The fishy stink of his armpits wafted up into her face. She worked impassive, having trained herself long ago to show no outward reaction to his various noxious fumes.

"Cowards!" he hissed, breaking the silence.

She flinched when he kicked a bronze greave; the leather and bronze shin-guard skipping and clattering across the tiles of the agora floor. Her eyes followed its path. She looked up and saw the frightened faces of the townsmen. She dipped the washcloth in the basin and returned to her task.

She saw Drimutes' eyes darting back and forth. "They are so very brave when they are collecting tribute," he growled, "but when faced with battle, more than half of the cowards fled, leaving us to fend for ourselves."

The other men grumbled their assent. Melissa had heard that some of the soldiers had slunk away, mostly the younger ones, while the commander had been scouting the barbarian horde. Others, including citizens, a fact that Drimutes did not bother to mention, had fled after Porphures reported what he had seen. But by far the largest exodus had occurred after the spreading of the word that both Ixos and Trimma had risen from death. It required no philosophy to conclude that the barbarians had also risen from the dead. It did, however, require a certain blind avarice to deny the evidence.

She smoothed the cloth along the back of his plump neck, the urge to throttle him causing her forearms to stiffen. She wanted to choke the news of Ergates' fate out of him, but even if she dared, her hands were too small to penetrate the mass of muscle and fat protecting his throat.

She closed her eyes and exhaled a measured, silent breath. She dipped the cloth into the basin. Anxiety gnawed at her guts. She attempted to distract herself by marking that he was employing his usual tactic. Start with a truth, or half-truth, and proceed to the lies. She wrung out the cloth and began to blot sweat from his shaggy legs.

Drimutes waited for the men to quiet down. "Their cowardice and their delays. If it was not for *his* wavering, we would all be safe on the road to the capital," he said.

Melissa, through a gnashing expenditure of will, kept herself from sucking in an appalled breath. Instead, she wrung out the cloth, twisting it until it was almost dry. *He* was the one to blame for the delay. She herself had heard him scheming with his cronies the night the commander had returned from scouting the horde. *'Let them leave,'* he had whispered to his men, *'We shall divide their land and goods between ourselves.'*

The opportunity had been too rich for him to believe that the dangers were credible. Once he had seen the horde for himself, he had insisted on a diplomatic mission, believing that he could purchase the goodwill of the invaders. He had derided Porphures' exhortations for an immediate evacuation. The commander had barely rescued Drimutes from that fool's errand, losing precious soldiers, as well as some townsmen, in the process. By the time they had regrouped from the fiasco, some of the most recent fugitives had returned, bewailing the undead barbarian horde, which had closed off the eastern routes and had torn runaway townspeople to shreds.

Melissa fended off her growing rage and concentrated on washing his feet.

"We have two options," he said. "Either we prepare for a siege and hope that this runner of his reaches the capital, and the Fat King deigns to send an army, or we make a push for the mountains."

The men clamored to express their opinions. She watched Drimutes lean back and fight to keep the smile from his lips. She tried to establish eye contact with him again, straining for that silent communication that her father and mother had enjoyed, a connubial benefit that she had never before achieved with Drimutes.

He caught her pleading look. For a second, while confusion warped his features, she felt a spark of hope. Then his befuddlement consolidated into outrage. She ducked her head and tensed her body, knowing what was coming.

He backhanded her, the blow producing a meaty *whack* against the side of her head. As she lay sprawled on the tiles, he stood up and pointed at the doorway, looming over her like a giant. "Be gone, woman! We men must counsel."

Her injured ear throbbed. She rose and gathered up her washing implements, hating the way she scurried out of the courtyard.

Furious, she paced back and forth in her chamber, then changed into her most humble clothing. She collected fresh washing gear and veiled herself, then slipped out of the house and hastened to the agora.

The blood-smeared soldiers shocked her to a standstill inside the entrance. The surviving eleven sat silently on the benches. Gore dripped from their sagging bodies and pooled around both their sandals and the pieces of armor they had managed to shrug off. Ergates was not among them, but the commander was. She hurried across the agora and placed her washing kit next to him. She knelt and began to strip his armor, starting with his greaves.

Porphures opened his eyes and, his voice raw with weariness. "Many thanks for your kindness."

She looked away, unable to bear the candid gratitude in his half-lidded eyes. She felt a seething shame that no one had sent so much as a single servant to tend to these brave warriors. She wiped away angry tears and focused on peeling off his armor. Every section she removed revealed bruises, both fresh purples and aged yellows.

"If we had possessed ten more veterans, we might have broken through," Porphures sighed. "The barbarians are inept warriors, but their numbers are far too great."

"If we had departed immediately..." one of his men said.

Porphures waved a dismissive hand at his man. On the follow-through he accidentally grazed Melissa. "My apologies," he said.

She bowed her head and removed the last of his armor. She tried not to admire his shape. He was handsome and well-formed, in spite of the filth and his exhaustion. His belly was taut, unlike that of Drimutes, who walked about as if on the verge of giving birth. She checked herself before her glance became a gaze.

She began to bathe him. The other soldiers, sluggish and quiet, unbuckled their own armor. If they were envious of her attention to their commander, she could not detect it.

Porphures submitted to her wordless directions, granting a docile lift of his hard arms so that she could get in deep. Once she had washed his head and torso, he stood, groaning on the way up. As she washed his legs, she set to working up her nerves to ask him about Ergates.

Her awareness drifted away from her scrubbing, so she didn't notice his swelling member until she almost butted his half-hardened penis with her brow. She raised an eyebrow and glanced up at him. He shrugged, the corner of his mouth stretching into a lopsided smile, which she thought made him seem boyish even with the grays dappling his charcoal beard.

"I am as astonished as you," he said.

She looked down, for once glad for the veil lest he see her blush, a response she had believed she was no longer capable of. She washed his calves and found the courage to say, "Have you word of Ergates?" She swallowed, but could not force the dryness down. "My mistress is distressed...her son," she murmured.

"Lady, your hair betrays your connection to the boy." His voice was low and husky.

She reached up and tucked an errant lock of hair back under her headwrap.

He cleared his throat. "He is unharmed. He volunteered to stand watch. He is a remarkable young man. He saved my life at least three times."

Shudders wracked her frame. She mastered herself, repressing a sob of relief, the effort bringing more violent shakes. He stooped, grasped her hand, and guided her to stand. "I thank you for your decency," he said. "Leave the basin and towels. I shall return them when it is discrete to do so."

She met his eyes. "There is talk of a push to the north."

He shook his head. "The horde is thicker to the north than it is to the east."

"Then we all are doomed."

"No, lady. We must only hold out until Pragmates returns. Even a small force of trained soldiers can turn back these strange and incompetent invaders. Take heart. Should the Fat King refuse aid, Pragmates will assemble a private company of elite warriors. He will return in no more than ten days."

Pragmates shrieked and stopped running. Another stitch of pain had exploded in his side, deep in his guts. He leaned over gasping, while pressing his palm into the shredding agony under the left side of his ribcage. He could ignore his throbbing soles and burning calves, but he could not run through these side-aches.

He groaned, regretting every wasted second. He looked up to renew his gratitude for the iron-gray overcast sky, the heavy cloud cover keeping the temperature down, the sun not beating directly on his head.

At least Helios burns me no more, he thought. He whispered a quick prayer for rain so that he might replenish his dwindling water supply. He had forgotten how desolate this portion of the road was, where the desert stretched lethal before greening again. He read the low, heavy clouds both as a sign that he was nearing the edge of the desert, and as a portent that his fortunes were improving. Perhaps he might find a horse he could use.

He straightened up and continued to massage away the stitch. He was anxious to resume his marathon, but experience had taught him that he needed a complete recovery or the pain would simply flare up again a few paces down the road. He closed his eyes.

Patience, he thought. He would save time by foregoing the bureaucratic delays certain to accompany any requests made of the Fat King. He would go straight to Porphures' martial allies. They would throw together a cavalry force which would speed to the polis. One good chariot charge would annihilate the barbarians.

He opened his eyes and blinked, then rubbed them. It was no mirage. There was a tiny figure on the eastern horizon. He stood and watched, disregarding the stitch, as the figure grew in size. He began to jog, hoping the traveler was a local and could tell him where he might procure a horse.

He slowed to a walk when he came within hailing distance. He called out and the traveler waved. The traveler wore a low-crowned brown leather hat with a wide, circular brim, the brim casting darkness over the traveler's eyes. His straight, broad nose protruded from the shadows of his hat, casting its own shadow over his long lips. The beardless man was half a head taller than Pragmates. His mantle, a brown several shades lighter than his hat, hung to his ankles. The toes of leather boots peeked out below. The mantle's sleeves descended past his hands. He lugged a bulky leather bag over his right shoulder.

The traveler dropped his burden on the road, the heavy bag sending up puffs of dust after striking the dirt. A lock of braided brown hair swung out past his left ear. The traveler tucked the long plait back into the neck of the mantle.

"Stranger, I advise you to turn back. Barbarians invade from the west," Pragmates said.

The stranger bowed his head. "My thanks for the warning. Do you flee these barbarians?"

Pragmates narrowed his eyes. "No. My commander sends me to the capital. I shall return with a force to meet the invaders in battle."

The stranger's lips curved into a smile. Pragmates could not say if the stranger was mocking him, until the smirking stranger said, "You do not flee for your life?"

Pragmates grasped his hilt. "Stranger, I say I do *not* flee."

The stranger knelt before him, clutching the warrior's knee with one hand, and the tip of Pragmates' beard with the other. The stranger bowed his head. "Forgive me, friend, I did not intend to offend. I have met soldiers fleeing eastward along this very road."

"Deserters," Pragmates said and spat into the dirt.

The stranger released Pragmates' beard and knee, then looked up, the wide brim of his hat still shading his eyes. "Indeed. I see now that you are a man worthy of honors."

The stranger crossed his arms and then opened them too fast for Pragmates to comprehend. Pragmates gagged and took two stiff, backward steps. He touched his hands to his throat and looked wide-eyed at the hot scarlet runnels on his fingers. He gawked at the stranger, who held the finishing pose of his blinding move, both arms out wide while sluggish droplets of blood oozed from the undulating blades of the two daggers, one in each hand.

Pragmates sank to his knees. The stranger wiped the blades on his thigh and then sheathed them inside his sleeves. He caught Pragmates as he pitched forward, then eased the dying man onto his back.

Pragmates reached up and grabbed the stranger's mantle as the man kneeled over him.

"Do not be troubled, friend, I shall perform the rites proper," the stranger said. "I shall lay you in a tomb unmarked to all but the Legitimati. It may be of some comfort for you to know that wild dogs and vultures savage the flesh of those cowardly deserters, and Hyperion will bleach their never buried bones. Let Duszeus glean whatsoever he is able."

"Porphures," Pragmates gurgled.

The stranger made shushing sounds. "Peace, soldier, your passage to the Isles of the Blessed is assured. Fear not for your commander, for I bear aid against the invaders. Close your eyes now. Your journey begins."

Porphures ignored the pale barbarous hands straining to reach him as he perched atop the easternmost wall with sufficient height to frustrate the starving, undead invaders. As the last rays of Helios skimmed over the horizon, he searched for the dust cloud that would signify the approach of an army.

Pragmates should have returned by now.

"Evil," he murmured; there was no other explanation. Pragmates had met with evil on the road to the capital, or the Fat King had done evil to his lieutenant. Porphures ground his teeth, thinking of Pragmates languishing in some dark prison, while the Fat King delayed, hoping that the undead barbarian horde would do his dirty work. Porphures vowed to all the gods that he would discover what happened to Pragmates, and that he would repay anyone, *anyone*, who used Pragmates in anything less than a worthy manner.

First I must pass through this calamity, he thought.

He shifted his eyes from the horizon, to the cemetery outside the absurdly low city walls. He watched the reeking invaders, most now completely naked, as the wretches dug like dogs, throwing up haphazard mounds of dirt as they sought out corpses with rotted and maggot-ridden meat still clinging to the bone. Early this very day the emaciated, blue-tinged cannibals had blundered upon the notion that the graveyard might yield their vile sustenance.

No one seemed to have witnessed how this particular corruption had begun. To Porphures, it had appeared that one moment, the bruised and filthy adversaries were milling about, clogging the thoroughfare and everywhere else they could worm their way into, stumbling around while scouring the polis for live meat, and the next moment a mob of mute barbarians was rioting on the east side of the polis. They scratched and clawed over decayed torsos and limbs, the whole spinning, drawing those on the periphery into the center of the silent confusion while expelling others.

Still, this macabre revelation that the undead barbarians' preferred nourishment did not attract those swarming the other precincts. Those yellow-eyed creatures continued to dodder through the unsecured portions of the polis, relegating the survivors to lofty roofs and the agora, as well as Drimutes' house and courtyard. Porphures had grown surefooted, balancing along the higher walls while moving from post to post.

He watched the revolting creatures commit sacrilege until it turned his stomach upside down. He wanted to make another vow, to re-bury those desecrated corpses, but he could not see a way to accomplish it.

He looked at the lock of soft, shiny black hair in his right hand. He realized that he had been stroking it between his thumb and forefingers, enjoying the silky texture. Two nights back, a servant girl had stolen into the agora, bearing this gift to him, claiming that her mistress wished him to carry the lock as a charm against bad fortune. He was not certain about the customs here on the outer rim, but in the capital, this sort of gift was meant to provoke a fairly specific response.

"Commander."

Porphures recognized the boy's voice and slipped the lock of his mother's hair into his tunic.

"The graveyard is that of the poor," Ergates said as he crouched down next to him. "Those that can pay make the journey into the mountains, so the mystics can usher them into the underworld."

"That is outrageous," Porphures said. He glanced at the boy, who glared at the scavengers. "I wish to attack as well. But if we wait, they shall starve," Porphures mused.

"Then we can walk out of here."

"I believe so." He took one last look at the eastern horizon. "What news of your father's temper?"

"His mind has turned down a dark path."

"He still favors the northern push."

"Yes. I overheard him arguing to abandon the women and children. He believes we can make it without them."

Porphures exhaled a weary breath. "I shall not leave them behind."

"Neither shall I. He believes the Fat King will not send an army."

"They would have arrived by now. Evil has befallen Pragmates."

Ergates bowed his head. After a moment, he raised his head. "What do you make of them?" He gestured to the undead barbarians below.

"I do not know. I know they kill and feast on human flesh, if they are able. They also feast on herd animals, and any other creature they are able to trap. I know that they can be killed so that they do not rise again."

"No, I mean …"

Porphures clapped Ergates on the back. "I know what you mean, Ergates. I have heard the whispers about your father's hubris. But I do not believe that this is a punishment from the gods. The Olympians would never allow their agents to desecrate graves thus."

"They rise from death…"

"Or they rise from sickness. We do not know. I have seen no signs that the gods are angry at us."

"So you believe some things happen by chance."

"I do. I believe…"

"*Ergates!*"

Porphures was well familiar with Drimutes' habitual and abrasive summons of his son. Ergates slumped, then sprang to his feet and began jogging along the wall. Porphures rose and followed the boy.

Drimutes awaited in the torch-lit agora. Porphures counted ten armed lackeys accompanying the town boss, who never seemed to go anywhere without an entourage, as if he feared treachery. Porphures reminded himself that the treacherous fear treachery most. Besides, there were four of Porphures' soldiers in the agora, and the rest a whistle away.

Drimutes stood with his hands on his hips. "I warned you about wandering Ergates." He slapped his son across the cheek, the *smack* resounding off the stone walls of the agora.

Porphures' mouth clamped shut. He told himself, soon enough, should they both survive, that the boy would grow large enough to repay his father's abuses. Yet he could also picture himself lunging forward a step and drawing his sword, the blade glittering in the sun before it sliced through Drimutes' neck.

He forced himself to look beyond that oh so satisfying blow. If he did such an action, whatever followed, a bloodbath would be assured. His remaining eight men would fight to the death. However, there were three times that many able townsmen. Maybe all would fight, maybe none. Maybe they would feign submission and plot an ambush.

Drimutes ignored the rage on his son's face, and squinted at Porphures.

"Soldier," Drimutes said to Porphures, who had noticed long ago that Drimutes never called him 'commander.' He held his position a few paces away, believing it better for everyone that he maintain a space greater than arm's length between himself and this puffed-up buffoon.

"We have counseled," Drimutes said. "We desire that you soldiers bivouac on the roofs. We believe there is too much mingling with the slave girls in the agora. We believe this *improper* mingling distracts the soldiers from their duty."

Porphures' mouth went dry. He searched the schemer's devious face for any indication that he knew, either of Melissa's gift or that his wife had bathed his bitter rival. Porphures could not penetrate Drimutes' standard mask of explicit scorn. However, he knew the man well enough to understand that if Drimutes did know, rather than a face-to-face battle for his honor, Drimutes would attack from a posterior angle.

Porphures ran his tongue around the inside of his mouth, working up moisture in order to speak in an even tone. From experience, he knew that in desperate times people became reckless. If she came to him in the night, he could not be sure that he would not stain both their honors. Drimutes might be watching for just such an angle.

Porphures realized he was gripping his hilt tightly. He let his hand fall away from his sword. "Perhaps it would be wise to do so," he said.

Ergates' chin dropped to his chest. With a honking inhale, he jerked his head upright. He let out a nervous laugh and looked down on the sea of blue-skinned, yellow-eyed creatures. The undead barbarians were especially dense below him, the frayed men and women glowering up at him with mute intensity, waiting for him to fall asleep and tumble into their stinking clutches. He could feel the feverish heat baking off them.

He looked beyond them to the east. The first rays of Helios signaled that his watch on guard duty was nearly over. Still no tell-tale cloud of dust. He guessed it would not be long before they ceased setting a watch. There was nothing to see but the shambling horde, thick around the polis, scattered to the horizon.

Beyond the throngs infesting the polis, the drift of the greasy-haired wrecks mesmerized him, and his eyelids were drooping again, when he detected deliberate motion. His eyes widened as a figure strode through the horde, the ripples of aimless undead barbarians parting before the wayfarer, but otherwise paying the stranger no mind.

A bungler tripped and fell before the stranger's feet. The downed barbarian flopped his stick-like limbs about, as if drowning in the dirt. The stranger halted, hunkered down, and hoisted the clumsy barbarian to his feet. The stranger gave the barbarian a gentle pat on the back before letting him stagger away.

With rising Helios at his back, shadows darkened the stranger's features, but when that odd, wide-brimmed hat tilted upward, Ergates shivered, certain that the stranger was staring right at him.

Ergates shot to his feet and hurtled along the cope stones. He leapt from the wall to the lofty roof that the commander was sleeping on. "Someone approaches!" he said as he shook Porphures awake.

"Is Pragmates here?" Porphures said and sat up.

Ergates bowed his head, unable to bear the sight of the hope dying in his commander's eyes. He swallowed heavily. "No, but come see."

The commander, not as nimble upon the walls, forced Ergates to slow his pace. When they arrived at the easternmost secure wall, the stranger was standing below. Ergates gaped. The noxious barbarians had withdrawn from the stranger, creating an open semicircle against the wall, while seeming to be oblivious of the fresh meat just a few feet away.

The stranger's broad-brimmed hat shaded his eyes as he looked up at them. His loose and tan mantle billowed around him. He stooped and hauled up a large leather bag the color of his hat. "Ho there, a hand, dear sirs," he called.

Ergates looked at Porphures, who wore a mystified expression. Porphures shrugged, and they reached down and pulled the bag up and placed it on the wall.

The stranger stretched his hands to them. "Assistance, I beg you, lest the *pharmakon* fail and they sense my presence."

They each took a hand and helped the stranger up. The clean-shaven man's nose and mouth, though well-formed, were prodigious, and they reminded Ergates of the masks that the comedians wore while capering on stage. The man tucked into his collar a handful of errant braids of brown hair, the weave of each slender strand both singular and as cunningly embellished as any eastern rug.

"Gather the men, time wanes," he said.

Ergates glanced towards the north wall of the agora. His father, scowling, faced the cluster of townsmen, who spilled out from under the portico to line the adjacent walls. He looked to the south.

Porphures and his eight surviving soldiers stood armed and ready. Ergates himself was pressed against the east wall. He had inched away from the nearest townsman, so that he was next to the barricaded entrance. He could hear the undead barbarians outside, their fingers probing, their ragged nails scratching at the stone and wood that clogged the passage.

The stranger sat on the tiles in the middle of the agora, reclining against his bulky bag, the brim of his hat canted low, as if he was snoozing. All eyes were on the stranger.

The distrusting expressions gladdened Ergates. He could not be sure, but within the gloom cast by the stranger's hat, Ergates believed that he detected a tiny, malicious smile playing over those long lips.

"We are assembled," the stranger said and raised his head. He bounded to his feet and turned all the way around. "Permit me to speak of my dreams."

Ergates narrowed his eyes. The stranger, apparently a mantis—a dream interpreter—spoke in a tone that seemed fermented and sickly-sweet, reminding Ergates of the time when he and Ixos, still whelps, had found a jar of spoiled wine and had dared each other to drink, passing the jug back and forth until they were senseless.

"Some believe the best course is to stay, endure the siege, and wait for the enemy to starve," Porphures said.

Ergates stared at Porphures, but the commander kept his eyes on the mantis. Ergates forced a cough, hoping to startle Porphures in case the mantis was beguiling him.

"In my dreams I have seen them devouring dirt," the mantis said. "Which, after all, contains the dust of corpses. They will outlast you."

Ergates uttered a quiet *pfft*. He had not witnessed the undead barbarians eating dirt. He frowned. They were filthy around their mouths, and only the gods knew what they did in the dark of night... He gave his head a quick shake, fearing that the intoxicating voice of the mantis was working on his wits

"If you do not go northward, you will all die," the mantis said. "One by one, as they snatch the weary and unaware from the walls. You have already lost some to carelessness. How many more comrades, sickened with the disease, do you wish to kill? Or perhaps they will finally press with such force that they break through a wall. But even if the walls hold, and you do not fall into their clutches, how long before hunger drives you to adopt their favored mode of nourishment?"

"How were you able to walk unharmed among them?" Porphures asked.

Ergates folded his arms across his chest. Porphures would not let this charlatan get away with it. Doubtless the commander would expose the mantis as some sort of spy.

"In my dreams," the mantis said. "I was shown the secrets of the pharmakon. Alas, the herbs and nectar are very rare, and I spent my meager supply in penetrating the horde. Now, I am as vulnerable as any of you."

Ergates bit his tongue. He wanted to call the mantis a liar. Even more, he wanted Porphures to do so.

The mantis turned to face the townsmen. "You must all go into the mountains. It is the only way. All other ways lead to total destruction."

Ergates studied Porphures. The commander, instead of looking angry and defiant, appeared to be weighing the mantis' words. Ergates could not understand why no one was asking the mantis why he had risked coming here in the first place.

"All must go," the mantis told Drimutes. "All will be needed. Everyone who is able to wield a weapon, be it a sword or distaff, an old woman's cane or a child's toy sword. Without everyone working as one, we shall never reach the mountains."

Ergates was not surprised at the reddening of his father's face. For once his father's stubbornness might be useful.

"But...not all will survive the journey," the mantis said.

Ergates recognized the look of calculation in his father's face.

"They are too thick about the walls," Porphures said. "Did your dream show how we are to get past them?"

Ergates straightened up. He chastised himself for not trusting Porphures to see through the dream interpreter's act.

"Indeed," the mantis said. He knelt and began unfolding his bundled bag. "Much like the pharmakon, I was shown this contraption in my dreams. We shall be able to launch a man through the air well beyond the walls to a place where they are not so thick."

Ergates' brow creased while he tried to reconcile the odd straps and rods with the stories he had heard of war machines that could lob boulders and burning masses at enemies. Even if the mantis' implements performed as he claimed, surely no man could survive the landing.

The mantis stood and held up fat swatches of leather. "These will pad his fall, and protect him from bites. He will run away, drawing a portion of the enemy along with him."

"Then another," Porphures said.

The mantis whirled, his loose mantle swishing, to face the commander. "Indeed. You see the stratagem now. One more is all that will be needed. Then the northern push can begin. You have battled them, Commander. You know they are feeble warriors. Two columns, one on each side of the women and children, and a straight push north." The mantis dropped the leather and shook his fist. "We can make it!" he declared.

Excited chatter broke out among the townsmen. Porphures stood impassive, his men silent behind him, maintaining discipline. Ergates edged around the barricaded passage toward the soldiers.

"What else does your dream show you?" Porphures asked.

The townsmen quieted.

"Much," the mantis said. He rotated, scanning each townsman. He continued to turn until he locked eyes with Ergates, whose bladder seemed to fill to a throbbing level in an instant.

The mantis stepped up to Ergates, never breaking eye contact. Dizziness and nausea roiled through Ergates.

"Here is our hero!" the mantis said, smiling. "Light, fast, yet strong. In my dreams I saw you—a noble and good young man—succeeding in this crucial task. The first to be launched, a great honor indeed."

The mantis looked deep into Ergates' eyes and Ergates thought of the river, swimming underwater, seeing the golden shafts of Helios filtering through the surface as he rose at the speed of bubbles.

"You are sensitive," the mantis whispered, then he raised his voice. "Fear will only serve you in this labor, my young friend. Future peoples will sing songs of your heroic deeds."

"My son will not be cast through the air!" Drimutes spat.

The mantis blinked his shadowy eyes. Hope glimmered within Ergates. He spun towards Drimutes, and Ergates felt like he could breath again. "I dreamed of you as well, Lord Drimutes," the mantis said.

The mantis pounced on his unfolded bundle and rooted around inside. He seized something and sprang towards Drimutes. Ergates craned his neck and saw that the mantis was holding a blackwood box. Ergates detected golden scrawls ornamenting the small box, but he was too far away to discern the shapes of the symbols.

"It is crucial that the mountain dwelling mystics receive this box," the mantis said. "So that they might stop the invaders once and for all. It is only right and proper that our chieftain should take this box to them."

Ergates watched his father swell as he accepted the box.

"I have seen that Lord Drimutes is the only one who will not look into the box. For if any one person should look into the box, other than the mystics, all will be lost."

Ergates sensed that the delivery of the box was the mantis' real purpose. Ergates felt in his marrow that the mantis did not care who lived or died along the way.

"You ask much," Porphures said.

The mantis wheeled around to face the commander. "I understand your reservations. After we launch our young hero, I shall be the next into the fray, if only to prove my goodwill. All what I shall do is provide you with an opportunity, my friend. If you do not see the worth of opportunity, then withdraw and let come what may."

Porphures gave the mantis a measuring look. "Well spoken."

The strength drained from Ergates' knees.

Grinning, the mantis turned to Ergates. "Now, let us prepare our young hero for his flight!"

Ergates flailed his arms and legs, his heart in his throat. The ground was speeding at him. He overshot the target, landing feet first on the edge of the clearing. He felt his knee twinge on impact, then he slammed into the nearest barbarians. He bowled through them with his eyes closed. The leather padding absorbed the bony blows and he flopped to a stop on his back.

He laid there until a shadow fell over his closed eyelids. He opened his eyes to see a slobbering barbarian bending toward him, mouth open wide, ready to tear into him. He raised his padded forearm. The barbarian's mouth yawned open, then he bit down.

Ergates scrabbled backwards and shook his arm free, ripping out several of the barbarian's blackened teeth. He struggled to his feet as something struck his padded back. He limped sideways, gritting his teeth against the pain in his sprained knee, and began to run.

Melissa had been told that they would reach the mystics' mountain stronghold before fast approaching nightfall. She hoped so. She looked up at the cliff face on her left, so titanic and steep that it made her feel a bit disorientated to seek the summit, but it was better than looking to her right and plumbing the depths of the jagged chasm below.

Staring at the path, which was both swept and level, and wide enough to walk on, she could see the drop in the corner of her eye, and the longer she stared, the more the path appeared to shrink, until it seemed like a tightrope, leaving her a misstep from certain death.

The toddler hitched against her and began to sob in her ear, squeezing his tiny arms tighter around her neck. She adjusted him into the crook of her arm, rubbing his back and cooing softly. He was an orphan now. The barbarians had taken his mother, as well as other mothers, fathers, and males too young to be fathers, and even a pair of soldiers. Only the children remained. Still, they could not prevent the children from seeing the barbarians snatch away their families, and pull those unfortunates into blood-hungry packs. She could still hear their screams and the sound of tearing flesh.

But worse than those pitiful wails were the pleas of bitten survivors, those who did not panic and run off into the horde, but stood fast and battled the enemy. The sound of sharp steel slicing through their throats and distorting their cries into gags and gurgles; those sounds still echoed in her ears. Every time she blinked she saw that awful pyre, which was scorched into the backs of her eyelids.

Melissa glanced over her shoulder at Porphures. She would not forget him gore-streaked in battle, but now, after cleansing himself in a clear mountain stream, with a small boy riding on his shoulders, he looked so much like a loving father. It gave her something to grab onto lest she drown in the darkness threatening to swamp her soul.

Behind Porphures, Ergates limped while holding the hand of a young girl. Melissa looked away as tears blurred her vision. It was a genuine miracle that Ergates still survived. She kept her eyes on the path and chastised herself for doubting that the gods were good.

She raised her head and glared at Drimutes, who walked at the forefront of the column. She lowered her head lest her rage overwhelm her. Shocking her, and she suspected, everyone else, he had fought like Ares himself. But his valor was not without stain. She and the other women had been keeping the children together while the men hacked at the undead barbarians.

Drimutes had spun toward her with his sword, ready to strike and with murder in his eyes, then he had looked beyond her, and the homicidal moment had passed. He had waded back into the fray. She had risked a glance behind her and had seen Ergates watching. She reckoned that some treacherous servant had gone whispering to Drimutes about her gift to Porphures. On the other hand, long before the handsome commander had arrived, Melissa had felt sometimes that her husband wished her dead.

The call to halt rippled from the front towards the rear of the column. Melissa craned her neck and saw that the pass ran into a set of stone steps, which climbed as lofty as a house. Three men stood on the landing above. Behind them, the passage darkened into the mountainside as if it was a cave.

Melissa had never before seen one, but she assumed that the trio were mystics. They wore white skullcaps and flowing robes of the same color. The one standing in front had a snowy beard that hung to his belly. The other two stood behind this wizened man, their beards brown and grown only to their chest. Each held a staff as tall as himself in their right hand, the butt end flat against the landing.

The intense relief nearly caused Melissa to swoon. They had made it. These holy men would usher them into their stronghold, and she would be reunited with her daughter, whom Drimutes had insisted on sending into the mountains, along with the other blossoming virgins of the polis, so as to prevent any violations by the tribute assessors. The mystics were expert at attending to young women, as it was the custom to send excess daughters from a family into their care.

Ergates stepped next to Melissa. He gave her a dark look, and she knew that he also believed that Drimutes had meant to kill her.

"The mantis is gone," Ergates said.

"What was his name?" Melissa asked.

"No one thought to ask."

Melissa cocked her head. "No one asked his name and where he was from?"

"And still more strange; no one has thought to ask why no one has thought to ask."

As she watched Drimutes ascend the stairs, she found it hard to believe that her husband would be so submissive, but right now, before her very eyes, he was doing the bidding of the mantis, handing the blackwood box over to the ancient mystic.

The mystic opened the box, then handed it to one of the younger mystics. The ancient mystic drew a scroll from the box. He unrolled the scroll and held it close to his eyes.

"The true reason we are here. To deliver a message," Ergates whispered.

"What else might lie in the box?" Melissa asked.

The ancient mystic re-rolled the scroll and placed it back in the box. He closed the lid, and shaking his head with a steady palsy, said something to the younger mystic who was holding the box. That mystic stepped forward and announced, "The impious may not tread on sacred ground. You are forbidden from progressing further."

Confused objections exploded from the train of survivors. "By Phoebe..." Melissa gasped.

She saw Drimutes charging up the stairs, ranting and waving his arms. The other young mystic, the one not holding the blackwood box, with blinding fast motion, twirled and rammed the butt of his staff into Drimutes' chest. Drimutes fell into the townsmen below him.

From behind she heard Porphures shout terse commands. He passed her, sword drawn, "Come, Ergates!"

She watched her son follow the commander and his soldiers as they worked their way to the front. The young mystic drove back townsmen with his stunning staff while the other two retreated into the dark passage.

Porphures appeared on the steps. He ducked a sweep of the mystic's staff and shouted a command. A second later, a pair of javelins arced over him and pierced the mystic. Porphures rushed up the steps and shoved the transfixed mystic off the landing, then man plunging into the chasm and out of sight.

The toddler in Melissa's arms started bawling and she looked behind her at the terrified children. Many were straying near the precipitous drop. She shuffled along the path, herding the children against the cliff wall, exhorting dazed women to help her.

Marshalling the women and children had left her exhausted by the time Porphures descended the stairs. She scrutinized him as he edged towards her. He was not bloodied, but she could imagine the smattering of fresh bruises under his leather armor. She could tell by the sorrow in his warm eyes that he had bad news for her.

"Ergates?" she asked.

"Is safe," he said.

She closed her eyes and felt the tension drain out of her.

"The mystics have fled into their stronghold. Their gate is too stout to force," he said.

She opened her eyes, understanding his meaning. They were trapped now, with the undead barbarians not far behind them, flooding up into the mountain.

"It is not hopeless," he said. "Come, let us gather the children."

Melissa ascended the steps last, the toddler still in her arms, which had gone numb from the burden long ago. She was surprised to see that the landing did not lead into a cave, but rather a short tunnel. On the other side, the pass widened into a small plateau, with a man-high brick wall running along the chasm side. Polished stone benches and tables were clustered around an oval-shaped altar, which dominated the middle of the plateau. The white altar was chest-high. In its center there was a soot-blackened depression.

At first Melissa could not reconcile the size of the milling throng to the few who had survived the devastating flight from the polis. Then she began to recognize the girls that the elders had sent into the temporary custody of the mystics. She spotted Ergates sitting with his back to her. His arm was draped around the shoulders of a girl who sat hunched over, her forehead inches from touching the table before her.

Melissa recognized her daughter's sleek black hair. "Sunnoia," she said.

She hurried over to her daughter, as Sunnoia turned at Melissa's approach. Sunnoia leapt up and the two women fell into each other's arms. The toddler, crushed between them, let out an angry squeal. Laughing, Melissa withdrew enough to hand the toddler to Ergates, then she pulled Sunnoia back into her weary arms.

Sunnoia, sobbing, whispered of rape and of rites both orgiastic and blasphemous. She spoke of molested virgins escaping the stronghold during the recent skirmish.

"They come!" a soldier called out from the tunnel.

"Mother, who comes?" Sunnoia asked.

Porphures trudged through the darkened tunnel and stopped on the landing. A torch wedged into the rock wall above his head, cast flickering light on the staircase. Halfway down, Drimutes sat alone, using his dagger to whittle a point on the recovered staff of the slain mystic.

Drimutes stopped carving and looked back over his shoulder, then turned back to his work. "Commander," he said upon seeing Porphures appear.

Porphures was bone-tired. On the other end of the tunnel, he was unable to keep from stealing glances at Melissa. Drimutes surely had nothing to say to him, so he decided that he might as well seek respite here, while waiting for the next wave of barbarians to arrive. His knees crackling, he sat down on the landing.

He massaged his aching thighs and listened to the rhythmic scrapes of Drimutes' blade against the ash staff. He could feel the weight of the puffy bags under his eyes.

"I did what I thought was right," Drimutes said in a sudden burst.

Porphures did not know what to say. Drimutes resumed his whittling.

"Aye," Porphures said.

"For the polis." Drimutes took a raspy breath. "My father's father founded the polis. He was born and raised in the capital. He loaded all his possessions and his entire family onto wagons and led them as far away as he was able, until he found this good land."

"He wished to live beyond the reach of the Long King."

"Aye," Drimutes said. "To live free. To enjoy the fruits of one's labor. He built the first houses. He sired the first children born in this land. He convinced others to come. The polis grew. Trade arose between the townsmen and the damnable mystics. The first tribute assessors came, with swords and with chariots, when I was a small boy. My father debated whether or not to move on, to cross the mountains and begin anew. My father was a great man. He traveled to distant lands. He returned from those excursions with strange goods, and rich flocks, and Melissa. He said that my mingling with her would produce strong children."

"Ergates is a noble and good youth."

"Aye. He favors his mother," Drimutes agreed.

Porphures did not say it, but he judged the boy fortunate in that regard.

"In that way, he is fortunate," Drimutes said.

Porphures managed to keep quiet, but he could not stop a bemused smile from spreading over his lips.

"All our work, my grandfather's, my father's, mine own, it ends here," Drimutes said and stopped whittling. "I should have foreseen the mystics' treachery."

Porphures could not bring himself to say comforting words to Drimutes, not even to tell him that this calamity was not his fault. Drimutes resumed whittling.

"We have more than enough warriors to hold this passage," Porphures stated.

Drimutes uttered a dry chuckle. "I may be no soldier, Commander, but I can see clearly that we possess no options which do not end in destruction. Should we hold the passage, we shall starve. Should we descend, they will surely overwhelm us."

"I fear some may cast themselves into the chasm," Porphures said as he stared at Drimutes' slumped back.

Drimutes froze for a moment, then tested the sharpened point with the ball of his thumb. "I shall die in this very spot. No foul barbarian will step foot on this staircase before I am slain."

Porphures rubbed his temples. He did not believe that their situation was as hopeless as Drimutes seemed to think. Tactics blurred through his mind. He intuited that there must be a way to combine tactics into a winning strategy—if he were not so exhausted...

Porphures raised his head at the sound of racing footfalls. A moment later, the forward scout came sprinting into the sphere of torchlight. "They are coming!" he called out.

Drimutes stood up and readied his newly-finished spear. The scout dashed up the stairs and into the tunnel while shouting the alarm.

Porphures struggled to his feet and drew his sword. He descended, his tired muscles protesting each step. He stopped at the bottom of the stairs and stood shoulder-to-shoulder with Drimutes. "Let them come," he said through gritted teeth.

Melissa raised her heavy head. The effort seemed great and it took what seemed like forever before her gaze was level. The insides of her skull felt dark and thick. The dampened sounds of the battle on the opposite side of the tunnel would not permit her to fall into a complete stupor.

She stroked her daughter's soft hair as Sunnoia lay next to her on the stone bench. She had leaned into Melissa's body and fallen into a light sleep ruined by twitches and whimpers.

Melissa rebuked herself for wallowing in despair when her precious child, having disclosed tearful and stammering revelations of the mystics' abuses, had already suffered far more than she had in less than half the years.

She gazed into the flames dancing on the oval altar. She reminded herself that she had birthed two fine children and was the wife of a chieftain. She looked at the terrified and exhausted refugees—children, girls, and women—huddled together on and around the stone benches. Melissa reckoned she was more fortunate than most, certainly more fortunate than every woman she had ever met. Melissa knew she was not the first to marry a cold man who was quick with the back of his hand.

Her eyes lighted upon one of the molested girls, now an orphan, who tossed and turned on the hard stone ground, alone. The girl was miserable, and flinched at every battle shout that carried through the tunnel. Melissa called the girl over and eased her into a place on the bench beside her. Sunnoia did not wake.

Melissa rose silently and picked her way through the clusters of non-combatants and paused at the mouth of the tunnel. The fight appeared to go well, the men holding the tunnel entrance, the fresh rotating with the spent, a stratagem that Porphures had installed, although she had heard that her stubborn and murderous husband was refusing to rest.

She listened to the shouts and grunts of the men, the slicing of blades and thuds of spears into diseased flesh, and she imagined the unnerving silence of the risen dead. Porphures had seemed undaunted, but the fatal countenances of many of the menfolk told her that the main host had arrived, and so custom dictated that the women and children shiver in the dark until the men failed.

She touched the dagger sheathed and hanging from her belt. She would not cringe in the shadows and wait for the starving dead to butcher and devour her. When the time came, she planned to muster her peers and rally them to fight with their knives, and if need be, their hairpins and fingernails. She bared her teeth and vowed to stay ready.

Stepping past the altar, she worried again that they might be committing some arcane sacrilege by burning wood in its cavity. With the potentially blasphemous fire burning, she feared to pray lest she offend the gods.

She approached the brick wall and looked beyond the black chasm, and tried to locate their abandoned polis under the starless sky. There were no cookfires, no lamp-lit houses to mark the location.

Looking at the nothingness, an unbroken black void, as if her home had never existed, her urge to pray dissipated. Ergates would die fighting. The gods would not even allow Sunnoia time to heal, much less the opportunity to birth her own children. She understood clearly now that the gods were cruel.

Her last shred of doubt concerned Porphures' late arrival in her life. She judged that if the gods had sent him to test her, then her constant day-dreams, about the many ways a husband could die and open the way for a new husband, had proved her a sinner.

But she could not discount the possibility that Phoebe, in return for her devotion, had granted her a boon. Perhaps without her yearning to seem worthy to Porphures, by now she might have cast herself into the chasm. Perhaps Phoebe meant her to understand that where there was life, there was also hope.

She heard scratching on the other side of the wall. She looked around and saw that she was alone at the wall. She frowned. She had not touched it.

She inched forward, intending to peek over the edge, when a flayed and bloody hand clamped on the top brick before her.

She sprang backwards while a strangled yelp burst from her mouth. The brick scraped loose under the mangled hand, then both flicked back out of sight. Something heavy thudded into the lower part of the wall. She stood, listening hard as silence followed. "No," she said.

She ignored her heart spasms and rushed to the altar. She plucked a half-burning stick from the fire and ran to the wall, to hold the torch over the drop. Dozens of yellow and bloodshot eyes glistened in the torchlight. Hunger-contorted faces glared up at her. One of the maniacal climbers yawed backwards, flailing without a sound, and while staring at her, plummeted out of the range of the torchlight, to be swallowed by the lower darkness.

Melissa flung the torch at the nearest climber, who had reached the bottom of the brick wall and was angling towards her. Sending up a shower of sparks, the torch bounced off the back of the climber. The torch threw off an orb of feeble light as it sank into the chasm, revealing swarms of the risen dead scaling ant-like up the craggy canyon.

She turned to sound the alarm, but shrieks of fear drowned out her voice. The women and children surged to her side of the altar as well. Through the chaos, she saw an undead barbarian lurch up to his feet, his broken arm dangling, while another one lay at his feet, convulsing, his body too fractured to rise. Melissa looked at the cliffs above. The risen dead were scaling downward, with more losing their handholds and tumbling toward the plateau below.

Melissa pushed through the terrified throng and found Sunnoia. She grabbed her daughter by the shoulders. "Go, tell Ergates!" she shouted and watched Sunnoia dart into the tunnel. She turned her back on the barbarians who were falling to the plateau to then begin climbing and struggling over the maimed, if their bodies allowed.

She drew her dagger and stalked toward the first barbarian scrambling over the brick wall. As she plunged her blade into his belly and felt the hot gush of fluid drench her arm, she thought it did not feel much different than disemboweling a bull either for a meal or sacrifice.

After performing a series of quick incisions, she jerked the knife free and his guts splattered on the stone floor. She ignored his weak gropes as he fell. Turning, she saw a hand appear on the wall. Melissa stabbed her dripping knife into the ragged hand as it gripped a brick on the edge. The knife's tip sliced through skin and slender bones and slammed into solid brick, the sudden stop sending a shock of pain vibrating up her arm.

She held onto the dagger as it rebounded off the brick and ripped free of the wounded hand. She watched long enough to be sure that her victim had fallen from the wall, then she hurried to the next attacker.

A barbarian had gotten his arms over the wall. He was hanging by his armpits and was trying to boost himself over. His face was a mask of blood, the tongue lolling out like a dog's, the eyes yellow and red, filled with hunger.

Melissa seized him by the hair and wrenched his head back. Most of his greasy long hair tore loose from his scalp in a grimy mass, but enough remained rooted so that her maneuver exposed his neck. She slit his throat with a practiced slash and dodged the arterial spray. She lashed her hand downward, flicking off most of the disgusting hair, which slapped against the stone ground. More barbarians breached the wall on either side of her. She turned to call for help.

Crippled barbarians were dragging children down to their snapping jaws. Some women were beating at battered and hobbling attackers, as others stood paralyzed. The risen dead continued to tumble onto the plateau, bowling into friend and foe alike, splashing in the spreading pool of blood. The chorus of grating screams did not drown out the cracking and splintering of bones and the popping of joints torn from sockets. A frantic woman, so gore-splattered that she was unrecognizable, fled past Melissa and leapt over the wall in hysterical terror.

Rage blinded Melissa. A hand grabbed her shoulder and she tore free and unleashed a frenzied assault on her attacker, as she let out a scream of fury.

Ergates swung his sword from his heels, and with an upward arc he lopped the head off a crawling barbarian. The headless body collapsed at his feet, partly within the plateau side mouth of the tunnel. On the follow-through, Ergates' blade struck a nearby corpse, wedging into the body's shoulder. He worked the sword back and forth, then tugged it loose, nearly falling over from the effort.

He righted himself and swayed, as the first light of Helios penetrated the tunnel. He blinked, seeing no more attackers, either standing or crawling over the jumbled landscape of hacked and chewed bodies.

He staggered sideways and looked behind him. Halfway down the tunnel, a torch guttered in a wall sconce and cast a hellish glow over his mother. She sat with her back against the wall and her knees drawn up to her chin. Blood matted her hair and dappled her profile, and dripped from her soaked smock, which clung to her skin. Her dagger's blade spiked out of her clenched right fist.

Beyond her, Porphures stood guarding the opposite mouth of the tunnel. Ergates watched as long as he dared, but no more barbarians engaged the commander. Ergates began to hope that the other end might be clearing, too.

He turned back to his responsibility. There were no attackers in sight, so he leaned on his sword and took a deep, shuddering breath. He stepped out of the tunnel, naked and stinking, blue-tinged flesh dominated the slaughter.

Scattered among the barbarian corpses, the picked-over ribcages and eyeless skulls of the devoured, flashed ivory under the waxing sunlight. He recognized that the majority of the stripped bones were prepubescent. The barbarians' first assault on the plateau had devastated the children.

He scanned the abattoir. He saw severed and gnawed limbs, and torn and beheaded torsos, all soaking in a lake of gore. He detected no motion, not even one lone fly feeding on the blood. He looked up at the cliff face and saw no one. He moved along the periphery of the plateau, stepping over corpses, until he reached the brick wall. He looked over, and saw no climbers. He returned to the tunnel's mouth. "There are no more!" he called out.

Porphures raised a weary hand. "Check for risers," he said. "I shall scout ahead. If the way is clear, we shall build a pyre."

Ergates watched the commander descend out of sight, then looked at his mother. She was still sitting with her knees drawn up to her chin. He wanted to join her, to sit and think of nothing, but the commander was right. There would be more risers.

He turned and began to wade in, seeking the infected. His sandals squelched in entrails as he struggled to find solid ground. The blood was ankle-deep around the altar. When he found a relatively intact non-barbarian, he stooped down and slit that unfortunate's throat. He plodded through his grim work, telling himself that if the situation was reversed, he would want someone to do him the same favor. He prayed he would not discover Sunnoia.

He had worked three quarters around the altar when he heard fabric flapping above him. He looked up and saw the mantis crouching on a slight outcropping that was barely wide enough for a crow to roost on. Ergates' first instinct was to cast his sword at the hateful mantis, but the man was too high.

"How does it feel to be a hero?" the mantis asked, smirking, his wide-brimmed hat tilted down and shading his eyes.

"You did this," Ergates said, glaring at the man. "You baited us. You put it in their minds to climb up and reach us."

The mantis nodded. "You are sensitive indeed to the world around you, boy, but easily distracted as I have shown here today."

Ergates scowled, opening his mouth to respond. Before he could, however, he felt teeth against his bare ankle and pain filled his vision. He glanced down and saw a child, no more than a toddler, with yellow and bloodshot eyes, wedged fast between corpses but stretching his neck, his teeth sunk into Ergates' skin.

Ergates drove his sword straight down and through the child's head, and the teeth immediately released. Ergates stumbled away and looked up.

The mantis was gone.

Leaping from the landing, Melissa let out savage howl and drove a spear through the mouth of newly-risen Drimutes. Corpses broke her fall. Rolling to her side, she watched Drimutes' risen corpse twitch in final death.

"Mother!" she heard Ergates call out.

She stood up and ran up the stairs and through the tunnel. She stopped when she saw him, when she saw the faint blue tint to his cheeks, and she saw in his eyes that he had been bitten. "Gods no!" she yelled.

She heard Porphures pounding toward her and dropped to her knees.

"Kill me. Please!" Ergates cried.

"I cannot," Melissa sobbed.

"Commander…" Ergates said when he saw Porphures appear.

She bowed her head, unable to watch. She sensed Porphures step past her, then heard a bony *thunk*. A body crashed into her and sent her sprawling. Scrambling to her hands and knees, she saw Porphures on his back, a spear jutting from the center of his chest. He gripped the spear with both hands and feebly kicked his legs.

She looked at Ergates and saw a weighted net drop around him and force him to the ground. Mystics encircled him as a quartet of mystics peeled away from the mob and seized her. They dragged her to the middle of the tunnel and pinned her down. She craned her head and saw another group surrounding Porphures, stabbing him with long knives.

The ancient mystic bent over her, his crinkled, bearded face blocking all else out. "You will receive the great honor of entering into the *mysterion*," he told her. "We shall record all that happened here, but you must never speak of it." He drew a razor from his robes. "To insure your silence, we must take your tongue. But be of good cheer, we shall nurture both your son and his transformation."

As the razor came down and blood filled her mouth, a single tear rolled down Melissa's face.

BLOOD AND THUNDER

KELLY M. HUDSON

When the man named Tom Wales came walking across the sand-blasted horizon, his long duster flapping in the swirling wind, neither of us were sure if he was going to be our doom or our salvation. In the end, I guess, he turned out to be a little of both.

He was a tall man, with angular features, born of rough-hewn stock from the mountains of Kentucky, and every bit of him was as tough as dried-out jerky. He had a hard way about him in every particular aspect. He had hard eyes, a hard stance, hard hands, hell, even his teeth seemed hard. He wasn't prone to humor, but he could surprise you now and then with a joke. At least, I always thought they were jokes. I could have been wrong. The main thing about him I remember most, though, was his eyes. They were gray like flint and betrayed nothing. When he looked at you with those eyes, he could be thinking about giving you money or killing you. There was never any way to tell.

My name is Randolph Carter, but most call me Randy. I come from Texas, on the western side, near New Mexico, and like everybody else left alive in this world, I got a story. But like most, my story is boring as hell, up until the dead rose and started chomping on the living. After that, everything changed quite dramatically.

I'm twenty years old and short. I used to be called Randy the Runt, but that was before, when the world was pretty normal, back when the dead stayed in the grave and didn't have the impertinence to rise again and chew on the flesh of the living. My height was never a problem with the ladies, though. I'm very handsome, with my blonde hair and blue eyes and cut physique. I had a friend in high school used to call me Hitler's Wet Dream. I suppose I was. But again, that was before. Now I'm just like everyone else, lucky to be alive and unlucky to be living. These are terrible times, the kind that do more than try a man's soul. They're apt to tear it apart.

I was with another guy, a boy named Paul. He was taller than me and strong as a mule, but he was maybe sixteen at the oldest. Paul was slow, and not just in how he moved. Sometimes I wondered if maybe he wasn't one of those zombies, just more clever than the rest. He was good in a fight, though. He could hammer the shit out of just about anybody or anything. Which was good, but it wasn't good enough for the predicament we were in.

Me and Paul, we were surrounded by about fifteen of those dead things. Some call them zombies, others have more and varied colorful names for them. I go back and forth. Zombie is the best fit, but sometimes I can be creative, too. I was having one of those creative moments right then, as a matter of fact, just as Tom Wales crested the hill and laid those cold gray eyes on us.

"Goddamn pus pickles!" I shouted, more out of desperation than any kind of heroism.

We didn't stand a fart's chance in a tornado. Despite my good looks and Paul's superior strength, there were too many for us. We would have died there if not for Tom and his intervention.

The zombies were generally pretty easy to kill, unless they got you cornered with superior numbers, which was how they had me and Paul. We were at the edges of the desert, somewhere either in New Mexico or Arizona, having paused at a rest stop along the highway to see if we could pilfer any food from the vending machines. They were empty, of course, but we had to try. Plus, we could refill our water bottles for the trek ahead. I decided to go ahead and take my last civilized dump before we got out into the wild, but was deterred when I discovered all the toilets were overflowing with things I couldn't describe. Also, there was no toilet paper left, and I'm not one to take a dump without something to wipe with. I was going to squat into a urinal and use a scrap of newspaper I found when Paul gave out a shriek like a woman having a baby. I yanked up my britches and ran back outside, only to see about ten of those things coming for him; there was no time to get an exact count.

I grabbed Paul by the arm and pulled him back with me. I decided we should head on around the back side of the rest stop and put the building between us and them. Only problem was, the desert pretty much surrounded us, and it was flat as a ten-year-old girl's chest, so there wasn't anyplace to hide. And one thing about zombies, once they spotted you, once you got on their radar, they wouldn't let go. They'd follow along, more dogged than a Texas Ranger.

Still, we had to think about surviving the next few moments and not worry about what came next. It was like that in this brave new world where there were more living dead than there were living. You had to keep moving forward. In the end, it was all that mattered.

Of course, when we rounded the corner, there were ten of those suckers standing around, milling about like a bunch of tourists with no place to go. Once they saw us, though, they began to get some nasty ideas in those rotten heads of theirs. I never once saw a zombie that didn't want to eat a person. Not once. I've even seen some that were just heads, lying on the ground and baking in the sun, and when they saw me, those teeth started chomping and they gave off that low hum they did when the dinner bell rang. Dinner for them was us, and we now had nowhere to go.

The zombies came around the side of the building and we were trapped between them.

"Well, hell," I said. "Looks like we got a hard fight ahead of us." I balled my fists and got ready while Paul grunted, sounding more tired than anything else. That was another thing you had to watch out for in this new world: weariness. I've seen many a good man and woman lay down their arms or shoot themselves in the head. Good people, too, the kind you'd want next to you in a fight. Sometimes it just got to be too much and they had enough. Once a person got to that point, there wasn't much you could do for them except get out of the way.

The zombies pressed in. We couldn't run, we couldn't hide. All we could do was fight. I pulled out my little hatchet I carried in a case strapped to my belt. It wasn't big and fierce, but I'd gotten pretty good with it. I could carve the average dead fucker's head open really quick, and as we all know, once you kill their brain, they're done for. That and fire are the only sure way to get rid of them. I suppose high quantities of acid would work, too, but who had access to something like that?

Stupid, foolish thoughts. I get them all the time, especially when I'm close to death. But I'd never been closer than I was at that point.

And it was then I saw Tom Wales for the first time, over on the edge of the horizon, staring out at us. Something shook within me, like my bowels were about to let go when I laid eyes on him, but I pushed those thoughts away. I didn't have time to mull over such things.

The closest zombie snapped his teeth together and lunged for me. I caved in his skull with two quick blows and his brains dribbled out the hole I made. He fell to the side, his fingers still twitching for me as he tumbled to the ground. Paul was busy bashing in some heads next to me. He'd found a baseball bat when we'd gone through Houston weeks ago and put it to good use. The power behind those swings was enough to knock the head off of anything, much less a zombie. It didn't take but one smack to do mortal damage. The first zombie's brains exploded out its ears from the concussion of the blow and the second one (a woman) had her rotted head cracked open. Her brains hung for a moment, dangling out like threads of spaghetti, before finally falling.

But there were too many, like I said. And despite me chopping down another two of them, they pressed into us and it went from a fight to kill them to a fight to keep their teeth from chomping you. If they bit you, it was all over. Oh, not at first. It took some time, depending on the health of the person. But I never saw anybody last more than three days after a bite. They got the fever and the chills and then they shit themselves to death. It wasn't pretty. And it was a hell of a bad way to go, because once you went, if your buddy didn't take care to smash your head in, you'd come back as one of them, and you'd stink of dried shit for the rest of your days.

Teeth nipped at my nose as this one ugly bastard lurched forward past the last one I killed and got in real close and personal. His face was smushed, like a bulldog, with his eyes pushed out and to the side, bulging like poached eggs stuck into the sides of his head. His teeth jutted out with no lips to cover them, so they clicked together like a tap dancer's shoes. He stunk to high heaven, a combination of rot and boiled flesh.

I backhanded him, sticking my leg out and tripping the ugly wretch so that he fell to the ground in a heap of moldy bones and clothes. But my victory was short-lived as the zombies behind him lunged for me, and I knew it was only a matter of seconds before one of them got hold of me.

A loud crack snapped over the air and three zombies next to me all fell as one, their brains popping loose from their heads like zits being squished. The gore washed up against me like a tidal wave and I gagged for a second, the stench of those rotting brains too much to bear.

Paul rallied next to me, grabbing two zombies by the head and smashing them together. Their skulls crunched like potato chips stomped by a boot and he let their bodies crumple to the ground as he spun to maul a couple of them coming up behind us.

More zombie heads exploded all around us and pretty soon, it was like we were standing in the middle of a bunch of water balloons. We were drenched in blood and brains as if it were raining on us. I kept fighting, and so did Paul, and before we knew it, those dead fuckers were dead for good, all heaped around us in a tangled mess of body parts and steaming brains.

Tom Wales was twenty yards away, guns pointed our way, smoke drifting from the barrels all lazy-like.

I dipped my head and smiled.

"Thank you, sir," I said. Like I said before, you could never tell if the man was going to nod to you or shoot you, not by the look in his eye. And I sure didn't want to come all this way and get shot for not properly thanking somebody for doing a good deed.

Paul grunted next to me.

"My name's Randy, and this here is Paul. Don't mind him, though, he don't talk much. I used to think he was mute, then I thought he was re-tarded. Now I just don't know," I said.

Paul punched my arm—hard. He didn't like when I said things like that about him.

Tom walked towards us, around the pile of dead bodies, and past us. He didn't say a word. I wondered at the moment if he was like Paul, a man prone to silence. What I didn't need to think about was what his guns could do for us. A fellow like that, he was a good shot, and he seemed to have plenty of ammo. In this world, what with all the pus pickles and scavengers, Tom Wales was the kind of friend any man would cherish.

So I ran after him.

"Mister," I said. "We sure do appreciate what you did. You think it'd be okay if we maybe walked with you a while? We seem to be headed in the same direction."

Tom stopped and looked right through me.

"Which way are you going?" he asked, his voice as cold as his eyes.

I pointed west. "That way," I said.

"I'm going that way," he said, pointing southwest.

"Yeah," I said, changing my pointing finger to follow his. "Like I said, we're going in the same direction."

He studied me for a long time, long enough for Paul to creep up behind me. One of the many good things about Paul was his loyalty. He had my back, regardless of the circumstances. We'd been in a lot of tight scrapes together and I was always thankful for him.

"You scavengers?" Tom asked.

"No, sir," I said. "We're survivors. We've been wandering for months now, trying to find someplace safe. Someplace that doesn't have any goddamn zombies running around."

"Ain't no such place," he said. He spat a wad of tobacco juice onto the chin of one of the dead zombies. Up till that point, I hadn't noticed he'd been chewing.

"It would be good if we traveled together, though," I said. I didn't want to beg, but I would have. "Three can keep each other safer than one or two. We can keep watch through the night a lot easier."

"I've been doing okay by myself," Tom said. "I don't see the advantage of a partnership."

"Well, Paul here, he's strong, see. And like you noticed, he don't talk much, so that's a good thing, if you like your peace and quiet. And I'm fairly smart and we're both good in a fight."

He didn't seem impressed. Maybe it was my small stature that left him a little under-whelmed.

"Plus," I said. "I don't sleep much. I only need about four hours a night. I've been that way since I was a little kid. So I could pull most of the night watch, when we needed one."

"Can you cook?" he asked.

"What?"

"Can you cook?"

I never had to answer a question like that before, but right then, the truth didn't matter. I would figure something out down the road, if I had to.

"Yes, sir. Best damned cook at Denny's, back when there was a Denny's. You ever eat at one of them?"

Tom nodded. "Gave me bad heartburn."

"Well, now, that wouldn't have happened, not at my Denny's," I said. Why in the hell had I picked Denny's? I should have brought up some fancy restaurant from back when the world was normal. But I guess you go with what you know, and I knew the menu at Denny's like the back of my hand.

Tom shrugged. "I'm going that way," he said, pointing west now. "I don't own the road."

He walked off and it took me a minute to realize that, while he wasn't exactly enthused to have us along, he also wasn't running us off, either. Or shooting us.

"Come on," I waved to Paul. "We got us a new friend."

* * *

We walked for hours through that hot sun, the sweat pouring off us like Mary weeping over Jesus, until the sun started to settle in the distance. We didn't pass much of any interest, just a few burnt-out husks of some cars and some dried, desiccated bodies. It was that way everywhere. There wasn't much to see, and then all the sudden, along would come some zombies, or a bunch of folks intent on robbing you.

Let me tell you, these weren't fun times to live in.

When the sun got so it was lighting up the western sky with shades of burnt orange and scarlet reds, we decided it was time to find some shelter. There was some good things about being out here like we were, where the land was flat in all directions. Nobody could sneak up on you, least of all zombies. If they tried, you could see them coming from miles off on a clear day. The bad side of it was the nights were colder than a witch's tit and it was hard to find a spot to hole up in. Usually, me and Paul would stop when we found some deserted place, like we thought the rest stop back there had been, and wait until morning. That hadn't worked out so good, as you know.

We sat in the sand and didn't have much to say to each other. I decided I didn't like the silence, so I got to talking.

"How about I go find some twigs and branches and such," I said. "We can have a good little fire to keep us warm."

Tom shook his head.

"Well, why not?"

He stuck a plug of tobacco in his mouth, swished it around some, and spat out a big wad.

"You seen any trees lately?" he asked.

I had to admit I didn't.

"But maybe we could find something else. An old house or a car or something that's flammable," I said. "Anything would beat the cold we're feeling. Plus, we could see if any zombies try and creep up on us."

"No, we couldn't," Tom said. He spat another brown chunk of spit onto the ground. "You light a fire and it gives you night blindness."

I hadn't thought of that. To tell the truth, me and Paul hadn't spent but a couple nights out in the elements since we'd set out on our little trek, and for those we hadn't had a fire, either. I hated those nights, when you only had the moon to see by.

I looked up. There wasn't going to be no moon tonight. I believe they used to call that the New Moon. I never understood that reasoning, seeing as there wasn't ever a moon to see. So how could you call it new if it didn't even exist?

"So we're just gonna sit here then, and let it get dark?" I asked.

Tom didn't say anything. He stood up for a moment, scanned the horizon in each direction, and sat back down, seemingly satisfied. He was dressed in a pair of old blue jeans, a pair of cowboy boots, that duster I mentioned before, and a black t-shirt underneath. He wore a backpack that had a bedroll lashed to the underside. What was in the pack, I didn't know, but I assumed it was ammo and nothing but. On his hips he wore his guns in holsters, like a real cowboy. I eyed those guns when he stood up and looked around. I didn't want him to think I was getting any funny ideas, but I was curious. They were Glocks, I could see that much. Other than that, I couldn't tell you much about them. I wasn't ever good with guns. I could shoot a shotgun fairly well, but hell, so could anyone. You just pointed and pulled, the buckshot took care of the rest. I spent most of my young life in school and then, when I got out, I had various jobs, none of which had anything to do with carrying guns. I didn't know about Paul, but I hadn't seen him ever act like he wanted a pistol, so I didn't question it much.

Tom pulled out his bedroll and set it up. It was just a thin blanket and it certainly didn't look warm. He laid down on it and used his backpack for a headrest.

"You got first watch," he said, and before I could say a word, a soft snore drifted from his face.

"He sure goes to sleep quick," I said, thumbing towards Tom and grinning at Paul. Tom snorted and the snore got louder. "No, sir. He don't waste any time."

Paul did the unthinkable. He kicked Tom's side, waking him. Tom sat up, his eyes red as hellfire, a growl on his lips.

"What?" he snapped.

"Uh," I said, and pointed at Paul, who leaned his head back and made some mock-snoring sounds. Tom got it.

"Sorry," he said, lying on his side. "Always happens when I sleep on my back."

And like that, he was out again.

I sat for a while, not saying much. There wasn't much to say. Paul was hell on a conversation, and the only other person willing to talk was sawing logs. I watched the sun set, absorbing each and every moment as the sky changed so many colors. There were a lot of fat, fluffy clouds floating by, and they moved like cotton blowing over a kitchen floor. They were white, then orange, then red, and finally purple, before they disappeared, the stars coming out behind them. I have to say, the stars were bright, and even without the moon, we could kind of see okay.

Watching that sunset put me in mind of the last time I'd seen something so pretty. It was hard to believe it was just two years ago, given how much had changed since. I had been watching the sun rise that time, not setting. It was the night of my Senior Prom, and my date, Sally Ann Watkins, was lying beside me on the hood of my car, an old Ford Mustang. We'd danced at the Prom, snuck in drinks and got properly shit-faced, and headed out to the quarry afterwards, where we let our tongues dance and our bodies follow. Sally was a nice girl but fairly plain to look at. I didn't mind, though, because even thought I was handsome, most girls didn't want much to do with me on account of my small stature. Besides, me and Sally had grown up as neighbors, until her family moved a few blocks away when we got to high school. We were close and it made sense we found each other when we both ended up without dates for the most important night of our lives.

It also made sense we'd lose our virginity to each other that same night.

I'm not ashamed to admit it took me so long. Lots of guys brag they lost their cherry a long time before I did, but I mostly think they're full of crap. Guys tell tall tales when it comes to women, and I wasn't in a big hurry, anyway. Sure, I wanted to do it, but the few girls I'd dated and tried with all shot me down. I never had a steady girl to keep working on, so it was basically a take my shot and see what happens kind of situation.

I didn't have to try too hard with Sally. We kissed and next thing I knew, her top was falling off and I had those succulent titties in my mouth. And then we were in the back seat somehow, like we'd teleported, and she was on top of me, her panties hanging from my left ear. She slid down on me and I'll never forget that hot wetness as it wrapped around me. I never felt so safe and loved in my life. It was over quicker than I wanted, but she didn't seem to mind. She smiled and laughed and we held each other for a long while. When the sun peeked over the horizon, we decided to get dressed and watch it.

I'll never forget the way she felt, all snuggled up next to me. It was the greatest single moment of my life. It was a shame we parted after that. She went off to college and I started up one those odd jobs I mentioned. In fact, we only talked to each other once after that night, and it was to wish each other well. Some nights, like tonight, I would think back on it and wish I'd done something more about the situation. But I knew if she'd wanted more, she would have said something.

Still, it was a regret wrapped in a warm remembrance, and it was in this memory I found I was drifting off to sleep. Blackness came quick, and I was happy for it.

I woke with a start, a rough and calloused hand over my mouth, pressing tight. I tried to scream but another hand grabbed my throat, throttling my intentions. My eyes flew open to see it was Tom who had his hands on me. His eyes were narrow and mean looking. As always, I couldn't tell if that meanness was meant for me or someone else. He leaned up and pressed his lips to my ear.

"Quiet," he whispered. "There's some of them around us."

He removed his hand and I listened. I could hear them, then, shuffling, bare and shod feet alike, kicking sand not more than five feet away. I never really understood how they knew when humans were around, but I always figured it was by smell or sight, and out here in the desert, with so much sand blowing around, it was hell on the senses. I had trouble seeing and smelling sometimes, so I couldn't imagine it was much easier for the pus pickles.

I sat and listened as hard as I could, trying to count how many different ones I heard. Once I got past twenty, I shuddered and stopped. I didn't want to know. After that many, the numbers didn't matter much. There wasn't going to be any escaping twenty or more, short of a shotgun and a handful of grenades, and even that wasn't much assurance.

I could see, like I said, but only about a foot in front of me. Once Tom had me awake and quiet, he leaned back, all silent like, and he might as well have disappeared. I couldn't tell if he was there or not. I wondered about Paul, if he was awake and being quiet like us two, but I couldn't really search for him.

I'd be lying if I told you I wasn't scared. It was maybe the second biggest time I'd been afraid for my life, and the first since the outbreak started. The worst was the initial night, when the dead rose and people were getting killed left and right. I was sealed up in that liquor store I worked in, huddled in the stock room, all the doors locked and the lights out, and I could hear the folks outside, howling for help. Some of them pounded on the doors but most of them were running past, like rabbits being hunted. It seemed to last forever, the cries of terror and panic, but eventually they all died off, only to be replaced by the moaning of the living dead.

They moaned then, when we were sitting alone in the desert, hoping we didn't have the bad luck of one of them stumbling over us. It was like being in the middle of a herd of cattle on the move.

Sand flew up next to me as a zombie stumbled. I felt the torn skin of its rotted leg brush my cheek. I stifled a scream. It paused, hovering close, and I could make out its long, gray form. All it had to do was look down and I was caught. It wavered, its body swaying back and forth. Twice its leg grazed a part of me, and both times I had to bite the inside of my cheek to keep from flinching or crying out.

The pus pickle staggered on, leaving me behind. I exhaled slow, my head spinning. To my right, I heard a slight sound, like a baby sighing, back in the direction Tom had disappeared to. It was followed by a low crack, like someone had stepped on a twig and was grinding it underfoot as quietly as possible. This was followed by the deepest silence I ever heard. It was so quiet, it was loud.

A wind picked up, spraying us with sand and then swirling off, following the zombies as they lurched away. They were gone within moments, off in search of warm flesh, never knowing how close they were to a mini-feast.

I didn't move the rest of the night, and when the sun peeked over the horizon, I glanced around to see what had become of Paul and Tom. Paul was fine, sitting just five feet from me, his eyes as big around as saucers. Tom was where I thought he'd been. At his feet was the body of a zombie, its head wrenched from its neck and slumped on its chest.

Tom was lying on the sand, snoring softly.

* * *

We ate a meal of some oatmeal me and Paul had scored some miles back. We mixed it with some of the water from our canteens, fried it over a fire we made, and let it slide down our throats. It was just enough to tease my stomach and make me even hungrier, if that was possible.

It was hard out here. Hard to find food, hard to keep it, and hard to go without it. I guess some folks might've dreamed about some big apocalypse where they'd have the whole world to themselves and it does sound good, until the food that's left spoils and the electricity doesn't work. Then you're screwed and that's where we were. That oatmeal was the last of our provisions, and I didn't mind sharing with Tom, seeing as he saved our lives twice, but when my bits were done and I saw him still eating, my stomach could've turned me into a Judas.

That's another thing about this God-awful world we live in. You might think you're a good guy, and you might try your best to do the right thing, but there comes a point sometimes where it's you and another person and only enough food for half of one of you. Then you find out real quick just how good and righteous you are.

I won't tell the story, 'cause I lived it and I'm ashamed of it, but I killed a man for food once. It was a while ago, and I feel awful about it, but it was either him or me. I know that for a fact 'cause he had the same look in his eye as I did.

So I did what I did, and that's all I'm gonna say about it.

Tom, he must've seen me eyeing him 'cause he smiled and let me tell you, if I thought for one second his eyes were cold, well, his grin was frigid. I knew I wasn't ever gonna try and test him, no matter what.

He reached into his backpack and pulled out a small bag of beef jerky. He tore it open, dropped a couple pieces in his mouth, and then handed the rest over to me and Paul. I couldn't believe our luck.

"Thank you, sir," I said and practically gobbled them down.

"Let 'em sit," Tom said. I must've looked at him queerly, 'cause he felt the need to explain further. "If you stick it in your cheeks, you can let it soak there, like tobacco, and the juices will feed you for a good long time."

I'll be goddamned, but that man was as right as Jesus.

We walked all day, not encountering much of anything. We passed by a couple more rest stops but they didn't have anything other than some broken down cars and dried-up bodies. We did manage to refill our canteens at one, which was lucky for us.

As we walked, I talked. Tom listened and grunted here and there, either to show me he was listening, or to tell me he didn't care.

"Yeah, me and Paul, we've been together for going on two months now. Is that right, Paul?" He nodded. I tell you, it was hell being stuck with traveling companions that didn't like to talk.

"So, yeah, we met back in Austin. Have you been to Austin?" Tom shook his head. I continued.

"Well, Austin sucks, and that's being nice about it. Whole place was just a-teemin' with fucking zombies, and the folks that were still alive were sealed up in buildings, not looking to let anyone else in. I guess they had a point and all, but it still bugs the shit out of me when people don't help others. Anyway, I found Paul there. And can you believe this big old, dumb son-of-a-bitch had a whole grocery store to himself?" I thumbed back at Paul, who grimaced at being called a dumb son of a bitch but grinned when I implied how smart he really was. Paul was like that. He was complicated.

"I don't know how he managed it, but no one ever tried to get in there, far as I could tell. Maybe they did and he killed them and folks got the idea that going over to the Save Mart was a one-way trip and decided to leave it alone. Me, I was from out of town, so I didn't know any better. I walked right up and pounded on the door. There weren't any zombies around, not right at that moment, anyway, so it was fairly safe. And here comes Paul, ambling up like he just can't believe what he's seeing." I laughed but no one else did.

"So I says, 'Open up, I'm hungry.' And that's what he does. He looks around, unlocks the door, and lets me in. That was the start to a beautiful friendship."

We walked a bit more, and when Tom didn't ask me how our little time in paradise ended, I decided to tell him, anyway.

"I bet you're wondering how we came to leave such a great place and end up here, out in the desert." When he still didn't take the hint, I shrugged and kept on going. Wasn't much else to do but walk, and talking passed the time.

"It was a sad day, but as they say, all good things come to an end. Our end was a motorcycle gang who decided they liked what they saw and wanted it. Me and Paul, we may not be the sharpest tools in the tool shed, but we know when we're outnumbered and outgunned. So we ran as fast we could out the back, but it didn't matter that we were giving up so easy, 'cause those bastards decided to give chase. We barely got away. To this day, I don't understand why they gave a shit about us. They got the store and everything in it."

"Cannibals," Tom said, as if it was the most sensible thing in the world.

"Pardon me?"

"They were most likely cannibals," he said. "They wanted to eat you."

I coughed and shook my head. I'd heard tales, but they were hard to believe.

"Men, acting like pus pickles?"

He nodded.

"I hope to God you're wrong, mister."

He didn't say anything, but for the briefest of seconds, a pained look crossed his face. I was going to push my inquiries further, but that's when we heard the gunshots, and our course of action changed forever.

They were over a rise about a quarter mile away. It was a small town, if you could call it that. To me, it was more a strip of about ten buildings along a road, with a few houses out back of them. Somewhere inside there, some one was shooting. We couldn't see them, but we sure could see the zombies.

There was about eighty of them, as I eyeballed them, and they were mostly clustered around a gas station at the front of the town. They clumped up together there pretty good and after another round of shots, I knew whoever was fighting, that's where they were fighting from.

I also knew that those folks were well and truly fucked.

But Tom didn't seem to think so and he pulled his pistols and jogged towards the area. There wasn't anywhere much to hide our approach and all a zombie had to do was turn around and we would be caught on sight. Still, they were intent on what was before them, not behind them, and despite their pernicious behavior, I never knew a zombie who had eyes in the back of his head.

Tom moved quickly towards the town, holstering his guns as he got closer. I guess he decided stealth was the best option, 'cause as he emptied his hands of the Glocks, and filled his right one with a machete he'd pulled out of his pack and his left hand with a hatchet hanging from his waist by a strap. He never bothered to look back at us to see what Paul and me were going to do.

I glanced at Paul and that dumb son of a bitch had ditched his backpack and grabbed his baseball bat. He was stalking after Tom, a big, hunched-over bastard with bad intent.

I watched them for a moment, then shrugged my shoulders and pulled my knife.

"Hell, don't bother waiting for me, boys," I said, as I jogged after them.

Tom was the first to attack. He slipped up behind two of them pieces of crap and slashed them both across their ankles, clipping their Achilles' heels. They both went down in a clump of dust. He moved on to another one, a few feet away, and did the same, chopping this one deep in the right hamstring. It tumbled to the ground.

I got what he was doing, and it made a whole lot of sense. Paul got it, too. He cracked three of them on their knee caps, taking away their ability to walk. We didn't have a lot of time; the element of surprise would only last a few seconds, probably less than a minute. If we could work through a number of them, immobilize the fuckers, then we could maybe make some headway on the rest.

I did my part. I slashed two zombies just below their calves. They were some tough, meaty ones, the kind that have been around for a good amount of time. Those things turn to gristle after a while and they don't rot the way they should. Most of them should be piles of compost by now, but for some reason they got longevity that don't make much sense. Maybe it's all the human meat they chomp on, maybe it's something else. In the end, it doesn't matter. It is what it is and you got to deal with it or get dealt with. I was too stubborn to give up yet, so I got busy doing some dealing.

Of course, my pus pickle wasn't being too cooperative. I cut the skin all right, and even got pretty deep, but I didn't do enough damage to make it fall. The damned thing turned around, its teeth gnashing together as it fixed to get a good bite of my shoulder. And it would have, too, if not for Paul. He saw my predicament and ran back to help me out. He swung for the fences with that one. Its head popped off and rocketed through the dry desert air, hitting the ground a good twenty yards away. It rolled off and ended up lying on the side of its head, its right ear resting against the hot sand.

Up ahead, Tom was making us look like damned fools. He'd carved through maybe a dozen of them before they caught on. Zombies ain't too bright and you can sneak up on them provided you're not wearing squeaky shoes. But even so, they're at their deadliest when there's a whole bunch of them, and despite our ninja-like maiming skills, there were still a lot left when they caught wind of us.

One of them, a nun, was the first to turn. She burped a dry gasp and the one next to her, a kid in a baseball uniform, saw us and made the same noise. It spread like rabies through the group until all of them were turned now, staring at us like ants marching on an abandoned picnic.

Tom threw his hatchet, splitting the nun's skull in two. Dry brains spilled out like moldy jelly, thick and heavy. He spun and used the machete to chop the little baseball kid's head off. He put the machete away and drew his guns.

The time for subtlety was over.

He mowed them down as they came. One, two, three, four, all the way up to almost fifteen before he popped his clips out and fished for more. Dead zombies lay in heaps all around, with more coming, heading straight towards him. Me and Paul, being good friends, weren't about to let our new pal take a fall. We ran up on each side of him, Paul with his bat and me with my knife. We had to do our fair share and besides, Tom had the guns and the ammo. We needed him a lot more than he needed us.

I'd say between me and Paul, we killed a good five of the suckers before his guns started roaring again. It was a beautiful sound, those shots, as they echoed across the sand and into the distance. It was a beautiful sight, too, seeing heads splatter and brains blow out high into the sky, or from the backs of their skulls, or from the sides, out their ears. As long as it was blood and thunder, it was a happy day.

The folks that were holed-up were in a gas station. Soon as they saw us coming, and all the zombie ass we were whipping, they ran out and decided to throw their weight into the matter. There were three of them and they didn't look like much from that short distance. I could see there was a fat Mexican with them, a woman so skinny I thought she might be a boy at first glance, until I saw she had some big ol' titties on her that threatened to tip her forward at any moment, and another fella who wore a business suit and a big, floppy hat, the kind Gilligan wore on that old TV show. The man in the business suit and the woman were armed with tire irons; the big Mexican had a big stick that reminded me of another TV show I was fond of when I was a kid: Walking Tall. I guess they'd run all out of bullets.

They dealt bloody vengeance, I tell you. One thing you learned in this screwed-up new world of ours was to kill and kill well. If you don't, hell, you're dead before you can even get started.

Between our two groups, we had the zombies pinned, with nowhere to run, even if they could. But they wouldn't, zombies never run away. They keep coming, like sharks, intent on eating what's in front of them, regardless of the odds or conditions. We cut through them, me and Paul, with Tom shelving his guns again in favor of that machete. At some point, he picked up his hatchet 'cause I recall seeing another zombie get its head split open, but it's hard to relate after the fact. Mostly what I remember was a blood-bath, with very little bloodshed.

These zombies were old enough now that when you cut them, they leaked like thick oil from a rusty car engine. The blood was black and congealed, coming out all ropy and curdled. We were covered in the gore and laughing about it all the way. I remember swinging that knife and kicking and punching every zombie I could get my hands on. It was a blur and then it was over in what seemed like the snap of a finger, and we were standing in the middle of over fifty zombies, the six of us, breathing hard and wiping the sweat from our brow. I was giggling and so was the woman. Everyone else seemed too tired to care.

Back behind us, the ones we crippled during our sneak attack were clawing at the sand, crawling towards us. Tom took them out, one by one, burying the hatchet in each of their heads. By the time he finished, I'd caught my breath and so had the others. It was time for introductions.

"I'm Randy," I said, sticking out my blood-caked hand for the woman to shake. I'm no fool. I make friends with the ladies first, just in case. She looked down at my hand like I'd just wiped my ass bare-handed after taking a particularly satisfying dump.

"I'm Wanda," she said, not shaking my hand.

"This here is Paul," I pointed at Paul. "And Tom." I pointed at him. "They don't talk too much, so I'm sure hoping one of you likes the fine art of conversation."

At this, the man in the business suit smiled. He had gold-capped front teeth and reminded me of someone I'd seen before.

"My name's Turner," he said. "And this fellow here is Barry."

That caught me by surprise. "A Mexican named Barry?" I asked.

"You got a problem with that, pendejo?" Barry asked, in perfect English.

"Nope," I said. I turned back to the white man in the business suit. "You look familiar. Do I know you from somewhere?"

His grin got so big I thought he'd swallow the sun.

"See?" he said, looking at Wanda. "I told you, honey. I was famous once."

Wanda rolled her eyes and walked away, back towards the gas station. She slung the tire iron over her shoulder and let it rest there, holding it lightly.

"Yeah, you know me, son," Turner said. "I'm Mighty Turner Burn, the rapper."

"Oh, shit," I said. I couldn't believe it. I should have known, what with the gold teeth. I glanced at Paul. "Turner Burn wrote that song, Big Bootie Ho's. It was real famous for a while."

Turner rubbed his chest. "You boys be nice to me, I might just rap you a few lines, show you my stuff."

Tom grunted and walked past us, following Wanda.

"What's his problem?" Turner asked.

"He's a vaquero," Barry said. "Cowboys don't talk much."

Barry went with Tom and the rest of us joined them. Me, I was happy as hell to have someone to talk to.

"Tell me about the good old days, Turner," I said. "You must've been knee-deep in pussy."

"You know it, son," Turner said, then he started telling his tall tales.

I could see why they'd gone to the gas station first. The place was a goldmine. I'd never seen a spot where nothing had been ransacked. It was like when the dead started walking and chomping, the folks in this town must have just run away together. No one stopped to stock up on anything, so that meant the gas station, with its little convenience mart, was stocked to the ceiling. Sure, the electricity had gone off, and that caused the meats and other perishables to spoil in the wall fridges, but all the other things, the junk food that was so crammed with preservatives they'd last through a nuclear war, that was all still there. That meant potato chips, goddammit, and candy, and for Tom, beef jerky that wouldn't quit. There was also cases of bottled water, which would come in handy, and sodas—which, despite being hot as hell, were still tasty, seeing as I hadn't had a Coke in a long time—and beer. Hell, yeah. Beer. I couldn't remember the last one I'd had, but I could sure see the first one I would enjoy.

By the time we got through sorting stuff and dividing it all out so that everyone got an equal share of what they wanted, night was falling, and that meant we'd probably need to hole up where we were. Which was just fine by me. I was looking forward to sleeping someplace with a roof over my head.

It got cold, like it does in the desert, and we decided to retire to one of the houses Wanda scouted out while we went through the goodies. She found a nice place, no zombies, with a fireplace and plenty of chopped wood to last through a winter. There was no electricity, but there was a sofa, a couple of beds, and a carpeted floor. Barry the Mexican fixed us a real good fire. With the shades pulled down, nobody could see inside and only the smell of the smoke gave us away. But hell, lots of places were still burning, places we'd left behind. The smoke wouldn't bring us any trouble.

We sat around in the living room, dividing up the watch so each of us only had to spend an hour outside, keeping tabs on things. We'd dug into our food and I was close to going into a sugar coma, what with all the Twinkies I'd ate and the Cokes I'd drank. That's when Barry broke out the beers.

"Cervezas," he grinned.

"Don't mind if I do," I said, taking one. Everyone but Tom filled their fists, and once the suds started flowing, so did the talk. We each told our stories, in turn, except for Paul and Tom, who remained silent. I spoke for Paul, though, and would've for Tom, but I didn't know a thing about him. I did tell how we were introduced and how there wasn't a finer man to have by your side in such trying times. I grinned, thinking I must've earned some suck-up points, but Tom never paid me much mind. He stayed by the windows, peeking out now and then, listening to us talk, but never joining in.

So each of them talked, and here's what they said, as best as I remember:

WANDA

"I was a waitress in Dallas, out at a Wendy's near the airport, and I didn't have much going on in my life when all the craziness came down. I'd just broken up with my boyfriend of one year, Eliot, and was feeling a bit blue about it. He was a good man, which was unusual for me, but he was also boring as hell, so I had to let him go. That night, the first night the danger came close, I wasn't doing too well. You all remember, the news was just full of stories about crazy people attacking each other, so most folks didn't go out at night, much less at all, and since I worked the overnight shift, that meant I wasn't making squat for tips. We'd get the usual cops and some military boys, but they never tip worth a damn.

"So anyway, that night, the first zombie I ever saw came walking right out of the bathroom and it turned out he was one of my only customers of the night, so there went that tip. Evidently, he went to use the toilet and had a massive coronary; at least, that's my guess. He could've had a stroke for all I know. What I did know was he looked just about the same as before he went in, except his skin was kinda gray and his eyes were glassy. He went straight for the cashier, bit the poor girl in the arm and tore himself off a chunk big enough to make a steak out of. The cops at a nearby table jumped to their feet and shot him in the head, but in doing so, some of their shots went astray, and they hit the cook and the manager, a geek named Marv who always tried to feel my ass. I wasn't too upset they died. In all the excitement, no one noticed at first they'd been shot and killed, so when they came back, they bit a couple of the cops and then it all went crazy.

"That was when I killed my first zombie. It was one of the other customers, a forty-year old businessman with a glass eye. I knew it was a glass eye the minute I saw it, and I don't know about you all, but when someone's got something fake about them, like a leg, hand, hook or an eye, it kind of creeps me out. Well, this businessman, I guess he got bit early on in the confusion and rose up quickly, his teeth chomping together, looking at me like I was more tasty than the Moon Over Miami I'd served him. Might be he was right, but he picked the wrong gal to fuck with.

"He lumbered over to me and at first, I froze, scared to death. I kept fixating on that eye of his and how empty it was. The thing is, the other eye, the good one, was turning the same way. I watched it cloud over with each step he took, until he was almost on top of me. I grabbed a clipboard on the counter behind me and spun around, smacking him on the side of the head. He pitched forward with a grunt and that glass eyeball of his popped out and rolled around on the counter like a marble, spinning in place. For some reason, I grabbed the eye and stuck it in my pocket and I've kept it there ever since, even though it got cracked a month ago and a piece broke off. It's my good luck charm.

"I ran right, jumped in my car, and started driving. I kept going until I ran out of gas and eventually, I found Turner and Barry. They're both nice, and I appreciate how they've never tried to rape me, which I hear is pretty common these days. They kept me safe from all sorts of bad things, but I'd like to think I've returned the favor.

TURNER

"Yo, you all know my story and shit. White boy from the ATL, come up out of the projects, my only friends a bunch of black kids with talent. We came up in the game, started out slinging drugs, turned out some chicks, and were having a real good time. Then we went and saw Jay-Z play up over in Charlotte and next thing I knew, it was like I was reborn. I didn't want nothing to do with 'that' life. I just wanted to tell my story, do my thang, rap out my lines. I was good, too, anybody'd tell you, for real. They called me the next Vanilla Ice, which kinda pissed me off at first, I won't lie. But then I went back and got his records and yo, that white boy was fly for his time. I held my head up after that. Weren't nobody in the game that was white and right but me and Eminem, and he's a sell-out fool. I made my records and wasn't nobody could touch me, even folks in my old crew. They came out, acting like I owed them something. I was like, better step off, you hear?

"I was the top of the world, then that tape came out of me pissing on those girls and that was it. I mean, it ain't right, yo. They was old enough. It wasn't like I was R. Kelly, pissing on some little girls. These were old women, all grannies and shit, and they liked it. But it crushed me, anyways, and it looked like I was out of the game. But here's the thing, yo, check it: I'm too big and too talented to not be in the game. MTV, they offered me a spot on their new reality show, The Big Bro Experiment. You hear of it? Naw, probably not, 'cause that stuff was so fresh yo, it hadn't even come out yet. It was about a bunch of us hip-hop moguls, all living under the same roof, with a fixed income and no amenities. It was like getting back to the streets, only it was all gonna be on film.

"That's why I was in Dallas, 'cause that's where we was gonna film it all. Matter of fact, I was on set, checking the house out, when some crazy bitch comes flying around the corner. She bit Snoop—he was gonna be the host—she bit him right in the ass. I laughed at first, but when he fell down, screaming for his life, the shit got serious.

"It all went to hell after that. I don't need to tell you folks. People started dying and zombies started rising, it was like a hip-hop Thriller video, what with all the beats playing in the background. I got the fuck up out of there and hit the road, and I been using my street survivor skills to stay alive ever since.

BARRY

"I used to believe in God, but now I don't know. If there is one, He's one big asshole. I do believe in the Devil, because I see him everyday, every time one of those dead things tries to bite me. They have to be from the Devil.

"I lived in San Antonio. I had a wife and three kids, all girls, and I worked as a car mechanic. I was good at what I did and was saving up money to get my own shop. I was living pretty good. I like America. I came across the border when I was a little kid with my mother, and she got caught and sent back but I got adopted. I don't know how or why that could happen, but it did. My new parents were white and they didn't like my birth name, Alejandro, so they called me Barry, after their favorite singer, Barry Manilow. You ever listen to Barry Manilow? He's good. I wonder if he got eaten, like so many others.

"My parents, they gave me a real chance in life and I took it. I went to college but dropped out when I got my girlfriend, Lourdes, pregnant. My parents were mad at me but it was okay. I worked hard and we got married and my parents forgave me, especially when they laid eyes on my little Rae, my first daughter. She had the prettiest eyes.

"I worked hard and like I said, I was always good with cars and engines, so I moved up. I even got offered the chance to work on a pit crew for an up and coming NASCAR driver. But I turned them down, because it meant I'd be away from home and my darling women. Me and Lourdes had three girls, Rae, Rochelle, and Rita, one year apart from each other. Rita was two years old when the dead started to come back to life. She died one night in her crib, smothered in her blankets. How that happened, I don't know. Later on, I realized maybe Lourdes killed her out of mercy. Lourdes was upset about the zombies. She thought they were God's judgment and we were all going to die.

"I don't know. Anyway, Rita was dead, but I didn't know it at first because she was back alive, you know? And…"

Barry started crying then, the poor bastard.

"I set her down to play with the other girls while I went to the garage to get something. The first thing she did was bite Rochelle and when Rae ran over, she bit her, too. I heard them all screaming and then Lourdes started crying and I came running, there was blood everywhere and I didn't know what to do.

"Lourdes did, though. She'd been in the bathroom when it all happened. She came out, saw the blood, and ran into the kitchen. She came back with a butcher knife. When I figured out what she was going to do, I tried to stop her, but she was too fast. She cut my hand bad."

Barry held his left palm up and showed us the scar.

"I fell down and hit my head. I wasn't knocked out, but I was dazed. By the time I got it together, my babies were hacked up and Lourdes was sawing on her wrists with the knife. She'd gone loco.

"There was blood everywhere. So I ran, and I haven't stopped, and I won't till I'm dead. That's why I don't believe in God anymore. Well, not really."

* * *

Those were their words, as best as I can remember. I wish we'd never shared our stories, once Barry finished. That beer didn't go down so good and began to feel all hot in my stomach. But I guess you've got to know the people you're running with, and it's best to know them up front. That way you can decide if you want to stick with them or not.

I slept like a rock that night and bitched like a rich girl when it was my time to get up and take watch. I wandered around outside, sitting and standing, sitting some more and walking, but I didn't see or hear anything, that is until it got close to the end of my time, and I heard a slight whimper come from the shed out back. Chills ran up my spine, but I didn't have a yellow streak to go with it, so I slipped on over and had myself a look. I couldn't see much, but I sure heard a lot.

It was Wanda. She was in there, getting it good from someone. Seeing as how the guy pumping her was so quiet, I figured it had to be either Paul or Tom, and since Paul wasn't the type to get a woman's panties off, I figured it must be Tom.

Good for him, I remember thinking. But I was also jealous. I'm not ashamed to admit it. I'm a man, and even though the world had gone to hell, it didn't mean I didn't have the same urges as before.

I went back and woke up Barry when my shift was over. When I got back inside and saw Wanda asleep in the corner, next to Tom. He was staring at me with those eyes of his. I never heard them go out or come back in. I nodded and smiled, and took my spot on the floor.

The next day, we went through all the houses, gathered up what supplies we could find, and huddled back together and went through the bounty at the original house. I have to tell you, we'd struck a gold mine. It really was like the folks in that town up and vanished, leaving behind all they owned. The whole deal reminded me of a story I heard a preacher tell one time, about the Rapture. In it, Jesus would come down and call the faithful home, leaving the rest of the world to stew in its evil, wicked juices. Times of calamity, disease, and judgment followed. Remembering that story, and seeing as how we found this little town, it made me wonder if this place was the only righteous area in the world, and God had called them up and left the rest of us to suffer for our sins.

It made as much sense as any other theory I'd heard.

We had ourselves a nice meal that night. Turner put together several cans of beef stew we found at different houses and warmed it over a nice fire.

"I was a good cook, once," he said, smiling broad, showing off those teeth. "When my career ended, I thought maybe this was the kind of shit I was gonna do. You know, go on some celebrity show and shit? But I never got the chance. Looks like I never will."

We ate well and felt full. We kept a regular watch on things, but there were no zombies around that we could see. After we were all stuffed and content, Wanda stood, saying she had a few words to say.

"I know we all don't know each other that well, but I want to tell you my intentions," she said. No one said anything, so she kept right on going.

"On my way out here, before I met up with all of you, I heard a radio broadcast, back when the radio still put out information," she said.

The TV's were the first to go, then the radio. I heard tell the internet was still up and running, but nobody was ever on it. I wouldn't know. I wasn't too fond of computers, so I never learned much about them except where all the free porn sites were. For a moment, as she talked, I wondered if I could find myself a computer and if one of those sites was still up and running. If so, I had myself a date.

"I heard of a preacher, from out west, who told of a place just south of San Diego, called Angelville, where lots of people had gathered and life was continuing as it had before," Wanda said. "It was my goal to make it there. It still is. I hope maybe I can convince you all to come with me. Maybe we can find this paradise together."

Nobody spoke for a long while. We just let the things she said soak into our brains like the stew was in our bellies.

After a time, I said, "I don't see why not. What the hell have we got to lose?"

"Well, white boy, we got a nice place here," Turner said. "We got enough food to last a long time."

"That's true," Barry joined in. "And from what I understand, there's been lots of talk about places like Angelville, and they've all been lies."

All eyes turned to Paul. He pointed at me, basically saying that where I went, he went. We all turned to Tom.

"Going beats the hell out of staying," he said.

More silence followed. Eventually, Turner said he would go along, and so did Barry. What else did they have to do?

We stayed a few more days right where we were, resting up and being happy.

On the third day, Tom took another one of his walks. He left in the early afternoon and didn't return until the sun was disappearing in the distance. None of us gave much thought or concern to his leaving; it was becoming old hat. Wanda cared the most, though. She'd go outside the house we were staying in, giving the horizon a good scan every hour or so, and come back in, disappointed. Each hour that passed made her look more haggard. I guess she was in love with Tom, which was the pits for me, 'cause I would've liked her to be in love with me, instead.

Eventually, he came back, like he always did. This time, he didn't look as grim as he usually did. He looked downright palsied. Tom called us all together and gave us a little talk. It was short and sweet, but the impact of what he had to say made all of us sick to our stomachs.

"A horde," he said, leaning against the living room wall, his eyes like flint.

"Chinga," Barry said, his eyes wide.

"I'll be damned," Turner said.

Wanda didn't say anything. She just sort of scooted over nearer to where Tom was.

"Excuse me for being the ignorant hick," I said, clearing my throat. "But what in the hell are you talking about?"

"A horde, motherfucker," Turner said, being his usual, helpful self. "The worst of the worst."

"Chinga," Barry repeated, crossing himself.

I looked around, still confused. I met Paul's eyes and he simply shrugged. He had no idea, either.

Wanda sighed. "I saw one once. They were moving along down Route 66. There must've been two or three hundred of them. They were all gathered together, shuffling along. I don't know where they were headed or why and I didn't care. I just steered clear."

"So I'm guessing a horde is a big ass group of zombies," I said.

"You can say that," Barry said. "I heard of them, but I've never seen one." He turned to Tom. "You say you saw them?"

Tom shook his head. "I saw where they'd been. Best I can figure, there was probably a hundred or more. Their tracks led off north, so I'm betting we're okay. But I could be wrong."

"Hordes destroy everything in their path that's human," Wanda said. "They're like locusts, and if you come across them, they will chase you until you give out."

"They're headed north?" I asked.

Tom nodded.

I sat back in my chair. "Good." I didn't like the idea of what I'd heard, but there wasn't much I could do about it. And besides, they weren't near us anymore, so we were okay.

Still, a part of me worried, like it always did. When it came to zombies, you could never get comfortable.

And not for the last time, I wondered why the hell Tom was always going off on his own.

We stayed in that town another couple of nights before we struck out again.

What lay before us was more desert. More sand and more hot sun. Before we left, Barry and Turner combed the town, looking for a car that would work, but what the people left behind was a bunch of junkers and vehicles drained of gas. It didn't matter if Barry could fix them up if there was no juice to run them on. So we gave up on that and went back to walking.

No one talked much. It was too hot. We made a few miles before night started coming up on us. Each of us had backpacks full of stuff so we didn't have to worry about water or food for a while, which was a nice blessing. You never know how much you take things like that for granted until you can't find it anymore.

At night, we set up camp. I noticed Tom walked way off in the distance, almost out of sight, back the way we came. I took this as my opportunity to chat with Wanda.

"So, you and him, huh?" I said, thumbing back at Tom. She was unpacking her bag.

"What of it, runt?" she shot back. She pulled a long beach towel out and flapped it in the wind, shaking it loose.

"I ain't judging. Just making sure I don't accidentally put my wiles on you and seduce you. I don't want to get shot or nothing," I smiled.

"You're a funny little man." It was a Spongebob Squarepants towel. The blinding yellow of his big, retarded face nearly blinded me.

"Why does everything have to be about my size?"

"I don't know, half-pint." She laid the towel out and sat down on it.

"There you go again. I'm beginning to take this personal."

"Good. I want you to know, no ifs, ands, or buts. I'm with Tom and I'll never be with you or anyone else."

"Well, you don't have to be mean about it," I said. She was really hurting my feelings.

"Yes, I do," she said. "You men, you don't understand anything unless it gets beat into you. So I'm beating it into you now like I did Turner and Barry before. There's no chance."

"Okay," I said, holding my hands up. "Jesus."

The others were about twenty yards away, fixing a fire for the food. It would be put out once it got dark. No sense in attracting any unneeded attention.

"Mostly, I wanted to make sure you were with him so I could ask you some questions," I said.

"About what?"

"About Tom."

"Talk to him, you want to know something."

"He's not exactly forthcoming with his words."

"So you figure he talks to the woman he's sleeping with."

"Tell me I'm wrong."

Her face screwed-up, like she was getting ready to blow a nose full of boogers into my face. Then she lightened up and relaxed, lying back on Spongebob's face.

"I suppose you're right. He does."

"I don't need to know much, just some basics."

"Like what?"

"Like, why does he do that, every night, even when we were back at the house? He stands off and to the side, looking into the distance, like he expects to see something."

She sighed. "That's personal."

"Well, goddammit, name me something that ain't personal in this fucked up world of ours?"

She chewed her bottom lip and caved. "I don't rightly know. All he'd ever say to me was that he had unfinished business, and was pretty sure it was following him."

"What the hell does that mean?"

She shrugged. "He won't say. I do know he used to be in the Army, and he was part of the group in Vegas."

Vegas.

Shit. We all knew about Vegas. That was one ugly scene, not that most of what went down once the dead rose wasn't.

Vegas was a real mess. The U.S. Armed Forces had decided to make their first stand against the living dead there and it turned into what those military folks affectionately called a FUBAR situation. There were too many tourists, too many families with kids, and too many zombies. When the regular folks got caught in the crossfire, that made more zombies.

I don't understand how we lost to a bunch of walking corpses, but we did. Not only us, but I heard tales of other countries falling apart, too. It was like a plague that, once it got started, there was no putting a stop to it. But Vegas, yeah, that was real bad, and it was then that I think everyone realized life as we knew it was over. Once the Army went down, with their tanks and planes and guns, what kind of chance did the rest of us have?

"Makes sense," I said, after chewing it over for a while. "He does have that thousand yard stare thing going for him. Is that what makes him so sexy?"

Wanda rolled her eyes and put her hands behind her head. The move made her boobs thrust up all sharp and delicious, and I knew she did it on purpose. She was showing me what I'd never have and also, by design, telling me that my looking at her tits didn't matter to her one bit. I might as well have been a dog or an old man, as far as she was concerned.

I gave up on her and wandered over to Paul. He was sitting in the sand, picking up handfuls and letting the grains run between his fingers. He seemed really caught up in what he was doing, so I left him to it. Sometimes I'd forget Paul was just a big kid.

Turner was running his mouth, telling Barry about a pair of twins he did, back when his record went gold.

"Oh, I was the man, dawg," he promised, flashing those teeth of his.

Barry listened, but you could tell it was a polite, half-listen kind of thing. Both of them were busy getting the food and their sleeping spots ready. I didn't really want to say anything to either of them. A blue mood had come over me so I decided to take a walk.

I didn't go far, but it was enough so I had some privacy. Thinking that made me laugh. Privacy. There was plenty of it to be had now. Along with plenty of flesh-eating dead and crazy humans. Not for the first time I felt myself on the verge of tears and I'm not ashamed to admit it. I cried the first night when I heard what was happening. It was like I woke up and I was in the start of some scary movie. But the movie didn't end; it just kept going on and on and on. I also cried the first time I killed a zombie. That may sound stupid, but despite what anyone might think, it's hard to kill something that looks like your next door neighbor, and in fact, was my next door neighbor. I thought he'd come over to borrow a power tool or something but what he really wanted was to chomp on my face. I beat him to death with a fire poker. It was the most disgusting thing I ever saw, his brains and skull spilt out all over my living room floor.

A cold wind rippled across the sands, swirling around and encasing me in its cocoon. I didn't mind so much. Sure, I shivered, but it was fitting. Life was a cold, cruel thing and one day, it would up and pull the rug out from under my feet like it does to everyone else. I just hoped I wouldn't come back as a zombie.

I was so caught-up in my thoughts that I didn't hear Tom sidle up next to me. Or maybe he was just that slick. Probably it was a bit of both, but when I turned and saw him, I nearly pissed my pants.

"Goddamn, you scared the bejesus out of me," I gasped. I thought I caught a slight grin from the corner of his mouth. But it was like watching lightning; there and gone in a flash.

"Wanda said you had some questions." His jaw was set and grim and he never looked at me when he spoke. Not then, and not in the ensuing conversation.

"Well, I wasn't trying to pry or nothing, but yeah, I am curious," I said, sounding a lot bolder than I felt. Mostly I was hoping he wouldn't shoot me in the head and walk off.

Tom didn't shoot me. He stood like a statue and hardly made a sound. When he finally did speak, it all came out in one long tumble, like he was the worst sinner on Earth and I was a priest hearing his confession.

TOM

"I grew up in Kentucky, down near the border with Tennessee. I was raised to be an Army man, through and through. My daddy took me hunting and fishing, teaching me skills that have saved my life time and time again. He did it because he was a racist, and he swore a race war was coming, when the Mexicans and the Blacks would rise up and put the white man down. He told me he was getting me ready for the day it happened, but he died of a heart attack when I was fifteen, so I guess he was spared something even worse.

"I joined the Army straight out of high school and never looked back. Despite how hard my daddy worked, I never bought his bullshit about Blacks and Mexicans. He was just an ignorant, backwoods redneck. But that doesn't change the fact I loved him.

"I did two tours in Iraq and one in Afghanistan. I've seen so much blood and sometimes I think it's all I see in my dreams. I've killed men, women, and children, and I've killed them for many reasons, but mostly to stay alive. Because that's what war is. That's what war does to a man.

"I was called back here, when it started to get bad. My unit, the 105th Ranger Regiment (we called ourselves Rangers 105), was shipped straight to Vegas. We were the vanguard of what was to come. When we won our victory over the living dead, we'd provide a template for the rest of this new war. But I suppose you know things didn't turn out like they thought.

"My unit, we were tight and I always thought we'd stay that way. There was Brick, who was a big black man built like a brick shithouse. And Bobby, who was great with bombs, a skinny toothpick from Georgia. Darren the Kid, who was the youngest and craziest, and Johnny, our leader. He was from Alabama, had the thickest accent, and was generally the toughest guy I ever met. They called me Outlaw, because my last name is like that Clint Eastwood movie. They were my brothers and I loved them like I loved my family.

"Until we got in a firefight outside the Bellagio. It was brutal. I won't bother with the details, but a lot of troops were turning and running, ignoring direct commands. Our unit was supposed to storm the east wing and rescue some people trapped inside but it was hard going, what with the other soldiers deserting or going berserk. No one will ever tell you this, but the real reason why we lost is two things: soldiers found it hard to shoot Americans, even if they were already dead, and soldiers lost their minds. I'd say a good fifty percent went crazy, and who could blame them. It was like something out of the Bible, all that bloodshed, and death, and bodies rising from the dead and eating the living.

"I never thought Rangers 105 would go that route, but I was wrong. When we went in to help those people trapped in the east wing in the Bellagio, we got caught ourselves. Some dumb shit outside lost it and started firing tank shots into the building. Before we knew it, the floor we were on collapsed and we were two floors down from where we'd started; with a whole mess of zombies. When they saw us, they got that look in their eye. You know the one; where you think maybe for a second they're not really dead at all, that there's still some intelligence in there. It's the kind of look that makes a man freeze just long enough for the teeth to get you.

"I won't go into details, but we were pinned in, stuck in a room we barricaded to keep the dead out. And during those few days, the Army pulled out and we were left behind. Leave no man behind. Yeah, right.

"The few days turned into a week and that turned into two weeks. We were barely surviving, and our rations had run out. To make matters worse, there was a family in the room next to us, also trapped. A man, probably forty, with a wife and two daughters, both teenagers. Sometime during our siege, Johnny went crazy. He got the idea that we shouldn't starve to death when there was food right next door. He was talking about the family, of course.

"Bobby was the first to join him and Darren wasn't far behind. That kid was always about living life and taking a risk, so killing some family he didn't know didn't seem that big of a deal to him. Brick was the last to join them, and when I said there was no way I was going to do it, they laughed. They thought I'd go along, like I always did. But I didn't.

"They bashed in the wall separating our rooms and killed the father right off. Shot him in the head so he wouldn't come back. Then they knocked around the Mom and the girls a little bit before Brick tied them up, using some rope we'd brought with us. They were made to watch as Darren skinned the father.

"They ate him, right in front of his family, no better than the zombies we were sent to kill. They didn't even bother to cook him. They just chopped off the fatty parts and went to town. Bobby vomited his first bite, but he got the rest down, no problem. Darren held up the man's left elbow, offering it to me with a laugh. 'Have a chicken wing.'

"It didn't take long for them to get to the girls. I won't tell you what they did before they carved them up, but if I was any kind of man, I would have stopped them. At that point, they'd already stripped me of my guns and I was pretty sure they had ideas about tying me up and eating me, too.

"Before they could, I broke the door open to the family's room and let the zombies in. They poured through, teeth clacking, and I ran like hell through the hole in the wall to our old room.

"It all happened so fast, the Rangers 105 didn't have a chance to get me. They were too busy shooting zombies. I opened the door, found some space to slip out, and went on the run. I gathered as many guns off of dead soldiers as I could and fought my way out of Vegas. It took me nearly two weeks to get free of the Strip.

"That's how I ended up out here."

When he finished, he looked over at me, those gray eyes still as cold as death itself.

"So, you think they lived, and are coming after you?" I asked.

He shrugged and looked off into the distance again. "Could be. I reckon it's possible. There were times when I was trying to get out of Vegas when I thought I saw one or two of them tracking me, but I could have been paranoid. Or maybe they were zombies and I saw them staggering around. I don't know."

"Still," I said. "It's something to be appraised of."

Neither of us said much to the other for a while.

"I guess I'll be going back to camp," I said. When he didn't say anything, I added, "For what it's worth. I don't think you had much choice. If you hadn't gone along with them, you would've become something less than human, and there's enough of that shit going around to last an eternity."

He didn't speak. He dug in his pocket, pulled out a pack of tobacco, shook it, tore off a pinch, and put it between his gum and right cheek.

"I reckon so," he said, before spitting a big juicy wad onto the desert floor.

That night was the coldest I'd felt in a long time. The moon was out again, more than a fingernail, less than a quarter, and it gave off enough light so you could see if you had to. It was a shame it didn't warm up a body, too.

I had the early watch, and when it was done, I rolled up in a blanket I'd snatched from one of the houses we'd searched, and fell right to sleep. I had horrible nightmares of babies being eaten and soldiers raping men, women, and for some strange reason, goats. Let me tell you, when I woke up to the sounds of someone screaming, I thought it was coming from me. It wasn't.

It was Paul.

He was pinned on his back with four zombies on top of him, their fingers scrabbling at his skin. They were poking holes in him, gouging his flesh. All four looked to have been women before they'd turned, and not one of them had a stitch of clothing on. They were starved, with their ribs poking through their brown, shriveled skin. The only places they didn't appear dried-up like prunes was where Paul's blood was splashing from his wounds, painting their dead flesh.

The worst was the zombie that had him by the foot. It was a man, also naked, and he was chewing on Paul's heel. He'd torn a flap off so the bone was gleaming in the soft moonlight and the piece of skin was flopping around on its lips, greasy and slick with blood.

My heart sank and I froze as I sat up and watched my best friend being torn apart. The thing was, it was too late to save him. Once those things bite you, you're done. It's over, brother. It's like they got extra nasty shit in their teeth, some kind of super-infection, and it'll burn through a man in less than two days.

Paul looked over at me, his eyes wide and his mouth open. The sounds I heard coming from his chest were the most awful I ever heard in my life. It was worse than listening to a dog get kicked, the way he was yelping, and his eyes, they were pleading with me. He was begging for my help but I was too scared and stunned to do anything.

Then his head exploded. I heard the report from the shot after the bullet struck. It echoed in my ears so loud that there's still nights I think I hear it, rattling around in my brain.

Paul's teeth and skull fragments erupted from the blast, peppering the zombie digging at his sides. His jawbone, broken in two by the concussion of the bullet, spun out and stabbed one of the women in the side of her head, sinking into her ear and killing her when it struck her brain. She fell to the side with a soft moan as the others, momentarily taken back by their feast blowing up in their faces, groaned and returned to feeding. Their faces and shoulders were littered with pieces of what was left of Paul's head, making them look like old, shriveled pin cushions.

The male zombie with the mouthful of heel flesh bent backwards as his head disintegrated, spraying the area around him with dried bits of skin of shattered bones. The flap of Paul's heel flew up into the air and fluttered back to the ground, settling like a feather on the chest of the zombie who was eating it. The sound of the gunshot rang out as it fell, the noise finally catching up with the damage the bullet had done.

Sudden fury seized me. I jumped to my feet, my knife in hand, and dove for those goddamn women zombies still chewing on my friend. I stabbed one in the back of the head, the point of the knife jutting out through her mouth, then pulled the blade free and slashed the throat of another one as it turned to hiss at me. That didn't do more than push it back for a second, but a second was all I needed. I jabbed my knife through its left eye, twisted it, and yanked it back out again. I got chunk of dried brain and half an eye for my troubles. I slashed the blade through the air, winging the refuse off, and went after the last one.

If the things had any kind of functioning intelligence at all, the last one would have gotten up and run for its life. But instead, she stared at me, all dumb-like, a bit of Paul's rib meat hanging from the corner of her mouth, her face peppered with bone bits.

I drove my knife into her left eye, did that twist thing again, and pulled it back out, the fire leaving me. When she fell to the side, twitching for a second and then dead for good, my heart went with it.

Barry cried out to my right and I saw a flurry of action as Turner ran at something in the corner of my eye. Tom stepped over next to me, gave me a grim look, and stalked off ahead, Wanda by his side. She had the tire iron in her hands and she looked like she was ready to give it a good work out.

I sat back and watched as my friends moved out to fight a dozen zombies, all bearing down on us. Like the others that had gotten Paul, they were naked, and it was kind of disconcerting to be attacked by naked zombies. Bad enough they were the living dead, but did we really need to see their dried-up tits and peckers, waggling in the wind?

I only watched for a moment. I had to get up and help, and that's what I did. I rolled Paul's body over and found his bat and picked it up, getting the weight of it. I was always jealous of his bat because it could do some major damage and still keep you at arm's length from those creatures. But now that I had it, I would have given anything to give it right back to Paul, if only he wasn't dead.

I held it by my side and glared at the naked zombies.

"This if for Paul!" I yelled and charged right into the midst of them.

My first swing took the head right off one of those suckers. Goddamn but the head flew like I was Babe Ruth. Its head smacked the face of one behind it, shattering that one's nose. As the first body fell, gummy black blood bubbling from its stump, I stepped into my next swing, nailing the one with the broken nose. I didn't knock its head off, but by God I sure put a nice dent in it. The thing's left eyeball popped out and slipped down its cheek, falling into the valley I'd made of its skull, rolling around as the zombie tottered for a moment, its brain dying. It fell over and then that was it. The others had killed the rest, making short work of them.

I was mad at first, feeling like I was robbed of my revenge, but I slowly realized this didn't have anything to do with revenge. It was about survival, and it was really the only rule left that meant anything. You survived. You made it to the next day, the next hour, the next minute, the next breath, if you could. It was all that counted. Because when you let your guard down, when you got caught by the short hairs, well, that was all she wrote.

Still, I was pissed. Someone had let us down. Someone had fallen asleep and Paul had been killed 'cause of it. I at least deserved some reckoning for that.

"Which one of you was it?" I asked, eyeing the four of them. I pointed the dirty end of the bat at them, brains and bone dripping off it like cheese melting over the sides of a sandwich.

No one said a word. They all looked at me like I was the crazy one. Well, I was going to tell them a thing or two.

"One of you lousy bastards fell asleep and got Paul killed," I said. "I think it's only the decent thing to do to step forward and own up to what you did."

They were silent. No one wanted to be a man and admit to their mistake. I was growing angrier by the moment.

"Goddammit!" I yelled. "Someone say something!"

Wanda pointed at Paul's dead body. I must've squinted at her something awful 'cause she finally spoke.

"I got off my watch and woke him up," she said. "He must've gone back to sleep."

And just like that, all my righteous anger ran off like a mouse being chased by a hawk. That dumb shit had fallen asleep and gotten himself killed. I shuddered, thinking about all the nights we'd spent out there alone, and all the watches he took where he might've gone to sleep, too.

"Shit," I said, spitting on the ground and walking away.

The next day brought more walking and more hot sun. I swear, my skin was getting so dark I was going to get confused for a Mexican if it kept up. But there wasn't much more to do than keep moving. Now we had a place to end up at, which was a blessing, because before I met up with these folks, I didn't have anything like that to look forward to. It was nice having a goal, an objective, and I hoped we all made it in one piece. I also hoped this place was right next to the ocean, and there were lots of pretty girls to look at, or at least one who'd call me her sugar plum and become my own.

It's funny. You can go through hell and high water and in the end, it all comes down to basic needs. You must have food, water, and companionship, and if you're really lucky, you get yourself a nice gal or guy to share other things with.

I glanced over at Wanda. There wasn't a chance in hell I'd be getting with her. She was all for Tom, and I couldn't blame her. I took a minute to look Turner and Barry over, but I'd never had felt a thing for another man and even now, I couldn't muster that kind of emotion. Turner kind of looked at me funny for a moment, like he knew what I was thinking and didn't approve, so I gave him a wink to rub it in. I heard him cuss under his breath and walk a few more steps away from me.

I missed Paul. The big bastard never talked, but he was like my shadow, and walking around without him made me feel empty and lost. I was glad for my new friends, but I still missed him.

That night came and went, and so did the next day and night. We walked forever and hardly talked when the sun was out, but come night, we would sometimes get into some lively conversations. My favorites were the ones Turner would get into with Barry. I'd sit and listen, grinning from ear to ear, as Turner told story after story about his days when he was famous. He almost always found a way to offend Barry, but having no place else to go, Barry would stick around to the bitter end.

One of those conversations went something like this:

"I ever tell you the time I got with three girls at once?"

Barry shook his head, his nose wrinkled with distaste.

"I don't know what you'd call it, like a four-ménage or something, but that's what it was. And let me tell you, esse, I was sticking shit in places I don't think they ever belonged."

"I'm no esse," Barry said.

"Shit, it don't matter none, homeboy. You gangsta 'cause you survived this long. Which is more than I can say for most of the world. So you an esse, hombre. Just accept it."

"Whatever."

"So, each one had different hair color; there was a blonde, a brunette, and a red-head. It was like that ice cream you used to be able to get. What was that shit called, son?" He looked at me.

"Neapolitan," I said.

"Yeah! That's the shit. I got all Neapolitan on them. I took the blonde and stuck her titties in my face while the brunette and the red-head took turns switching out on my front and backside, if you know what I mean."

Barry looked like he'd been forced to swallow a green lemon, slice by slice.

"One of my boys said I should've had the blonde sit on my face, but damn, son, I don't play like that. I don't munch the rug, knowwhutI'msayin'?"

The look on Barry's face got worse.

"So, I got tired of that position and we changed things up. I swear, esse, I had my finger up one ass, my dick in another, a toe in the blonde's mouth, and one of my fingers was busy picking the red-head's nose. I never heard so much moanin'!"

Barry got up at that point and walked away.

"Shit. That boy is too tight inside. He ought to appreciate a good story."

"I do," I told Turner. "Tell me more."

After another long trek, we discovered what happened to all the people in the town we'd found abandoned.

Wanda was the first to see them, as she crested up a short little hill and stopped in her tracks. The desert had evened out some and was rolling into more hospitable terrain. Early that morning we came across some scrub brush and later, some actual grass. It wasn't much, but it sure was a sight for sore eyes.

She held up her hand to signal us to slow down and be quiet, so we did and joined her by her side. There was a slight valley below us and we got a good eyeful of what she'd seen.

There was a ring of cars and trucks, all pulled into a tight circle. All I could think about when I saw it was those old cowboy movies, where the wagon train circles up and they fight the Indians. It was the same thing for those poor folks, only it wasn't Indians they were fighting, but zombies. Maybe there were some Indian zombies mixed in, I don't know, but it was the living dead they'd fought.

And what a fight it must've been. The valley was littered with dried-up old corpses, all of them missing parts of their heads. There must have been about forty of them in all, and they'd been dealt a mighty defeat.

But as I looked closer, I could see they'd really won. The survivors from the town had fallen, either one by one or as a group, and were all zombies now themselves. They milled around their cars, moaning and shuffling. There were probably ten of them left, and their bodies were riddled with bites. Most of them had big chunks taken out of their arms or legs. One was a little girl, both her cheeks missing. She was sitting on a tricycle and ringing the bell on the handle.

We backed away, slowly. There was no need to engage them, not if they hadn't sensed us, so we made our way around the valley and kept going, hoping they would stay where they were.

"I don't understand it," I said, shaking my head.

"Understand what?" Barry asked.

"Why they'd do something like that. I tell you what, if I get bit, the first thing I'll do after I get the one that got me is put a gun to my head and pull the trigger. Ain't no way I'm coming back like that."

"Maybe they're Catholic," Barry said.

"What the hell does that have to do with anything?"

"For Catholics, suicide is a mortal sin. There is no forgiveness for such an act."

"I thought Jesus forgave everything," I said.

Barry shrugged.

"Huh," I spat. "It's still stupid."

* * *

We spent that night about a mile away from them, and all of us were on edge. Hell, we had been since Paul died. It was something else, how you could meet some folks and within a day or two be best pals. They'd hardly known Paul long at all, but I could tell it took something out of each one of them, even Tom. There were quiet spaces, even amongst the talking, that I just knew were moments when all of us were questioning our mortality. It's hard not to when you're literally staring death in the face all the time.

Wanda sidled up next to me that night. She was my watch relief and I was glad she was awake. I didn't have to go shake her, unlike any of the others. Her and Tom, they seemed to have some kind of internal clock. I always wanted one of those but I never learned how to do it.

Turner was lying on his back forty feet away, snoring. Every now and then he'd say something in his sleep, things like, "Bitch, where my money?" Barry was five feet away from him and I could never really tell if he was out or not. He slept sitting up, hunched over, and I had to believe it did horrible things to his back, but he never complained. So I didn't think about it much, except when he did it, and then I thought it looked weird. Tom was off by himself, asleep.

Wanda sat up close to me, closer than I'd ever expect. It kind of made me uncomfortable. When she spoke, it was in whispers, so I got the idea it wasn't that she wanted to get close to me, she just didn't want the others to hear her.

"He's the first man to be nice to me," she said. I didn't need to ask who. "He doesn't talk much but that's all right. My last boyfriend, he was a real chatterbox, kind of like you."

"He surely wasn't as handsome as me," I smiled.

"No. but he was taller, and that counts for something."

"Again with the short jokes."

She shrugged. "All the men I've been with, they've been rotten somehow. Only two have raised their hands to me, and then it was only once each. The others, it was like something was wrong inside them and they expected me to fix it somehow. It's not like that with Tom. He's all broke inside, worse than the rest, but he accepts it. He doesn't mull it over or let it turn him bad, not like most men."

"You got a low opinion of men," I said.

"Yes, I do. You would, too, if you went what I went through."

"I suppose so. I've had a few girls break my heart, but nothing like what you're talking about."

"You're younger; you haven't been through it yet." She laughed, a bitter bark. "Probably won't, neither. The world ain't what it used to be."

I had nothing to say to that. When you're right, you're right.

"The first man who laid a hand on me, Darrell Thibodaux, was a car mechanic I dated back about seven years ago. He was like the rest, dark and full of pain over something or another, but he could be real nice sometimes. He used to like to take me out for eat ice cream. I thought is was really sweet, until one night we got some vanilla cones and was sitting in his pickup truck, licking away, 'cause it was a hot summer night and the ice cream was melting fast."

"You're making me hungry for ice cream," I said.

"Hush. So we got to talking and he said something I didn't like." She paused a second. "Funny thing is, I don't remember what it was he said. I just remember taking offense and telling him so and next thing I know, he smacks the side of my mouth so hard my nose starts bleeding."

"Jesus," I said. "Ain't no call for that."

"No, there isn't. I remember sitting there, watching the blood drip from the tip of my nose onto my ice cream, ruining it, watching as the blood swirled in with the white iciness and then melted down my closed fist. I got so mad I couldn't see straight. I turned on that bastard and shoved my cone as far up his nose as I could. He screamed. Can you imagine that? Like a little girl, like I'd been the one to slap him. The ice cream got up in his nose and I guess it was real cold, but I wasn't done yet. I punched Darrell Thibodaux in the balls so hard that the ice cream I shoved up his nose shot out and splattered the windshield. I got out and walked home after that and never spoke to him again."

"The moral of the story is, don't come between you and your ice cream," I said.

"Damn right," she said.

"What happened with the other fella that hit you?"

Her nose twitched. I couldn't tell if she was about to laugh or cry.

"That's a story best left for another time. Besides, isn't it about time for you to get some sleep?"

Wanda was something else. She could be so forthcoming and then turn cold a second later. It was like we were all on her time. I couldn't blame her, though. There's no way of imagining what it could been like for her, always having to keep men from trying to rape her. But I like to think she'd grown closer to me. After all, she did talk to me more than anyone but Tom.

In any case, she wasn't going to talk any more, so I turned in. It took me a long time to fall asleep that night. I kept thinking about what she'd told me. I went from feeling sorry for her to proud of her. I was glad she was with Tom. She'd finally found a man her equal. She didn't need anyone, but she was better when she had someone good by her side.

Her and Tom, they were good together.

I thought about an old girlfriend of mine, the first one I had after high school. Sally Jenkins. At the time, she was the one for me. I imagined we'd get married and have kids and live a great life, but she went away to college and we lost touch with each other. Last I heard, she was engaged to some Korean fellow that went to school with her. I wondered if she was still alive, and if so, if she was still with her fiancé. I hoped so. I hoped I would find the both of them in that little paradise we were headed to. I hoped they were happy as hell together.

I also hoped I'd find someone for myself while I was at it.

Sometime during all that hoping and wishing, I fell asleep.

They came for us the next night.

It was on Turner's watch. He never saw them. He was sitting still, looking around, keeping his eyes and ears open, when a rifle butt conked him on the back of the head. He yelped and went out like a light.

My first recognition of what was going on was when rough hands shook me awake. I thought it was my daddy, come back from the dead to make me suffer for not mowing the lawn like I was supposed to. I reckon it was all a product of some strange dream I was having, but when I called out, "Leave me alone, Daddy!" I woke to the sound of harsh laughter.

"He's calling for his daddy," someone said. It was Bobby the Bomb, I'd come to find out a bit later. "What a pussy."

When I snapped to, I looked around and saw my companions were all awake, and not one of them was amused by my outburst.

"What the hell is going on?" I asked.

A huge black man stepped over to me. He was so big, he ate up the whole, starry sky.

"Daddy's come home," he said. It was Brick who was talking to me. The others laughed at what he said.

"Where's Tom Wales?" a young-looking man asked. He was Darren the Kid. It took me a moment, but finally the realization of what was happening tore through the cobwebs of my sleepy mind like a bullet through a box of cotton swabs.

"Holy shit," I blurted, unable to contain my tongue. "You're the Rangers 105."

A shadow moved around Brick, tall and lithe, quick as a cat that's had its tail stomped on.

"What did you say?" the man asked. His eyes were dark, blacker than coal. I knew he had to be Johnny, their leader.

"Me?" I said, trying to play dumb. "I didn't say nothing. I talk a lot of gibberish. If you knew me well at all, you'd know that was as true as the day is long."

"This motherfucker is getting on my nerves," Brick said. He leaned forward and cracked his knuckles. "Let me twist his head off and drink his dumb-ass blood."

Brick was the size of a real house, not a shitter. Tom's description didn't do him justice. He was wearing old army fatigues, torn at the shoulders and just above his thighs, making him look like one of those professional wrestlers that used to be on TV. The arms and legs coming out of his outfit were something else. The arms rippled with muscles and were about as big around as my thighs. His legs were truly tree trunks, gnarled and ugly, ash-gray at his knees, like he'd been kneeling in the remains of a cremated body. His face was damned ugly too, all ruts and valleys and big, fierce eyes. And his breath...God Almighty, but it smelled like garbage wrapped in shit. I know this 'cause he leaned in so close I gagged. He looked like he could crack an elephant like it was a walnut, and kill it with one puff of his breath.

Bobby the Bomb was a regular-looking guy; white, with a mop of black hair and nice, tanned skin. He wasn't big but he wasn't small, more like average all around, except for being so skinny. But he had a stare to him, and later, when I got a closer look, I saw he had a squiggly scar that ran across his right cheek like a lightning bolt. He was dressed in standard Army fatigues, although they were so spotted with dried blood, they didn't really function as camouflage anymore, unless he liked to hang out in a slaughter-house.

Darren the Kid was about as young-looking as anyone I'd ever laid eyes on. In fact, if I hadn't already been told a little about him by Tom, I would have sworn he was twelve years old. He had a baby face, soft and sweet, with big brown eyes that could seduce Jesus with their innocence. He was slight of build, too. The guns at his side, the rifle slung around his shoulder, and the pistol he had pointing at my friends, all told me he was a crack shot.

The sandy blonde hair on top of his head only made him look all the more angelic.

Johnny leaned down, getting closer to me than even Brick was, and tried to stare me down. How he stayed in that cloud of stench Brick called his breath, I'd never know. Maybe he was used to it by now.

"Tom's been talking, hasn't he?" Johnny asked.

Like I said before, he had black eyes, and they liked to swallow a person up. When he put that gaze on you, it was hard to notice anything else about him. But I did my best, observing just in case I found something that could help me out. Turns out, there wasn't much there. He had black hair, like his eyes, and it was shaved close to his skull. His jaw was solid and cut, sharp at the point of his chin, and it matched the nose riding above his thin mouth like a rocket shooting across the horizon. He wore the standard Army garb, like the rest, but his was much more kempt. In fact, of all of them, he was the one who was still most like a soldier. His shirt and pants looked like they'd just been starched and his boots gleamed in the moonlight, reflecting my face back at me. He was tall and thin and moved like a panther.

"Who's this Tom you're referring to?" I asked, trying to delay the inevitable.

I heard the crack before I felt the pain, and my head shot to the left and I spit out a tooth before I realized I'd been hit. He was quick. In fact, his hand flew out and back so fast I wasn't exactly sure I hadn't imagined it.

"Don't fuck with me," Johnny said.

I spat a wad of blood onto the sand.

"Please, mister, leave him alone," Barry said. God bless that big Mexican. He was trying to help. "We don't know anything."

Johnny glared at me before turning to Barry.

"We've been traveling with this Tom Wales, that's true," Barry said, suddenly shriveling under the gaze of the leader of the Rangers 105. "But we know nothing about him."

Brick laughed. At first, I thought it was a cough, but the smile told me otherwise.

"He might not have said anything to them, but he's been talking to this little bitch, that's for sure," he said, pointing at me.

Johnny turned back to me. "Whatever you know, best spill it, son," he said. "It'll go easier on you if you do."

"Is that what you told that family? Did you tell their daddy that before you raped his little girls?" I snarled. I don't know where all my spit and vinegar came from, but it rose up hot and vile in my throat like a bucket of steaming vomit.

It only made Johnny smile.

I'd never seen a grin like that before. I read about it, in some cheap novels, about how some rotten son-of-a-bitch was so evil that when he smiled, you thought the Devil himself was standing before you. Well, that's what this was like. Corrupt, soul-destroying evil radiated from those perfect teeth of his. I knew right then he didn't give a damn about anything, even himself. All he cared for was misery and destruction. The more he could dole out, the better.

I'd like to say I was tough about the whole deal, but in the face of it, I wilted like a flower in the hot sun.

"He only told me about you guys," I said, defeated. "He didn't tell me much, just that you were brothers and what you did in Vegas. And how he left you."

"Did that punk ass bitch tell you how he tried to kill us?" Brick snapped.

I nodded. I couldn't lift my chin; it must've weighed a ton. My eyes bored holes into the desert floor. I could feel Johnny staring at me, weighing my words, and then he was up and gone.

"Tie them up," Johnny said. "We'll wait and see when he comes back."

The rest of the night was uncomfortable, to say the least. We were tied back to back, arms behind us and tied not only together, but to the person next to us. Our feet were tied together, too, so there was no way we were going to plot some kind of *'altogether, let's stand and run'* kind of escape. Besides all that, one of those bastards had a gun on us at all times.

Turner slept most of the night, leaning on me and giving me a real bad cramp in my shoulders. It wasn't his fault; he was still out from being slugged with the butt of a rifle. Barry was behind me and Wanda was on my other side. She kept giving me nasty looks, as if somehow I'd sold her and Tom and all the rest of us out. I felt bad, but I wasn't a hero, not like that.

As the sun rose, I got a better look at what was going on all around us. I saw that it was only Johnny and Brick with us after a while, that the other two had gone off somewhere. They came back when dawn was just starting to get warm, driving up in an Army truck and a Jeep. There was a giant, shiny machine gun mounted in the back of the Jeep and it gleamed in the early morning sunlight the way a muscle car would have after getting a good wash.

"You like the big gun?" Brick said, noticing that I'd seen it. "That's a Gatling gun, one of the newer kinds. You know how many bullets it can shoot per second?"

I shook my head.

"Enough to make you think you stuck your head inside a beehive," he laughed.

Bobby and Darren got out of the vehicles, parking them close enough for access but positioned just right so the view in all directions wasn't hampered.

Johnny walked back over and knelt before me.

"Is this usual? Does Tom take walks like this every night?" he asked.

I nodded. Wanda jabbed a bony elbow into my ribs.

"Bastard," she hissed.

Johnny turned his smile on her and I had the distinct mixed feeling of reveling in the way she wilted before his grin, just like I had, and feeling real sorry for her.

"Here's the thing, honey," Johnny said to her. "We've been tracking you for a long time. We look at his footprints, and we know they're his from the tread. We know he goes out and reconnoiters every night. So your friend here, if he'd lied to me like he tried to before, I would have cut his throat and let him bleed all in that pretty hair of yours."

He chuckled, and if I thought that smile was from the Devil, then his laugh was worse.

"And I would've hated doing that, because we have plans for you," he said.

"Boss!" Bobby yelled. Johnny's head snapped up and followed to where Bobby was pointing. I did, too.

In the distance, opposite the sun, Tom stood, real far away, but close enough to show us it was him.

Johnny stood up and cupped his hands to his mouth.

"Good to see you, Tom!" he yelled. "We stopped by to have some fun with your friends."

About that same time, Turner woke up. I was glad, because in addition to leaning his big ass on me, he was also drooling all over my arm. It was running down in rivulets, sticky and gross.

"What's going on?" he muttered.

"You drooled all over me," I said.

"We're in a heap of shit," Barry said.

Johnny snapped his fingers and Brick leaned over us, blocking the newly born sun. He grabbed a handful of Wanda's hair and yanked her up. We went with her and I was amazed to see he was lifting our entire group with one massive arm.

"Your little girl here, she was true to you by keeping quiet!" Johnny yelled. "So quiet she tipped me off that she had a thing for you. So I tell you what: come on down here and be a man and I might let her go."

Tom stood still, as heat waves rose up off the desert floor, making the image of him waver like he was some kind of mirage.

"You know we mean business, but we'll give you a demonstration," Johnny said. He snapped his fingers and Darren ran over, knife in hand. He cut Turner loose and shoved him away from us. Turner pitched forward, eating sand.

"He's all yours, Brick," Johnny said.

"Hell, yes," Brick laughed. He let go of us and we fell into a heap. We were hardly settled before Darren was scrambling over us, tying us back together. Brick lumbered over to Turner, who was trying to get back to his feet.

"What you want, punk?" Turner said, crowing tough. I'll give it to him. I would have been pissing my pants about then.

"I recognize you," Brick said. "You was one of them white rappers, stole his beats from the brothers."

"I didn't steal anything," Turner said, thumping his chest. "I'm the real deal."

"White trash piece of shit," Brick hissed. He raised his fists and struck a boxing pose. "You little wannabe niggas make me sick to my stomach. I'm gonna enjoy stomping the shit out of you."

"Bring it, bitch," Turner growled.

I don't know where he got his bravado from, but I was pretty damned impressed.

For all of a minute, it was a real fight. The two men circled each other, Brick jabbing occasionally, getting the feel of his opponent, and Turner responding.

"We gonna dance, or are we gonna fight?" Turner spat.

Brick lunged forward, straight into a resounding jab by Turner. Brick's head bounced back as something snapped in his mouth. He spit out a tooth and grinned, blood dribbling down his chin.

"You pissed him off now, boy!" Darren yelled.

Turner lashed out two more times, catching Brick on the chin once and square in the chest the other time. Brick took the blows and laughed at each one. He never backed off, standing right where he was.

I could see the look coming onto Turner's face. It was the look of a man who just gave his best effort and found he'd come up short. Way short. He screamed and threw a roundhouse, clobbering Brick on the side of the head.

I heard another snap, only this time it wasn't anything on Brick. It was Turner's wrist. That fat hunk of meat snapped in two from the blow, followed shortly by Turner's screams. He staggered back, holding his flopping hand, his eyes about to blow out of his head.

Brick laughed. He punched Turner twice: once in the stomach and once in the ribs. Turner went down. It was like watching a sack of potatoes thrown off the side of a building. He collapsed, his legs buckling, and went straight down into the sand. Brick kicked him numerous times, each blow breaking bone. Turner tried to cover up, but it was too little, too late.

Barry was screaming next to me, a constant barrage of Spanish slurs flying from his mouth. I wasn't sure which was faster, his spit or his language. He tore at the bonds holding us together. That man was ready to die for his friend, but he couldn't get loose to do it.

Meanwhile, Brick had rolled Turner onto his back and was pummeling his head with a flurry of punches. Turner cried out once but that was it. After that, I heard snapping bones and teeth. Those sounds died off to be replaced by the whap of something wet getting pounded, over and over again. Seconds later, the wetness was exchanged for dry fists thumping sand.

I had to look away. My stomach roiled inside of me and I was afraid my dinner from the night before was about to come flying out. I also pissed myself a little, I'm ashamed to admit, but I was scared to death. I'd seen a lot of fucked up things since this whole zombie stuff started, but this was by far the worst. When I managed to look up again, I saw there was nothing left of Turner's head but a long red smear across the sand. There were wads lying here and there, probably clumps of flesh, bone, and brains, but I couldn't tell what they were, to be certain.

Brick dug around in the wetness at his knees and pulled out a pair of shiny golden teeth. He held them up and laughed.

"I beat your ass, nigga!" he screamed. He pocketed the teeth, rose to his feet, and wiped his knuckles clean on his pants.

Barry buried his head into his chest, whimpering like a kicked dog. Wanda didn't say anything. She stared at Tom, who hadn't moved, as if she was trying to tell him something with her mind.

Johnny smiled at Brick and turned back to Tom.

"You see how it is now!" he yelled. "You come over here, turn yourself in, and we let your friends go. You don't..." he moved quickly over to Wanda. He grabbed her by the hair and yanked her to her knees. To her credit, she never made a sound, even though I know it must've hurt like hell.

"You don't," Johnny repeated. "And your woman gets it next. And it's gonna be worse than those two girls in Vegas, I can guaran-fucking-tee it."

All eyes shifted to Tom, but he didn't move. He stood stone still and I began to wonder if maybe we were all looking at some kind of cardboard cut-out. I came to hope so, praying he was sneaking up behind those bastards, ready to deal their death with a fistful of hot lead.

Instead, the man who hadn't moved, who was tougher than anyone else I ever met, turned and walked away, disappearing over the horizon.

My heart sank. I won't lie. I started praying to God again, for the first time since the whole world went to Hell, and as usual, the man upstairs had better things to do with his time. Still I kept going, hoping I could nag him into doing something.

Wanda sank back to the ground when Johnny let her go. She didn't say a thing and neither did Barry, who was too busy crying. The bad guys huddled up, all but Johnny, who stared out into the distance where Tom had been. He had the look of a boy who'd lost his dog.

Suddenly, Tom appeared again and everyone sat up, expectant.

"Let me think on it!" Tom yelled across the distance. "Give me an hour."

Bobby whirled around, his face tight and stressed.

"It's a trick, boss. He's up to something."

"True," Darren said. "He can be crafty."

"Just say the word, boss," Brick said. "I'll go after him myself."

Johnny chuckled. "No. Let's give him an hour." He waved at Tom, who waved back, then disappeared again.

"He can't do much anyway," Johnny said. "Besides, I'd like a little challenge."

A half hour went by before the natives got restless. And when that happened, it meant bad things for the rest of us.

"I want to fight," Darren said. "Watching Brick got my dick hard."

"Shit, son, watching me do anything makes your dick hard," Brick laughed.

"True," Darren said. He pointed at Barry. "I want to kick the Mexican's ass."

Barry looked up at him. He squinted and grinned. "I would relish killing you, gavacho."

Darren shook his head. "See, I haven't ever killed a Mexican. I feel it's my patriotic duty, considering how those piece of shit wetbacks used to come steal jobs from honest, hard-working Americans."

Johnny waved his hand. "Have your fun, but don't take too long." He cracked his neck and walked away, towards where Tom had first appeared. "I need you all sharp for whatever Outlaw's going to pull."

"Cut the spic free," Darren said to Brick. "I'm hungry for some tacos."

Brick did it and Barry got first to his knees and then his feet. Darren moved in but Barry held his hands out.

"Hold on a minute," he said, rubbing his hands together. "Wait until the feeling comes back into my hands."

Darren laughed. "How about that? This brown-skinned turd thinks he's got a chance!"

"More than a chance, pendejo," Barry said, eyes squinting. "More than a chance."

Darren waited all of a minute before speaking again. "You ready now, or are we waiting on something else?"

"I'm ready," Barry said.

Darren charged him, fists balled, a dynamo of quickness and energy. Barry fell back into a pose I'd never seen before. He stood with his legs parted and turned sideways, holding out his right hand like a knife.

"Hi-ya!" Barry cried and flung his left hand out. He chopped Darren in the throat. He reeled away, choking, his hands at his neck.

"I know kung-fu," Barry said, smiling. "Mexican kung-fu."

He leapt forward and kicked Darren in his left ribs and on his right thigh. Darren yelped and ran away, still gagging from the first chop.

"Get 'em, Barry!" I yelled. My heart swelled with pride in my chest, watching that Mexican take it to Darren. I should have known it wasn't going to last.

Brick stepped forward and smacked Barry on the back of the head, sending the poor bastard sprawling across the sand. He hit him from behind, so Barry never saw it coming, and hit him so hard he scrambled Barry's brains for a while.

"Tie him back up," Brick said to Darren, who took a few minutes to recover from his beating. He gasped for air and nodded.

"I can't believe some bean-eater whipped your ass," Brick said, shaking his head as Darren passed by him to haul Barry back to our group.

Darren tied a babbling Barry back up when Bobby the Bomb returned. He'd been gone for a while, off on each side of our small camp, digging in the dirt. He smiled and gave Johnny a big thumbs up.

"They're all set, boss," Bobby said. "He tries to drive anything at us and it'll blow all to hell."

"Good work, Bobby," Johnny said. His cold eyes turned to us, staring at me a moment before tearing away and glaring at Wanda. As he looked at us, I noticed that not once did he break a sweat. The rest of us were drenched in this hot sun, but not Johnny. He stood around like it was a cool day in October.

"When this is over," Johnny said to Wanda. "I'll take you as my woman."

She said nothing. Bobby the Bomb kicked me in my kidneys and laughed.

"And I'm gonna make you my woman," he said to me.

"Not if I get to him first," Brick laughed.

"Come on!" Bobby cried out. "You'll split him in two with that dick of yours. You get sloppy seconds."

"True," Darren said, rubbing his throat. "But that's your fight. I want the Mexican."

"Ain't you had enough?" Brick asked.

"I was just getting a taste," Darren said.

"Well, I'd like to let you fine gentlemen who are planning on ripping me a new asshole know a little something," I said. "I got what they call the clap, and it's been burning my dick for some time now. You go sticking anything into me, you're gonna come out all fucked-up."

Bobby laughed. "We got condoms, dipshit," he said.

"No lube, though," Brick said. "Too bad for you."

I didn't have a comeback for that, and I certainly wasn't looking forward to getting raped. I glanced at Wanda but she wasn't looking at me, she was staring off into the distance. I followed her gaze and saw Tom, back where we'd last seen him, walking slowly towards us. He had his hands up.

Johnny snapped his fingers and his men moved. They all grabbed their guns and drew a bead on Tom. Now, I'm not good with guns, so what they all had looked like M-16's to me, but what the hell did I know?

Tom was too far away for them to hit accurately with their machine guns, so I wasn't too worried about him. Not yet, at least. Darren snatched up a sniper rifle and took aim. I supposed he was a great shot, but I hoped not. Johnny stood at the front of them, peering at Tom as if trying to look through him.

"He's up to something," Johnny muttered.

I certainly hoped so. He better have been. I was tired of sitting in the hot sun, sweating my ass off and wishing either to be dead or free. Barry groaned next to me and I shoved him with my shoulder.

"Better shape up, muchacho," I said. Speaking Spanish must have raised his spirits, 'cause he let loose with a whole stream of Mexican. I couldn't understand what he was saying but I was glad to see the goofy grin on his face.

"Get ready," Wanda said, through gritted teeth.

"Huh?"

Her hands came free. I saw a broken glass eyeball in her hand, and a smile on her face.

No one was watching us; they were all focused on Tom. Too bad for them. Wanda moved quick and quiet, snatching up a knife Brick had left stuck into the ground a few feet from us. She cut me free and then Barry. We made our move, scrambling for whatever we could grab to defend ourselves with. I found Paul's bat, Wanda grabbed another knife, and Barry sat where we'd left him, still babbling in Spanish and smiling a mile wide.

"Hold on," Johnny said, and I froze, sure we'd been caught. When no one said another word, I looked up, and what I saw made my jaw drop.

Cresting over the hill behind Tom were some zombies—lots of zombies. They were following him.

"What the fuck?" Darren spit.

More came, one by one, two by two, until they dotted the landscape like ants on an anthill. There must've been a hundred of them, with more coming every second. And there were even more, not directly behind him, but spread out wide to the left and right, circling in.

I knew what he did then, and it was the craziest thing I'd ever seen. He'd gone off and found that horde of zombies he'd told us about and led them here. I don't know what his plan was beyond that, but it sure seemed like it couldn't get any more insane.

Tom kept a good twenty yard distance between him and the zombies, walking at a pace that matched theirs. He had his hands up, and as he walked closer, I could see the grin on his face.

"Fuck this," Brick said, turning towards the Jeep with the machine gun mounted on the back. "I'm outta here."

Wanda was there to greet him. With a big smile…and her knife. Brick's face fell as she jammed it straight into his balls. He screamed like a girl and dropped his gun.

His scream set everything into action. Darren spun around, as did Bobby. They were raising their guns but were too late.

I threw the bat and cracked Bobby right between the eyes. He managed to fire a shot, but it thumped into the ground at his feet as he fell in a heap, his arms and legs shaking, blood spurting from his broken nose.

Darren sighted me with his rifle and I knew I was a dead man. I was out in the open, exposed and helpless. He smiled as his finger tightened on the trigger, but that was the last thing he did, 'cause the front of his face split open just below his nose and erupted in a gush of blood and teeth. He pitched forward, the rifle dropping harmlessly by his side.

Twenty yards away, Tom had drawn his guns and shot Darren dead.

Wanda screeched as Brick, acting on instinct, slapped the shit out of her. She went flying to the left and crumpled into a ball. She was out before she hit the ground. Brick stumbled around, knife jutting out of his crotch like it was his dick, screaming bloody murder. He seemed to forget all about the gun at his feet as his groin spurted hot blood with each beat of his heart.

This ruckus snapped Barry out of his funk. He stopped muttering Spanish and jumped to his feet. When he spotted Brick, he grinned and launched his body at him, crashing into the big man and taking him down.

My attention got divided several ways at this point. I glanced at the truck and the Jeep, considering which one to jump into and make a getaway. I also was aware of Wanda, on the ground, not moving, and Barry, on top of Brick, ripping his face off. Then, of course, there was Johnny, who the entire time had never taken his eyes away from Tom and the zombies bearing down on us.

It was like he sensed what I was thinking and turned. Johnny pointed the pistol in his hand and shot out two of the truck tires, making it impossible to drive. He spun and blew out two tires on the Jeep, too, before Tom shot him. The bullet thumped Johnny in the right hip, spinning him away from facing the vehicles and back to looking straight on at Tom.

He was ten yards away, the zombies twenty yards behind him. He stopped and stared at Johnny, dropping his guns to his sides.

Johnny grinned. "You want a showdown, Outlaw?" He laughed, blood flecking his lips. "That's just like you."

Tom nodded slowly.

"All right, then," Johnny said, setting his face to grim.

Time froze.

Tom and Johnny faced each other, both with a gun in their hand. A bead of sweat rolled down Tom's face, riding his nose and dripping off like a skier jumping off a ramp. Those eyes of his, those gray, deadly eyes, bore into Johnny's, full of cold hate.

Behind Tom, the zombies closed in. Ten feet from him. Eight feet. Five.

"Draw!" Johnny screamed. His hand shot up, lightning-quick.

Tom's was already up and firing.

Johnny's back exploded between the shoulder blades. Blood, bone and bits of organs showered out of the hole the bullet made, slapping the ground wet and hot. His head went next, the bullet Tom fired ricocheting inside and erupting out the right side, just above the ear. I could hear it in there, pinging, until it blasted out, taking a good chunk of brains with it.

Time unfroze.

A zombie reached for Tom and he spun, shoved the muzzle beneath its chin, and fired. The top of its skull flew up and out. It fell but the others were nearly on him. Tom fought back, punching and kicking but they were too many.

He was about to go under when Bobby the Bomb sat up, getting his senses back. Blood trickled down his face, splitting it in two, running from a long gash the bat had made when it struck. It ran along the valley of the scar on his face, making a bloody lightning bolt.

Bobby turned, saw the zombies, and stuck his hands into his pants. He pumped them like he was taking the time to jack off before he stopped and smiled, his hand coming back out holding a remoter detonator.

Suddenly, a large area behind him, right in the midst of the encroaching zombies, exploded, earth and body parts shooting into the air.

The force of the blast rocked the area, shaking Tom loose of the zombies on him and knocking me to my ass. Bobby looked behind him and grinned as body parts flew up into the sky in a geyser of thick blood and brittle bones.

Probably about sixty of the pus pickles had been taken out with the blasts. Since there seemed to be close to two hundred now—with more coming over the hill—it was a dent, but not a significant one.

I snatched up Johnny's gun and got ready to fire, but where to shoot? I'd seen a lot of bad shit in my life, but right then and there, I was in the thick of the worst of it. I felt like a booger in a room full of people that loved to pick and eat my kind, and they were all drooling as they moved in closer.

The zombies were twenty feet in front of me and around thirty were coming up on my right. To my left, they were thirty yards away, giving me a little cushion. But as slow as they were, they were cutting off just about any escape, except right behind me, and that was going to be gone soon, too.

Tom had rolled with the blast and gotten away from the closest of the dead, but he looked dazed and was still trying to stand when a straggler—a girl missing her left arm—came up behind him, bared her teeth, and bit his wrist.

Tom yelped and punched her so hard he shoved her nose up into her brain, killing her immediately. He looked at his wrist, at the blood bubbling from the wound, and I could see the realization flash across his eyes: he was a dead man. He looked up at me, paused, and said his peace.

"You get Wanda and clear out of here," he ordered me. "If you don't get her safe, I'll come find you when I turn, and I'll eat your goddamn face off!"

My heart was heavy in my chest but I didn't have much time to react; the zombies were pouring around us. I met his eyes one last time, nodded, and ran over to the prone form of Wanda, who was just now coming to. On my way over, I kicked Barry in the ass, knocking him off what was left of Brick.

Barry had taken the man's head off, ripping the flesh from the neck until he dug his way down to the spine. After that, he planted his feet on the big man's shoulders, placed his hands under the chin, and pulled until the head popped free. He picked up the head and punted it like a football into the oncoming horde of zombies. Barry didn't seem to notice them as he turned back around and started clawing at Brick's muscular chest. It was right around that time that I kicked his ass and shook him out of his trance.

He looked up at me, over at Tom, and then at the zombies. He fully understood what was happening now and the old Barry came back. Well, almost.

He did take the time to run over at Bobby, who was struggling to get to his feet, and stomp his knees until they snapped. Bobby rolled around on the sand, screaming, as the zombies moved in.

And they were close now. For a second, I couldn't see our way clear, but then a slight passage opened, and we went for it.

Barry stooped down and scooped a handful of guns that had fallen by the side, one of Bobby's and a couple of Darren's. He ran up to us and handed me two of them.

I stepped on something hard and looked down. It was Wanda's lucky glass eye. I took the time to pick it up and slip it into my pocket before me and Barry got on each side of Wanda and hauled her to her feet. She was really out of it; her eyes circling in her head like some kind of cartoon character. But we didn't have time to revive her. We had to get the fuck out of there.

It only took about fifteen yards of running to get out of the main group, and none of them got closer than occasionally snatching at my shirt. Once we were clear, I passed Wanda over to Barry so I could take a moment to look back on what was happening.

We were about fifty yards from the action. Almost all of the zombies were swarming around Tom and Bobby the Bomb, like flies buzzing on shit. A handful of pus pickles were stumbling after us, but they were still a safe distance away. More zombies came over the hill but their numbers were petering out. I'd guess there was close to two hundred of them left, after the bombs went off and the stragglers caught up, each one as deadly as the next.

I watched as they swarmed over where Tom and Bobby were, and I waited until both disappeared out of sight, before turning to leave. I heard a few gun blasts, but they were muffled by the sheer press of bodies.

I was heavy of heart as the dead swallowed the only man I'd ever considered a real hero. I couldn't believe it was ending like this; that the toughest, greatest man I'd ever known was getting chomped on by a bunch of worthless zombies. It was a terrible way to go, and I figured if a man like Tom Wales was going to die like that, then what kind of a chance would someone like me have?

When we reached the crest of the hill, a good distance from the feeding frenzy below us, Wanda finally came to her senses. She started screaming and fighting against Barry, but he held her tight. She wasn't going anywhere.

"He's dead," I said, the words heavy on my tongue. "I saw him get bit."

Wanda howled but she stopped fighting.

"He told me to get you to safety, and I reckon that's just what I better do," I said.

The words were hardly out of my mouth when we heard the first burp of automatic gunfire below us. We all turned as one, our jaws dropping to the ground.

Tom Wales was standing on the back of the Jeep, bloodied and gouged in a hundred places. His left arm hung limp by his side, almost torn off, connected only by a thin flap of skin. His right hand was on the Gatling gun, his finger pressed down on the trigger.

Tom Wales was mowing down the zombies like a man possessed.

The gun was trying to buck wild against him and it looked like at any moment it was going to come flying out of his control, but he used his hip and chest to keep it as steady as he could. A swath of zombies went down before him, their bodies buzzing apart like he was wielding a giant lawn-mower blade. Pieces of dead bodies flew everywhere. I couldn't make heads or tails of most of what was spinning through the air, but those parts were almost as deadly as the bullets themselves. They blasted several zombies, peppering them with splintered bones and chunks of fat.

We watched in awe as Tom dealt the final death to dozens and dozens of the creatures, then pressed onward. I didn't know how many rounds that gun carried, but I hoped it was a million. We were so caught up, we almost forgot about the zombies that had broken off from that group and were coming for us.

A fat one lumbered in front of me, his nose and ears gone and the skin of his face pulled back so the teeth seemed to point forward like needles. I raised the gun I held and blew those teeth and that head to hell.

The thunder of the gun and the shower of the congealed blood broke us from our reverie. I glanced at Barry and Wanda, meeting their eyes.

"Let's go," I said.

"Well, why not? It's time for some payback," Barry said.

Wanda whooped and we marched down the hill, straight into the teeming fracas that was threatening to swallow Tom Wales whole. I passed Wanda a gun and we started firing together

If I compared our different assaults and what they accomplished, the one mounted by Wanda, me and Barry amounted to barely anything. Tom's on the other hand, was like a giant hand had swatted the zombies from the sky. He was doling out bullets like there was no tomorrow and we tried to keep up, but mostly we stayed to the backside of him, keeping the zombies from creeping up on him and taking him out.

It wasn't long before I ran out of ammo and so did the others, but that didn't slow us down. We used the butts of our pistols and the stocks of the rifles to bludgeon as many as we could.

Everything was a haze of blood. It was everywhere. The zombies dribbled black blood like clotted motor oil, and damn if it didn't feel good to see it flowing by the bucketful.

Tom screamed out and our heads jerked up to see what was going on. Two zombies had broken through and were tearing a hole in his stomach while the other one was biting a hunk from his leg. It was all Tom could take. He let go of the gun and staggered back, beating at the zombies on him with his single fist.

I ran for him. I lowered my shoulder and bulled my tiny ass past ten of the creatures, knocking them down, plowing through the mass of dead flesh. Before I knew it, I was up on the Jeep, swinging with the battered gun butt in my hand, caving in the head of one of the zombies on Tom and kicking the other off him.

Our eyes met. For the briefest of seconds, everything seemed to stop.

"You came back," Tom said.

"That I did," I replied. "Now, show me how to use this goddamn thing."

It took no time at all to learn how to pull the trigger on the Gatling gun and even less to aim it. Before I knew it, the zombies were falling by my hand. My heart leapt in my chest as a savage fury beat inside me, pulsing through my veins and filling my head with waves of pounding thunder.

I killed close to another four dozen of them before the bullets ran out, and I wouldn't have noticed if not for the hand that fell on mine. I looked up and it was Wanda, her face and body drenched in black blood, her eyes as cool as a morning breeze.

"They're done for," she said.

I looked around. There was at least thirty or so zombies left, but most were wounded and staggering a good distance away. Barry was picking through the Army truck, throwing out gun after gun. I later found out he and Wanda had gotten in there and came back out armed to the teeth. Their firepower plus mine had turned the tide.

At my feet, Tom moaned.

Wanda and I looked down as one. Tom was on his back, his skin ash-gray to match his eyes, but there wasn't nothing of Tom Wales left. He'd died and come back as one of them, and it was only his grievous wounds that were keeping him from rising up and attacking one of us.

"We need to take care of him," Wanda said. She handed me a Glock she'd gotten from the truck. "You do it, I can't."

"Okay," I agreed. I aimed the gun at his head and fired, sending Tom Wales on his journey.

That's about where this story ends. We stocked up on weapons and provisions, as much as we could carry, and headed off, leaving the carnage behind. None of us got bit, which was a miracle, and we all counted ourselves lucky.

Barry told me how they had dug out the guns to help out, and Wanda told us both how she'd hidden the glass eye when we were set upon by the Army guys. It took her a long time to cut through those bonds, but she had, and in doing so, saved our lives just as much as Tom had.

I handed her the eye back.

"My good luck charm," she smiled.

We continued our trek towards the place called Angelville. I pray it exists, and I pray when we get there, I'm greeted by a bunch of big-breasted blondes eager to know the pleasures of a very short but very blessed young man.

I'm leaving this account in the bottle you found and I hope it provided good reading for you. If we're lucky, and we make it further, I'll leave another chapter somewhere on the road of our journey. If not, well, you know how it goes.

In any case, I hope you're fortunate enough to meet such good friends as I did. A man would count himself lucky to make one friend like the ones I had, much less the four I'd found. Turner was a good man, tough and loyal. Paul was my best buddy, and a truer friend I never knew. Barry was a Mexican who spoke near-perfect English and knew kung-fu and would never give up on his pals. Wanda was the toughest of us all, and she was also the glue and spit that held us together. And Tom...well, he was a hero. He fought off the bad guys, the living and the living dead, to keep his friends safe.

I can only hope it wasn't in vain.

ABOUT THE WRITERS

Kelly M. Hudson grew up in Kentucky watching cowboy movies and loving rock and roll. He currently lives in California and is the author of two novels, The Turning, and Men of Perdition, both published by Living Dead Press and available at Amazon.com. You can find out more about Kelly and his work by visiting www.kellymhudson.com where you'll find links to stories he's had published and how to find him on Facebook and Twitter.

Adam P. Lewis is an author within the horror genre. He has written numerous short stories, essays, and reviews published by Wicked East Press, Pill Hill Press, Living Dead Press, Static Movement, Dark Quest Books, and Ambrotos Press. Follow him at http://www.facebook.com/adamlewis518.

Alan Spencer is a horror author from Kansas City. His novels include "The Body Cartel," "Inside the Perimeter: Scavengers of the Dead," "Ashes in Her Eyes," and "Zombies and Power Tools." Keep an eye out for his forthcoming book "Cider Mill Vampires." Seek him on Facebook or e-mail him at: alanspencer26@hotmail.com

Patrick MacAdoo is an author of supernatural thrillers. He currently lives in Portland, Oregon. His influences include Stephen King, Elmore Leonard, Shakespeare, Plato, and David Milch. He is currently seeking a publisher for his novel, "Big Box Byzantine." You can find Patrick on Facebook and email him at aspergo321@aol.com

Rick Moore's stories have appeared in numerous anthologies, including 'The Undead: Flesh Feast', 'History is Dead' and 'Cthulhu Unbound' (Permuted Press), the Stoker Award nominated 'Horror Library 3' (Cutting Block Press), 'The Beast Within' and Harvest Hill (Graveside Tales), 'Embark to Madness' (Coscom), 'Bound for Evil' (Dead Letter Press), and in several anthologies from Living Dead Press. Recently Rick joined Dark Moon Digest as an associate editor. His story 'Kindread' appeared in the third issue of the magazine.

Originally from England, he now lives in Phoenix, with his wife Ruth and three cats.

Go to http://www.myspace.com/zombieinfection for updates on published works and to contact the author.

BOOK OF CANNIBALS 2: THE HUNGER
Edited by Rebecca Besser

Forbidden meat, but the sweetest when you take a bite...

Dark desires remain hidden deep in the human consciousness, waiting to be set free. Why not let them?

What recipe would you use to cook your neighbor? What cut of your girlfriend would you try first? Would a human steak be more tender on the grill than any you've tried before?

No matter how you boil it, roast it, or grill it, human meat is what we're serving up. Cannibalism at its best and worst are contained within this book.

Will you be able to stomach the contents as the innocent are served up for your dining pleasure? Or will you cringe with disgust at the wicked and twisted creations the sadistic chefs and butchers are making for your palate?

Next time you sit down for a meal at your neighbor's house, or are enjoying a cookout at your friend's, will you look at your plate and wonder...is it human?

MONSTER PARTY
Edited by Anthony Giangregorio

Zombies, vampires, werewolves and ghosts are just a few of the monsters in this anthology.

But this isn't any anthology, you see, this is a party.

Or to be more to the point…a *Monster Party*.

Ever wonder what would happen if a werewolf and a zombie squared off? Or perhaps a vampire and a Frankenstein monster? Or better yet, how about a world where every conceivable monster is real and humans are their prey?

If those burning questions have been driving you mad, then look no further than this book.

So go on over to the buffet table, grab yourself a plate (the shrimp looks good) and get yourself a drink, and enjoy the fun ride that is the *Monster Party*.

THE WAR AGAINST THEM: A ZOMBIE NOVEL
by Jose Alfredo Vazquez

Mankind wasn't prepared for the onslaught.

An ancient organism is reanimating the dead bodies of its victims, creating worldwide chaos and panic as the disease spreads to every corner of the globe. As governments struggle to contain the disease, courageous individuals across the planet learn what it truly means to make choices as they struggle to survive.

Geopolitics meet technology in a race to save mankind from the worst threat it has ever faced. Doctors, military and soldiers from all walks of life battle to find a cure. For the dead walk, and if not stopped, they will wipe out all life on Earth. Humanity is fighting a war they cannot win, for who can overcome Death itself? Man versus the walking dead with the winner ruling the planet. Welcome to *The War Against Them*.

ETERNAL NIGHT: A VAMPIRE ANTHOLOGY
Edited by Anthony Giangregorio

Blood, fangs, darkness and terror...these are the calling cards of the vampire mythos.

Inside this tome are stories that embrace vampire history but seek to introduce a new literary spin on this longstanding fictional monster. Follow a dark journey through cigarette-smoking creatures hunted by rogue angels, vampires that feed off of thoughts instead of blood, immortals presenting the fantastic in a local rock band, to a legendary monster on the far reaches of town.

Forget what you know about vampires; this anthology will destroy historical mythos and embrace incredible new twists on this celebrated, fictional character.

Welcome to a world of the undead, welcome to the world of *Eternal Night*.

DEAD HISTORY 2
A Zombie Anthology
Edited by Anthony Giangregorio

From the dawn of mankind, the walking dead have been with us.

The greatest moments in history are not what they appear.

Through the ages, the undead have been there, only the proof has been erased, documents destroyed, and witnesses silenced.

The living dead is man's greatest secret.

In this tome, are a few of the stories of what really happened all those years ago. History isn't alive, it's dead!

INSIDE THE PERIMETER: SCAVENGERS OF THE DEAD
by Alan Spencer

In the middle of nowhere, the vestiges of an abandoned town are surrounded by inescapably high concrete barriers, permitting no trespass or escape. The town is dormant of human life, but rampant with the living dead, who choose not to eat flesh, but to instead continue their survival by cruder means.

Boyd Broman, a detective arrested and falsely imprisoned, has been transferred into the secret town. He is given an ultimatum: recapture Hayden Grubaugh, the cannibal serial killer, who has been banished to the town, in exchange for his freedom.

During Boyd's search, he discovers why the psychotic cannibal must really be captured and the sinister secrets the dead town holds.

With no chance of escape, Broman finds himself trapped among the ravenous, violent dead. With the cannibal feeding on the animated cadavers and the undead searching for Boyd, he must fulfill his end of the deal before the rotting corpses turn him into an unwilling organ donor.

But Boyd wasn't told that no one gets out alive, that the town is a death sentence. For there is no escape from *Inside the Perimeter*.

DEAD RAGE

by Anthony Giangregorio
Book 2 in the Rage virus series!

An unknown virus spreads across the globe, turning ordinary people into bloodthirsty, ravenous killers.

Only a small percentage of the population is immune and soon become prey to the infected.

Amongst the infected comes a man, stricken by the virus, yet still retaining his grasp on reality. His need to destroy the *normals* becomes an obsession and he raises an army of killers to seek out and kill all who aren't *changed* like himself. A few survivors gather together on the outskirts of Chicago and find themselves running for their lives as the specter of death looms over all.

The Dead Rage virus will find you, no matter where you hide.

CHRISTMAS IS DEAD: A ZOMBIE ANTHOLOGY

Edited by Anthony Giangregorio

Twas the night before Christmas and all through the house, not a creature was stirring, not even a. . . zombie?

That's right; this anthology explores what would happen at Christmas time if there was a full blown zombie outbreak. Reanimated turkeys, zombie Santas, and demon reindeers that turn people into flesh-eating ghouls are just some of the tales you will find in this merry undead book. So curl up under the Christmas tree with a cup of hot chocolate, and as the fireplace crackles with warmth, get ready to have your heart filled with holiday cheer. But of course, then it will be ripped from your heaving chest and fed upon by blood-thirsty elves with a craving for human flesh! For you see, Christmas is Dead!

And you will never look at the holiday season the same way again.

BLOOD RAGE

(The Prequel to DEAD RAGE)

by Anthony Giangregorio

The madness descended before anyone knew what was happening. Perfectly normal people suddenly became rage-fueled killers, tearing and slicing their way across the city. Within hours, Chicago was a battlefield, the dead strewn in the streets like trash.

Stacy, Chad and a few others are just a few of the immune, unaffected by the virus but not to the violence surrounding them. The *changed* are ravenous, sweeping across Chicago and perhaps the world, destroying any *normals* they come across. Fire, slaughter, and blood rule the land, and the few survivors are now an endangered species.

This is the story of the first days of the Dead Rage virus and the brave souls who struggle to live just one more day.

When the smoke clears, and the *changed* have maimed and killed all who stand in their way, only the strong will remain.

The rest will be left to rot in the sun.

KINGDOM OF THE DEAD
by Anthony Giangregorio
THE DEAD HAVE RISEN!

In the dead city of Pittsburgh, two small enclaves struggle to survive, eking out an existence of hand to mouth.

But instead of working together, both groups battle for the last remaining fuel and supplies of a city filled with the living dead.

Six months after the initial outbreak, a lone helicopter arrives bearing two more survivors and a newborn baby. One enclave welcomes them, while the other schemes to steal their helicopter and escape the decaying city.

With no police, fire, or social services existing, the two will battle for dominance in the steel city of the walking dead. But when the dust settles, the question is: will the remaining humans be the winners, or the losers?

When the dead walk, the line between Heaven and Hell is so twisted and bent there is no line at all.

RISE OF THE DEAD
by Anthony Giangregorio
DEATH IS ONLY THE BEGINNING!

In less than forty-eight hours, more than half the globe was infected.

In another forty-eight, the rest would be enveloped.

The reason?

A science experiment gone horribly wrong which enabled the dead to walk, their flesh rotting on their bones even as they seek human prey.

Jeremy was an ordinary nineteen year old slacker. He partied too much and had done poorly in high school. After a night of drinking and drugs, he awoke to find the world a very different place from the one he'd left the night before.

The dead were walking and feeding on the living, and as Jeremy stepped out into a world gone mad, the dead spotting him alone and unarmed in the middle of the street, he had to wonder if he would live long enough to see his twentieth birthday.

THE CHRONICLES OF JACK PRIMUS
BOOK ONE
by Michael D. Griffiths

Beneath the world of normalcy we all live in lies another world, one where supernatural beings exist. These creatures of the night hunt us; want to feed on our very souls, though only a few know of their existence.

One such man is Jack Primus, who accidentally pierces the veil between this world and the next. With no other choice if he wants to live, he finds himself on the run, hunted by beings called the Xemmoni, an ancient race that sees humans as nothing but cattle. They want his soul, to feed on his very essence, and they will kill all who stand in their way. But if they thought Jack would just lie down and accept his fate, they were sorely mistaken. He didn't ask for this battle, but he knew he would fight them with everything at his disposal, for to lose is a fate worse than death.

He would win this war, and he would take down anyone who got in his way.

CLAN OF THE BIGFOOT

ANTHONY GIANGREGORIO

THE PLACE TO GO FOR ZOMBIE AND APOCALYPTIC FICTION

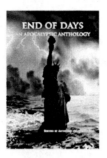

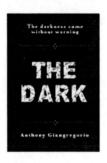

LIVING DEAD PRESS

WHERE THE DEAD WALK

www.livingdeadpress.com

CPSIA information can be obtained at www.ICGtesting.com
265615BV00007B/25/P